Jennifer Moore is a freelance writer, novelist and children's author. She was the first UK winner of the Commonwealth Short Story Prize and was previously shortlisted for the Greenhouse Funny Prize. Her short fiction and poetry have appeared in numerous publications on both sides of the Atlantic, including in the *Guardian*, *Mslexia*, *The First Line*, *Fiction Desk* and *Short Fiction*. *The Woman Before* is her debut adult novel.

THE
WOMAN
BEFORE

JENNIFER MOORE

ONE PLACE. MANY STORIES

HQ
An imprint of HarperCollins*Publishers* Ltd
1 London Bridge Street
London SE1 9GF

www.harpercollins.co.uk

HarperCollins*Publishers*
1st Floor, Watermarque Building, Ringsend Road
Dublin 4, Ireland

This paperback edition 2022

1
First published in Great Britain by
HQ, an imprint of HarperCollins*Publishers* Ltd 2022

Copyright © Jennifer Moore 2022

Jennifer Moore asserts the moral right to be
identified as the author of this work.
A catalogue record for this book is
available from the British Library.

ISBN: 9780008535391

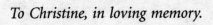

To Christine, in loving memory.

'No one ever told me that grief felt so like fear.'
C. S. Lewis, *A Grief Observed*

Chapter 1

Fern wasn't surprised to find her dead sister waiting at the bottom of the stairs. Five months and three days and she still saw her everywhere. Correction, she *thought* she saw her. *Imagined* she saw her. Dr Earnshaw, the latest in a succession of so-called grief experts, set great store by such distinctions. But then Dr Earnshaw didn't have a twin, did she? She'd admitted as much at their first session. Never had a twin. Never lost a twin. Never stood on the clipped golf-course green of the new cemetery as half her soul – the better, brighter half – disappeared into the rain-clagged ground without her. How could Linny have gone without her?

'Oh, sorry!' said the estate agent. Julie, was that her name? Janet? June? Something beginning with J, anyway. Fern had forgotten it as soon as the introductions were over. It was usually Sonia who conducted the viewings – Smiley Sonia as Paul called her – but she was off sunning herself in Cyprus for two weeks. Paul was away too, on business: something urgent and last minute in Brussels, leaving Fern to do the second viewing on her own.

'I er . . .' The estate agent seemed flustered, chin tipped back in shock, as if *she* could see Linny too. But that was impossible. Dr Earnshaw said it was all in Fern's head, her brain's peculiar way of dealing with the loss and guilt. Not even Paul believed her.

And yet there she was again – Linny – large as life, waiting by the bottom stair as if she'd been expecting them. Only now that Fern looked again, she realised it wasn't her sister at all. Nothing like her. True, she had the same long blonde hair, the same startling blue eyes – even bluer than Linny's in fact – but her features were all wrong. And that too-big Fair Isle jumper, that certainly wasn't Linny's style. It must have been a trick of the light.

'I'm Gemma,' said the estate agent, recovering her composure, 'from Thomson & Harvey.' *Gemma.* Of course. Not a 'J' at all. 'And this is Mrs Croft,' she added, gesturing towards Fern. 'Sorry, I didn't realise there'd be anyone in. When I spoke to your husband this morning he told me you'd be gone all day.'

The woman who wasn't Linny looked blank for a moment, as if she couldn't understand what Gemma was telling her. 'My husband?' And then something clicked into place behind her eyes and she nodded. 'Yes, I see,' she said, glancing over Gemma's shoulder to the freshly painted front door. 'I didn't realise I'd be here either.' Her voice was low and clipped, with a slight tang of accent. Scandinavian maybe?

'Nice to meet you anyway, Mrs . . .' Gemma glanced down at the client sheet on her clipboard. 'Mrs Rochester.' She reached forward with her right hand, ready to shake, but the woman didn't seem to notice. And then the moment was broken by a tinny ringtone coming from the estate agent's pink leather handbag. 'Gosh, I'm sorry. I'm going to have to get this. We're ridiculously short-staffed today . . . Hello?'

Fern stared at her own feet, at the scuff marks on the toe of her left shoe, trying to look as if she wasn't listening. As if the conversation was taking place in another room entirely.

'. . . But I've only just got here. Can't someone else do it?'

The Victorian patterned floor tiles were nicer, the colours crisper than Fern remembered from her first visit: a repeating geometric star pattern in terracotta, cream and blues that reminded her of her mother's old patchwork quilt. Perhaps they'd had a thorough clean and polish since last time. Or maybe she'd been too deep in the fog of her own thoughts to notice them properly when she came before. But Paul was right, they did make for an impressive entrance. Exactly the sort of period feature Linny would have liked. *Would have*, thought Fern, catching herself in surprise. Past tense. That probably counted as progress in Dr Earnshaw's book, but it didn't feel like it. It felt like a betrayal. Besides, what if she didn't *want* to accept what had happened? Didn't *want* to move on? Not even for the sake of the baby?

I'm sorry, she thought, hands slipping down to the gentle curve of her stomach. Another betrayal. *I didn't mean it.* That's why she was here, after all. For the sake of the baby. For the sake of her marriage.

'. . . But what about Mrs Croft?' Gemma was saying. 'She's come all this way especially . . .'

The baby kicked back on cue: a gentle rippling sensation somewhere inside her that might almost have been wind.

'. . . What, and ask her to come back later? How's that going to look?' Gemma turned away towards the hall mirror – an ornate monstrosity in antique gold – shielding her mobile with her other hand. Now there were two embarrassed estate agents hissing into their phones. 'Fine,' she said at last, rolling her eyes at her own reflection. 'I'll be there as soon as I can, though the traffic was pretty snarled up coming out.' She jabbed at the screen with a manicured finger and swung around again, sighing. 'I'm ever so sorry, Mrs Croft, but we're going to have to reschedule the viewing for another time.'

'I can show you round if you'd like,' the woman told Fern. 'Seeing as I'm here.'

Gemma sighed again. 'Thank you, Mrs Rochester. You're a life saver. As you know, Thomson & Harvey guarantee agent-accompanied viewings at all times but . . .'

'Really, it's fine,' said the woman. The tiniest of smiles flickered across her mouth and was gone again. 'We'll manage without you.'

Gemma was already slipping her feet back into the high-heeled shoes she'd shed on the way in. 'If that's all right with you, Mrs Croft?'

Of course. What difference did it make *who* showed her round? Paul had already made up his mind, although he wouldn't admit it. *Please, Fern – another look, that's all I'm asking. I've got a feeling about this one. We could be happy there. I know we could.* A new house. A new start. That was the answer to all their problems apparently. *Somewhere away from all the painful memories.* Away from Linny, more like – that's what he *really* meant.

'Yes,' Fern said out loud. 'That would be lovely. Thank you.'

'And if you have any further questions, don't hesitate to . . .' The estate agent was already halfway out the door as she was saying it, before anyone could change their mind. The rest of the sentence disappeared with her as the latch clicked back into place, stopping the sudden draught in its tracks.

'So,' said the woman, with a smile, her face angled towards the mirror. It was a proper smile this time though. 'Here we are then. Just the two of us. Or rather the four of us.' Her voice tilted up at the end, as if it might have been a question rather than a statement. Fern didn't quite follow – was she counting their reflections? Her own mirrored smile looked forced and out of place, as if it would rather be somewhere else. But then the woman smoothed down the front of her knitted jumper to reveal a neat matching bump of her own. 'You're expecting too?' she asked. 'Yes?'

'Oh, I see,' said Fern. 'Yes. That's right. Five months, though I'm barely showing yet. At least, I didn't think I was.' *You need to start eating more.* That's what Paul and his mother kept telling her. *You need to think about the baby now.*

'Me too,' said the woman. 'My baby's the same age, I mean.' Her hands moved together as she spoke, fingers interlocking to form a basket around the base of her belly. A human cradle. 'My first,' she said. 'Sofia.'

Five months and three days. That's how old Fern's baby was. Sometimes it made it better to imagine new life sparking into existence at the exact moment Linny's had shuddered to a halt. It was a comfort of sorts, a precisely timed blessing in the face of a sprawling eternity without her. But other times it made it worse, so much worse – almost as if Linny, or fate, or whatever it was that sent her bike skidding sideways into the lorry's wheel arch, knew there wasn't room enough in Fern's heart for the two of them. Which was nonsense, of course. But knowing it was nonsense didn't stop her thinking it. Didn't stop her blaming herself.

'I'm Marte, by the way,' said the woman. It seemed an odd sort of name to Fern's English ears, hovering somewhere between 'mutter' and 'martyr'.

'I'm Fern,' she answered, dragging her thoughts back from Linny to the matter in hand. New house. New start. It *would* get better, everyone said so. 'Thank you for doing this – I hope I'm not keeping you from anything. A quick whizz round will be fine, honestly, just to refresh my memory.' *Just so I can tell Paul I came.*

'No need to rush,' Marte assured her. 'I've all the time in the world.' Which was just as well really, because time slipped away surprisingly fast as they made their way from room to room, taking in the wide bay windows and high ceilings. Marte's quiet, unassuming manner made a pleasant change from the usual estate agent patter. She seemed happy for Fern to discover the house's selling points for herself – from the original tiled fireplaces to the impressive plaster coving – staying firmly in the background, always a few steps behind. It *was* a lovely house, despite the dubious decorating – Fern could see that now. Especially when the wind gave up rattling at the window frames and the sun came out, bathing the bedrooms in a soft yellowy light. Maybe in time they really *could* be content here, the three of them.

'Ideal for a nursery, don't you think?' said Marte, following her into the smallest bedroom. A heavy oak desk stood against one wall, and a dark-stained bookcase on the other, its shelves groaning beneath endless books on the First World War. But yes, the space itself was just right. Fern could almost picture it: freshly painted walls with an alphabet border – like the one they'd had when they were little – brightly coloured curtains and a mobile over the cot. Maybe a changing table in the corner.

'Perfect,' she agreed. 'You're not tempted to stay?' She couldn't remember what Smiley Sonia had told them about the Rochesters, if indeed she had, but it seemed like an odd time to be moving, with a little one on the way. Not for her and Paul, of course, that was different. It made absolute sense for them, on paper at least, especially with his new job. And in another lifetime – in an alternative reality where her sister's bike had swerved to the right, colliding with a traffic island instead – Fern might have been all for it. Excited even. No more cramped city living or endless flights of stairs to climb. Somewhere proper to work – somewhere other than the piled-up kitchen table. And a spare bedroom for Linny to stay over whenever she wanted, boyfriend and all, given the size of it. Not that Fern ever got to meet the last one – the flashy chap in the city, who broke her sister's heart.

'Me?' said Marte, staring past Fern to the sash window. Her smile had faded. 'No. I'm ready to move on.' She seemed on the verge of saying something else, as if she was weighing up a more intimate explanation of her circumstances, but then thought better of it. 'Don't get me wrong, it's a wonderful house. I think you'll be very happy.'

Happy? Fern could hardly remember what that felt like. She followed the other woman's gaze, looking out at the last of the roses along the back wall and the ruins of the old folly beyond. The crenellated tower, the one that gave the street its name, was barely visible through the dense tangle of ivy.

'At least I hope you'll be happy,' said Marte. She made it sound like a done deal, as if they'd already put in an offer. Already signed on the dotted line. 'With your baby girl,' she murmured.

Fern felt a gentle flurry of kicks inside as if the baby was listening in too, signalling its approval. It could just as easily have been a warning, of course, although she didn't think of that until later. And it was later still – much later – when Fern realised she hadn't actually mentioned the baby's gender. Officially speaking she didn't even know. Paul was adamant he wanted it to be a surprise, but it was a girl, all right. It had to be. Little baby Linnette. Yet somehow, much to Fern's queasy unease, Marte had known it too.

'Your beautiful baby girl . . .' Marte added softly, gazing at Fern's belly with a peculiar, hungry look in her eyes.

Chapter 2

Marte and her matching baby couldn't have been further from Fern's mind as she sat in the stuffy solicitor's office, the warm plastic seat sweating under her thighs. She was thinking of Linny, reliving their fight for the millionth time, as if the script might have rewritten itself in the intervening months. But the scene played out the same as it always did, with the same stupid, drunken words shooting out of Fern's mouth before she could stop them: *'Don't you play the martyr with me . . .'*

I didn't mean it, Fern wanted to explain, catching sight of Linny through the large internal window. Her sister's hair was in a low ponytail today, held in place by the familiar red scrunchie she'd worn all the way through junior school. *I didn't mean it. You know I didn't.*

'Mrs Croft? Is everything okay?'

Fern blinked, bringing her attention back to the here and now – to what Dr Earnshaw and her husband liked to call 'reality'. Devoted Darren, as Paul had christened their appointed solicitor on account of his bright-eyed enthusiasm for the job, was waiting to shake her hand.

'Gosh, sorry,' said Fern, her stomach catching on the table as she struggled to her feet. 'I didn't notice you come in. I was miles away . . . Nice to see you again,' she added, wincing inwardly at the clamminess of his palm in hers. She'd have been happy to go down the online conveyancing route, but Paul had insisted. After the recent cock-up on his boss's house purchase – a cock-up that had nearly cost him his hefty deposit – Paul wasn't taking any chances. He seemed to think old-fashioned face-to-face meetings were some kind of guarantee of competence.

'And you,' said Darren, beaming as always. 'Thank you for coming in. It shouldn't take too long – just a few more bits of paperwork to go through. Can I get you some tea or coffee before we start?'

'Not for me, thanks,' said Fern, who hadn't been able to stomach the smell of coffee since her early run of morning sickness.

'I'm fine too,' said Paul, who'd also forsaken coffee for the duration of the pregnancy. Fern knew he missed it though and was grateful for the sacrifice.

'Right then,' said Darren, eagerly. 'Let's get stuck in, shall we?'

Fern's attention drifted back to the internal window, watching her sister's ponytail swinging behind her as she strode away up the corridor, while Darren talked through the tedious forms and endless jargon.

Come back. Wait for me. But Linny was already gone.

'Now then,' said Darren. 'This fixture and fittings form's rather exciting. It even comes with its own appendix and pictures.'

'Pictures?' Paul repeated. 'What kind of pictures?'

'Furniture, mainly. A few electrical items too.' Darren pushed a neat pile of black-and-white printouts across the table. 'It's all in there.' Fern recognised the oak desk as Paul flicked through the first few sheets; it was the one from the small bedroom – the nursery – with detailed measurements and a suggested price of eighty-five pounds printed underneath. And now suddenly she *was* thinking of Marte, recalling the peculiar look in the woman's eyes as she stood beside that same desk, staring at Fern's stomach.

'Oh look,' said Paul, flicking on through the pile. 'There's that big gold mirror from the hall. I remember that.'

Yes, Fern remembered that too. She remembered how tightly Marte had cradled her own stomach as they stood there together, reflected in the glass. She remembered the wistfulness in her voice when she said she was expecting her first baby: Sofia.

'I've never seen anything quite like it, to be honest,' said the solicitor, 'but it does make a certain kind of sense. As you probably know, the vendors are relocating overseas – a retirement complex in Florida, I believe – so they won't be taking much in the way of furniture with them. You've got first refusal on the whole lot, even down to the piano. In fact, I think the piano's a gift if you want it. There's something in the notes at the back about having it retuned . . .'

Fern blinked. Retirement? No. That wasn't right. Marte couldn't have been much older than she was. Mid-thirties at most.

'I see.' Paul nodded, as if he'd been expecting something like that. He checked his watch. 'Do we have to decide right now?'

'Not at all,' said Darren. 'Obviously the sooner we get the paperwork back to their solicitor, the sooner we can fix a date for exchanging contracts. But no, take them with you and have a proper look through at your own convenience. If you do have any questions though . . .'

'Sorry, why did you say they're moving?' asked Fern, thinking she must have misheard.

'It's to do with Mrs Rochester's health, I think,' said Darren. 'The estate agent mentioned something about warmer climes during our last catch-up. I'm afraid I don't really know any of the details.'

Something twisted in Fern's stomach, but it wasn't the baby. Not this time. 'They have a daughter living there though?' she asked. 'At the house, I mean. Marte?' But even as she was saying it, the twisting feeling in Fern's stomach tightened. If Marte was the owners' daughter why hadn't she said anything? Why didn't she set Gemma straight? *No, Mrs Rochester's my mother. I'm afraid she's out for the afternoon.* That's what Fern would have said in that situation. It's what *anyone* would have said.

Darren was sifting through another pile of forms. 'Ah, here we are, the Rochesters: Mr Geoffrey Allan and Mrs Caroline Mary. No, no other adults permanently registered at that address.'

So Marte didn't even live there? *But I saw her,* thought Fern. It didn't make any sense.

The rest of the meeting passed in something of a blur. Fern was too busy thinking about the mysterious Marte to pay proper attention to much else. Too busy trying to remember exactly what it was she'd said. *My husband? Yes, I see . . . I didn't realise I'd be here either.* Maybe there'd been some kind of emergency – something to do with the *real* Mrs Rochester's health, that had brought Marte to her parents' house that day – and she'd been too preoccupied, or simply too embarrassed to set Gemma straight. Yes, that must be it, Fern decided, ignoring the lingering sense of unease in her guts. Ignoring the fact that the Rochesters had chosen to retire to the other side of the world when they had a new granddaughter on the way.

There were more forms to go through. Endless forms. Something about access to the old folly. Another round of signatures. Fern felt the beginnings of a headache behind her eyes and regretted not asking for a glass of water when Darren was offering out drinks. But then suddenly the meeting was over and Paul was on his feet, muttering about heavy traffic and commuting times. A fresh round of enthusiastic handshakes and they were heading back down the stairs again.

'Sorry, I just need to pop in here before we go,' said Fern, pointing to the ladies'. 'Won't be long.' She pulled out her phone as soon as she'd locked the cubicle door behind her and typed 'Marte Rochester Crenellation Lane' into the search engine. It didn't get her very far though. Not a single hit that included Crenellation Lane. Swapping the road name for 'Westerton' didn't help matters either. She switched over to the images tab, instead, to discover an entire gallery of Marte Rochesters. None of them bore any resemblance to *her* Marte though. Then again, even assuming she *was* the Rochesters' daughter, Marte might be married, with another name altogether.

'All right, sweetheart?' asked Paul, as Fern joined him outside. He gave her a worried smile, stroking a strand of hair out of her face. 'You seemed a bit distracted in there. This *is* what you want, isn't it?'

No, thought Fern. *This is what* you *want.* But she didn't have the heart to say it out loud. She could see the worry and concern written across his face and couldn't bring herself to add to it with her true feelings about the move or her new concerns over who the mysterious Marte was. Not after everything she'd already put him through in the last few months. Fern missed the old Paul – the Paul who made her laugh and looked at her with passion, rather than pity, in his eyes – and didn't want him thinking Marte might be another figment of her grieving imagination. Unless Marte really *was* all in her head, just like they said Linny was . . . No, that was impossible. Gemma had seen her too.

'I'm fine,' she told him, forcing a smile. 'Just tired.'

'Make sure you take it easy then.' Paul leaned in to kiss her cheek. 'I shouldn't be too late tonight. We can go through the furniture forms then if you want . . .'

'What?' Fern winced as a blonde cyclist cut across the junction behind him. It was fine though – she cleared the oncoming traffic with time to spare, disappearing off down a side street. Yes, it was fine. It wasn't Linny.

'The furniture forms,' Paul repeated. 'We'll have a look through them tonight and see if there's anything we want. That dresser in the dining room, maybe?'

'Yes,' agreed Fern, although she didn't remember any dresser. The physical details of the house had receded into a series of unconnected snapshots over the last few weeks: the beautiful, tiled floor in the hallway; a black-and-white wedding photo on the sitting-room bookcase; yellow light spilling through an upstairs window; the fading roses along the top level of the garden by the old folly.

'And the piano, of course,' said Paul. 'That's a bit of a bonus. Oh, speaking of which . . . Did you see the link I sent you to that new playlist?'

Fern fished in her pocket for her phone, remembering the CD compilations Paul used to make for her when they first got together, with a special meaning or significance to every chosen song.

'You'll have to ignore the cheesy title,' he added, sounding slightly sheepish. 'Although it's true.' Fern glanced up to see him blushing: a proper red-cheeked blush that made her want to reach out and kiss him – *really* kiss him – like the old days. 'It's called "Beautiful Tracks for my Beautiful Wife".'

Fern felt her own cheeks growing warm at the compliment. 'Oh,' she said. 'Thank you, that's lovely.'

'It's nothing much really. Just some nice relaxing piano music I thought you'd enjoy. I thought it might be good for the baby, too,' Paul said, touching his hand to Fern's belly. 'Someone at work said that babies can remember a tune they hear regularly during pregnancy for up to four months after the birth. Sort of like a calming trigger track.' He pulled his hand away again. 'I thought it might be worth a try.'

'Thank you,' Fern said again. 'I'll give it a listen in the car now.'

'And you're okay getting back on your own?' Paul checked, like he always did these days, as if Fern was too frail, or too pregnant, to be trusted behind the wheel. Driving wasn't a problem though. Driving took up all her concentration, keeping her mind firmly in check. It was when she was sitting in the passenger seat that it happened – the imagined swerve of lorries into their path, the sideways glimpses of twisted metal and buckled wheels.

'I'll be fine,' she said, studiously ignoring the blonde on the opposite pavement. *She* wasn't Linny either. 'I might even make a bit of a detour out to Crenellation Lane. Just a quick drive past to have one more look . . .' In truth, it was really a detour to the estate agent's Fern had in mind, hoping that Gemma would be able to shed some light on Marte. *Of course I didn't imagine her. How could I have done?*

'I'll see you at home later,' she told Paul. 'Have a good afternoon.'

Fern linked her phone to the car music system and pulled up the new playlist – anything was better than the local radio station, with its incessant adverts – skipping straight on to track four, Satie's 'Gymnopédie, No. 1', ears straining for those first pianissimo chords as she checked her rear-view mirror. Ah yes, there they were. Beautiful. The baby kicked inside her when the melody came in, almost as if *she* recognised it too. Perhaps it was worth giving Paul's theory a try – there was no denying music's power to trigger memories. Listening to those first few bars, Fern might almost have been back in Mrs Jackson's front room, some sixteen years earlier, squeezed onto the piano stool beside Linny, one hand apiece on the keyboard and the spares draped round each other's waists. It wasn't a duet of course, not really, but that's how they'd often learned their tunes to begin with. It was easier that way. More satisfying. Fern had forgotten quite how much she loved this piece. Maybe she could relearn it – both hands this time – if they took the Rochesters up on their offer of a piano.

Fern was still replaying the piece in her head as she entered the estate agent's.

'Mrs Croft?' Smiley Sonia looked up from her monitor, painted nails paused on the keyboard and painted lips stretched into their usual ready smile. 'What a nice surprise. What brings you all the way out here?' Today's lipstick was brighter than ever: a vivid orange to match her chiffon scarf and topped-up Cypriot tan, teamed with a plain white blouse and navy skirt. All she needed now was one of those funny peaked caps and the air hostess look would be complete.

'Hi Sonia. I was hoping to speak to Gemma actually. I just wanted to double-check something about the second viewing she did with me while you were on holiday.' Fern scanned the office but there was no sign of Gemma. 'Is she in today?'

Sonia shook her head. 'Not 'til the other side of the weekend I'm afraid. Hubby whisked her off to Paris as a surprise for their anniversary. He's such an old romantic. Are you sure it's nothing I can help you with?'

'I don't know. The thing is, Gemma had to get back to the office, so Mrs Rochester showed me round instead, only . . .' Only what? *Only it wasn't Mrs Rochester after all, it was someone called Marte. I just want to find out who she is and make sure I didn't imagine the whole thing.* It sounded ridiculous now, even to Fern.

Sonia beamed. 'Mrs Rochester? She and her husband only just left! You must have missed them by moments.' She pointed through the window towards a grey-haired couple in matching blue anoraks, heading into the baker's on the opposite side of the street. 'Yes, look, there they are.' Sonia stood up and waved, trying to get their attention, but they were fully focused on the pasties and cakes under the counter. 'What was it you wanted to know? Perhaps you can ask her in person.'

What was that woman doing in your house? That's what Fern wanted to know. *Is she your daughter or not?* 'Perfect,' she said out loud. 'I'll see if I can catch them. Thank you.'

Fern reached the baker's just as the Rochesters finished their purchase.

'After you,' said Mr Rochester, holding the door open for Fern as she stood outside, trying to think what to say. How to begin. She caught a glimpse of brown eyes flecked with gold, of faded black amongst the greyness of his hair. He didn't look anything like Marte.

'Oh no, it's okay, I'm not coming in,' Fern said, stepping sideways out of the way. 'I was waiting for you, actually.'

Mr Rochester looked confused. 'Waiting for me?'

'I . . . I wanted to talk to you about your daughter.' *I'm Fern Croft.* That's what she should have said. *My husband and I are buying your house.* Somehow those weren't the words that came out of Fern's mouth though.

'I'm sorry.' The poor man looked even more confused. 'But I don't have a daughter.' Maybe he thought Fern was there to claim him for herself. A long-lost love-child dredged up from his misspent youth.

'We don't have *any* children,' added Mrs Rochester, a thin, frail-looking woman with watery grey eyes. She didn't look like Marte either. 'You must be thinking of someone else . . .' She broke off, clutching her hand to her heart as if she was in pain. 'Dear me, I'm afraid we need to go.'

But then Fern was the one apologising, backing away down the pavement in confusion. Marte wasn't their daughter. Which meant . . . Fern didn't know *what* it meant. 'Sorry,' she stammered. 'Sorry to have bothered you.' She couldn't have made more of a mess of the conversation if she'd tried. It was too late to stop and explain about Marte now though. Too late to find out if *they* knew who the mystery woman in the house had been. It was too late for any of that because Fern had already turned on her heel, scurrying off down the street like a crazy woman. Which was exactly how she felt.

And when she took the promised detour along the elegant, tree-lined cul-de-sac that was Crenellation Lane, when she peered over the low hedge to see a blonde woman in a Fair Isle jumper in one of the upstairs windows, she took that as certified proof: crazy, crazy, crazy. Dr Earnshaw was right. This had gone on for too long. She had to get a hold on her imaginings, acknowledge them for what they were and move on. She owed it to Paul and their unborn child. And she owed it to herself. Fern skipped back through the playlist to the Satie track, stole one last glance up at the window – the suddenly empty window – and drove on.

Chapter 3

Fern and Paul talked that night. Really talked. Not about dressers and pianos – at least, not at first – but about everything that had been going on in Fern's head. About the strange second viewing and her humiliating encounter with the Rochesters. The whole complicated mess. She'd underestimated Paul though. He had more faith in her sanity than *she* did.

Marte must have been the cleaner, that's what Paul said, refusing to give any credence to the alternative: that somehow – even with Gemma there – Fern had imagined the whole thing. And she wanted so badly to believe him – to have her lurking sense of unease rationalised away – that she lapped it up gratefully, nodding like an obedient child as he brushed her anxiety aside.

The cleaner! Of course!

'But I'll talk to Sonia again if it makes you feel better,' Paul promised. 'There'll be a simple enough explanation, sweetheart, you'll see. And we'll change the locks on the doors as soon as we move in. First thing. That's if you still want to go ahead with it all?'

Fern nodded again. 'Yes. Of course.' And the funny thing was, she wasn't just saying it this time. Maybe she really *was* finally ready to leave. The flat seemed to have grown smaller and more oppressive than ever as they sat talking. Less homely. And all the good times she'd had there with Linny – and Paul, of course – they weren't what Fern remembered anymore. The tiny open kitchen no longer reminded her of crazy cocktail sessions and hungover fry-ups after boozy nights of dancing. Now, when she looked at the marbled counter top, Fern saw the unwashed dishes from that drunken anniversary dinner, abandoned in the wake of Linny's call. The dishes that were still sitting there when *the* Phone Call (capital P, capital C) came next morning. Even the big mirror propped up against the living-room wall – the one Linny had rescued from a skip during a famously drunken night out – had become a relic of sadder times. All Fern thought of now when she looked at the mirror was her and Paul in their funeral outfits, the strain reflected in his face as he struggled to hold her upright. She remembered her own face reflected in the glass – already so much thinner than Linny's, even then – stripped of every last trace of colour as she buttoned up her black jacket.

Or perhaps, Fern thought, surprising herself at the notion, it was the other way round. Perhaps the new house on Crenellation Lane, with its pleasing symmetry and high ceilings, had been busy worming its way into her affections while she wasn't looking.

'Yes,' she said again, to prove she meant it this time. The idea of staying put without Linny seemed worse, somehow, than moving on without her. The greater of two evils. 'I'm still not convinced it's the magic cure you're looking for but perhaps a fresh start will do me good. Do *us* good. A step in the right direction, anyway.'

Paul held her then – properly held her, not like a fragile china thing he was scared of breaking – burying his face in her neck. It was only when she felt the rhythmic shuddering in his shoulders that Fern realised he was crying.

'Hey, no snotting on the new maternity top,' she said, trying to turn it into a joke as she lifted his head and kissed away his tears. 'It's only a house.' But there was nothing funny about the sight of Paul crying, his brown eyes scrunched up in misery. For all his sensitivity to Fern's emotions, he rarely let his own get the better of him. He'd cried when his father, Graham, had rung to say he was getting married again. Fern remembered that all too clearly. But they'd been tears of anger and frustration, of worry for his mother, Tina. And of course he'd cried when he heard about Linny, who'd been the official second woman in his life for as long as he and Fern had been together. But Fern had been too deep in her own private grief to pay much attention. Paul was usually the one holding *her* up, not the other way round.

'I loved her too, you know,' he said, his face still buried in the curve of her neck, snotty tears and all. Fern stiffened, thinking of that last phone call. Of the last thing she ever said to her sister. 'But I love you more,' he sobbed. 'And the baby. I just want you back, Fern. I want it to be like it was before. Like *we* were before.'

Only without Linny.

'I know,' she said, wiping away her own tears with the flats of her palms. 'That's what I want too.' She wanted it to be six months ago. She wanted to unsay her spiteful final words and make everything all right again. She wanted to take a sledgehammer to her sister's bike, to strap her to a chair and stand guard over her for as long as it took for fate to give up and move on. *That's* what she wanted. But if she couldn't have that, then maybe a fresh start for the two of them – the three of them – was the next best thing.

'Let's do it,' said Paul, later, when they finally settled down with the pile of furniture printouts. 'Let's put in an offer for the whole lot. New start. New everything.'

'Someone else's old things, you mean?' Fern laughed, feeling lighter than she had in a long time.

'New to us, though,' he said. 'I'm just thinking it's a big house to fill and we'll have better things to worry about when we get there than furniture shopping.' He leaned in sideways, cupping his hands around her belly, and Fern had a shivery flash of Marte standing in the hallway, cradling her bump through her jumper.

'Get off,' she said, pushing him away. 'Stop it.'

Paul drew back, looking hurt and puzzled.

'It tickles, that's all,' Fern lied. 'Sorry. What were you going to say?'

He shrugged his shoulders as if he was shrugging off her rejection. 'It's not like we can't afford it.'

He was right, of course. With the sale of the flat and the balance from his uncle's estate, their new mortgage would be half what they were paying now. And with Linny's life insurance money they could have paid it off altogether if they wanted. Not that Fern would. Blood money. That's what it felt like to her.

She glanced through the sheets of photographs, flicking them against her thumb like a children's flip book. 'Really?' she said, stopping at a 1970s hostess trolley in mock-walnut with a flower-tiled top shelf. '*That's* what you want in your lovely new house?'

Paul grinned. 'It's a period piece, that is. Mum had one just like it. Perfect for all those dinner parties we won't be having with our imaginary friends.' The grin withered on his lips as he realised how that must have sounded. 'I meant, because we don't know anyone there yet . . . that we don't have anyone to invite. That's all. I wasn't talking about . . .' He sighed and shook his head, eyes closed against his own clumsiness.

Wasn't talking about who? Linny? Or Marte? Spoilt for choice with a crazy wife like her. But Fern took his hand and forced herself to smile, to let it pass, not wanting to endanger their new rapport. 'I knew what you meant,' she said. 'But I still think the trolley's a crime against good taste.'

He squeezed her fingers gratefully, the relief evident on his face. 'Okay, you win. Everything *except* the hideous hostess trolley.'

Nothing else seemed to happen for a long time, save for the steady succession of bin bags bundled off to the charity shop (five years' worth of misjudged holiday souvenirs and unwanted gifts from Paul's mother), and heated conversations with Sonia and Darren about hurrying things along. Fern left all the badgering and chasing-up to Paul though. He was better at that sort of thing, refusing to back down for the sake of politeness. She left the whole Marte issue with him as well, too embarrassed to face Sonia again after her undignified run-in with the Rochesters. But nothing more was ever mentioned. Fern wasn't sure if that meant Marte really was just the cleaner after all, or whether Paul forgot to follow it up. Either way, he clearly wasn't worried – *a simple enough explanation, you'll see* – so Fern did her best to put it out of her mind too. And then everything kicked off all at once and she had far more pressing concerns than mystery blondes and awkward encounters outside the baker's. Like how to pack up five years' worth of living in the space of a fortnight. Thirteen days and counting.

She dropped all pretence of working, packing away her paints and desktop easel along with everything else. The children's books she was supposed to be illustrating – a beautiful hand-painted nature series – would have to wait. A few more days wouldn't make much difference to her missed deadline now anyway, and if the publishers kicked up a fuss then Anna, her agent, would deal with it. Anna was a world-class expert when it came to dealing with fuss and at smoothing things over on her clients' behalf. It would be different once they were in the new place, Fern promised herself, sealing down the flaps with brown tape. Once she had her own room to work in, with that lovely yellowy light coming through the windows, there'd be no stopping her. No more distractions, real or otherwise. Not until the baby came, anyway.

'I'm sorry,' she whispered, as a frowning Linny drummed silent fingers against the cluttered tabletop. How long had she been there? 'Please don't look at me like that,' she begged, her mind slipping back to that last night. To their last conversation. 'It was a stupid thing to say. You know I didn't mean it. Please Linny. You have to believe me.' But Linny, being Linny, said nothing. She was already gone.

The last week was especially hard going. Boxes, boxes and yet more boxes. Entire second walls of cardboard and tape bearing down on her from all sides. Fern couldn't physically have done it on her own and was relieved when Paul managed to wrangle some extra days off work for the final push. It was good to have him there, the two of them working alongside each other like a proper team – a proper couple, again – but even though she left all the lifting to him, her entire body still ached with exhaustion. All that kneeling and squatting and ferrying things from room to room was taking its toll, not to mention the strain of last-minute worries, wondering whether they had forgotten to do something. Any lingering doubts she might have had about the new house – about strange pregnant women lurking in the hallway to show people round – were swallowed up in a more general longing to be in and settled. All Fern wanted now was proper space to walk around again and a good night's sleep. And for the endless, endless packing to be over.

'Ready?' Paul asked on Thursday morning, as they stood amongst the emptiness of their old lives, the last box safely tucked away in the back of the removal van. Already it felt like the flat belonged to someone else. As if it had moved on without them.

'I think so.' Fern took a last look at the sangria stains on the sitting-room carpet – what a night that had been! – and the stiletto boot-cracked tile above the fireplace (Linny's boot, naturally), and nodded. Ready as she'd ever be. And there was Linny herself, leading the way in skinny jeans and her favourite black T-shirt, slipping out through the open front door without so much as a backwards glance.

'Goodbye,' said Fern, out loud, addressing the flat and any last memories still trapped within its walls. There was no need to say goodbye to her sister though, she realised, with a peculiar mixture of dismay and relief. It was quite clear Linny was coming with them.

Chapter 4

The baby stopped kicking as soon as the right hand's plaintive melody came in, hypnotic notes winding sinuously over Satie's low pianissimo chords. It was like magic – musical witchcraft. Fern couldn't tell if it was the tune itself, whether the baby really was listening out for 'Gympnopédie, No. 1', or if it was simply taking its cue from her. Something happened inside her chest, inside her head, every time she heard it, but the feeling was hard to put into words. An emotional easing. A sense of letting go, even as the memories came flooding back, stronger each time: the bony jut of Linny's hip against hers as they squashed together on the piano stool; the chipped pink polish on her sister's nails (strictly against school uniform codes, of course, but that never stopped Linny); the cloying scent of Mrs Jackson's too-strong perfume, mixed with wood polish and roast dinner. Fern shut her eyes – just for a moment – and breathed in. She could almost smell it now.

She was waiting for the removal van to finish its complicated turning manoeuvre, left hand twitching as the music swelled inside the car, fingers searching out the once familiar notes. She reached along the dashboard for the low G, floating her hand back to the steering wheel to complete the major seventh chord. Yes, that was it. Then a low D and back up to A, C sharp, F sharp.

The same repeating two-bar pattern for whole lines at a time, plodding away under Linny's melody. Linny always got the tune when they played together, but that was all right by Fern. She'd been happy enough in her sister's shadow – a shy, unassuming frond beside the double pink blooms of Linnaea, the twinflower.

Ah, but who would have guessed the notes were still there after all this time, hardwired into the skin of her fingers, as if they'd been hibernating? As if *she'd* been hibernating, her younger piano-playing self still furled up tight inside her adult shell. And now there was a new little Linette inside her too, and everything was going to be all right. Maybe that's what the music was trying to tell her. It might not feel like it now – with dark chords still clustering round her every waking thought – but it was going to get better. A new house. A new start. Her, Paul, the baby, and Linny. And even as she sat there behind the lorry, fingers still moving along invisible keys, Fern knew her sister would be waiting there to welcome them. Proper, grown-up Linny, this time. No chipped nail varnish for her.

One last clumsy reverse, tyres growling with the effort, and the removal truck finally made the turn into Crenellation Lane. Mrs Jackson's perfumed front room faded away to lines of bare-branched trees and white Victorian villas, while Satie retreated into the background. This was it. No going back now. The driver sounded his horn in triumph, blasting the baby into wakefulness as he leaned out of the cab window, fist-pumping the air. Paul answered from behind with a short *parp* of his own, having somehow managed to get all the way out to the estate agent's to pick up the keys in the time it had taken Fern to crawl up the dual carriageway behind the lorry. And now all three of them went rolling round the corner in convoy, to find a tall blonde figure blocking the road in front of them.

Funny, for a moment Fern thought it was Marte, a jagged breath catching in her throat as the forgotten worries came rushing back to find her. *There she is. It's happening again.* But only for a moment. It was Linny – of course it was – she could see that now. Her hair was down this time, blowing loose around her shoulders, and she'd swapped her skinny jeans and T-shirt for a short red dress and heeled boots. Yes, Fern could see her sister as clear as day, but she still couldn't work out what she was doing in the middle of the street, ignoring the heavy lorry rumbling towards her.

'What's Aunty Linny up to?' she asked the baby out loud, keeping her voice bright and singsong. Her stomach felt hard and alien under her hand. 'What's she looking at?' It wasn't them, that was for sure, and it certainly wasn't the seven-and-a-half-tonne truck bearing down on her from behind. And of course, the driver couldn't see Linny either, could he?

'Come on,' she shouted through the windscreen. 'Move.'

The baby squirmed on cue, dragging an elbow against the tightness of her belly, but Linny didn't budge. She wasn't going anywhere.

'Hurry up!' Bewilderment gave way to panic as their convoy drew closer. Closer. Much too close. And still Linny stood there.

'Get out of the road!' Fern was yelling now, both hands off the steering wheel, batting at the air to get her sister's attention. But Linny was too busy watching the red Audi reversing into the opposite drive. Staring after it, stupidly, waiting for history to repeat itself.

'Linny!' Vomit rose in the back of Fern's throat as the corner of the cab smashed into her sister's side, white hot pain ricocheting through her own hip and up into her spine. *No. No. Please no.* It was just like before. Just like the day she . . . she . . .

Fern hadn't been there when the lorry hit but she'd lived it a thousand times since. Seen it. Heard it. Felt her sister's body crumpling like paper beneath the screeching wheel. But only in her head. Only in her dreams. This was different.

'Linny!' Fern didn't stop to think. Didn't stop to remind herself it wasn't real. *Couldn't* be real. 'Linny!' She was already halfway out the car door, engine still running, seat belt still tangled round her belly, screaming for her sister.

'No!' Months of barely bottled-up grief came tearing out of her throat in a raw howl, like an animal, as she flung herself towards the empty space where Linny had been.

'Linnaea!' Another shout from behind. Someone else calling for her sister. But it was too late.

Afterwards Fern remembered faces: the startled panic of the removal man as he slammed on his brakes; the wide-eyed shock of the man in the red Audi, their new neighbour; and Paul's face, bleached with fear, lips mouthing silent curses – or was it prayers? – as he leaned over her, scooping her up in his shaking arms. But not Linny's face. Linny had already disappeared under the truck, already vanished back to whatever dark corner of Fern's fevered imagination she'd sprung from. Only it wasn't just Fern this time, was it? That second cry – 'Linnaea!' – surely that meant she *wasn't* mad after all? Paul must have seen her too.

But that was all she remembered: the jumbled faces and the cry. Everything else was a blur, save for odd snapshots of clarity amongst the blanketing fog of her pain. Someone must have taken her inside, sat her down on the sofa once it was unloaded, and placed a mug of hot sweet tea in her hands. *World's Best Sister* it said on the front. It wasn't one of theirs. And Paul must have supervised the rest of the unpacking without her because the removal men were already shouting their goodbyes from the safety of the sitting-room doorway, not wanting to intrude on her recovery. On her craziness.

Six o'clock in the evening now. Time seemed to have melted into itself as she'd sat there, watching cardboard boxes bumping along the hallway. Listening to Paul shouting up the stairs about dented furniture and scratched wallpaper. Somewhere along the way the television had arrived in the corner of the room, still swathed in its protective wrapping. Fern didn't remember that, but she remembered the tea. More tea. Inevitable trips to the toilet. Someone taking her blood pressure, patting her on the arm and smiling. Small talk about the baby. About due dates and names. Paul coming to check on her like a poorly toddler with a temperature. Like a sick puppy. And now here he was again, easing himself onto the sofa beside her, sweaty and sour-smelling. He looked shattered, poor thing.

'How are you feeling?' he asked.

'Better, thanks,' Fern said, blinking back the memory of her sister standing there as the truck came rumbling down to meet her. The tea was finally starting to kick in, clearing a path through the fog in her head. She drained what was left of her latest cup, screwing up her nose against the sweetness. It had gone cold already, but she forced it down all the same, letting the sugar and caffeine bring her fully back to her senses. Yes, physically she *was* feeling better. But emotionally? It was too soon to tell. It wasn't like the other times she'd seen Linny; she knew that much. Until now they'd merely been snatches, glimpses out the corner of her eyes, teasing reminders of everything she'd lost. But this time had been real. Real and raw, hollowing her out from the inside all over again. Even now the emptiness was so overpowering it was a relief to feel the baby kicking, to know it was still there.

'Don't ever do that to me again,' said Paul, turning towards her, eyes wet, hands clutching at her knees. 'Promise me, Fern. I don't think I've ever been so scared.' This from the man who'd bailed out of a stag do skydive at twelve thousand feet.

Fern nodded, swamped by a sudden gush of guilt. No wonder he looked so tired. So lost. This wasn't how their fresh start was supposed to go. Things had finally been better between them these last few weeks – *she'd* been better – and now . . . She balanced the empty cup on the arm of the sofa and peeled away his hands, bringing them up to her lips. 'I'm sorry,' she murmured. 'I'm so sorry.'

'I don't know what I'd do if anything happened to you.' His voice sounded raw and jerky. 'The sooner we get you an appointment with that local counsellor Dr Earnshaw recommended, the better.'

'But . . .' *But I'm not crazy. How can I be? You saw her too.*

'Please, Fern. If not for me, then for the baby.'

She opened her mouth to protest – *I heard you calling her name. Surely you believe me now?* – but something held her back. Maybe Paul was still in shock. In denial. Perhaps that was a conversation for tomorrow instead, given everything he'd been through.

'It's going to be all right,' she promised, wishing she could believe it. '*We're* going to be all right.' But the music-inspired calm she'd felt in the car – the sense of hope – had splintered into a thousand tiny Linny-shaped pieces. How many months to put them back together this time?

Chapter 5

Sleep, when it finally came that night, brought little relief. Fern found herself back out in the road again – a strange, dream version of Crenellation Lane, with the estate agent's on one side and their old flat on the other – only this time she was sitting at a piano and there were two blonde figures waiting for the lorry in their matching dresses: her sister *and* Marte.

Fern broke off from practising her scales to warn them but her dream legs refused to cooperate. And then the red Audi was there, just like before, as the lorry picked up speed, hurtling along the road towards them, faster and faster. For a moment it looked as if it might miss them altogether, but Marte reached across, shoving Linny under the wheel with a shrieking cry of *'Linnaea!'* before wiping her hands down on her enormous pregnancy bump and heading back to the house.

One disturbing scene melded seamlessly into the next. Marte was in her old Fair Isle jumper again now – the wool straining over her distorted belly – with Fern's favourite slippers wedged onto her feet. She was giving them a guided tour of the upstairs rooms, pointing out her favourite spots as if they'd all be living there together. She'd even picked out her own bedroom under the eaves, all decked out like a nursery, complete with a barred cot and red baby blanket. For a moment Fern thought it was for them – for Linette – but her own belly seemed to have shrivelled away to nothing. To emptiness.

'My baby!' she cried out, pointing to the growing pool of blood by her feet. 'My baby!' But it was too late. Much too late.

And then the baby started crying and Fern woke with a sudden rush to a strange room. A few wild moments of panic – the bed, why was it back to front? and the baby, where was the baby? – then her eyes adjusted to the darkness, to wakefulness, and she remembered where she was.

The crying became a whining hot water pipe on the other side of the wall. Paul lay flat on his back beside her, snoring softly to himself. And the baby? The baby was fine, wriggling away like normal, pressing down on her bladder until it forced her out of bed.

It's okay, she told herself, blinking away the memory of Marte's face – of the look of triumph in the woman's eyes as the blood lapped around Fern's cold, bare feet. *It was just a dream.* Noisy plumbing and too much stress. That's all. Just a dream.

Friday was already well under way when Fern woke again to an empty bed and the sound of a crackling radio playing to itself in another room. The attic, perhaps? Maybe Paul had unearthed his old portable radio from one of the boxes and was retuning it, without much success by the sound of it. A breathy lullaby-style song battled against the crackling waves on a loop – the same childlike tune over and over – and then died away altogether. He'd be better off with the digital one she'd bought him for their first anniversary, but Fern had no idea which of the endless boxes that had ended up in.

I should go and help him look for it, she thought, blinking herself back into consciousness, feeling every bit as exhausted as she had the night before. How could it be 9 a.m. already?

A face-shaped stain leered down at Fern from the ceiling as she lay there, its yellow-brown jaws stretched into a hollow yawn. She certainly hadn't spotted *that* period feature when Marte showed her around the upstairs rooms – she'd been too busy making polite noises about the tiled fireplace to think of looking up. Yes, Marte must have been standing just there, at the end of the Rochesters' bed, Fern realised. She could still picture her now, the details fresher than ever after last night's dreams, from the shadows under the woman's eyes – such blue, blue eyes – to the silver flower-shaped studs in her ears and the pulled stitch on the front of her jumper.

Fern shivered under the duvet (Paul had muttered something about resetting the central heating last night, but it didn't seem to have worked), steeling herself for the day ahead and the once-simple task of getting herself vertical. Climbing out of bed was a complicated enough procedure already – she could hardly imagine what she'd be like by forty weeks. But even though her body felt more sluggish and alien than ever, yesterday's onslaught of grief seemed to have dissipated in the night. It was as if the horror of what she'd seen – the sheer terror of losing her sister all over again – had worked its way out through her nightmares, to be blinked away again under the yawning yellow face above her head. Now, when Fern forced her mind back to the scene with the removal lorry, there was relief mixed in with the horror. Relief that Paul had finally seen Linny too, which meant she wasn't crazy after all, not this time – unless they both were . . .

Paul's side of the bed was cold. Already up and at it, no doubt, in his bid to get everything straight before he went back to work on Monday. He must have showered and dressed as well: the bathroom mirror was a fog of steam, a finger-traced heart waiting for her in the middle of the glass. *Sweet*, Fern thought, if a little sinister-looking where the outline had started to run. He really was trying, she knew that. Trying to find a way back to before. And maybe now they stood a proper chance of making it work, she told herself, with his cry still ringing in her head: *Linnaea!*

Yes, things would be better now that he believed her. Who knew, maybe that was Linny's plan all along. Perhaps the whole gruesome drama of yesterday had been her ill-judged way of knotting the pair of them back together. A sign of forgiveness.

It's okay. It doesn't matter anymore. Be happy.

The pipes started up their whining again as Fern ran a basin of water. But it was a low-pitched moan this morning, a sullen drawn-out grievance. Nothing like the crying baby she'd heard in her sleep. *Thought* she'd heard. She splashed at her face, rinsing away the last vestige of her dreams, trying not to think about the ingrained dirt clinging to the outer ring of the plughole, magnified by the water. Trying to ignore the stray hair she'd just spotted, still tangled round the chain, and the half-circles of soap slime behind the taps, that must have escaped the ministrations of the cleaning cloth. Perhaps the Rochesters had been too caught up with last-minute packing to finish the job properly. Or maybe it was their mysterious cleaner, Marte, cutting corners on her last day, knowing her employers wouldn't be around to care. Either way, a proper scrub and bleach were top of the to-do list, Fern decided.

The towels hadn't found their way to the bathroom yet. She dried her face on a piece of loo roll, wondering how Paul had managed after his shower. Maybe he'd drip dried his way around the house, indulging in a spot of naked unpacking. Ha! That'd give the new neighbours something to talk about. Something *else* to talk about, rather. The image made her smile – her first proper smile since they'd arrived. She padded back into the bedroom, slipping yesterday's cardigan on over her nightie, before heading downstairs in search of naked husbands wielding box-cutting equipment. If she was quick, she might catch him in the act.

She stopped, halfway down, at the sound of voices coming from the hallway.

'I'm sorry I didn't get the chance to pop over and see you yesterday. To apologise.' It was Paul. Not quite so naked after all then, hopefully. Fern shrank back into the half turn of the staircase, listening. 'It wasn't exactly the arrival I had in mind,' he said.

'Don't worry on our account,' came a deep-voiced reply. The man in the red Audi, Fern guessed. He must have had a *great* view from his drive. A proper ringside seat.

'As long as everyone's okay.'

'Yes, she's fine now, thank you,' said Paul. 'Sleeping peacefully. I think it was the shock more than anything.'

'Of course,' agreed the other voice, as if that was his diagnosis too. 'I just bumped into April now, the nurse at number ten?' He made it sound like a question rather than a statement of fact. 'She said she gave your wife the quick once-over afterwards?' Another question, although Fern couldn't tell which bit needed clarifying – her married status or the extent of her check-up. 'Blood pressure and what have you,' the man added. 'And the baby.'

It occurred to her she ought to go down and introduce herself. *Hi I'm Fern. The crazy pregnant lady who tried to get herself run over yesterday. Yes, that's right. The one screaming in the street for her dead sister. It's nice to meet you.* But she didn't. She merely shifted position, manoeuvring herself along the stairs in order to hear better.

'Yes,' said Paul. 'Lucky she was on hand. I've managed to get us an appointment with the new midwife this morning to make doubly sure everything's okay, but I don't think there's any cause for concern. Just shock, that's all,' he said again. 'Nothing a good night's sleep won't cure.'

'She gave *me* a bit of a shock too! What was she doing out there?'

'She thought she saw a cat,' Paul told him, the lie slipping out so easily Fern wondered if he'd been practising it in his head.

A cat? That's what we're calling my sister now, is it? You saw her too, remember.

'It must have been a trick of the light or something. Pregnancy hormones,' Paul added. 'You know . . .'

Hormones? Ah yes, of course. If in doubt, blame them.

The man cleared his throat, suggesting women's hormones were the last thing he wanted to think about at that time of the morning. 'Just as long as she's okay,' he said. Fern pictured him backing away from the front door. Trying to make his escape. 'And the baby.'

'Yes,' said Paul. 'Thanks for coming by, and sorry again. I'm Paul, by the way. And my wife's Fern. We'll have to have you over properly when things calm down a bit.'

'Fern?' The man sounded surprised, as if he'd been expecting something more exotic. As if Fern was too timid a name for the sort of woman who threw herself at lorries. 'We used to have a dog called Fern. Lovely old thing she was. Beautiful red setter.'

Nice, thought Fern, suppressing the sudden urge to giggle. *Your wife reminds me of a dog I used to know. Dead now, of course.*

'I'm Richard,' said Dog Man, changing the subject.

Red Setter Richard, thought Fern to herself, wondering if Paul was thinking the same. They used to have shared secret nicknames for everyone they met – a harmless (if childish) development of the 'one-word game' Fern used to play with Linny when they were young. It had been a decidedly half-hearted affair lately though, with the exception of Smiley Sonia and Devoted Darren – yet another part of their lives that seemed to have died along with Linny. But maybe the move, with an entire street full of new neighbours to meet, would breathe new life into the old nickname game as well as their marriage.

'Good to meet you anyway,' said Red Setter Richard. 'I'd better go – Kerry will be wondering where I've got to. I'm supposed to be on leave this week, but it's been nothing but jobs . . . It'll be a relief to get back to the office on Monday! Let us know if you need anything. Local tips . . . the proverbial cup of sugar . . .'

Fern hauled herself back onto her feet as Paul came to meet her on the stairs, fully clothed, thank goodness. Fully dry. She remembered the heart he'd left her on the mirror and smiled.

'Ah, you're up,' he said, tipping his head forwards to kiss her belly. 'I was just coming to wake you. That was one of our new neighbours from across the road, Richard, the one with the red Audi. He seems like a nice enough chap.'

Just plain Richard. No nickname yet then.

'Yes, I heard,' said Fern. 'I didn't want to come down in my nightie though.'

Paul tugged at the front of his shirt. 'These are yesterday's clothes, I'm afraid. Bit grim really.' He sniffed at his left armpit, wrinkling up his nose in distaste. 'I was hoping to have a shower this morning but I couldn't find any towels. You don't remember which box they're in, do you?'

Fern stared at him in confusion. But the steamed-up bathroom . . . the dripping heart in the mirror . . .? She shivered. It didn't seem quite so sweet now. Far from it.

Chapter 6

No dripping heart. No steamed-up glass. Nothing. Just their own reflections – two bewildered faces with matching shadows under their eyes. His and hers tiredness chic.

'If it wasn't you, then how did it get there?' asked Fern, addressing the empty mirror.

Paul shrugged. She hated it when he shrugged. 'I don't know what you expect me to say. I didn't touch the shower, all right? I didn't steam up the mirror and I certainly didn't draw any hearts on it. Whatever you saw it's long gone now.'

Whatever you thought *you saw.*

'Linny,' Fern said, realisation hitting her like a physical punch in the chest. What other explanation could there be? 'It must have been Linny.' Did that mean she'd forgiven her?

'No, sweetheart, no. Please don't start this again.'

'Her way of telling me it's okay . . .' *Please, please let it be Linny.* Fern reached out to the glass as if she might still catch her sister's touch. But it felt like any other mirror.

'Give me strength,' said Paul. 'She didn't draw the heart, okay? It had probably been there for ages. It must have been greasy or something, that's why it didn't fog up like the rest of the glass.'

36

Fern shut her ears to his logic, which was flawed anyway. It still didn't explain how the mirror had steamed itself up all on its own. 'Just like with Mum,' she murmured. She and Linny saw signs from their mother in all sorts of places after she died. Hidden messages spelled out in secret codes only they knew how to interpret – in the mess of graffiti along the old train line, in the pattern of raindrops down the classroom window, in a bowl of spilled cornflakes. Only when their father took them to see the child psychologist, Linny pretended they'd made the whole thing up. Pretended it was just a game they played to keep from missing her so much.

'Listen to me.' Paul rested his hands on her shoulders, spinning her back round to face him. 'You've got to stop this. It's not healthy. Not for you, not for us, and definitely not for the baby. He or she needs a mother who's here – living in the real world – not off in some grief-stricken La La Land.'

Why was he being like this? 'But you saw her too yesterday, out in the street.' Wait, maybe that was the problem. Maybe this was his way of dealing with it, with the fact that Fern had been right all along, shutting himself off to the very idea of Linny in the hope that it would all go away again. No heart. No steamed-up mirror. No dead sister-in-law disappearing under a lorry.

The sun moved behind a cloud, pitching the room into sudden gloom.

'What are you talking about?' said Paul. 'All I saw was you – the woman I love, the mother of my unborn child – trying to get herself killed over . . . over nothing. Over a figment of her imagination. I *honestly* thought you were getting better. I thought . . .' He took his hands away and covered his eyes, sinking down onto the edge of the bath like a broken old man.

Part of her wanted to reach out and touch him. Wanted to wrap her arms around his neck and bury her lips in his unwashed hair. But the rest of her was too angry. 'You *saw* her,' she insisted. 'I heard you calling her name.' It was just like her mother all over

37

again. Only this time it was Paul denying he'd seen anything. Not Linny.

Paul shook his head. 'No. You didn't.'

'Linnaea. That's what you said. You *shouted* it. Just after the lorry . . . after she . . .'

'I mean it, Fern. You've got to stop all this,' he repeated, head still buried in his hands. 'If you won't do it for me then at least do it for the baby. Otherwise . . .'

Otherwise what?

He didn't say. At least, Fern didn't wait to hear if he did. She left him rocking backwards and forwards on the rim of the bath, before she said something she'd regret. Before she let rip with an otherwise of her own. *You've got to stop treating me like I'm crazy otherwise I'll . . .* because what *was* her otherwise? *I'll go and live with my crazy dad in the care home? Go and live with my dead sister in the cemetery? Go back to the flat we just sold and raise the baby on my non-existent earnings?* She didn't have an otherwise, did she? She was trapped here whether she liked it or not.

The kitchen was looking remarkably unpacked already. The fake wood units, with their fake gold handles, were every bit as old-fashioned and ugly as Fern remembered, but at least they were usable now, without teetering piles of boxes stacked across the worktops. Paul must have been up and at it for hours, slaving away while she slept. A grudging sense of guilt almost sent her back to the bathroom to make up with him, but she held her ground. Why should *she* have to apologise? He was the one talking down to her like some poor delusional, unfit mother. *She* wasn't the deluded one though. Not this time. Unless . . . Unless she'd imagined Paul calling out her sister's name along with everything else? Like Linny? Like Marte? No. Of course she hadn't.

Fern searched through the cupboards until she found the mugs and decaffeinated tea bags, then planted herself at their newly inherited kitchen table to wait while the kettle boiled. A breeze caught her as she stretched out her legs: a sudden chill running all the way down the right side of her body, as if the back door had blown open. It was still firmly locked though. There was no imagining that. Fern could see the double bolts from where she was sitting, top and bottom.

'Linny?' she whispered. 'Is that you? Are you there?'

No answer. Of course there wasn't. What was she expecting? Supernatural music and a voice calling her from beyond the veil? Ha! Wait 'til Paul caught her trying to start a conversation with thin air! No, Linny hadn't suddenly come back as some kind of Halloween ghoul, just because they'd moved into an old house. Linny was still Linny, the other half of her whole, watching over her like she always had. Watching her. Waiting for her. Wiping hearts onto the new bathroom mirror . . .

Fern headed over to the back door – its lower panels all steamed-up from the just-boiled kettle – and traced a matching heart of her own on the misted surface, holding her breath as she waited for Linny's reply.

Nothing.

I'M SORRY, she wrote underneath, scrunching up the 'y' to make it fit the space.

Still nothing.

Come on. Give me something, here. Anything. Just to prove I didn't imagine it.

But if it was proof Fern wanted, she was out of luck. She made the tea while she waited, forcing down a couple of biscuits by way of breakfast, watching the slow bleed of letters down the cooling pane.

Please, Linny. Linny?

She wiped the glass clean again at the sound of Paul's footsteps on the stairs, blood rushing to her cheeks as if she'd been caught doing something incriminating. Like trying to commune with the dead . . .

'Kettle's not long boiled,' she said, as he came into the kitchen, freshly showered and dressed. He smiled at her as if nothing had happened. As if everything was normal between them. Fern forced a matching smile of her own – too tired and confused to fight anymore. 'You found the towels then?'

'They were up in the attic room for some reason,' he said. 'Even though the box was clearly labelled BATHROOM. I don't know what made me think of looking up there, but it was a good call.'

Fern had a sudden flashback to her dream, to the barred cot and red baby blanket waiting under the eaves for the mysterious Marte. She remembered the cold look on the other woman's face as she'd stood there, watching Fern's baby leaking out of her, dripping away through the attic floor. She shivered, a fresh chill running down the other side of her body as Paul bent over and kissed the top of her head like a peace offering.

'You might be better off with baths for the time being though,' he added. 'The water pressure's all over the place and the temperature can't make up its mind. Scalding hot one moment, then freezing cold the next.' He sat down beside her, rubbing at an ingrained coffee ring with his finger. 'That's old houses for you, I guess. Might have to get a plumber to take a look if I can't sort it out myself.'

Fern thought about the whining pipes crying in the middle of the night. Yes, the sooner they got the plumbing sorted out the better. 'I'll ring round on Monday,' she offered. 'Once we've got ourselves a bit straighter. Maybe your friend Richard can recommend someone local.'

'I'm sorry,' said Paul. And there it was, finally, the apology she'd been waiting for. The admission. *I did see your sister yesterday. I do believe you about the mirror.* Only it wasn't that at all.

'I'm sorry to be going back to work so soon,' he finished, 'leaving you with all of this.' He gestured towards the kitchen cupboards, as if they were the real source of her problems. 'It'll be worth it though, once we're settled. You'll see. Things are going to get better from now on.'

Fern let him nuzzle into her, breathing in the fresh tang of his deodorant against the lemony sweetness of his shower gel. *Her* shower gel, in fact, but who was counting? She let him whisper his love into the curve of her neck, the words tickling at her skin.

I don't want to talk about Linny and the lorry anymore. That's what he was *really* saying, wasn't it? *Please, let's just move on.*

Then stop treating me like I'm crazy. Like I imagined the whole thing. Please, Paul, before this tears us apart for good.

'I love you too,' she whispered back, hoping that love was enough. Hoping that their new start wasn't the beginning of the end.

Chapter 7

There was a man waiting for them on the doorstep when they left the house a short while later, after another cup of tea and a quick change of clothes. A thickset man in shorts and T-shirt, with dark, curly hair and a round, childlike face. Was this Red Setter Richard coming back for some more neighbourly nosing?

'Ah. Sorry,' said the man, staring at Fern's stomach. No, it couldn't be Richard. The voice was all wrong. Too hesitant. Too clumsy. 'I was just coming to see you, to introduce myself.'

'We're on our way out, I'm afraid,' said Fern. Was this how things worked on Crenellation Lane? One person after another coming to gawp? Or was that level of welcome reserved for women who threw themselves at removal trucks? She felt a pang of nostalgia for the anonymity of their old life – for the self-imposed isolation she'd hidden in since Linny's death. Fern couldn't even remember the last time she'd seen her old neighbours. Everyone in the building had kept such different hours.

'Okay, I'm Sean,' said the man, shifting his weight from one muddied walking boot to the other, refusing to take the hint. 'I don't know if the Rochesters mentioned me?'

Sheepish Sean.

'Hi, good to meet you, Sean. I'm Paul, and this is my wife, Fern. I never actually met the Rochesters but you did, didn't you?' Paul asked turning back to Fern.

'Sort of,' she admitted, blushing at the memory. Maybe if she'd seen fit to introduce herself to them properly that day outside the baker's they might have got round to such niceties. 'It was a lady called Marte who showed me round though . . .' Fern's throat tightened as she said the woman's name, the memory of last night's dream still praying on her mind. But she ploughed on regardless. The sooner she knew for sure who this Marte was, the sooner she could forget about her again. 'We think she might have been their cleaner.'

'Who? *Marte*, did you say?' Sean's eyes narrowed in confusion.

Fern nodded, although his reaction made her doubt herself. She'd replayed that second viewing in her head so many times afterwards – had searched for her so many times on the internet – that the woman's name had cemented itself into her brain. *Marte. Marte. Marte.* It hadn't even occurred to her until now that she might have got it wrong. Might have misheard. 'Yes, that's right. At least I *think* that's what she said. Do you know her?'

Sean rubbed at a bit of dirt above his eyebrow as he considered his answer. Fern noticed another splatter of something mud-like nestled in the crease of his chin. Perhaps he'd been for an early morning hike along the river, splashing through puddles. That would explain the walking boots too.

'No,' he said at last, shaking his head for extra emphasis. 'They didn't have a cleaner as far as I know. Just me.'

Paul shot Fern a worried look as the man reached into his pocket for a business card, pressing it into her hand. She knew that look all too well. He'd been so certain Marte was the cleaner – that there was a rational explanation for what she was doing at the house that day – but now he'd be forced to reconsider the alternative. *It's all in your head.* That's what he was thinking, wasn't it? *Just like Linny.*

43

'I'm a gardener,' Sean added, in case Fern couldn't read the card for herself: **Sean Hoskins, Garden Landscaping and Maintenance.** 'I do most of the houses here on the lane and round about.' He pointed up the road towards a newer red brick property with an ornate topiary hedge. 'I only live over there, you see. We're practically neighbours.'

'Lovely,' said Fern, still battling with this new information about Marte. *Non*-information, rather. Not the Rochesters' daughter. Not their cleaner. Who else did that leave? 'We'll give it some thought.' They probably *could* do with a gardener once they were settled, given that their combined horticultural experience was limited to the pot of basil on their old kitchen windowsill. That had withered away to brown stems after Linny died though.

Sean ploughed on with his sales pitch as if he hadn't heard. 'Been doing your garden for years now, carrying straight on from one owner to the next. I was hoping you might be interested in keeping me on? Very reasonable rates . . .'

'As I say, we'll definitely think about it once we've unpacked and had a chance to see what needs doing out there,' Fern told him. 'Do you know the woman I mean though?' she added, turning the conversation back to Marte (if that really *was* her name), still hoping he could explain away the confusion. 'You must have seen her around the place. She's tall – about my height I'd say, with long blonde hair. And pregnant. A friend of theirs, maybe?'

'Sorry, Sean,' said Paul, cutting her off short. 'We really do need to get going.' Was that the real reason though, or was he just embarrassed by Fern's questions? Embarrassed by Fern full stop? 'I'm sure we'll be in touch soon about the garden, but for now if you'll excuse us . . .'

'She had a bit of an accent.' Fern ploughed on, refusing to be sidelined. She had to know, one way or the other. *I didn't imagine it. How could I have done?* 'Swedish, I'd say at a guess . . .'

'I'm sorry, no idea,' said Sean. He backed away down the path, taking his cue from Paul, stepping instinctively over the raised paving flag halfway along. 'Nice to meet you both,' he added with a cheery wave as he reached the gate. 'You know where I am if you need anything – gardening or otherwise.'

They took Paul's car to their 10.30 a.m. antenatal appointment because there was more room in the boot for shopping on the way home. That was the official reason anyway. Nothing to do with the last time Fern had been behind the wheel.

Paul wanted her to see the new counsellor Dr Earnshaw had recommended too – a Dr Susannah Culvert over in Westerton. The more medical experts the better as far as he was concerned. But Fern refused to be rushed into it. Refused to go back down that route until she'd had a chance to process everything properly. There'd been something different about Linny the day before that she still couldn't quite put her finger on. As if she'd had a reason for being there. Right there on that spot. A reason why Paul could see her too, even if he denied it afterwards. And now there was the mirror message to think about as well, not to mention her newly resurrected worries about Marte . . .

Fern scanned the length of Crenellation Lane from the safety of the passenger seat, hoping for another glimpse of her twin. For some kind of clue to make sense of it all. Why now? Why here? But there was nothing. Just houses and trees and neat privet borders. No sign of Linny heading up from the T-junction, and no sign of her in the rear-view mirror. Nothing of the elusive Marte, either. The entire street was empty save for the retreating figure of Sean, turning in through the gap in his crenellated hedge.

'I thought you'd decided to let this Marte nonsense drop,' said Paul as they passed the driveway with its red Audi, cutting through the empty space where she'd last seen Linny. The empty Linny-shaped space inside Fern's chest throbbed in recognition. *Oh, Linny.*

'I didn't decide anything of the sort,' she said, prickling at Paul's choice of words. *It's not nonsense. I need to know what she was doing there.* 'You told me you'd talk to Sonia about it. I'm guessing you didn't though.' The words sounded more antagonistic than she'd meant. *You saw Linny too. Why won't you admit it?*

'I'm guessing I had other important things to think about,' said Paul, defensively. 'Like moving house. Like looking after you.'

'I don't need looking after.'

'Yes,' he said. 'You do.' He took a deep breath. 'Which is why I'm asking my mum to come down for a bit.'

What? No! Not Tina, thought Fern. Anyone but her. Only there wasn't anyone else was there? One dead sister, one equally dead mother, a father lost in the warren of his own memories and another lost to the charms of his new French wife. And Tina. That was the total sum of their combined families. Fern had never noticed the gaps in their support network while Linny was alive, and why would she? Linny was somehow mother, father, sister and friend all rolled into one. With her and Paul by her side why would Fern need anyone else? But now? Now it was just the two of them, drifting in and out of understanding, waiting for the baby to fix them back together. And then there was Tina, who'd been desperate to come and 'help' from the moment she knew Fern was pregnant. There might not have been enough room at the flat – not for more than a couple of nights on the sofa bed. But now? Now they had room to spare.

'No,' said Fern. 'Please don't do that. I know you're worried. I know you think I'm being erratic. But I'm not going to let anything happen to me . . . or you,' she added, stroking her bump through the tightening fabric of her maternity dress. 'Am I now, Little One? You tell Daddy. We don't need Granny babysitting us, do we?'

She glanced out of the window as they passed a woman on a bike. Long blonde ponytail and no helmet. It wasn't Linny. Where *was* Linny?

'It needn't be for long,' said Paul. 'Just while we're getting ourselves straight.' He turned off the volume on the sat nav. 'Let's face it, we could do with an extra pair of hands. We haven't even bought a cot yet.'

'No,' she told him, her voice firm. 'That's the *last* thing we need.'

'Okay, maybe only a Moses basket to start with, but even so . . .'

'No, I mean your mother's the last thing we need. The last thing *I* need, anyway.'

'What about me?' he said petulantly. 'Has it ever occurred to you that *I* might want a bit of extra support? It hasn't been easy for me either, you know.'

'But this is supposed to be *our* new start. You and me.' Fern could feel the moral high ground slipping away under her feet. 'Please, Paul.'

What if he was right though? What if she really *did* need babysitting? What if it *was* all in her head – Linny and Marte and the heart on the mirror – and she was officially too unhinged to be trusted on her own anymore? Seeing Linny everywhere these last few months was one thing – that was grief and guilt playing tricks on her mind, just like Dr Earnshaw said. But conjuring up a whole new person out of nowhere – talking to her, following her around the house, comparing baby bumps, for goodness' sake – no amount of grief could explain *that*. And if her brain could invent something as crazy and convoluted as an imaginary house viewing, what else was it capable of? What if she couldn't be trusted with her own baby?

Fern forced the thought away again. There had to be a rational explanation for Marte being in the house that day – she just hadn't found it yet. She hadn't found *her* yet, either online or in real life. But she would. She had to, for her own sake, as much as Paul's. *See? I didn't imagine it. I'm not mad.* And finding the answer would be much easier without Tina breathing down her neck. After all, *everything* was easier without Tina.

Paul didn't respond.

'At least let's talk about it properly first. Tonight, maybe? I'll do us a Bolognese and we'll pick up some garlic bread . . . maybe some more of that wine if it's still on offer.'

47

No wine for her, of course. Fern hadn't touched a drop since she first found out she was pregnant, albeit three weeks too late for the poor sozzled little life inside her. Three weeks of pouring in whatever alcohol she could lay her hands on in an attempt to dull the pain. But the baby looked fine on the scans, thank goodness – the perfect size for her dates, they said, with no obvious developmental issues.

Paul still didn't answer. He was concentrating on the road, waiting for a gap in the traffic. Or maybe he was avoiding the question.

'So what do you think?' she said, as they swung across the now empty lane, tyres crunching on the gravel of the surgery car park. 'We'll talk about it tonight, shall we?'

Still nothing.

'Maybe she could pop down for a few days nearer the birth . . .?'

'I already spoke to her,' said Paul. 'She's booked on the Saturday afternoon train.'

Saturday afternoon? But that's tomorrow! A wave of anger swept through Fern as she sat there, trying to process the full horror of the situation. How could he have gone behind her back like that?

Chapter 8

Paul had timed his Tina thunderbolt to perfection. What could Fern say, sitting there in the waiting room with two other pregnant ladies (neither of whom bore even a passing resemblance to Marte) and an assortment of coughers, sniffers and rash-scratchers? It wasn't an appropriate place for an argument and he knew it, but that didn't stop the angry questions buzzing round Fern's head: *What do you mean, you've already asked her? When was that, exactly? While I was out of it, yesterday? Or this morning while I was still asleep? Why didn't you check with me first?*

She knew the answer to that last one, of course. He hadn't checked with Fern because he'd known exactly what she'd say. Tina was fine in small doses – she meant well, and she no doubt had their best interests at heart – but forty-eight hours with the woman was Fern's limit. All that fussing and fidgeting and questioning every tiny thing she did . . . it was exhausting. And the prospect of becoming a grandmother had only made her worse. Fern had heard her on the phone, her thick Norfolk accent belting out across the tiny flat, riding roughshod over everything Paul said: *Are you sure you want to put in an offer on somewhere right now? Wouldn't it be better to wait until after the birth? It's going to be enough of an upheaval without adding to it even more* . . . And now she'd be in Fern's ear about every little thing too: *Are you sure you should be eating that? Have you checked it's pasteurised . . .? I'd have thought you'd be winding down from work at this stage, not starting a new project . . .* Only it would be worse than ever once Paul filled her in on the lorry incident, priming her for her new role as Fern's minder. No, jailor, that was more like it.

The first of the pregnant ladies disappeared into the examination room opposite, leaving her chatty neighbour in search of a new talking partner.

'When are you due?' she asked, shuffling along the row to sit next to them.

'The twenty-seventh of December,' said Fern, trying to keep her irritation with Paul out of her voice. It wasn't just the prospect of Tina turning up on their doorstep (although she'd be lying if she said she wasn't dreading it). It wasn't even the fact he'd gone behind her back to issue the invitation. It was the emotional blackmail. That's what really got her. *What about me? Has it ever occurred to you that I might want a bit of extra support?* That was all for show, wasn't it? He'd sat there, letting her waffle on about talks and garlic bread, knowing it was already a done deal.

'A Christmas baby?' cooed the woman. 'Gosh. How lovely.'

Really? thought Fern. There were plenty of places she'd rather spend the holidays than a labour ward. Not that it mattered, of course. A nice, healthy little girl was all she cared about now – the actual date was neither here nor there. Besides, Christmas without Linny would be no Christmas at all. No carol karaoke between the pub and Midnight Mass. No silly stocking gifts to unwrap in their pyjamas, while Paul rustled up his festive fry-up. No joint present for Dad, delivered to the care home in matching Santa outfits. Dressing up was Linny's thing, not Fern's. Linny was the one who made it fun. She was the one who made *everything* fun.

'How about you?' Fern eyed the bulging balloon of the woman's belly. She looked ready to drop at any moment. Drop or pop – one of the two.

'Any time now,' said the woman eagerly, as if squeezing out an entire human being was something to look forward to. 'I've been practising my hypnobirthing techniques all morning, just in case.'

Hypno-what?

'I'm having a water birth at home,' she went on. 'Using focused breathing and visualisation. What about you? Are you going natural too?'

Flopping around a glorified paddling pool, panting along to whale music? Fern couldn't think of anything worse. 'I'm not sure yet,' she answered. 'We only moved here yesterday. I haven't had time to sort out a detailed labour plan yet.'

'I *thought* you must be new.' The woman nodded to herself. 'You get to know the faces coming here regularly.'

Including Marte? Presumably if she was local she'd be registered with the same community midwife team.

'I'm Nicky, by the way,' said the woman.

New Age Nicky, mused Fern, thinking about the hypnotherapy and visualisation. No, wait. Natural Birth Nicky, that was better. The game wasn't as much fun on her own though.

'I'm Fern,' she said, 'and this is my husband, Paul.' The introduction was lost on him though. He was too busy replying to work emails on his phone.

'So whereabouts have you moved to?' asked Nicky.

Fern tried to think of a useful landmark, but nothing came to mind. 'It's about ten minutes' drive from here. Crenellation Lane?'

'You're kidding me! *I* used to live on Crenellation Lane when I was doing my teacher training. The house with the big bay windows and the folly over the back wall. Next door to that raunchy crime writer . . . Jane someone . . . no, Jessamy Jane, that's it! Do you know the one I mean?'

'We haven't met all the neighbours yet,' said Fern. Maybe it was time they did though. Maybe this Jessamy lady knew Marte. 'But I know the house you mean. That's *our* house,' she said, glancing back at Paul. He was still staring at his phone. 'Number seven.'

'Gosh. Small world, eh?' said Nicky, clearly tickled by the

coincidence. 'That's where I met my husband actually. He was a friend of one of my housemates. It was multi-occupancy in those days – all mature students – but I think the landlord sold up not long after we moved out. I bet it's a lovely family house now.'

Yes, thought Fern. *As long as you don't mind dodgy plumbing and creepy stains on your ceiling.* 'You'll have to come round some time,' she said out loud, 'and have a look at the place. I'd love to hear more about what it was like back then.' In truth, the thought of entertaining a stranger made Fern feel palm-sweatingly anxious – her world had shrunk so much since Linny's death that *any* social interaction made her worried – but she knew she needed to make an effort. Plus it would be the perfect opportunity to ask Nicky if *she* knew Marte from her time on Crenellation Lane, without Paul listening in and judging her. Not that he was showing any signs of listening in at the moment. His absorption in his phone was plain rude.

'That sounds lovely,' said Nicky. 'Although it might have to wait until after the baby arrives now,' she added, launching into a blush-inducing monologue on her daily perineal massage programme and the likelihood of sex bringing on labour. '. . . It makes sense when you think about it, of course. Semen's wonderfully rich in prostaglandins.'

Fern didn't *want* to think about it though, not in a crowded waiting room. But there was no stopping Nicky now. 'And of course, nipple stimulation produces oxytocin . . .'

'Right, yes, of course,' murmured Fern, trying to imagine Marte sitting in the same waiting room, having the same conversation. But the Marte she remembered had been too softly spoken and reserved to make perineal small talk in public. Too self-contained. And as for the Marte in her dream . . . no, Fern didn't want to think about her.

'Oh, that's me,' Nicky broke off as she was called through into the consulting room, hauling herself up onto her feet. 'It was lovely to meet you, Fern.'

'You too. Oh wait,' said Fern. 'What about your number? So we can fix a time for you to come round.' *So I can ring you later and ask you about Marte.* She reached into her pocket for her phone and opened up her contacts list.

'Yes of course, good idea,' said Nicky, reeling it off at such speed that Fern's finger could hardly keep up. 'Good luck with the house,' she added as she reached the door.

Fern was still busy typing. 'Thank you, yes. Good luck with the er . . .' *The whale pool sex and nipple twiddling.* 'With everything.'

But it was too late. Nicky had already gone.

The new midwife, Beverly, seemed nice enough. Hands a little on the cold side, maybe, a touch too chirpy during the prodding stages, but yes, perfectly nice. *Bubbly Bev.* She reminded Fern of their old piano teacher, Mrs Jackson, although she couldn't quite explain why. Maybe it was the no-nonsense haircut, short and functional to the point of masculinity, or the creases round her smile. It could even have been her flowery perfume. But everything was fine, Beverly said, that was the important thing: Nice healthy baby, nice healthy mum. Just so long as Fern kept her blood pressure down, which meant no more stress from now on. Huh! Chance would be a fine thing.

Paul had finally put his phone away but was quiet to the point of sullenness during the appointment, feigning fascination with a *Questions to Ask Your Birth Practitioner* leaflet. Hiding behind it, more like, trying to keep a low profile after dropping the Tina bombshell. He left all discussion of hospital dates and pain relief options to Fern, although when she came back from the toilet with her urine sample, he and the midwife seemed deep in conversation.

Beverly took the sample tube from her with exaggerated care, as if it were a precious commodity – or maybe a dangerous one – heading over to the sink to check it for protein. 'I was just telling your husband about our social group,' she said, dipping in the test strip. 'A fortnightly get-together for expectant mothers and their partners out on the Petsworth Road. There's a little private room at the back of the Queen's Head . . .'

Fern could picture it all too clearly. An entire bar full of natural-birthing, whale-hugging nipple-twiddlers.

'Yes, that's all fine,' said Beverly, waving the test strip in the air by way of demonstration. She emptied the tube into the sink and washed her hands, before returning to her theme. 'Our next one's on Tuesday. Seven-thirty. It might be a nice way of getting to know some of the other local mums, seeing as you're new to the area . . . A good support network's so important, particularly in those first few weeks.'

'Yes, I can imagine,' said Fern. On the one hand the last thing she wanted to do was sit in a pub discussing intimate massage with a bunch of strangers. But on the other hand, *she* might be there. 'It would be good to meet people with similar due dates,' she added, with a sly glance at Paul. But he was fully focused on his leaflet again, as if it contained the answers to all their problems: *What can I do to make my wife sane again? How can I convince her Mum's visit's a good thing? What were the towels doing in the attic?*

'I might have met one of your group already,' Fern ventured. 'Marte, I think she said her name was.'

'Not this again,' said Paul under his breath. But Beverly didn't seem to have heard.

'Martha?' she said. 'Hmm. Not as far as I know. Unless she came last time when I was away . . .'

'No, *Marte*,' corrected Fern. 'At least I *think* that's what her name is. I'm guessing it's Swedish or something.' That was the name she'd been typing into Google on her phone, anyway. Not that it had got her very far without a surname.

'Ah, now, wait a minute, we did have a Norwegian lady – what was she called again?' The midwife sucked her bottom lip. 'It *could* have been Marte . . . Mind you, that was a good few years ago now. She went back home to have the baby if I remember right.'

'Come on, Fern, let's not get into this now,' said Paul. 'I'm sure Beverly's very busy with appointments.'

Fern ignored him. He might be happy to let the matter drop

but he wasn't the one dreaming about the woman, was he? *His* sanity wasn't in any doubt. 'She's about my age, I'd say. Long blonde hair. Blue eyes.' *Wears a Fair Isle jumper and does a good line in impersonating house owners.*

'Really?' The midwife must have been thinking about *her* long blonde hair and blue eyes. 'Are you sure you're not twins?' she joked. And then her face fell as she noticed Fern's expression.

Paul let out a soft choking sound. 'I'm afraid Fern's twin is no longer with us.'

She's still with me. Fern fought back the tears already stinging to get out. *Always has been. Always will.* 'It's er . . . it's still a bit raw,' she managed.

'Oh, I am sorry,' said Beverly, blushing. 'How awful. I didn't mean to upset you . . .' She looked genuinely horrified.

'No, no, you didn't. It's fine, really.' Fern told her, but the tears were off and rolling now despite her best efforts. 'It's just pregnancy hormones,' she sniffed, cringing even as she said it. *Hormones. You can always blame them.*

Beverly reached for the box of tissues on her desk, tugging out an entire handful and thrusting them at Fern.

'Here,' she said, cheeks still flaming red. For someone so used to dealing with hysterical women she seemed surprisingly awkward, patting Fern on the elbow as if she was frightened to touch her properly. *Not so bubbly anymore.* 'I think we're all done anyway,' she added. 'How about I give you a few moments to yourself while I go and get ready for my home visits?' She passed the tissue box on to Paul. 'Good luck with the unpacking and what have you . . .'

Paul reached over and squeezed Fern's hand as the door shut behind the midwife. But Fern's fingers stayed limp in his, her anger over Tina rushing back. She was angry at herself too. Angry for crying like that in front of a stranger. How was she supposed to prove she didn't need Paul's mother babysitting – didn't need that new grief counsellor in Westerton – if the mere mention of the word 'twin' was enough to send her into meltdown?

55

Chapter 9

It was almost eleven o'clock by the time they left the surgery. Fern was already heading for the car when she realised Paul wasn't behind her anymore. She turned to find him talking to a short, dark-haired woman in an oversized puffer jacket, who waved back at her as if they were old friends. Who was *that*?

Fern retraced her steps to join them at the bottom of the disabled access ramp, racking her brains as to who it could be. Someone from the estate agent's maybe? Not Gemma, unfortunately. But then she spotted the nurse uniform peeking out the bottom of the woman's jacket, and it all fell into place. It must be the lady from up the street – the one who checked her over after the lorry episode. April, was that what was she called? It was funny, her face didn't seem at all familiar to Fern – she must have been more out of it than she'd realised – but she did recognise her voice.

'Hello again,' said April. 'Glad to see you looking so much better today. How are you feeling?'

'Good thanks. Back to normal now.' Whatever *that* was. 'Thank you so much for taking care of me yesterday.'

April batted her gratitude away with another wave of her hand. 'I hardly did anything. Just happened to be passing and wanted to make sure you were okay. That's all.'

'Well, I really appreciate it.'

'Yes,' agreed Paul. 'We both do. You should come over for a drink or something later. Dinner maybe? Let us thank you properly.'

April smiled. It was a nice smile – warm and genuine. 'Nonsense, you've only just moved in. The last thing you need is extra guests to entertain. You'll have to come to me instead,' she said. 'I'm having a bit of a get-together tomorrow afternoon as it happens, to celebrate the end of my kitchen renovations. Sounds silly, I know, but it's the first big project I've taken on since my husband passed away. Bit of a milestone, in that sense.' Her smile faded for a moment but she pushed on into the next sentence before either of them could react. Not that she wanted their expressions of sympathy anyway, Fern guessed. What good did they ever do anyone? 'It won't be anything very fancy,' April went on. 'Just a few friends and neighbours – a few drinks and nibbles. But it'll give you a chance to meet some of the other people on the lane.'

The prospect didn't fill Fern with much enthusiasm. A whole room full of people judging her at once. *Yes, that's her. Ran straight out in front of the lorry, I heard.* She couldn't even sell it to herself on the basis that Marte might be there, because judging by Beverly's response she wasn't local after all.

'About three o'clock,' said April. 'It'd be lovely to see you if you fancy a break from unpacking.'

'Three? Oh, that's a shame,' said Paul. 'That's when my mum's train gets in.'

It was? 'Well, I'd love to come,' said Fern, surprising herself, petty point-scoring somehow winning out over her natural dislike of parties. 'Is there anything you'd like me to bring?'

'No, no, just yourself. That'll be grand. Number ten, that's me. The one with the tatty hedge!'

'You don't use Sean to do your garden then?' said Paul, changing the subject as if he didn't care whether Fern came to meet his mother from the station or not. 'He's been round this morning, touting for business.'

'Sean Hoskins?' April hesitated for a moment. 'No, not for me, I'm afraid.'

Paul raised his eyebrows. 'Really? Isn't he very good then?'

'Oh no,' said April. 'He's very thorough. He does my friend Kerry's garden – Kerry and Richard from up the road – and it's always immaculate. But nurses' wages don't quite run to a gardener, I'm afraid,' April finished, looking embarrassed. 'Especially now I've blown the last of Pete's insurance on a new kitchen!'

Fern felt another surge of sympathy for her, sensing the pain hiding behind the flippancy.

'Anyway,' said April. 'I'd better dash or I'll be late for clinic. Those blood tests won't take themselves! See you tomorrow,' she told Fern.

'Lovely,' said Fern, although in truth she was already regretting her decision. April seemed warm and welcoming enough – *Amiable April* – but having to make small talk with a room full of judgemental strangers was the last thing Fern felt like. Unless she turned the small talk round to Marte, of course, which would be easier without Paul there . . . Just because Marte wasn't local enough to be registered at the same doctor's, didn't mean the locals wouldn't know her. Yes, thought Fern. *Someone* must know her. Someone must have seen her at the Rochester's house before, and be able to explain what she'd been doing there that day.

I'll try calling Nicky first, Fern decided, making a silent bargain with herself. *She might know Marte from one of her antenatal classes – from pregnancy yoga or something. And if she does, I'll make my excuses about the party. But if* she *can't help me, I'll go to April's and find someone who can.*

She waited for Paul to say something when they got back to the car, but he didn't. At least he didn't say anything about the party, or about Fern being out when Tina arrived. Maybe he was grateful for the chance to fill his mother in while it was just the two of them. *She's really lost it now, Mum. You should have heard her screaming after that truck like a mad woman. It's lucky no one was hurt. And then there's the whole business with the mirror. Not to mention this Marte nonsense . . . Some mysterious woman she claims showed her around the house, who no one else has ever heard of . . .*

'I thought maybe I'd drive out to that big Tesco near your dad's care home to stock up,' Paul suggested. 'I can drop you off there on the way – save you trawling round the supermarket – and I'll pick us up some lunch for afterwards. What do you think?'

'Thank you, that sounds good,' said Fern. In an ideal world she'd have made her excuses and rung Nicky from the car while Paul did the shopping, but how could she refuse a visit to her father? It felt like an age since she'd last seen him and so much had happened since then. The 'Marte nonsense' could wait. 'Though just for the record,' she added, 'I'm still furious with you about your mum.'

'I know,' said Paul. 'And just for the record, I still think it's for the best. You heard what the midwife said. A good support network is really important.'

Support for who, exactly? thought Fern.

Friday morning at the care home was just like any other morning, save for the scent of cooking fish emanating from the kitchen. Fern's father was on surprisingly good form for once though. He recognised Fern as soon as she walked into the residents' lounge, his face crinkling with pleasure.

'Hi Dad,' she said, breathing an inward sigh of relief. Thank goodness it wasn't going to be one of 'those' days. Fern leaned over to kiss his cheek before pulling up a chair beside him. He smelled of coal tar soap – some things never changed – with a faint top note of garlic. Time was he wouldn't touch the stuff – could smell it in their cooking the moment he walked in the door – but maybe his taste buds had grown as confused as the rest of him. 'How are you feeling today?'

'Not bad,' he said, with a shy smile. 'Not bad at all.' He shifted stiffly in his chair, eyes turned towards the door, as if he was waiting for someone.

'Everything all right?' Fern asked, following his gaze. There was no one there. Maybe he needed the toilet – he could be a bit funny about that when he had visitors. Heartbreakingly coy. 'Do you want me to fetch one of the carers? See if I can find Anne for you?' Anne had always been his favourite. She reminded him of his mother, he often said – of Grandma Etta. That was on a good day, of course. On a bad day he thought she *was* his mother.

'No, I'm fine.' He turned his attention back to Fern. 'I was just looking for your partner in crime. Are you all on your own today, then?'

'I'm afraid so,' she said. 'It was the big move yesterday, so Paul's down at the supermarket, stocking up on essentials. Do you remember I showed you those photos from the estate agent's last time I was here? The double-fronted house with the bay windows? You said it was a bit like your nanna and grandad's place.'

Her dad looked confused. 'No,' he said, 'I mean Fern. Where's Fern today?'

Oh dear. Maybe he wasn't having such a good day after all.

'*I'm* Fern,' she said, keeping her voice bright and singsong. 'It's me, Dad.'

He thought about that for a moment, then laughed, uncertainly. 'Oh yes, of course you are. My little Fern. I still remember the day you were born . . .'

Here it came again. Of all the loops his mind ran on, this was the one he slipped into most often.

'. . . By the time I got back from Manchester you were already there,' he told her, 'the two of you cuddled up together in the same cot, like peas in a pod.' Yes. Always the peas, which was funny, because neither one of them could stand the things. Linny

60

used to hide hers in her skirt pockets, emptying them out onto their bedroom windowsill later for the birds. 'Your mother was dozing – she must have drifted off before I arrived – so we let her sleep. I was too scared to even touch you though. I just sat there, watching your tiny chests moving up and down. My little blonde angels . . .'

'There might be another blonde angel in the family soon,' Fern said, stroking her stomach. 'I think Paul had fair hair too when he was little, though you'd never guess it to look at him now.'

'Paul?'

'That's right. He's going to be a daddy soon and you're going to be a grandad. That's exciting, isn't it?'

But it was no good. 'Where's Fern?' he asked, staring at the empty seat beside her.

'*I'm* Fern.' A little less singsong this time, maybe. 'It's me.'

'Of course you are.' Another laugh. 'I knew that! So where's Linny?'

No, please not this again. Fern took a deep breath, fiddling with the armchair. 'There was an accident, wasn't there, Dad? Do you remember?' If only *she* could find a way of forgetting too.

'An accident?'

Sometimes it was all right. Sometimes it was the very thing that brought him back. *Of course*, he'd say. *My poor baby girl. You must miss her so much.* And even though it hurt to name it – to speak the accident out loud – it was worth it to share the loss with someone else for a while. Someone who'd known Linny as long as she had; who'd dabbed calamine lotion on their matching chicken pox spots; who'd swung them both round together, round and round and round, in their favourite 'dizzy helicopter' game; who'd taken them into the big bed with him after their mum died, singing his little peas to sleep each night when he must have been falling apart inside.

But not today. Today it *wasn't* all right. His face grew dark, even as he said it – 'What accident?' – panic already twitching at the corners of his mouth, eyes widening in fear. 'Where is she? Is she okay?'

'Oh, Dad, she's . . . she's . . . Don't worry, she's fine,' said Fern, bottling it at the last minute. She turned her face away so he wouldn't see the tears. 'Just a little bump that's all.'

He let out such a long, shuddering sigh of relief, she knew she'd done the right thing. 'Thank goodness for that,' he said. 'She'll be in later then, will she?'

Fern closed her eyes. It felt cruel lying to him. Cruel not to. And the sad truth was it probably didn't matter either way. Chances were he'd have forgotten again by the time she left. Like it or not, the good days were getting fewer and further between. She almost envied him in a way though. Not the Alzheimer's obviously. She wouldn't wish that on her worst enemy. But there were times, like now, when he got to have *his* Linny back again. Times when she'd never even gone, like in that poem the celebrant read at the funeral:

Death is nothing at all,
I have only slipped away into the next room.

It wasn't just a metaphor for Dad, was it? Linny really *could* be in the next room. Really *could* be coming in later to see him.

'I'm not sure,' Fern said. 'Maybe.'

Perhaps there was a kindness even in the cruellest of diseases.

'I'll never forget the day you girls were born,' he said, the tension easing back out of his face as he slipped into the same old cycle, 'though I missed the actual birth itself. By the time I got back from Manchester you were already there . . .'

Oh, Dad, thought Fern. It broke her heart every time now. Every single time.

She went to the bathroom while he was choosing his lunch options, glad of the break and hating herself for feeling glad. It was so much lonelier on her own, without Linny there to share the burden. To turn his endlessly repeating loops into something to smile at – Birth Story Bingo, that's what they used to play – instead of desperate reminders of how far he'd already gone. How lost he was.

Anne stopped her on her way back to the lounge to ask how the move had gone.

'Not too bad, thanks,' Fern told her, as an elderly lady hobbled down the corridor towards them, her dressing gown gaping open to reveal the sagging weight of her naked breasts. *Apart from my little suicide performance in the street. And imaginary messages on mirrors that only I can see . . .* 'It's going to take a while for it to feel like home, but we're in now, that's the main thing.'

'It'll be nice for your dad having you a bit closer. He's always so much perkier after you've been. Like the other day – when was it, Monday? – he couldn't stop talking about you. Telling everyone, he was: *I've seen my girl again . . . my lovely girl.* You clearly made his day.'

'But I wasn't here on Monday,' said Fern, shrinking back instinctively as the old lady began plucking at Anne's sleeve. The smell of rose perfume permeating the air and mingling with the fish was almost overpowering. 'I haven't been able to get here for the best part of a fortnight. Too busy packing.'

Anne rubbed her chin. 'That's funny. I could have sworn . . .' She paused, turning her attention to the old lady as the sleeve-plucking intensified. 'What is it, Maisie? Are you all right?'

'It's not me, it's *her*,' said Maisie, pointing a skinny finger at Fern. 'You have to tell her. Tell her to stop.'

'Sorry,' said Anne. 'She gets a bit confused sometimes. This is Fern, Maisie. William's daughter. We were just talking about her—'

'I know who she is,' Maisie interrupted, her puckered lips pursed with frustration. 'She's the one that brings them all, isn't she?' Her watery gaze flicked from Anne to Fern and back again. 'I don't want them here anymore though. I don't like them.'

'All right, Maisie love,' said Anne. 'Let's get you back to your room, shall we? See what's happened to your nightie.'

'Please,' the old woman begged, making a sudden lunge for Fern's stomach. 'I don't like the way they look at me.'

'Come on, that's enough now,' said Anne, steering the woman away. 'Sorry,' she mouthed again over her shoulder, the remains of their conversation evaporated away in a cloud of rose and confusion. 'I'll catch up with you soon.'

Fern watched them go, the imprint of Maisie's bony fingers burning into her belly. Anyone else would have written the poor woman off as crazy, seeing things that weren't really there. But then Maisie wasn't the only one who did that, was she? Had she recognised something in Fern? Some kind of kindred spirit? Was that Fern's own future right there, stumbling back down the corridor muttering to herself?

She forced the idea away for the nonsense it was – the poor dear would probably have said the same thing to anyone. Wouldn't she? – and focused her thoughts on what her dad had told Anne, instead. *I've seen my girl again . . . my lovely girl.* What if he meant Linny? First Paul and now Dad! She enjoyed a short-lived burst of excitement – more proof that her sightings weren't all in her head – before the rational side of her brain kicked in again. Poor old Dad was hardly a poster boy for sanity these days, was he? He could even give Maisie a run for her money on a bad day. Perhaps he'd got confused, remembering something from weeks before as if it had only just happened. Or perhaps he'd had a visit from someone at work – one of the girls he used to mentor before he got ill – or Moira, his old neighbour. Fern wasn't the only one who came to see him. There were plenty of people around who still remembered the *real* William Evesham, not the poor husk of a man who didn't even know what day of the week it was half the time.

It was no good asking him of course – by the time Fern got back, he'd gone again, retreated into the warren of his own mind, leaving a stranger in his place.

'All right, Dad? What did you go for in the end? Fish pie or jacket potato?'

He stared at her, blankly.

'Anne was just telling me someone came to see you on Monday? Who was that then?'

Still nothing.

'She said it was your girl . . .' Fern made a mental note to check the visitors' book on her way out. See if she recognised any of the names. 'Did you mean me?'

'My girl,' he said, eyes sparking into life. 'My girl always comes to visit me.'

'That's right, Dad,' she agreed. 'I do.'

'My girl,' he said again, but he wasn't looking at Fern. He was staring past her at the window. At the yellowing net curtains and the naff ornamental fruit. 'Are *you* married?' he asked suddenly, eyes flicking back towards her as if he'd only just noticed she was there.

'Yes. I'm married to Paul, remember? You gave me away at our wedding. And you did a lovely speech, afterwards, saying how proud Mum would have been. About me and Linny being the reason you kept going. You made everyone cry!'

He didn't remember, of course. Fern was pretty certain he'd forgotten who *she* was again, but it was less painful to play along. To pretend.

'You take good care of that husband of yours,' he said earnestly, leaning forwards in his chair. 'You hold on to him tight, and you love him as hard as you can. Because you never know how long you've got together.'

'Okay, Dad. I will. I promise.'

'You never know,' he said, his voice cracking as he hunched back down into his chair. Back into himself. 'You never know.'

Fern bit her lip and nodded, surreptitiously dabbing away a stray tear as she turned to leave.

Chapter 10

Dad was right, of course. You never knew how long you had left with the people you loved. Fern was living testament to that. She'd give anything – *anything* – to take back her last phone conversation with Linny. To unsay her last words: *'Don't you play the martyr with me. I know what you've been doing. I've seen the way you look at him.'* That wasn't Fern talking though – not really – it was the bottle and a half of red wine she'd polished off at dinner. The dinner Linny had just hijacked, leaving Paul muttering under his breath about there being three people in their marriage, as Fern headed into the bedroom clutching the phone to her ear. It was all those months of jealous insecurity she'd thought were behind her, bubbling back to the surface at the merest mention of *him* – the secret boyfriend Linny refused to introduce her to. So secret Fern didn't even know his name. So secret that for a moment there – a blind, stupid moment she'd always regret – she'd found herself imagining the unimaginable. Thinking the unthinkable.

Of course it wasn't true. How could it have been? Linny would never do something like that to her. And neither would Paul. But Fern wasn't thinking straight that night. She was thinking how much more affectionate Paul had been while Linny was tied up in her clandestine relationship, as if he was compensating for something. She was thinking about that conference he'd been to the same weekend Linny was away. Thinking about all those late nights at the office. About years of easy in-law intimacy bubbling over into something more . . . *Three people in this marriage.* And then, when Linny told her she'd made a mistake ending it when she did, when she said she was lonely and wanted him back, something snapped inside Fern's head.

You don't understand what it's been like these last few months. It's all right for you. You've got Paul. Good old faithful Paul.

Don't you play the martyr with me. I know what you've been doing. I've seen the way you look at him.

Fern knew it wasn't true even as she was saying it. She must have done. But when Linny laughed, when she snorted down her nose as if she'd never heard anything so ridiculous – *Paul? Your Paul?* – Fern didn't join in, laughing the whole thing off like the joke it was. She didn't take it back. Didn't apologise. She ended the call, angry tears already spilling down her cheeks as she flung the phone onto the sofa, then poured herself another glass of wine.

But afterwards, after drunken sex that didn't prove anything she hadn't already known – of course it was her Paul wanted, not Linny – the full ridiculousness of what she'd said finally caught up with her. Fern lay there in the room-spinning darkness, wishing she could take it all back. How could she have said something like that? How could she have *thought* it? The two of them together . . . Queasiness swam inside her stomach at the idea that Paul might have overheard. At the thought of poor Linny, hoping for a bit of moral support from her sister – from the one person who knew how lonely she'd been these last months on her own – and having *that* flung in her face. She'd have to try and catch her first thing in the morning, Fern told herself. Try and put things right again. Only she never got the chance, because *that* was the morning Paul suggested trying for a baby, which is exactly what they did, hangover and all. She never got the chance to take back

67

her poisonous nonsense – *'Don't you play the martyr with me,'* – and tell her sister what she *really* meant: *'I love you, Linny. The world makes no sense without you. I make no sense without you.'*

Dad was right. You never knew. So, for that whole afternoon, whenever her anger and frustration with Paul threatened to bubble over again – *of course we're up against it. That's because you invited your bloody mother to stay* – Fern bit her tongue and said nothing. And even when she ran herself a bath that night and found another heart waiting for her on the mirror, she kept it to herself this time. Just like when they'd got back from the child psychologist's all those years before, after her mother's death. When Fern found the grease-smeared kiss her mother had left for her on the oven door, and those secret whispers hidden in the static between radio channels. Fern hadn't told anyone about *them* either, not even Linny – not after what she'd told the psychologist lady. *It's just a game we like to play when we're feeling sad*, Linny had said. *We won't do it again.* But it hadn't felt like a game to Fern.

Keeping her mother's secret signs and hidden messages to herself hadn't made them any less special though, any less comforting. So why should it be any different now, when Linny was the one leaving them for her to find? Fern could take solace from knowing her sister was still with her (even if she hadn't put in a physical appearance yet today), still loving her, despite that last awful phone call. And Paul? Well, Paul could hold on to his own brand of comfort by *not* knowing.

Fern traced an L in the middle of the heart – L for Linny; L for Linnette – then stepped out of her dressing gown into her freshly scrubbed bath. No more stray hairs. No inherited tide mark under the taps – Paul was nothing if not thorough when he took over the cleaning. She'd protested at first, dismissing his concerns about breathing in bleach fumes 'in her condition' as fussy and overbearing. The sort of thing Tina would say. But she'd relented soon enough, when she realised her stomach was too big to reach the bottom of the tub. She'd slipped off to the kitchen to ring Nicky instead, only to discover that she must have missed a digit when she'd typed the number into her mobile. So much for that plan. It looked like Fern was going to April's party whether she liked it or not.

Ah yes, that was better. The endless unpacking had taken its toll, along with the emotional strain of the last twenty-four hours and her frustration over Nicky's number, but Fern could feel the tension easing away again already. She closed her eyes and sank down even lower, letting the water lap at her chin. No more Marte. No more Tina. Just the warmth of the water and the gentle fizz of foaming bubbles popping around her ears.

They'd done it, she realised. They'd actually done it. Made the move they'd always talked about. Packed up their city lives and headed for a new start in the countryside. Okay, so the outskirts of Westerton wasn't *proper* countryside as such, but there were woods at the top of the road, the river a mere ten-minute walk from their front door, and a mature split-level garden with terraced lawns and shrub-filled borders just outside the window. It was impressive enough now, with the roses chopped back and the deciduous bushes shedding their leaves for winter. Fern couldn't wait to see it in the spring. Perhaps they *should* give Sean a try, seeing as he already knew the plot. He'd presumably know what bulbs were planted where, and which dead-looking things were genuinely dead, and which were pretty summer shrubs in waiting.

Maybe next year they could plant tomatoes and peppers along the bottom wall, if there was room, Fern thought. Fresh salads straight from the plot. Perhaps a blackcurrant bush too for making jam. Or raspberries. In fact, there might still be apples on the trees at the back now. She'd have to have a proper explore. And then there were the two sloped lawns to think about too, come the spring. They'd definitely need help with them. Fern couldn't be lifting a mower up and down those steps all day – even if they *owned* a mower – not with a baby to look after, and Paul would be too busy at work.

'Unless we keep Granny on as our gardener,' she murmured, stroking her hand across the bulge of her bellybutton. 'Fix her up a little bed in the shed so she doesn't get in our way. What do you think? Shall we banish her to the garden?'

The baby kicked back, conspiratorially. A gentle flurry at first followed by a sudden jerk – a hard knee to the ribs – as the bathroom door flew open.

Shit. Fern nearly jumped out of her skin, shoulders rearing up out of the water in shock. But it was only Paul, come to check on her.

'Do you want a cup of tea bringing up?' he asked, sticking his head round the door.

'No, I'm good thanks. I won't be long.'

'You haven't got the water too hot in there, have you? You're looking a bit flushed.'

That's because you caught me making jokes about your mother.

Paul could do a pretty good impression of Tina himself, when he put his mind to it, fussing and clucking like an overbearing mother hen.

'Lukewarm at best,' she told him. 'No need to worry. The baby's fine. We're both fine.'

She waited until he'd gone back downstairs, then twisted the cold tap on with her big toe. Maybe the water *was* a bit hot after all, given how steamy the mirror still was. Better to be on the safe side.

The mirror . . .

That was strange. From where Fern was sitting – half-sitting, half-lying, with the edge of the bath digging into the curve of her spine – it looked like an 'S' in the middle of the heart she'd drawn. Not an 'L' at all. 'S' for 'sister'? 'S' for 'sorry'? *Sorry for leaving you.* But by the time she'd hauled her ever-expanding bulk back out of the bath, the glass had cleared again.

It found its way into her dreams that night though. Only this time it wasn't the bathroom mirror that was steamed up, it was the TV screen. Tina was beside her on the sofa, trying to watch one of her craft programmes, moaning because the picture kept misting over. There was no sign of Linny but there was *someone* there, someone neither of them could see. Someone's finger drawing a fresh heart across the screen as they sat there, with a dripping 'S' through the middle.

There was something very wrong about that 'S'. Even in her dream Fern knew it was a bad sign. The baby didn't like it either. She could tell by the tightness in her stomach – a tightness and a pummelling sensation, like tiny fists trying to hammer their way out. But every time she wiped the offending letter away, it came back, bigger and bolder than ever.

The man who came to fix the problem – an odd hybrid of Sean and Red Setter Richard, with an ancient-looking remote control – said they needed the code word to clear the screen: a name beginning with 'S'. *Sean?* No. That wasn't it. *Sally? Simon? Sandra? Steven?* None of them were right, either. Then somehow Marte was there, in Fern's slippers and an old dress of Linny's, grabbing the remote control out of his hands to enter a name of her own. *S-O-F-I-A*, she spelled, saying each letter out loud. But ugh, her mouth. Her mouth was a gaping black hole. No teeth, no tongue, just a long tunnel of darkness stretching away down her throat. And then suddenly the television set exploded in a ceiling-high pyrotechnic blaze, taking Marte and Tina with it. That's when the baby started screaming.

Baby. There was no baby. Only her own, who was lying peacefully for once, letting her poor old mum get some sleep. But Fern was wide awake now, listening to the screech of the pipes, trying to breathe through the fluttering, pounding sensation in her chest. Just a dream. Another dream. Dr Earnshaw said vivid dreams and nightmares were common in expectant mothers (something else to pin on pregnancy hormones), but the ones she'd had in the old flat had been nothing like these. These were raw and visceral and real.

Paul stirred, rousing briefly, nudging at her elbow with his clenched fist.

'All right?' he murmured.

Fern's face was damp with sweat, cooling now in the night chill of the room. 'A bad dream, that's all,' she said. The clutch of panic in her chest was easing already; the horror of Marte's face – of that black space where her mouth should have been – blurring at the edges as the nightmare receded. 'And those pipes,' she added. 'The sooner we get them looked at the better. Can't you hear them?'

But Paul didn't say anything. He let out the tiniest of moans, somewhere in the back of his throat, and then settled back into a light nasal snore.

The nightmare that was the real-life Tina, and her imminent arrival, dominated the next morning. No leisurely Saturday lie-in with the papers to mark their first weekend in their new house. No enjoying the views of the garden from their new kitchen, over a nice plate of scrambled eggs and bacon. No time for any of that.

Paul was already working like a demon when Fern got up, transforming the spare room from moving-day dumping ground into a suitable space for a guest. The built-in bookshelves in the alcoves were almost full, and the stack of flattened boxes on the inherited double bed had reached critical teetering height. Fern's heart sank at the sight of the chest of drawers from their own bedroom newly installed along the far wall. It made it look as if Tina was moving in for good. Maybe she was. Maybe that was something else he'd neglected to mention. She beat a hasty retreat before she said anything inflammatory, heading for the toilet. On the plus side, the bathroom mirror was behaving itself perfectly this morning. Utterly heartless.

'I'm just popping into town to pick up some flowers for later,' she told him, once she was dressed and breakfasted. Once she'd scrubbed around the kitchen sink and hunted out the horrible rose-patterned teapot Tina had given them for their third anniversary. Paul was still hard at it – he'd moved on to hanging pictures now – crunching and popping his way across a carpet of discarded bubble-wrap.

'That's a good idea.' He looked surprisingly pleased to hear it. 'See if you can get some freesias. They're her favourite.'

'Really? How do you know that?'

'That's what Dad always gave her on their anniversary.'

'What? *Oh,*' said Fern, the penny finally dropping. 'I meant for April actually – I don't want to turn up empty-handed – but I can buy some for your mum as well if you want.' There was a secret language to flowers, wasn't there, she thought mischievously: different blooms imbued with different meanings. Perhaps she could find one that meant 'stop interfering, this isn't your baby' – dandelions perhaps? Stinging nettles? – with a few sprigs of 'go home soon' and 'don't outstay your welcome' to complete the bouquet. 'I might have a bit of an explore while I'm there,' she added, 'but I won't be too long.'

By 'explore' Fern meant going back to the estate agent's to ask Gemma about Marte. She wasn't about to tell Paul that though – she didn't want him to think she was obsessed.

She'd weighed up calling them the day before, after her aborted attempt to ring Nicky, but it was too late by then. The office was already shut. An in-person visit might be better anyway. It might be easier to drop Marte into conversation face to face and get the proof she was looking for. Proof that Gemma remembered seeing her too. Proof that Fern hadn't imagined the whole thing, that she wasn't as crazy as Paul, and any of the new neighbours who'd witnessed her performance on moving day, seemed to think. Maybe that was all she needed to get Marte out of her head, taking the nightmares with her. That was the theory anyway. The hope.

Chapter 11

Fern was so deep in thought coming down the path, a few minutes later – planning out what she was going to say to Gemma when she got there – that she almost walked straight into the scowling woman on the pavement.

'Sorry,' she said, as they began the traditional shimmy of awkward encounters, both stepping one way, then the other, in a sideways Hokey Cokey. Her partner wasn't in the mood for dancing though, judging by the expression on her face. Anyone would think Fern had gone out of her way to engineer the collision.

'Sorry,' she said a second time, flashing the woman an apologetic smile. 'I was miles away.'

Me too. That's what Fern would have replied in that situation. Or, *no, no, it was my fault. I wasn't looking where I was going.* Or simply returned the smile and carried on walking.

But the woman didn't do any of those things. She stood staring at Fern's stomach with a look somewhere between longing and hatred, lips turned down at the edges and nostrils flared.

'Pregnancy hormones,' said Fern. Again. She really had to stop doing that. But then she started gabbling instead, which was even worse. 'I don't know whether I'm coming or going at the moment . . . only moved in a couple of days ago and I've got the mother-in-law arriving today . . . boxes everywhere . . . a million jobs to do . . . I'm . . . I'm Fern by the way.'

It occurred to her, too late, that the woman might not even live on the street. She'd probably just introduced herself to a complete stranger – some grumpy woman who happened to be cutting through from the woods on her way to somewhere else. *Smooth*. But she needn't have worried. At least, not about that.

'Yes,' said the woman, finally dragging her gaze back to eye-level. 'I know exactly who you are.'

'Oh.' Had she watched the moving-day performance as well then, or simply heard about it on the Crenellation grapevine? Didn't people round here have anything better to talk about? Mind you, Fern reasoned, raunchy crime writers aside, the street seemed a pretty quiet, backwater kind of a place. Someone throwing them-selves at a removal lorry was probably the single most exciting thing that had ever happened there. Slightly more gossip-worthy than what Sean was doing to get rid of the aphids on everyone's rose bushes, anyway.

She waited for the woman to return the introduction, but she didn't. What she said was: 'I didn't realise you were pregnant though. When's it due?'

Fern bristled at her pointed use of the word 'it'. She made the baby sound like a library book. 'The twenty-seventh of December.'

The woman's face softened. But only a fraction. She still looked like she'd swallowed a lemon – a big, spiky lemon at that. And then she stalked off, without another word, crossing over the road and heading up one of the opposite drives – the one with the red Audi parked on it. She must be Red Setter Richard's wife Kerry then, Fern realised. April's friend, with the immaculate garden.

Fern stood and watched her go, feeling oddly shaken by the encounter. If she'd been dreading the party before, she was double-dreading it now. Had she and Paul done something to offend the woman, already, without knowing it? Parked in her favourite space? Failed to hire Sean on the spot? Or was she just worried about crazy women lowering the tone of the neighbourhood? That's when Fern realised she was doing a pretty good impression of a crazy woman right now, staring after her like some kind of stalker. So she smoothed down the collar of her coat and walked down to the car, trying to rationalise the whole thing away. Perhaps Kerry was equally unpleasant to everyone – the bad-tempered *yin* to April's cheery *yang*.

The piano music playlist kicked in automatically as soon as Fern switched on the engine. Panic sparked in her chest – just for a moment – as she remembered the last time she'd been listening to it, but then the rippling Debussy melody took over and she relaxed again. No lorry today. No Linny. *Still* no Linny. It had been two days now, she thought with a pang. Two whole days without so much as a glimpse of her sister's face. It wasn't like Linny to stay away so long . . . Fern didn't want to think about that now though. And she *definitely* didn't want to think about Richard's wife anymore. Right now she was a woman on a mission: a Marte mission. Everything else would have to wait.

The traffic was painfully slow heading into Westerton, and Fern regretted not leaving earlier. If she hadn't stopped to clean the sink and play 'hunt the teapot,' she'd have been halfway there by now, with the added bonus of missing Killer-Stare Kerry. She parked behind the Town Hall, hurrying straight down to Thomson & Harvey's in the hope of catching Gemma before she got tied up with viewings. Hurrying was putting it nicely, of course. It was more of a comic waddle, with extra panting, and Fern was glad of a road-crossing rest by the baker's to catch her breath. No Rochesters picking out cakes in there today, just a weary-looking mother and her twin toddlers in matching outfits. Identical twins . . .

Nope. No thinking about Linny. Just Marte.

Fern caught a gap in the line of cars and crossed over to the estate agent's, wishing she'd stopped at the public toilets en route. She seemed to go from nought to sixty in as many seconds these days when it came to needing a wee. Still, too late now. There was Smiley Sonia, waving through the glass, hurrying across to open the door for her.

'Mrs Croft! This is a nice surprise. How did it all go on Thursday?'

'Good, thanks,' said Fern, casting a surreptitious eye round the office, looking for Gemma. But apart from a young man collating pages as they came out of the printer, and the dim outline of someone moving around in the back office, everyone seemed to be out on viewings again. 'Couldn't have gone better,' she lied. The estate agent's was one place, at least, where no one knew what had happened. One place where no one knew *her* – where she could still pretend to be normal.

'Oh, I *am* pleased. Your husband was filling me in about your sister when he came to pick up the keys. I had no idea. I'm so sorry.'

Thanks, Paul.

'Still,' said Sonia, 'a new start might be just what you need. Such a lovely house too. Ideal place to bring up a little one.'

'Yes,' agreed Fern.

'So, what can I do for you today? Or is it purely a social visit?'

'I . . . I . . .' Fern's carefully rehearsed speech trickled away to a light stammer. She shook her head, as if to dislodge the right words, to restart her brain, and tried again. 'I wanted to ask Gemma something actually. Is she in today?' This was starting to feel like déjà vu.

Sonia shook her head. 'I'm afraid not. She's been signed off work with a broken leg. Took a nasty tumble down some steps, poor thing. Is it something I can help with?'

Fern could see the puzzlement behind Sonia's pink lipstick smile. Coral pink to match her perfect nails and butterfly scarf. *Why do you want to talk to Gemma? Why not me?* 'It may not be for a while, but I could get her to give you a ring when she's back, maybe?' she offered.

'That would be great, thank you,' said Fern, inwardly cursing her bad luck. She wanted answers *now*. 'Actually, there *is* something you can help me with,' she added, in a sudden burst of inspiration. 'Do you have the Rochesters' contact details? I'm not sure their mail redirection's kicked in properly yet because we're still getting letters for them.' That was the biggest lie yet. 'Must have been five or six this morning.'

'Let me see,' said Sonia, heading over to her desk. 'Please, take a seat.' Coral-pink nails tapped away on her keyboard like shiny crab claws. 'No . . . we don't seem to have their new address on file. Mind you, I'm not quite sure how that would work with forwarding stuff on anyway. What with it being a whole different mail system over there.' Sonia leaned an elbow on the desk, nails tapping at her teeth this time, as she pondered the full ramifications of a transatlantic house move. 'We've got their mobile numbers though. Maybe if you brought the mail into the office, I could give them a call. Ask them what they'd like us to do with it.'

'Or give *me* their numbers and I'll ring them myself,' Fern offered, although she didn't hold out much hope. It was probably against some client confidentiality rule.

'Sorry, I can't give out that kind of information,' said Sonia.

Fern nodded. It made sense really, otherwise sellers would have to answer to every little thing their buyers were unhappy with. *How come you didn't mention the screaming pipes or the dodgy water pressure? Why didn't you warn us about the psycho lady over the road?* But maybe there was another way . . .

'Ohhhhh,' said Fern, dragging the sound out long and tremulous. She leaned forwards in her seat and clutched at her stomach.

It worked. Sonia's face was full of concern. 'Are you all right?'

'No . . . I er . . .' Fern shut her eyes and breathed out through her mouth. And again.

Sonia was already round the desk, crouching on the floor beside her. 'Is it the baby?' Her perfume was floral and sickly, strong enough to add a touch of genuine dizziness to Fern's performance. 'Do you need a doctor?' she asked, her hand hot on Fern's wrist. 'An ambulance?'

Fern shook her head. 'No, really . . .'

'Or I could ring your husband for you?'

More head-shaking. 'No, really,' Fern said again. 'I'll be fine, thank you.' She opened her eyes and smiled, as if the worst of the crisis had passed. 'Just came over a bit funny there for a moment.' Lies, lies and more lies. 'You couldn't get me a glass of water, could you?'

'Yes, of course. Maybe a biscuit or something too? I'll see what I can find.'

'Perfect, thank you,' said Fern, feeling predictably guilty at her deception. What she couldn't have predicted, though, was the sense of exhilaration that came with it. She was really doing this, wasn't she? She was actually going through with it.

'I won't be long,' said Sonia, heading for the back room. 'You stay there and take it easy.'

Fern did nothing of the sort. The second Sonia was through the door, she swivelled the computer screen round to her side of the desk and tugged her mobile out of her bag, with a quick glance over at the young man in the suit to check he wasn't watching. She didn't have long. There it was on the screen: contact number for Mrs Caroline Mary Rochester. Fern snapped off a photo and checked her phone screen. *Shit*. She must have been too close. The picture was fuzzy, with a weird rainbowed ripple of light across the middle that rendered half the digits unreadable. *Try again.* She forced herself to slow down this time, to make sure it was properly in focus before she pressed the button. Yes. That was better.

Fern swung the screen back round, the crazy thumping in her heart reaching all the way up to her temples, and returned her phone to her bag. Only then did she allow herself another glance towards the printer. There he was, still collecting sheets up out of the tray. Still sorting. Still stapling. And there was Sonia, heading back into the office with a glass of water and what looked like half a packet of custard creams wedged under her arm.

'Here we go,' said the estate agent, smiling. She handed the glass to Fern and retook her seat on the other side of the desk. 'Feeling better?'

Fern took a few sips of water and nodded. 'Little bit shaky still,' she said, which was true (although not for the reason Sonia imagined), 'but I'll be fine in a minute. Thank you for the drink.'

'You're welcome. We can't have you collapsing on us, can we?' Sonia unwound the biscuit wrapping and offered the packet to her. 'Custard cream?'

'Why not? Thank you.'

Sonia didn't take one herself though. 'I thought you'd gone into labour, for one horrible moment,' she said, adjusting the angle on her screen.

Fern stopped chewing and held her breath. Could she tell someone had moved it? Would she guess what had happened?

But no, Sonia kept on talking as if nothing had changed. 'I thought Declan and I might be delivering our very first Thomson & Harvey baby together!' She turned towards the printer. 'What do you reckon, Dec? Think we'd make good midwives?'

Declan dragged his attention away, briefly, from the task in hand – just long enough to grunt and offer up a gormless grin – and then he was lost to them again.

'He's new,' Sonia whispered. 'Now then, where were we? Ah yes, that's right, trying to work out what to do with the Rochesters' mail. What's the time difference in Florida, I wonder?' She tapped a few more keys. 'Oh, that's no good. Orlando's five hours behind. They might still be asleep.'

'Do you know what? It's fine,' said Fern. 'Don't worry about it. I'm sure the redirection will kick in soon enough, and if not, I'll take it up with the Post Office. It all looks like junk mail so far anyway. Probably not worth disturbing them for.'

'Florida,' said Sonia dreamily. 'All right for some, eh? Hopefully the sunshine will work its magic. Caroline was in a bit of a bad way when they came to drop off the keys.'

'A bad way? What do you mean?' Fern remembered how frail Mrs Rochester had looked that day outside the baker's. How she'd clutched her hand to her heart as if she was in pain.

'I don't know.' Sonia's expression was decidedly *un*-dreamy now. She lowered her voice to a confidential hiss, although she needn't have bothered on Declan's account. He was still busy sorting and stapling. 'Didn't like to ask, really,' she said. 'Perhaps it was just the stress of the move . . . Let's hope so, anyway.'

Yes, thought Fern, taking another sip of water, forcing it down. Her own throat felt pinched and dry suddenly. *Let's hope so.*

Chapter 12

Fern took the long way back to the car, after a stop at the toilets, following the stream of Saturday morning shoppers up the high street in the hope of clearing her head. The call would have to wait until later. She'd been so intent on stealing the number (adrenaline still coursing through her body even now) that she hadn't stopped to think about the time difference. It was a good job Sonia was on the ball – that was a lucky save. A 6 a.m. phone call to inquire about a strange woman in your house – your old house at that – wouldn't be the ideal start to anyone's day.

She paused to catch her breath, halfway up the hill. The road's name sounded oddly familiar – where had she seen it before? Ah yes, of course. Shortford Terrace was where Dr Susannah Culvert's practice was. The new counsellor Paul wanted her to see. Fern weighed up going to check if they were open, popping in to make an appointment while she was passing, but something held her back. Perhaps it was the thought of having to start again with someone new. Going back over the same old ground as before. *My sister. My twin. My other half. Yes, I still see her. No, it's not all in my head. Of course I want to get better and move on. I do. Only . . . only . . .*

Maybe she'd be better waiting until she'd got this Marte business sorted and freed up some much-needed head space. Maybe *then* she'd feel up to laying herself bare in front of another stranger. To reliving that last conversation and the crushing guilt and shame she'd been carrying around with her ever since. *Don't you play the martyr with me.* The Martyr . . . Marte . . .

Fern blinked in surprise. She hadn't made the connection before, but it seemed so obvious now. Blindingly obvious, the two words sitting almost the same on her tongue. Martyr, Marte. *Don't you play the Marte with me.*

No. It's just a coincidence, she told herself, sweeping her gaze along Shortford Terrace as if daring the absent counsellor to suggest anything else. *Just a coincidence.* But what if it wasn't? What if the guilt had become too much for her, taking on a life of its own? A walking, talking, pregnant life of its own? It was all very well clinging to the fact that Gemma had seen Marte too, but the estate agent was proving nearly as elusive herself.

I saw her though. I did. I saw her.

Fern tucked herself in against the window of a hardware store, shutting her eyes against the sudden dizzy whirl of paving stones. And there she was again – Marte – standing at the bottom of the stairs, gazing over Gemma's shoulder towards the front door. *I didn't realise I'd be here either*, she said. Yes, Fern could still hear her now, as clear as anything – the low clipped tone of her voice, the careful placing of every word. She hadn't imagined it. *Please tell me I didn't.*

She opened her eyes again, tentatively, relieved to see the paving stones back in their proper place. No more swirling. *Just a coincidence*, she told herself again, pushing on across the junction with Shortford Terrace and carrying on up the high street. By the time Fern reached the top of the hill, she was feeling better again. *Mentally* better, anyway. *Physically*, she was a panting, back-aching mess. She stopped for another rest outside a smart-looking independent bookshop, admiring the colourful window display. She'd have to come back for a proper browse later in the week and see if they stocked any of the books *she'd* illustrated. That was always exciting.

Fern shuffled along the pavement to make room for a man in a mobility scooter, when she caught sight of something in the hospice shop, next door. It was a large-scale map of Westerton – an old, framed one – tucked into the window between a rocket-shaped lava lamp and a blue ukulele. She leaned in for a closer look, belly brushing against the glass. There was no date as such, unless it was hidden away behind the frame, but it looked genuinely old. Victorian maybe? Edwardian?

The general layout of the town had barely changed as far as she could tell, give or take the odd shopping centre and pedestrianised precinct; although the outlying housing estates were a different story. But it was Crenellation Lane itself Fern was most interested in. There it was, snaking its way into the top corner of the map, hugging the boundary of the old Gillyhead Estate. There was Gillyhead House, now a boutique hotel and mini golf course, and there (when she really pressed her nose in close and squinted hard) was the folly at the back of their garden.

There was no price on the map, at least none that she could see from outside, so she went in to enquire, thinking it might make a nice present for Paul. An I'm-still-mad-about-your-mum-and-everything-else-but-I-know-I'm-a-nightmare-at-the-moment-and-I-do-love-you peace offering.

'Ooo yes,' said the elderly lady at the till – a tiny sparrow of a woman with the electric-blue glasses of a twenty-something and a shock of pink hair. 'I know the one you mean. Lovely old thing, isn't it? Only put it in there this morning.' She squeezed out from behind the counter, skinny legs incongruously clad in neon orange and black leggings and high-top trainers, and tottered over to the window. She had to climb right into the display to retrieve it, catching the ukulele with her elbow in the process. A couple of the strings twanged against something as it headed floorwards, landing with a muffled thump on a pair of flowery wellies.

The old lady bent down to rescue it, then turned her attention back to the map. 'Let's see then,' she said, turning it over to examine the handwritten price label on the back. 'Ah yes, eighteen pounds. That's right. I remember now.'

That's a bit steep, isn't it?

She handed the map to Fern with exaggerated care, like a baby she was frightened of dropping. 'Worth it for the frame alone, I'd have thought,' she said. 'Proper quality, that. And in such good condition too.'

Really? The horrible, moulded frame was the worst thing about it – Fern had been thinking of getting a replacement if it proved to be a standard size – but she nodded and mmm'd in all the right places and thanked her for her trouble. There didn't seem to be any question of her *not* buying it now, overpriced or otherwise, given that the old lady was already tottering back to her counter. She tucked the map against her chest and carried on round the shop, on the off-chance of finding a suitable frame replacement there and then. Something a bit cheaper, hopefully.

What she found instead was a box of piano sheet music (including the collected works of one Erik Satie), a pair of maternity jeans and a pretty wooden mobile for the nursery, with brightly painted birds and bears.

'Goodness, haven't you done well?' exclaimed the old lady. She handed Fern her change, then disappeared down behind the counter, muttering something about bubble-wrap and yesterday's hopeless volunteer moving everything around. She finally re-emerged with an ancient copy of *The Times*, wrapping the map in endless sheets of newspaper before tying it with green wool.

'There,' she said, standing back to admire her handiwork. 'That should do it. Now to find a bag big enough to put it in!'

'Don't worry,' said Fern, aware of the small queue building up behind her. She'd already caught a couple of stray sighs and tuts.

'I'll be fine carrying it.' But the old lady refused to be hurried. She unrolled a dubious-looking Bag for Life for the jeans and piano music, humming under her breath as she slid them in, then stopped when she got to the mobile.

'Lovely this, isn't it?' she said, holding it up to the light and watching it spin. 'Really pretty. Do you know what you're having?'

Death glares from the other people in the queue?

Second thoughts about that map?

'A girl,' said Fern. 'At least that's what it feels like.'

'Mother's intuition, eh? I'm sure you're right.' The lady spun the mobile round again, sending painted horses galloping after the bears. 'Did you see that box of baby clothes in the corner? They're all girls' ones. Newborn, I think.'

Fern had seen them, yes. They looked brand-new too, which was what had put her off. Unworn baby clothes felt like an unspoken tragedy. A curse.

'I'm not sure I can carry anything else,' Fern joked, feebly. *Please don't tell me how you got them. I don't think I want to know.*

'They all came in together,' said the lady, as oblivious to her discomfort as she was to the queue's growing impatience. 'The baby clothes, the mobile and a beautiful little book of nursery rhymes, though we've already sold that, I'm afraid.'

'Gosh, is that the time?' Fern made a big show of checking her watch. 'My husband will be wondering where I've got to.' Not exactly the subtlest of hints, but the sighs behind her were getting louder and longer all the time. Still too subtle for the old lady though, it turned out.

'Bit of a funny story, actually,' she went on. 'A retired couple brought them in the weekend before last. They found them in their attic room when they were packing up to move – a whole box of baby stuff tucked away in a cupboard behind a pile of old suitcases. They didn't even know it was there.'

'The cupboard, you mean?' asked Fern, drawn into the story despite herself. 'Or the baby things?'

'The cupboard,' said the lady, which, by logical extension, meant the baby things too. 'They must have seen it when they first moved in, I suppose, but it got covered up with other things and they forgot all about it. And the box itself was tucked right into the corner, under the eaves. Goodness knows how long it had been there.'

'You find all sorts of forgotten stuff when you move, don't you?' Fern wondered if it was too late to change her mind about the mobile. It looked clean enough – presumably the shop checked everything was in good condition before they put it out for sale – but the thought of baby things tucked away in the attic reminded her of her dream. The one with Marte and the cot.

'That's the funny thing though. They didn't *have* any children. And nor did the people who had the house before.'

'Gosh, that *is* funny,' agreed Fern. *Creepy, some might say.* The mobile was looking less attractive by the second.

'Lovely couple, they were,' said the old lady. 'Donated all sorts of stuff over the last few weeks. A big carload every other day.' She stretched out her hands to indicate exactly how big these carloads were. 'Moving to America, you see – didn't want to take it with them.'

America? Fern's breath caught in her throat, but she kept her voice bright and casual. Tried to, anyway. 'Really? Whereabouts?' Maybe it was just a coincidence. Maybe people were always retiring to the States in this neck of the woods.

'I'm not sure,' said the lady. 'I don't think they said.' She slid the mobile into the Bag for Life and pushed it back across the counter. All done, finally. Only now Fern was the one who didn't want to go, not without knowing for certain.

'What about the box of piano music?' she asked. 'Was that one of theirs too?'

The lady thought for a moment. 'Yes, I think you're right. They said they were leaving the piano behind for the new people, but they weren't sure they'd want the whole music collection as well.'

Fern felt oddly woozy again. A *real* funny turn this time. 'S-sorry,' she stammered, her tongue too big for her mouth all of a sudden. 'I've come over a bit dizzy. Is there somewhere I can sit down?' Maybe it was karma for faking it at Thomson & Harvey's.

'Yes, yes, of course,' said the old lady, shuffling out to help her. 'You have gone a bit of a funny colour.' She guided Fern to the storeroom at the back of the shop, and into a battered green armchair. 'There you go. You sit yourself down there 'til you're feeling better. No rush. And I'll come back and check on you once things quieten down a bit.' She took a few steps backwards, head cocked on one side. 'Yes, that was one of theirs too, now I think about it.'

'The chair, you mean?' asked Fern. That definitely wasn't in the list of furniture the Rochesters had given them. Maybe it wasn't them after all then. Thank goodness for that.

'No, we've had that old thing for ages. I mean the hostess trolley,' said the lady, pointing to the Seventies monstrosity behind Fern's elbow. Mock-walnut with a flower-tiled top shelf. 'We don't have room for it in the shop at the moment,' she added, lowering her voice as if she didn't want to hurt its feelings, 'though between you and me I think it's hideous. *I* wouldn't buy it.'

Fern shook her head, weakly, orange flower tiles swimming in and out of focus.

'No,' she agreed. 'Nor would I.'

Chapter 13

Fern was right about Paul wondering where she'd got to. Not that she blamed him – it was almost one o'clock by the time she got home. But then, once he'd satisfied himself that she and the baby were all right (Fern didn't mention the funny turn in the hospice shop), he moved on to wondering how she'd managed to forget the flowers. April's *and* Tina's.

'But that's what you went in for,' he said, looking genuinely confused.

'Yes,' Fern agreed. No arguing with that one. At least, not without telling him about Sonia. About Marte. She thought of Mrs Rochester's number burned into her phone, radiating out guilt and deceit through the leather of her handbag, hot like her own flushed cheeks. But then she shivered instead. Because now she couldn't think about Mrs Rochester without thinking of those forgotten baby clothes hidden away in the attic. In *their* attic.

'I thought I'd have a bit of an explore first,' she said. 'And then I got distracted . . . it's something for you, actually.' She padded back into the hall to retrieve the newspaper-wrapped map, hoping he'd forget about the flowers once he saw it.

'What is it?'

'You'll have to open it and see,' she said, trying not to think about the abandoned baby mobile, now residing at a different charity shop on the other side of the road.

'Wow, that's fantastic.' Paul handed the discarded newspaper wrapping back to Fern. 'Where did you find it?'

The Rochester Reject Store. 'A charity shop on the high street,' she said. 'I spotted it in the window when I was walking past. Look, you can even see our house on it. Well, the folly, anyway.'

'Thank you,' he said, kissing her. Eighteen pounds well spent after all. 'It's perfect.'

It hadn't occurred to Fern at first – not until Paul carried it through to the dining room and hung it on the waiting picture hook over the fire – that the map might be another of the Rochester's unwanted items. Maybe she'd seen it that day with Marte, without taking it in properly, filing it away in her subconscious while she was thinking about something else. Maybe *that's* why it caught her eye in the window.

'Look at that,' said Paul, pleased as anything. 'It covers up that darker patch perfectly. The exact same size. In fact, wasn't there a map of some sort here when we first looked round?'

Fern shivered again at the thought. Maybe she could ask Mrs Rochester about it when she called her. Start with the map, by way of an icebreaker, and then build up to Marte. *Who was that woman in your house?* Why *was that woman in your house? I need to know I'm not going mad. Please, just tell me.*

'Are you sure I can't change your mind?' asked Paul, scooping up his car keys after a late lunch. 'Mum's really looking forward to seeing you.'

'Hmm? What's that?' Fern was trying to work out where that crackling radio noise was coming from. It was the same off-station singing she'd heard the day before – the same breathless tune fighting to make itself heard above the growling crackle of interference.

'I can't tempt you with a ride out to Blatchford?' said Paul. 'The chance to experience the heady delights of the station car park for yourself?'

Fern shook her head. She was just waiting for Paul to leave so that she could call the Rochesters.

'No,' she told him. 'I'd better show my face at April's party now that I've said I will . . .' She broke off, listening for the radio again. 'Is it coming from one of the boxes in the attic do you think? Maybe we left the batteries in an old bedside alarm clock or something.'

Paul frowned. 'What are you talking about?'

'That radio,' said Fern. 'Can't you hear it? It's the same tune as yesterday morning – almost like a lullaby – but it's too crackly to make out the words.'

'I can't hear anything,' said Paul. 'I'm not sure I've really got time to look now, either. I don't want to be late for Mum.'

'No, that's fine,' Fern told him. 'It's not important. You get off.'

It *wasn't* important. Not compared to finding out the truth about Marte, once and for all. Fern waited until she heard Paul's car pulling off the drive and then fetched her phone from the kitchen. It would be 9.30 a.m. in Orlando now. Perfect. She pulled up the photo she'd taken in the estate agent's and copied Mrs Rochester's number down onto a piece of paper, together with the international dialling code.

This is it, she thought, as she typed it into her phone with shaking fingers. *This is where I finally get to find out who Marte is and what she was doing in the house that day.*

The number rang. That was a good start. A far better start than when she'd tried calling Nicky.

It rang and rang. Fern felt a belated pang of guilt as she imagined Mrs Rochester struggling down the stairs to answer it.

Come on, Fern begged. *Please pick up. Please.*

'Hello, welcome to the voicemail service for . . .'

Fern didn't even hear the rest of the automated message. She didn't think to wait and leave a message of her own after the beep – not that she'd have known what to say anyway – she was too busy swearing under her breath. Too busy cursing her continued string of bad luck. All she wanted was an explanation as to what Marte was doing there that day. Proof that she really *was* there that day. Why did it have to be so hard?

She ended the call and took a deep, steadying breath. Maybe the Rochesters were still jet-lagged from the move. Maybe she'd have more luck trying again later. And in the meantime, there were new neighbours to meet – and interrogate on the sly – at April's. It didn't matter how Fern got the answers she was looking for as long she got them. One way or another, it was time to knock this Marte business on the head. To put her doubts and confusion behind her and say goodbye to the bad dreams that came with them.

Fern was full of renewed resolve as she waddled over to number ten clutching the bottle of cheap fizz the Rochesters had left by way of a welcome present. It wasn't as good as the flowers she'd meant to buy, but it was too late to worry about that now.

April ushered her inside, full of compliments for her maternity dress, for the healthy colour in her cheeks and (rather embarrassingly) for the cheap bottle of fizz.

'A woman after my own heart, I see! Thank you. I'm so glad you could make it,' she said, leading Fern along a familiar-looking hallway towards the kitchen.

The pretty tiled floor was exactly the same as theirs, with the same carved white bannisters finishing in an ornate swirl at the bottom of the stairs. There was even a mirror in the equivalent spot just inside the front door. But April's house felt lighter, somehow. Brighter. The difference must have been in the décor – in the clean lines and neutral shades she'd chosen, in stark contrast to the Rochesters' heavy colours and patterned wallpapers. And her new kitchen, with its pale shaker units and stone worktop, was nicer still.

'Wow,' said Fern, nodding to the man by the sink, who was nursing an impressively large glass of red wine. What wouldn't she give for a matching glass of her own? 'This is lovely. Really light and airy. Really spacious.' Was that the right response? It was hard to tell without knowing what the kitchen was like before.

'Super, isn't it?' agreed the man. He was a big bear of a fellow, with a generous swathe of dark hair and the gently rounded belly of someone who enjoyed their food. Not fat, as such, but not quite as trim as the neat cut of his neck and shoulders suggested. 'We'll all be getting ours done the same now!' He put down his wine and stepped forward to shake Fern's hand. 'Hi there, I'm Eddie. You must be my new neighbour. Fern, isn't it?'

'Yes, that's right. Good to meet you.' She waited for him to let go again, but he didn't.

'Sorry I haven't been round to say hello yet.' There was a rich, velvety quality to his voice, and he seemed very sure of his own charms. 'Been working to a bugger of a deadline. Only just got the last chapter sent off now.'

'Eddie's our resident author,' April explained. 'Bit of a local celebrity on the murder-romance writing circuit.'

'For my sins,' said Eddie, hand still clasped tight around Fern's, the flesh of his thumb pressing into her palm in a way that felt tinglingly over-familiar. Flirtatious.

'And our resident Lothario,' April added, smiling. 'The Casanova of Crenellation Lane – that's what we call him. New lady friend every week.'

Come to Beddy Eddie, thought Fern, suddenly wishing Paul was there too. They should be meeting the neighbours together like a proper couple, storing up joke nicknames and secret observations to share with each other in private, later. But then she remembered about Marte, and the need for answers, and the feeling passed again.

'Lady friend?' Eddie scoffed. 'I'm not sure they've ever been called *that* before.' He grinned. 'And it's not every week by any

93

stretch of the imagination. Fortnightly at most.' He finally released Fern's hand and picked up his glass again, laughing. It was an easy, good-natured laugh that shook the soft swell of his belly.

'You'll have to watch out,' April told her. 'He's got a bit of a thing for blondes . . .'

Blondes like Marte?

'. . . and brunettes,' she added, nudging him in the ribs with her elbow. 'And redheads . . .'

Eddie batted her away, still laughing. 'Don't believe a word she says. You know what nurses are like for making stuff up. Oh no, wait, that's writers, isn't it?'

Fern laughed too, relaxing into the conversation. He seemed friendly enough – a little too friendly if anything – which was a welcome relief after her recent encounter with Kerry.

'I'm a model citizen really,' he added, leaning in, lowering his voice as if he and Fern were part of the same conspiracy. 'Perfect man-next-door material. No loud music. No nasty yapping dogs. And I'm always around to take in stray parcels for my more gainfully employed friends and neighbours.' He broke off for another sip of wine. 'Which is probably why I'm on first-name terms with every delivery driver in Westerton. One of the many advantages of working from home . . . That and not having to get out of bed 'til midday if I've had a late one.'

'It's hard to keep up the momentum sometimes though,' said Fern, thinking of the boxes of art materials still waiting to be unpacked. Anna was going to have her guts for garters if she didn't get a move on. Even *her* super-agent negotiating skills could only stall the client for so long. 'I work from home too – as an illustrator. I'm currently doing a series of children's nature books but I'm hopelessly behind, what with the move and everything.'

What with my sister dying and me going to pieces . . .

Thursday. That was the last time Fern had seen Linny, which was two full days ago now. It wasn't like her to stay away so long.

'So does that mean we've got writers on both sides of us?' she asked. Two writers and an illustrator in the middle, like some kind of book sandwich, although Nicky's old neighbour might be long gone by now, of course. A lot could change in six years. 'I heard there was a lady writer living next door to us too – at least there used to be. Somebody-or-other Jane, I think her name was.'

Eddie grinned. 'That's me. Jessamy Jane at your service.'

Oh. Fern felt stupid, without quite knowing why.

'Terrible pen name, I know,' he said. 'But a bit more romantic-sounding than Edward Gumley. *Anything* sounds better than that. I'm not sure Mr Gumley would sell quite as many copies as Ms Jane, somehow.'

'Oh, I don't know,' April began. 'It might appeal to the—' She broke off suddenly as the doorbell rang. Three short sharp rings, like some kind of code. 'Gosh, look at me. I haven't even got you a drink yet. What a terrible hostess. Be a dear, Ms Jane, and sort Fern out with a glass of something while I go and let Kerry and Richard in. I want to ask them about that old worktop in my garage, before everyone else gets here.' She seemed pretty certain who was at the door. The three rings really must have been a code, after all, like Linny always knocking to the rhythm of David Bowie's 'Sister Midnight' riff. (Probably the Iggy Pop version, knowing Linny.) 'There's Coke and lemonade kicking around somewhere,' April added as she headed for the hall, 'and juice and sparkling elderflower in the fridge.'

'I take it you've already met Kerry and Richard, then?' asked Eddie, pulling open door after door in search of the elusive refrigerator.

'Sort of,' said Fern, thinking about her abrupt conversation with Kerry that morning and the sound of Richard's voice drifting up the stairs the day before. And who could forget her performance at the end of their drive on Thursday? 'Why do you ask?'

Eddie turned and grinned at her. 'Because of the expression on your face when you heard their names. You looked properly panicked. I'm guessing you didn't exactly hit it off?'

'I er . . .' *No. Not exactly.*

'Aha!' Eddie let out a cry of triumph. 'Here we go. What can I get you then? It looks like we've got orange juice . . . apple juice . . . cranberry and something-or-other . . . the famous sparkling elderflower . . .'

Fern was slow deciding. Partly because he was right – she *did* feel panicky at the thought of facing Kerry again – and partly because she didn't fancy any of them, especially.

'Sorry,' said Eddie, taking her indecision for something else. 'Writer's nosiness. Bad habit, I'm afraid. Always trying to work out what makes people tick. Always looking for the unsaid things in every conversation. You should tell me to mind my own business. That's what everyone else does.'

'Oh no, it's fine. I'm not sure Kerry likes me very much, that's all. Perhaps we got off on the wrong foot.' *Not only the wrong foot – the wrong leg.* 'I'll just have some water, please.'

'Of course,' said Eddie, shutting the door. He straightened up and leaned in close, breathing out a hot cloud of sour-sweet wine. 'Nothing to do with you, I'm sure,' he whispered. 'They've been trying for a baby for a while now. I suspect Kerry finds it hard being around pregnant women sometimes.'

Fern was surprised by the force of her own relief. There'd been so many dark thoughts crowding in on her over the last few days – the baby clothes in the attic, the horrible dreams, Kerry's rudeness and Tina's imminent arrival (not forgetting Marte, of course, the new star of her one-woman worry show) – that it felt good to be able to cross one of those worries off. *It's not me she's got the problem with then. Only my bump.* Hopefully Eddie could shed some light on the Rochesters' mystery house guest as well – two worries for the price of one. Fern just needed to find a way of working her into the conversation.

'Oh, that's good to hear,' she told him. 'I mean, I'm really sorry for Kerry and Richard, obviously,' she added, blushing as she corrected herself. 'But I'm glad it's not something *I've* done.'

'I shouldn't think so. They've been going through a bit of a rough patch all round this last year,' Eddie went on, the epitome of indiscretion. Indiscretion was good though. With any luck he'd be just as forthcoming about Marte. 'And I rather think it's taken its toll . . .' He rolled his eyes, treating her to another mischievous grin. 'On all of us.'

He broke off at the sound of voices in the hallway. 'Here they come,' he murmured. 'Crenellation Lane's answer to Tom and Daisy Buchanan . . . only without the *Great Gatsby* glamour. Better change the subject.'

'The Rochesters,' Fern said, jumping in quickly while she had the chance. 'The people who lived in the house before us. Did you know them well?' *Did you know Marte?*

'Geoff and Caroline? That *was* her name, wasn't it? Didn't really know them at all, to be honest. They seemed nice enough but very much kept themselves to themselves. Barely spoke two words to them the whole time they lived there.' The doorbell rang again. Just the one ring this time though. 'Not that they were there very long, of course.'

'I see,' said Fern, trying to hide her disappointment. How long was not very long? A few years? A few months?

'I'm not sure she was that well,' said Eddie, tapping the side of his head. 'Up here, I mean. Maybe that's why they left so soon. Or maybe it's me. Maybe I scare everyone off! You must be the fourth lot of new neighbours in as many years.'

Fern bristled inwardly at his offhand dismissal of the poor woman. He'd probably say the same thing about her if he knew. More head tapping. But she kept talking, hoping he might be able to tell her where the baby clothes had come from, if nothing else, which of the many previous owners they must have belonged to. Maybe then the idea of them festering away in the attic wouldn't seem so creepy. 'They found a whole box of stuff in the loft when they moved out . . .' she began. But that was as far as she got, because suddenly the kitchen was full of people: Kerry, Richard and April, and a family of red-headed boys following in their wake. They weren't from the street though, as it turned out. Not proper Laners.

It was funny to finally meet Richard in the flesh, after the removal lorry debacle and the whole red setter conversation Fern had eavesdropped on the day before. He seemed nervous as they shook hands, staring at a fixed point just above her left cheek, and disappointingly un-setter-like in appearance. Despite her brief glimpse of him through the car window, Fern had still pictured him with a full head of glossy russet locks, but in reality he had cropped dark hair, with creeping streaks of grey. He peeled his palm away from hers with unnecessary speed, muttering something about getting a drink as he shuffled off. Perhaps it wasn't nerves after all then, but embarrassment. Embarrassment for her, after the moving-day incident, or for the obvious waves of dislike his wife was sending out, like cartoon laser beams of hate.

Kerry's rudeness didn't bother Fern nearly as much now she knew what lay behind it though, and the awkwardness of their second encounter was mercifully short-lived. No sooner were the basic introductions over – 'Yes, we've already met' – than the doorbell rang again. And again. April's light and airy kitchen was becoming less airy by the minute, and Fern found herself with plenty of other things to concentrate on than the Brantleys' chilly welcome. There were endless introductions – the local dentist, a librarian, a pair of teachers, a hospital porter – and more names than Fern could ever hope to remember. Endless questions on due dates, baby names, and unpacking progress. Endless missed opportunities to quiz people about Marte. The woman was a lot harder to work into polite conversation (without coming across as some kind of weird obsessive) than Fern had anticipated. And the few people she *did* manage to ask were no help at all. They didn't seem to know any more about the Rochesters' mysterious guest than Sean had.

As the afternoon wore on, Fern's mind slipped back to what Eddie had said. It hadn't struck her at the time – she'd been too focused on the Rochesters – but four different house owners in four years? That wasn't normal, was it? Why hadn't anyone at Thomson & Harvey seen fit to mention that little detail? Or Devoted Darren, come to that? It must have all been there in the paperwork. And what was it, exactly, that kept driving everyone away? Something more serious than noisy pipes and dodgy water pressure, she guessed. Something much worse than faces on ceilings and the odd mysterious draught.

Nibbles were nibbled. Drinks were drunk and smiles were smiled. So much so that Fern's face was aching almost as much as her back when she finally admitted defeat. She wasn't going to find the information she needed like this. She'd have to think again. And in the meantime, there was Tina to contend with, and the initial barrage of fussing and clucking and pointing out everything Fern was doing wrong for a woman in her final semester. She might as well go home and get that over and done with.

'Thank you for having me,' she said, cornering April in the utility room, where she was topping up the peanuts and crisp selection. 'It's been really lovely, but I might sneak off now if that's okay. Don't want to incur the wrath of the mother-in-law.' She felt a twinge of guilt as she said it – Tina might be many things but wrathful certainly wasn't one of them. 'The baby's giving me a bit of gyp too.' *Gyp?* Where on earth had that come from? Maybe she was turning *into* Tina. 'I think a lie down might be in order.'

'Completely understand,' said April, smiling. 'You go and put your feet up. But listen, you know where I am now. Pop round for a cuppa any time. Always up for a bit of company when I'm not at work.'

'Thank you.' Fern could already picture the two of them bonding over chocolate digestives and the latest Eddie gossip. *You'll never guess who I saw coming out of his house this morning . . .* And even with this latest lot of worries about the house – the house

99

that saw everyone off within a year – there was a schoolgirlish glow of new-friend happiness in her chest as she returned the smile. Maybe, deep down, April was lonely too – after all, she'd lost someone recently as well. The other half to *her* whole. Or maybe she was just nice.

'I'd love to,' Fern said. And this time she meant it.

Chapter 14

Tina. By Saturday evening, she was already everywhere: a dowdy omnipresence of shapeless cardigan and elasticated skirt, with an ever-ready frown of disapproval lurking behind her home-cut fringe. It was such a big house as well. Fern couldn't understand how her mother-in-law managed to be quite so in the way all the time. It seemed to be a special skill of hers – her not-so-secret superpower.

What's that? Someone wants to get a mug off the shelf? A spoon out the drawer? Engage cupboard-blocking shield at once.

Pregnant woman desperate for the toilet, you say? Aha! This calls for an emergency three-hour bath.

But there were, to Fern's surprise, some upsides to her mother-in-law's constant presence. Tina brought a no-nonsense normality to the house, forcing out irrational fears – of some kind of curse on the property, or dead babies' clothes in the attic – by the sheer force of her equally no-nonsense personality. By the sheer volume of her endless commentary on what needed doing, and when. *You'll have to strip those window frames right back next summer and give them a new coat of varnish. That's the problem with old wooden ones. And that carpet will need changing once the baby's off and crawling. You don't want him rubbing his little face in that.*

Her face, thought Fern.

No, there was no room for the unexplained with Tina in residence. Not that first evening, anyway. And no chance to sneak away and try calling the Rochesters again.

Tina's influence didn't extend to dreams though, unfortunately. Marte was back, banging at the door of the locked attic cupboard, crying to be let out. *Tum-t-tum-tum-boom*, she hammered. *Tum-t-tum-tum-boom*. It was the same rhythm as the riff in 'Sister Midnight', Linny's knock. For one glorious moment Fern thought it *was* Linny. She broke open the door – crowbarred it open with splintering fingernails – and threw her arms around her sister.

Oh, Linny, thank goodness. I thought you were dead. I've missed you so much.

But then she felt her twin's belly swelling against her own, felt the rough wool scratching at her bare arms, and drew back in horror. It was Marte, blue eyes fixed unblinking on the swinging mobile above their heads, bleached white fingers reaching upwards in a gesture of longing. 'My baby,' she whispered, over and over again. 'My baby, my baby. *My* baby.' Round and round went the mobile, until Fern couldn't tear her eyes away either. A dizzying whir of colourful horses and bears, spinning faster and faster, with no little one there to see them. Because now it was the baby locked in the cupboard, crying for Marte. Crying for Fern. Crying and crying.

Even Tina couldn't keep the dreams away. But the sound of her flushing the toilet – twice, no less – and shuffling round on the other side of the wall in her ancient sheepskin slippers, turning taps on and off, made the darkness that greeted Fern on waking less oppressive somehow. There was comfort in the racket her mother-in-law was making. Something to give the screaming pipes a run for their money.

* * *

102

Sunday saw a more relaxed start to the day – more relaxed than the day before anyway. No more scurrying around getting ready for Tina, hunting out hidden teapots, because she was already there. She was already planted in the kitchen chair that Fern had come to think of as *her* chair. Already drinking stomach-churning coffee out of Fern's favourite mug, while holding court on the perils of *over*-parenting, whatever that might be.

'Ooh, shut the door behind you, love,' said Tina, pulling her dressing gown tighter around her chest. 'It's ever so draughty in here. I thought I'd better wait to get washed and dressed until you were up, though. Didn't want to disturb you if you were catching up on lost sleep.'

'Catching up would have been good,' agreed Fern, yawning on cue. 'Try telling that to the baby though. And that blooming radio. I swear it's coming from our attic.' So much for escaping city sound pollution. What with the screaming pipes in the middle of the night and the banging radiator, the new house was far noisier than their old flat.

Paul frowned. 'A radio? Like the one you heard yesterday?'

'Yes,' she said. '*Exactly* like that one.' She paused for a moment, listening. 'It's still going now. Can't you hear it?'

His frown deepened. Fern guessed that was a 'no'.

'I can't hear anything,' said Tina, before he could answer. 'Mind you, I've had a bit of a cold this last week and that always does funny things to my ears. Must be all that phlegm swooshing around my system. Tea?'

Straight from phlegm to tea. Lovely.

'In a bit, maybe. I might head up to the attic first and see if I can work out where the noise is coming from. It's really starting to get on my nerves.' Not that the prospect of a trip to the attic filled Fern with much enthusiasm. Not with Marte's midnight appearance still so fresh in her head. She half expected to see the mobile swinging from the ceiling when she got there, just like in her dream.

103

'No, you stay down here and keep Mum company,' said Paul. 'I'll go. Don't worry,' he added, looking oddly worried himself. 'We'll get to the bottom of it.'

He was as good as his word too, finally reappearing some three-quarters of an hour later clutching a filthy-looking baby monitor. 'Look what I found, tucked away in the cupboard – right in the corner under the eaves.' He wiped at the cobwebs on his jumper. 'I had to wriggle all the way in on my tummy to reach it. But that solves the mystery anyway. It must have been picking up a station from somewhere else.'

Tina pulled a face. 'It's a wonder it still works, given the state of it. Goodness knows how old it is.'

'Yes,' agreed Paul, opening up the back to reveal heavily corroded batteries. 'But I'm pretty sure that's our culprit. It must be – there's nothing else up there.' He made a big show of taking the batteries out and putting the whole thing in the bin. 'There we go. Hopefully you'll be able to sleep a bit better now.'

First the abandoned box of newborn clothes. And now a monitor. What next? An actual baby?

'Yes,' said Fern, feeling more disturbed than ever. She was thinking of the crying coming from the attic cupboard in her dream. 'Thank you.' The whole thing begged more questions than it answered. That was only *half* a baby monitor – the receiver. What had happened to the transmitting bit? Why would someone leave one half behind and not the other? And why hadn't Paul been able to hear it too? But by the time Fern popped out to the car later that morning, to collect the Satie piano music she'd bought, she had other things to worry about, starting with the discovery of a steaming dog turd on the doorstep. To be fair, it wasn't steaming anymore by the time Fern found it – almost tripping over the thing on her way out – but Paul certainly was.

'What kind of person lets their dog crap on someone else's doorstep?' he said. He must have asked the same thing three times in as many minutes, fuelled by a growing sense of disgust and disbelief.

They stood there in the doorway, all three of them, staring down at the offending offering as if they'd never seen anything like it.

'Don't even *think* about clearing it up,' Tina told Fern (who hadn't been thinking anything of the sort). 'Not in your condition. You let Paul take care of it.'

Fern was happy to oblige, edging round the offending 'present' while Paul headed back to the kitchen in search of a carrier bag. She could still hear him when she reached the car – '*but who does that sort of thing?*' – opening up the boot to retrieve the forgotten piano music and maternity jeans. There'd been something vaguely sinister about the Satie book yesterday – as if it had been infected by the unwanted mobile, or Mrs Rochester's illness – but today, with Tina on the scene, it was a regular book of piano music. Nothing more. Nothing less. And half an hour working on 'Gympnopédie, No. 1' would be a welcome break from comments on the state of the carpet in the dining room, and those 'Arctic draughts' still playing havoc with her mother-in-law's neck. Yes, a nice bit of Satie might be relaxing for Fern *and* the baby.

Someone heading down their neighbour's path – the neighbour who wasn't Eddie – caught her eye as she closed the boot. This could be her chance to introduce herself, to find out how well *he* knew the Rochesters and the mysterious pregnant woman. Fern was already halfway to their gate when she realised her mistake. It wasn't her neighbour at all. It was a delivery driver. And there couldn't have been anyone at home, either, because the man was still clutching the parcel in his hands.

'I'm guessing he's out?' Fern asked, thinking she could offer to take the parcel in. 'Or her,' she added, realising she didn't actually know *who* their other neighbour was. He or she hadn't been at April's party, Fern knew that much. 'I could take it for you, if you'd like. I live next door,' she added, pointing back towards her own house.

'Nah. This one needs a signature,' said the delivery driver. 'Thanks anyway.'

Fern retraced her steps, waddling back past the car, and that's when she spotted it: a neat scratch in the paintwork, running all the way along the front passenger door. Wait, *two* scratches. That couldn't be an accident. What sort of person keys your car while their dog craps on your doorstep? Was this the start of an intimidation campaign to get rid of her and Paul? Some local weirdo who didn't like the idea of outsiders moving in? Maybe that's what happened to the Rochesters *and* all those other owners before them. Perhaps they were scared off by the neighbourhood nutter. Fern had a sudden image of Marte – the twisted, psychotic version of Marte from her dreams – running a knife along the door under the cover of darkness, smiling demonically to herself. Then she shook the thought away again for the nonsense it was. Kids, that was all. Local kids with nothing better to do, and a dog with badly behaved bowels. Or a badly behaved owner. One of the two.

'Makes you wonder what sort of neighbourhood you've come to,' said Tina, unhelpfully. 'Whether it's really the sort of place you want to bring children up in . . .' She made it sound like there'd been stabbings in the street. Riot police called in to break up a gangland shooting. 'I mean, you expect this sort of thing in the city, don't you? But not all the way out here.'

'It'll be kids, that's all,' said Fern, firmly, surprised to find herself the voice of reason for once, even if she was still trying to convince herself at the same time. Just kids. Not neighbourhood gangs. Not some local weirdo with an out-of-towners grudge. Not the dreaded curse of number seven, Crenellation Lane, working its weird voodoo magic. And definitely, definitely nothing to do with Marte. 'They've probably done the same to half the cars on the street,' she added. 'And I very much doubt anyone's trained their dog to poo outside our house on purpose. Probably just let it off the lead and didn't notice. There are loads of people with dogs here.' That seemed to shut Tina up. For a few minutes, anyway.

Turds, car-scratching and mystery baby monitors aside, it was still a nice leisurely morning. Surprisingly so, given how much Fern had on her mind. And it was made all the nicer by an unexpected appearance from Eddie, bearing a personally signed copy of *Blood Lovers* by Jessamy Jane. The cover was generically dark and moody, with sinister-looking woods in the background and the title picked out in blood-red type above a dead blonde girl in the centre. At least, Fern assumed she was dead, although she looked surprisingly fresh and dewy-skinned for a corpse.

'Thank you,' she said, reaching past Paul to take the book from Eddie, after the men had made their introductions, then turning it over to read the blurb on the back. 'That's so thoughtful.' It sounded like the literary love-child of Ruth Rendell and Mills & Boon: sexy Scandinavian au pair disappears in a cloud of scandal, only to be dug up in local woodland three months later. Enter stunning female detective Rosella Ransom and her dashing main suspect . . . 'So this is what you get up to in your lonely garret, is it?'

'Afraid so. Load of old tripe, to be honest, but it pays the bills. Beats an honest day's work.'

'I'm sure it's very good,' said Fern, although it wasn't the sort of thing she'd usually go for. Mind you, she'd barely read anything since Linny died. Happy endings felt trite and wrong and the alternative was no better when she was still too deep in her own tragedy to take on anyone else's. 'Thank you,' she said again, genuinely touched by the gesture. 'I might even start it tonight.' A nice bit of murder for some light relief from the dark dreams she'd been having.

Eddie grinned. 'I wouldn't bother if I was you. Seriously. Only brought it round as a joke, really. An excuse to meet your good husband and your . . .' He raised his eyebrows at Tina, who'd materialised in the hall behind them. '. . . Sister?'

Oh, but he was a charmer. Cheesy – very cheesy – but still charming. And Tina was lapping it up.

'Mother,' she said, patting her hair and preening. 'Paul's mother, that is. Tina Croft,' she added, edging past Fern to shake Eddie's hand. She giggled – a high-pitched, girlish giggle Fern had never heard before – as Eddie leaned forwards, taking her fingers in his and raising them to his lips. The Casanova of Crenellation Lane indeed. Wait until April heard about *this*.

'A pleasure to meet you, Tina Croft,' Eddie murmured, his voice slow and syrupy. Anyone would think he was flirting with her. Maybe he was. Maybe that's what happened when you dreamed up debonair heroes for a living, thought Fern. When you spent too long viewing the world through their dark, smouldering eyes . . . all those beautiful, feisty women throwing themselves at your feet with one sensual sweep of your hair . . . He might not have the taut physique of a romantic hero, but Eddie could certainly give his dashing main suspect a run for his money in the charm stakes. But if he was the brooding anti-hero, who did that make Tina? Not the sexy Scandinavian au pair on the cover, that was for sure.

Fern found herself giggling too – all the tension of the last few days spilling out of her in a sudden flash of silliness. In her mind's eye she was already recreating the scene for April over tea and biscuits, exaggerating Tina's reaction and playing up Eddie's flirtatious drawl. Faeces *and* flirtation – their new doorstep was getting all the action this morning.

'I'm glad you're here actually, Eddie,' said Paul, cutting through the merriment. 'I wouldn't mind picking your brains for a moment. Have you had any trouble with dogs on *your* property?' he asked, dragging the conversation back to his new favourite subject.

Eddie frowned. 'Trouble? What sort of trouble?'

'Fouling,' said Paul, the outrage still there in his voice. Still fresh. 'Someone left a turd on our front step this morning. Right there,' he added, pointing. 'Exactly where you're standing.'

Eddie took a swift step backwards and Fern giggled even harder. *Icked-out Eddie.*

'No,' he said, pulling a face. 'Nothing like that, thank goodness.'

What about non-existent pregnant blondes? Any problems with them? Fern wanted to ask – and would *already* have asked if it wasn't for Paul and Tina breathing down her neck. But she'd left it too late now: Eddie was already making his excuses: 'I promised my agent I'd have those rewrites finished by first thing Monday morning.' His entire body language had changed, and he seemed very keen to go suddenly. Perhaps he wanted to get back home and check his shoes for stray traces of dog poo. The mental image made Fern smile, despite her frustration at the missed opportunity to question him further.

Her good mood carried her all the way into Sunday afternoon, through the disappointing discovery of the piano's terrible tuning, and on towards a rare moment of freedom. Of long-awaited opportunity. Tina and Paul were both busy upstairs, measuring the nursery for furniture, which meant Fern was finally off the leash. Finally free to sneak off and call the Rochesters again. And this time, if there was no reply, she'd make sure she left a message asking them to ring her back. One way or another she was going to get the answers she needed and put the whole Marte business to bed, once and for all. No more fruitless Google searches. No more quizzing the neighbours. No more nightmares. Onwards and upwards.

Chapter 15

Fern left a note on the kitchen table – *Popped out for some fresh air. Back soon* – and headed off up the road, with the Rochesters' number already saved onto her phone.

She checked out the other cars parked on the roadside as she went. Nope. No scratches. No signs of vandalism. She must have been unlucky, that's all. Or maybe it didn't even happen in the street. Maybe it was in the car park in Westerton and she hadn't noticed at the time. She *had* been a little preoccupied.

Someone on the other side of the road broke off from hosing out their bins to wave at her – someone from April's party, presumably – sending water spraying up their garage door in a wide arc. Still no sign of Linny though. It had been three whole days now.

Where have you gone? Why can't I see you anymore?

It was the first time Fern had ventured this far up Crenellation Lane, other than to turn her car round. The houses were even bigger if anything, though not necessarily smarter. Especially not number twenty-three, whose jungle of a front garden was enough to give Sean nightmares. And then, just like that, the houses ran out and the pavement became a narrow path, high-hedged on both sides, snaking off into the shadowed gloom of the woods.

The remains of Fern's good mood disappeared too, along with the sunlight. She felt oddly conspicuous as she picked her way across the rutted mud and puddles in an old pair of gym trainers – this was proper welly territory now – even though there was no one there to see her. Yes, conspicuous and cumbersome, panting with the effort as the path rose sharply, twisting itself round the thick roots that had burrowed up to the surface, like gnarled human limbs from some tacky horror film, refusing to stay buried.

Trees flanked her on the left – sycamores and oaks mainly, judging by their dropped leaves – while the high hedge ran on to her right, following the border of the old Gillyhead Estate. According to the map she'd bought Paul, the path opened out onto parkland soon, to wide open space, but who knew what sort of changes the last hundred years or so had wrought. It could be a dead end now, for all Fern knew. Or a housing estate. Or nothing. The same endless path stretching on forever.

And then, just as she was about to admit defeat, to start retracing her steps, the path took a final twist round to the left and the trees melted away like magic. Fern found herself on an open ridge of land, with views down to the river on one side, and the smooth green contours of the Gillyhead House golf course on the other. And there, straight ahead, stood an even more welcome sight: a bench.

It took her a while to catch her breath, and a little longer still to steel herself for the phone call, her stomach a knot of nerves and her head full of fresh worries. What if they'd taken out new phone contracts with an American company by now? What if yesterday had been her last chance and she'd blown it by not leaving a message? Eventually she stopped scrolling through junk emails on her mobile – no messages from Linny hidden in there either, not unless she taken up slimming supplement sales in the afterlife – and called the Rochesters' number.

One ring.

Two rings.

Three. Four. Five.

Come on, come on.

Six rings.

Seven.

'Hello?' The woman's voice at the other end of the line sounded a long way away. Not quite a whole ocean, but still a good distance from a Sunday afternoon bench in Britain. It sounded tired, too – tired and irritated, with a tinge of suspicion. All that, somehow, squeezed into a single word: *Hello?*

'Oh. Hello,' said Fern. 'Sorry, I wasn't sure this number would still be working. Erm . . . is that Caroline? Mrs Rochester?' *Don't screw it up this time*, she was thinking. *Say what you came here to say. Spit it out.*

'Who is this?' asked the woman, sidestepping the answer with a return question of her own.

'My name's Mrs Croft. Fern Croft. The new owner of your old house. The one on Crenellation Lane,' she added, redundantly. *In case you'd forgotten where it was.* 'I was just—'

'How did you get this number?' The voice was waking up now. Not quite so tired anymore. Angrier.

Shit. Fern didn't want to get Sonia into trouble. But what else could she say? *I stole it?* Probably not the best way to gain the woman's trust.

'It was . . . it was on some of the paperwork.' Was that vague enough? 'I'm sorry to bother you – I'm sure you're busy settling in, just like us.' Fern kept on talking, blurting out whatever nonsense came into her head, in an effort to smooth over the awkwardness. 'I hope the move went well by the way. Oh, and thank you for the bottle of fizz. That was a really nice gesture.' Fern hadn't even thought to leave anything for the couple buying their flat. They'd have to make do with a cracked tile over the fireplace and some sangria stains on the carpet. 'Anyway, the reason I'm ringing is er . . .'

112

She forgot all about Paul's map. Forgot about warming up to the Marte question by asking if it was the same one they'd taken to the charity shop. But even if she had remembered it wouldn't have changed anything. Now that she was here – now that she was actually doing it – Fern just wanted to get it over with.

'This might sound like a funny question, but when I was looking round your house . . . not now, I mean ages ago, when we were still thinking about buying it . . . I erm . . .' Oh, for goodness' sake. Why was it so hard? 'Well, the thing is, the estate agent had to go, so another lady showed me round instead. Marte.' *There. Done it.* 'She did a good job and everything, but . . . but, no one here seems to know who she is. Which wouldn't really matter, only erm . . .' *Only what? Only I'm nosy?* That's what the woman was going to think, wasn't it? 'Look, this is probably going to sound a bit weird, but I've been having these horrible dreams . . .' Perfect. Not nosy at all, just plain mad.

'Sorry,' interrupted Mrs Rochester. 'What did you say?'

Which bit? thought Fern. *The estate agent? Marte? The nightmares?*

'Marte,' she blurted out, plumping for the mystery woman. 'Who is she, and what was she doing in your house?' And there it was. Finally.

Her questions met with silence at the other end of the line. A long silence.

'Hello? Mrs Rochester? Are you still there?'

More silence. And then a funny wheezing sound like someone struggling to breathe. Sonia was right – the poor woman didn't seem very well at all.

'Mrs Rochester,' Fern said again, remembering how she'd clutched at her chest outside the baker's. Maybe she had a weak heart. 'Are you okay? What's wrong? Is it something to do with Marte?'

'Mar-te,' whispered the woman, her voice a slow strangled echo. And then a new voice came on the line: a man's voice.

113

'Who is this?' he demanded.

Here we go again.

'How did you get this number?'

'I'm sorry,' said Fern. 'I didn't mean to cause any trouble. I'm just trying to find out who Marte is.'

'Leave us alone,' snapped the man. 'Don't call us again.' And then the line went dead.

Fern dropped the mobile away from her ear as if it was hot, burning hot, her fingers shaking. She wasn't sure exactly *what* reaction she'd been expecting, but not that. Definitely not that.

The shaking had spread to the rest of her body now. What was wrong with her, for goodness' sake? Why was she such a neurotic mess? Fern knew the answer to that. It was written across her every trembling bone; etched into the gaping hollow within. No matter how big the baby grew, it still wouldn't fill that empty space inside of her. There weren't enough babies in the world for that. *Linny. Oh, Linny.*

And now she was crying again. Ridiculous. Crying and whispering her sister's name into the silence. *Linny. Linny. Linny.* And even though she'd promised herself she wouldn't do it anymore – promised Paul and Dr Earnshaw that she'd deleted it off her phone – she found herself opening up the music app, clicking on the playlist marked LAP (Linny's Answer Phone), and pressing 'Play'. The quality wasn't quite as good as the original, but the original was long gone now, disappeared into the ether along with Linny herself.

'Hi there. You're through to Linnaea Evesham. I can't come to the phone right now but if you'd like to leave a message after the beep I'll get back to you as soon as possible. Unless this is another of those mis-sold PPI calls, in which case you can stick your message up your—' BEEP.

'It's me,' said Fern. The phone was back up by her ear, even though she knew how stupid it was. She knew. She really did. 'I just wanted to hear your voice. I just wanted to – oh, Linny.

Nothing's right without you. *I'm* not right without you. I can't even make a phone call without cocking it up. And now Tina's here and . . . and . . . and you're not. Not even like you were.' She'd already deserted her once by dying. Why would she want to do it again? 'Where are you?' Three days and not so much as a glimpse. 'Is it the new house? Don't you like it here? Is it Paul? Is it because he's pretending he didn't see you? Pretending . . .' Pretending what, exactly? Pretending he couldn't see dead people? Pretending he wasn't as crazy as her?

'I thought maybe you'd been to see Dad. That's what he told Anne . . . Said he'd seen his girl again.' But that was before, Fern realised. Before the thing with the removal lorry. 'Am I right? Have you been to the care home?'

Linny said nothing. She never did.

'Please, Linny. Don't leave me now. Don't leave me.'

Of course not, you idiot. How can I? This is us we're talking about. You and me. Always and forever.

Fern willed her to say it. *Waited* for her to say it, the mobile pressed so tight against her ear that the stem of her earring dug into her neck. Waited and waited. You and me. Always. Forever.

But there *was* no forever anymore, was there? Not for them. Linny was gone and Fern was stuck here without her. With Paul and Tina and Marte. She might not have got the answers she needed from the Rochesters, but the woman's name had meant something to them, she was sure of it. Why else would they have reacted like that? Which meant Marte was real. She was out there somewhere – she had to be. It was just a question of finding her.

Chapter 16

Fern passed dog-walker after dog-walker as she headed back down the path to Crenellation Lane, including some familiar faces. Sunday afternoon was clearly the designated exercise time in local canine circles and Fern found herself sizing up everyone she passed as a potential suspect for the unwelcome gift on the doorstep. But the people she recognised from April's party were nothing but friendly when they spotted her, which ruled them out of the investigation. Not that she *was* investigating. Not really. It was Marte she was interested in. She managed to turn her brief conversation with the hospital porter – whose name Fern had already forgotten – round to the mystery woman, but that was a dead end too. He'd mainly been on night shifts since he moved to Crenellation Lane and had never met the Rochesters.

Sean stopped to say hello to Fern as well, but he was only interested in talking about gardening contracts. His yappy little Yorkie jumped up around her legs while he replayed his sales pitch, barely pausing for breath. And even though Fern *had* been thinking of taking him on, on a trial basis at least, the pushiness of his manner was starting to put her off the idea. She was saved from any further decisions by the appearance of an even yappier specimen, who came chasing up the hill towards them, looking for a furry partner in crime. The newcomer turned out to be Richard's dog, despite looking nothing whatsoever like a red setter. *Scruffy-Terrier Richard*? No, that didn't work at all – he was somewhat slower up the path than his pet, and the two dogs were already circling each other aggressively, like boxers, by the time he arrived.

'Oh, hello again,' he said, sounding surprised to see Fern there. A bad surprise, judging by his pained expression, but perhaps that was more to do with his uphill chase than any personal dislike on his part. That's what Fern told herself, anyway.

'Hi. Nice to see you,' she lied, forcing her own face into something approximating a smile, as another rush of misery threatened to overwhelm her. *Oh, Linny. I don't fit in here. I belong with you.* 'Lovely weather today.' The three of them – Fern, Sean and Richard – made awkward small talk for a minute or so while the two dogs snapped and growled, and then Fern made her excuses, speeding up her waddle down the final section and back out into the space and light of Crenellation Lane.

But she didn't go straight home. She couldn't face Tina's fussing right now, or Paul demanding to know what was wrong – he could always tell when she'd been crying. Fern walked back along the other side of the road instead, down to April's house, determined to make her trip count for something. She hadn't had a chance to ask April about Marte at her party – hadn't wanted to monopolise her when she had so many other guests to look after – but she did say Fern could pop round for a cuppa anytime. And the idea of making a proper friend on the street was an added attraction. Someone who understood what it was like to lose somebody. Who knew what it felt like to have an empty hole inside them that nothing else could fill. Maybe a friend to share the grief was exactly what Fern needed. The closer she got to April's front door, the more hopeful she felt. Maybe *this* was the new start she'd been looking for – an answer to the Marte mystery and a blossoming new friendship.

April's car was right there on the drive – a blue Golf with an NHS window sticker on the rear windscreen – but there was no answer when Fern rang the bell. That wasn't particularly odd in itself, but she could have sworn she saw someone at the dining-room window a few moments later: a dark outline pressed against the glass for a moment, and then it was gone again. She waited a polite amount of time – long enough for April to have run up and down the stairs twenty times over; for a hundred laps of the kitchen – and then knocked, just to be sure.

No luck. And no luck at Eddie's either, when Fern stopped off to see if *he'd* be able to shed any more light on the Marte mystery. Even if he didn't know the Rochesters very well, he might still have seen their elusive Scandinavian friend coming and going. But no, he wasn't answering his door, although his car was still on the drive as well. Maybe he was too busy working on those rewrites for his agent to answer. Or perhaps he and April were out for a walk together. Then again, maybe Eddie was the real reason that April hadn't answered, Fern thought, recalling the figure she'd seen at the dining-room window. Remembering the pair's flirtatious banter the day before and the amount of wine Eddie had been putting away. Maybe one thing had led to another after the party and April had finally succumbed to the Casanova of Crenellation Lane herself, as a temporary relief to her loneliness.

The thought of April and Eddie's friendship – platonic or otherwise – made Fern feel oddly jealous, which was ridiculous given that she'd only just met them. She'd been letting her imagination run away with her again, hadn't she? Imagining that she and April would somehow be kindred spirits because they'd both lost someone. Yes, ridiculous was the word for it. She was a grown woman, for goodness' sake, not the new girl at school, trying to fit in. Not that she'd ever had to face that, of course. Not with Linny. Everyone always wanted to be friends with *her*, which meant they all had to be friends with Fern too.

She felt even more like a schoolgirl afterwards, like a sly teenager, creeping back through her own front door. Though if Fern was the teenager, what did that make Paul? Her parent? Her keeper?

'We're upstairs,' called Tina, before Fern had even shut the door behind her, as if she'd been watching out the window. 'Come and see.'

Fern prised off her muddy trainers with her toes, too weary and too sorry for herself to bend all the way down to unlace them. And then she heaved herself up the stairs to find the others, grumbling inwardly as she went. What was so important that it couldn't wait until she'd sat down for a bit? Until she'd fortified herself with some tea and biscuits? Maybe they'd discovered another hidden cache of baby clothes. How horrible would that be? Or a Go-Back-To-Where-you-Came-From brick through the bedroom window, after the poo incident failed to get the message home. Or maybe . . . maybe it was Marte they wanted her to see. Maybe she'd moved herself into the attic while no one was looking, just like in Fern's dream, and Tina and Paul were up there discussing due dates with her. And even though Fern was only being silly – teasing herself as she went with ever more ridiculous scenes – the image still sent shivers down her spine.

'In here,' said her mother-in-law, sticking her head out of the back bedroom. Not one of the front rooms, with a proper spying view out of the window, as Fern had suspected. There was nothing to see from the back of the house apart from the garden and the crumbling folly beyond.

Tina stepped to one side as Fern arrived, gesturing into the room like a circus ringmaster. 'Ta da!'

Fern wasn't sure what she was supposed to be looking at, initially. Were there different curtains in the window, maybe? Had they swapped them with the ones in Tina's room? But then she spotted the desk from the nursery, all set up with

119

her lamp and table-top easel, and a large noticeboard hanging behind it.

'We thought we'd make a start on your office for you,' said Tina. 'Your studio, I mean. Then you can get going with work again whenever you're ready.'

Really? Fern certainly hadn't been expecting *that*. What happened to lectures about maternity leave for the self-employed? About needing to take things easy for the sake of her blood pressure, and the baby?

'But we can move the desk somewhere else if the light's not right,' said Tina, studying her face anxiously. 'I know these things are important. You just say where you want it. And we can get rid of that noticeboard if you don't like it. Paul found it in the attic when he was looking for that baby monitor earlier. We thought it might be good as an "inspiration board" or whatever it is you arty types call it.' She paused. 'You're not keen, are you?'

'No, it's great,' said Fern, meaning it. 'Perfect, in fact. Thank you.'

Tina beamed. She looked so pleased with herself, so relieved that Fern felt bad for wishing her away.

'I really am here to help you, love,' Tina told her. 'So you let me know what you need. Even if that's just making the odd cup of tea and keeping out your way so you can get on with things. I'm a big girl. I'm sure I can amuse myself.'

Wow! *What did you say to her?* Fern wondered, catching Paul's eye behind his mother's back. *And why the heck didn't you say it sooner?*

'Thank you,' she mouthed. Maybe it really would be all right after all. Maybe they could survive the next week – or however long Tina was planning on staying for – without coming to blows. Perhaps it *would* be useful to have another pair of hands around the place, just while they were finding their feet.

Paul grinned. He looked even more relieved than his mother. 'You're welcome,' he mouthed back.

Tina's helpfulness didn't stop there, either, which was how Fern found herself relaxing in another bath after dinner that evening, hot cup of decaf tea (in *her* mug) on one side of the tub, and a trio of new aromatherapy tea lights on the other. Special pregnancy-safe ones, apparently, 'because you have to be extra careful with these things when you're expecting'. Who knew? The relaxing piano playlist Paul had made for her was playing on shuffle setting in the far corner of the room, well away (at Tina's insistence) from any electrocution risks, and even though the quality was a little tinny without a proper speaker, it was still lovely. *All* of it was lovely – the music, the bubbles, the candles – a proper oasis of peace and pampering after all the ups and downs of the last few days. So relaxing, in fact, that Fern didn't give the idea of messages on the steamed-up mirror a second thought. She closed her eyes, resting her hands on the wet curve of her stomach as the soaring Satie melody washed over her, breathing out a soft sigh of contentment.

'What do you think, Little One? Are we going to be all right when Daddy goes back to work tomorrow? You, me and Granny?' It would be better once *she* got back to work too. Maybe that's what she needed – something real to get her teeth into and stop her mind spinning off in ever more neurotic directions. 'You, me, Granny and Linny,' Fern corrected herself. It had been half a week since she'd last seen her sister now. Surely she wouldn't stay away any longer?

No, she wouldn't. No sooner had the thought played itself out in her mind – Linny's name still hovering on her lips – than it happened. Right then and there, as the last D minor chord of 'Gymnopédie, No. 1' died away to nothing. There was a moment's silence – maybe two – and then Fern's phone rang. But it wasn't her regular ringtone, 'Morning Breeze' or whatever it was called. And it wasn't the silly one Paul had sneaked on there for a joke during a drunken night out with the three of them – *this is your husband calling. Answer the phone, dear.*

This is your husband calling. It was Iggy Pop's 'Lust for Life': Linny's ringtone.

No. It couldn't be. But it was.

Fern's breath caught in her throat. Linny! *Wait. I'm coming. I'm coming.*

Chapter 17

Heart pounding, Fern couldn't launch herself out of the bath quick enough. Her body had become a wet, slippery lump – all bump and elbows – and the water a solid force trying to push her back down. Trying to keep her under. But she fought her way up, skin skidding and squeaking against the curves of the tub, hauling herself up on the crest of her own mini-tidal wave. Water sloshed over the carpet as she broke free, candles kicked across the room in its wake. She didn't stop to check which way up they'd landed. Maybe if she had, she'd have caught the flame before it got a proper hold on her towel. And maybe, if she'd stopped to think, she'd have realised what a ridiculous notion it was anyway. But she didn't stop. And she didn't think. At least, not logically. *She got my message* – that's what Fern was thinking – *she got my message and now she's ringing me back.*

Everything seemed to happen at the same time. Catching her foot on the edge of the bath as she scrambled out. Tumbling headfirst towards the floor, hands clasped instinctively over her belly to cushion the baby. The dancing flicker of yellow out the corner of her eye as she went down. The smell of burning. Could she already smell burning or did her brain fill in that detail afterwards? And still the sound of Iggy Pop, ringing in her ears, belting out his lust for life. The sound of Linny calling.

But Fern couldn't reach the phone. Not with her head wedged against the towel rail. Not with her stomach squashed beneath her and the flame creeping up the towel inches away from her hair. Wet hair, but even so.

Wait for me, I'm coming.

Fern yanked her head back and rolled sideways, away from the fire. Something didn't feel right. A raw pain in her temple and a tight twist in her trailing leg. And something else. Something was wrong. No time to think about that now though. She dragged herself up on to her knees, on to her feet, and lunged for the flaming towel, catching it at the fireless edge and flinging it into the bath.

She hobbled across the room to her blaring phone, left ankle buckling beneath her with every step, and reached up onto the shelf to retrieve it. That's when she realised what it was – what was wrong with the whole situation. Iggy was still singing. He hadn't cut off after the designated ring time and her answer-phone hadn't clicked in. It wasn't a call at all, was it? Just another track like the Satie before it. But even as the realisation kicked in, like a dull ache inside her squashed stomach, she was already swiping the screen to answer.

'I'm here. It's me.'

Iggy kept on singing.

'Linny.'

And singing.

'Linny.'

Fern must have played her favourites list on shuffle by accident, Iggy Pop and all. But realising her mistake didn't stop the blind, desperate hope, burning inside her.

'Linny! Are you still there?'

Of course she wasn't. She never had been. Fern stood, naked and dripping, staring at the little screen until her eyes blurred, willing it to light up with her sister's photo. The one she'd taken that night they went out for break-up drinks, to help Linny get over *him*.

'Look,' Fern had said, showing her sister the picture she'd just snapped. She was still smiling in it, despite the heartache, eyes still sparkling even after an entire bottle of Prosecco. 'Look how beautiful you are. Much too good for him,' she'd added, as if she knew who he was. As if she'd actually met him. But it was true, nonetheless – Linny *was* too good for him. She was too good for everyone.

'You're kidding me, right?' said Linny, laughing. 'Have you seen the colour of those bags under my eyes? I look like I've done ten rounds with Mike Tyson. As for my hair . . .'

'Beautiful,' insisted Fern. 'So beautiful I'm going to set it as your new profile picture.'

'What? You don't want *that* flashing up every time I ring. Mrs Halloween Ghoul Eyes staring out your phone at you whenever you go to answer . . .'

'Mrs Beautiful Eyes,' Fern had told her, firmly.

The picture was still there, stored away on her mobile with all the others (backed up on her laptop and external hard drive to be on the safe side). But it didn't flash up now, no matter how hard Fern stared at her phone. And then Iggy was gone again, booted off by Debussy.

Idiot, she thought, cursing her own stupidity as she shook herself back to sense. The whole bathroom could have gone up in flames if she hadn't caught that towel in time. The whole house. And as for throwing herself out the bath like some kind of sumo stunt woman . . . What if she'd knocked herself unconscious? How would she have put the fire out then? She could have damaged the baby, landing on her stomach like that. Fern's insides ached and throbbed just thinking about it. She *hadn't* hurt the baby though, had she? Oh God, what if she had?

'You're okay in there, aren't you?'

The baby wasn't moving. Why wasn't she moving?

'Come on now, sweetheart. Give me a little wriggle, so I know you're okay.'

Nothing. No kicks. No elbows grinding against her belly. Just stillness.

'Seriously now. Time to wake up.' Fern put her hands to her stomach and jiggled from side to side. And when that didn't work she scrolled back through her mobile until she found 'Lust for Life' again. She turned up the volume as loud as it would go and pressed the phone against her stretch-marked belly.

Drum intro – nothing.

Drum and guitar. Still nothing.

Wait, was that a kick? Yes. A something anyway.

Thank goodness.

And again, and again. Stronger now. Kick, kick, kick, kick, almost in time to the music. Maybe she was going to be a rock chick like her aunty.

'Good girl. That's it. Good girl.'

The baby was all right. *Thank goodness.* No harm done. Apart from a burned towel and a twisted ankle. And possibly the start of a bruise on her forehead. Fern crossed over to the mirror to check out the damage but it was too steamed up to see. It *was* only steam though. No heart. No letters. She turned back to the window instead, pulling up the roller blind. Not very far, given her state of undress, just enough to open the bottom sash and get rid of the condensation. Just enough to see the dripping message scrawled across the glass. There were five letters this time: S O F I A.

'Paul!'

The window stayed shut but somehow the cold was in her anyway, shivering through her as she tore open the bathroom door and screamed for him to come and see.

'Paul!'

He came thundering up the stairs to find her, Tina chasing behind, words already tumbling out of his mouth in a senseless stream of panic: 'I'm coming, stay there. What is it? Is the baby okay?'

'Look,' Fern cried, as he rounded the top step, swerving sideways to find her in the doorway.

But Paul was looking at her instead, his eyes bulging with fear, front teeth bared and lips turned down at the edges. 'What is it? What's happened?'

'There,' she said, pointing at the window. 'See?'

'What is it?' he said again. 'What am I supposed to be looking at?'

'The name on the glass,' she said. 'It's *her*. I know it is.' She didn't know how, or why – and maybe she didn't want to – but she knew it was her all right.

'Not this again,' said Paul, terror draining away to something more like anger. 'Please, *please* tell me we're not doing this again. I thought you'd gone into labour early. I thought something was wrong. I thought . . . I don't even want to *say* what I thought. But not this. Not this *Linny* nonsense again.' He spat her name out like it was something hateful. Something dirty.

'No. Not Linny.' It was Marte. It had to be. That was the name she'd chosen for her baby. Fern could still hear the wistfulness in the woman's voice as she said it: *Sofia*. 'Look,' she said, grabbing hold of his shirt and tugging him across the room to see.

'There's nothing there, for crying out loud,' he snarled. 'There never is. It's all up here.' He tapped the side of his head, just like Eddie had done at the party. Only with more aggression, his whole face screwed up in rage. And, unlike Eddie, he wasn't talking about Mrs Rochester. He was talking about her.

The worst thing was he was right. There *wasn't* anything there. Not anymore.

'I saw it,' said Fern, shaking all over with the unfairness of it. 'You have to believe me.'

'Look at you,' said Tina, bustling in with one of the towels from the guest room. 'Shivering like anything.' She stepped between them, forcing her body in front of her son, as if to shield Fern from his anger. 'Come on, pop this round you, love, before you catch a chill.' She draped it over Fern's shoulders, overlapping the edges across her chest as if she were wrapping up a child after a swim. *Making a sausage roll,* as Fern's dad used to say when they were little. 'And don't you go upsetting yourself. That's not good for the baby, is it? Or your blood pressure. I'm sure it's a simple misunderstanding.'

'I told you,' said Paul, rounding on his mother. 'This is exactly what I'm talking about. She's getting worse, not better. Seeing her in mirrors. Seeing her in windows. Chasing after her in the street . . . And what on earth's been going on in here?' He scooped up the blackened towel – what was left of it, anyway – and pulled it, dripping, from the bath.

'I caught one of the candles when I was getting out,' said Fern. 'It's only a towel. No harm done.'

'No harm done?' repeated Paul. 'So busy looking for your stupid messages you nearly burn the house down? And what's that on your forehead?' The questions came faster and faster as his fury gathered pace. Not that they really were questions – more like accusations. 'Why are you bleeding? What have you been doing up here?'

'Shh,' said Tina. 'That's enough now. Can't you see you're upsetting her?'

'*I'm* upsetting *her*? Oh, for crying out loud.'

'Look.' Tina kept her voice steady, hugging her arm round Fern's towelled shoulder as she took charge of the situation. 'Let's all calm down a bit, shall we? You go and get yourself dressed, love. Get into your nightie and dressing gown. And you,' she said, addressing Paul, 'you come and help me in the kitchen. We could all do with a nice cup of tea.'

But Paul wouldn't be told.

'Tea?' he growled. 'We need more than a sodding cup of tea to fix this one. We need . . .' He shrugged his shoulders. 'Fucked if I know. I give up. I can't do this anymore.' And with that he stormed out of the bathroom, flinging the towel at the mirror as he went. Fern heard him on the stairs – still storming, stomping like a tantrummy teenager all the way down. And then, after a slight delay while he stopped to put his shoes on, to grab a coat and pick up his keys, he slammed the front door behind him.

Chapter 18

Fern was still cold, even in her dressing gown, with the duvet pulled all the way up to her chin. She felt cold on the inside too – numb – as if the chill had worked its way right into her bones. Into the very heart of her. And for once she was glad to have her mother-in-law there. The last thing she wanted was to be on her own as she shivered in bed, her ears straining for the sound of Paul's key in the door. So much for their new start together – they hadn't even made it to the end of the weekend. Sunday night had never looked lonelier.

Tina pressed a cup of tea into her hands and perched on the edge of the bed. 'I'm sorry,' she said. 'I was only trying to help. I didn't *mean* to interfere, but I've gone and made things worse, haven't I?'

'It wasn't you,' Fern assured her, although Tina was having none of it.

'I should have kept out of it,' she went on. 'Should have left you to work things out between yourselves . . .' She gave a short, wry laugh. 'Not exactly my strong point though, is it? Keeping out of things?'

Fern was too miserable to agree. Not even inwardly. 'It's not your fault,' she said. 'It's mine.' It was true. Her fault for thinking

Paul would believe her. Her fault for thinking it was real. Any of it. Even though she'd swear on her own life (if not the baby's) that it was.

Tina shook her head. 'I haven't seen him like that since . . . well, since he was a lad. A moody teenager. Forever slamming doors and storming off into the night.' She smiled at the memory. 'But he always cooled off soon enough. I'm sure he'll be back once he's stomped it out. A bit of a walk, a bit of fresh air, then he'll turn round and come home again, tail between his legs. You wait and see.'

Fern wanted to believe her. Wanted to think it would all blow over like a regular row. They'd had enough of them over the years (usually over Linny, gobbling up too much time and attention), but she'd never seen Paul lose it like that. Never seen that wild blaze of anger in his face – not against her, anyway. What if they couldn't come back from it this time? What if she'd used up all her chances, baby or no baby? What if *he* didn't come back? Or – the thought struck her as a physical spike of pain behind her eyes – what if she didn't want him back?

No. Of course she did. Didn't she? It wasn't Paul talking to her like that – shouting, rather – it was his fear. Fear for the baby. Fear for her, unravelling before his eyes. That's what *he* was frightened of, not some creepy message on the window he couldn't even see. Maybe if he had seen it things would be different.

'I didn't imagine it,' she told Tina. 'It was right there on the glass.' But even now she was starting to doubt herself. Starting to wonder whether she needed help.

'I know it was, love. I know.'

A flicker of warmth flared inside Fern's chest. 'You saw it too?' *It wasn't in my head? You mean, I'm right and Paul's wrong, and he's a bastard for walking out like that?*

'I couldn't see anything much from where I was,' Tina admitted. 'I was too busy worrying about you catching cold. But if you say it was there then I believe you.'

131

The hopeful flicker snuffed itself back out again. Fern knew when she was being humoured. Patronised.

'Paul takes after his father when it comes to this sort of thing, I'm afraid,' said Tina. 'Shying away from things he can't understand.'

That wasn't exactly news to Fern. After all, he still swore blind he hadn't seen Linny in the road, despite having called out her name.

'Graham was just the same,' said Tina, referring to her husband of thirty years in the past tense, as if he'd died rather than traded her in for a younger, Frencher model. Maybe he *was* dead to her now. 'If he couldn't see something, then it couldn't be there. Simple as that.'

Fern liked Graham – more than was strictly loyal, given his treatment of Tina and, by extension, Paul. She'd always found his quiet cynicism a welcome respite from his wife's intensity while the two of them were still together. But she nodded, nevertheless, as if that same cynicism was something to be avoided at all costs.

'Paul's never lost anyone close to him,' said Tina. 'Never *been* that close to anyone, come to that. Apart from you, of course.'

Until now, thought Fern miserably. No one would call them close right now.

'We never meant for him to be an only child but that's the way it worked out. It's funny, I'd convinced myself I was having twins but it was just wishful thinking.' Tina shook the thought away again. 'But to *lose* a twin. I can't even imagine . . . It would be stranger if you *didn't* still see her. I mean, a bond like that . . .'

She was trying, she really was. Fern appreciated the effort – the sentiment – even if her mother-in-law's bluntness left something to be desired. Maybe that's what made her open up. Or perhaps it was simply the need to tell someone her side of the story. Someone with less of a vested interest in Fern's sanity than Paul. Marginally less, at any rate.

'It wasn't Linny,' she blurted out. 'Writing on the window, I mean. It was Marte.' There. She'd said it, although the name might not mean anything to Tina anyway. Had Paul mentioned her obsession with the unknown woman in his gripes about her mental state?

'Who?' asked Tina.

Clearly not. Fern took a deep breath and plunged into the story from the very beginning. From the moment she first saw the woman, to the fact that no one could tell her who Marte was, or what she'd been doing there that day. She told Tina about her twisted dreams; the other messages on the mirror; her call to Mrs Rochester. She even told her about the baby clothes in the attic, which she couldn't help feeling were somehow tied up with Marte too.

'I wish I could brush the whole thing off like Paul and forget about it,' she finished, 'I really do. But he doesn't see the same things that I see, and he never met her. She was standing right there.' Fern pointed to the far end of the bed, almost spilling her tea in the process. 'As real as you are, I swear. Only . . . only now it's as if she never existed except in my head. And the more I try to get her *out* of my head, the more . . .' She sighed. 'Oh, I don't know. I can't explain it. None of it makes any sense.'

'Sometimes it's hard to know what's real and what isn't,' said Tina. 'It's not always as clear cut as people think, is it? Not when you really love someone. When you lose someone . . .'

But what's losing Linny got to do with Marte? Fern turned back towards her mother-in-law, surprised to see tears glistening in the other woman's eyes. She wasn't talking about Fern's loss anymore, was she? She was talking about her own.

'Who is it?' Fern reached across the covers, wrapping Tina's clenched fingers in hers. 'Who do you mean?'

'My baby,' said Tina, softly. 'My first baby.' She pulled a lopsided smile, half nostalgic, half sad – the smile of an older, longer-settled grief – her other hand slipping down to the loose, middle-aged swell of her own belly. 'It's silly, really,' she said. 'It's not like he was ever alive, not to the rest of the world. I lost him before anyone knew I was expecting. But *I* knew. I knew him like I knew myself. And I loved him.'

'That's not silly at all,' said Fern. On the contrary, it went a long way to explaining Tina's endless fussing and pregnancy lectures. 'I'm sorry, I didn't realise. Paul never mentioned it.'

'He doesn't know. No one does. I even lied on my forms when I was expecting him. Said it was my first pregnancy, though the doctors could probably tell it wasn't.' A tear trickled down her cheek. 'I never told Graham, or my parents. Not even the baby's father, although he didn't stick around for long anyway. I don't know why I kept it secret, really. Scared, I guess. Scared of what people would think.'

It was hard to imagine Tina being scared of anything.

'And afterwards it was too late,' she went on. 'There wasn't much point then, anyway. Why sully his memory with other people's prejudice?'

Fern forgot about Marte for a moment. Forgot that Paul had just walked out on her. She was too swept up in her mother-in-law's story, in this new softer, secret side to her. To have gone through something like that all on her own, carrying the burden of grief all this time. And then to have chosen *her* to share it with.

'You must have been young to deal with all that on your own,' she said, trying, and failing, to work out the timeline in her head.

'Not so sweet sixteen,' admitted Tina. 'But even now, all these years later, I still think I . . .' She broke off, shaking her head. 'You'll think I'm barmy.'

'No,' Fern told her. 'I won't. Trust me.'

'I still think I feel him. Inside me, I mean. It's usually just before I go to sleep, or first thing in the morning, when I'm still waking up – like a warm weight in my stomach. A sense of something – someone – nestling inside of me, all curled up a like a cat.' She laughed, embarrassed by her own admission. 'Which is nonsense, of course, utter nonsense. But then, none of it ever made any sense. I felt him long before it was medically possible and I still felt him afterwards. It wasn't like that with Paul.'

'Did you ever see him?' Fern asked. '*Do* you see him?' She wanted the answer to be 'yes'. To know it wasn't just her.

Tina shook her head again. 'No, nothing like that. I mean, I can picture him as clear as anything – how I imagined he'd look when he was born – but no, he's never been more than a feeling. I did go to a medium once, at least that's what she called herself, but that was years later when I was expecting Paul. I felt guilty, like I was cancelling him out, replacing him with a better model.' She rolled her eyes. 'Like I said, utterly barmy. But I knew I wouldn't be able to relax into motherhood properly until I'd made my peace with him.'

'And did it work? Did the medium manage to reach him?'

But the front door clanged before Tina could answer, making them both jump.

Paul! He was back.

'There,' said Tina, dabbing her eyes with a tissue. 'What did I tell you? Home again already, with his tail between his legs. But listen, drink up that tea before you go anywhere and no rushing on the stairs.' It looked like normal Tina was back again then. Regular service resumed. But Fern did as she was told, swigging down the entire cup before she began the complicated process of hauling herself out of bed. She could have waited for him to come to her, but she didn't. She thought of Young Tina, all hollowed out with loss and no one to share it with, and followed her mother-in-law downstairs to set things right again. Slowly, though, obviously. No rushing.

Only it wasn't Paul. It wasn't anybody, as it turned out. It must have been the clatter of the letterbox springing shut again as someone posted a note through the door. For a crazy moment Fern thought the bit of paper in Tina's hand might be some kind of leaving note from Paul. Maybe he hadn't just stormed out after their row but left for good. Maybe the move hadn't been a new start for him at all, so much as a last-ditch attempt at saving their marriage. One last chance . . . a chance she'd just blown in spectacular fashion. And now this was his cowardly way of saying goodbye without having to deal with the consequences of his words . . .

No. Fern blinked the idea away for the nonsense it was – marriages didn't end in hurriedly scrawled letters pushed through the door – and shuffled down the hallway for a closer look. It was a political flyer, that was all. Except it wasn't. Fern was close enough now to see that someone had blacked out half of the blurb in thick marker pen. And the remaining words spelled out a threatening message:

███████████ GET ███ OUT. ███ ███WE DON'T WANT ███████ ███ ███ YOU ███ HERE. ███ ███ ███ ███ LEAVE ███ ███ ███ NOW.

Fern shivered. If this was someone's idea of a joke – the verbal equivalent of a turd on the doorstep – it wasn't very funny. The longer she looked at it the colder and sicker she felt.

'Why would someone want to send you that?' whispered Tina, dropping it back onto the doormat as if it had singed her fingers. 'Who do you think it's from?'

There was only one way to find out. Fern's mouth was dry, her hands shaking, as she opened the front door – just a crack – and peered into the darkness.

Chapter 19

The street was quiet. Eerily quiet. Whoever was out there had already slunk away through the shadows, leaving Fern blinking blindly after them. Unless they were still there, waiting in the darkness. Watching. She forced the thought away again, shivering even harder now as she tugged her dressing gown tighter.

Tina was all for calling the police there and then, but Fern wasn't so sure. What could *they* do? Question everyone on the whole street? In the entire area? They had bigger fish to fry than tracking down some sick freak with a marker pen. Besides, if she went to the police that would make it more real somehow. It would mean giving into her fear. And it was funny, but seeing the terrified look on her mother-in-law's face, while the image of the younger, vulnerable Tina was still fresh in her mind, made Fern feel braver. It made her want to be more like Linny, for a change, and less like herself. Linny wouldn't hide behind her own front door, shaking like a victim, would she?

Fern picked up the offending bit of paper and screwed it into a ball. Then she opened the door wider and flung the thing out into the road as hard as she could. 'You forgot this,' she shouted after it. 'It can't be ours, because we're not going anywhere.' And then she lost her nerve when she saw the outside light come on in the house across the street, and bolted back inside, breathless with her own sense of daring.

It didn't last long. The front drive had been empty and Fern realised with a jolt that Paul wasn't just cooling off with a walk round the block; he was behind the wheel. She thought about the glass of wine he'd had with his dinner – it *was* just the one, wasn't it? What if he was driving, angry *and* over the limit? What if he did something stupid?

By the time she'd heaved herself back upstairs to check her phone – hoping, praying, for a message from him – the sick feeling was back with a vengeance. Paul still hadn't called. Still hadn't texted. If only they *could* 'get out' like the anonymous flyer-defacer wanted them to. Go back to the familiar safety of the flat and their old, well-worn life. Even the shadow version they'd been living since Linny's death had to be better than this, with Fern doubting her own sanity more than ever, and Paul too angry to stay in the same room as her. The same *house* as her.

'Fern, love,' Tina called as she followed her up the stairs a couple of minutes later. Her pale cheeks and lips belied the false cheeriness in her voice. She was obviously still shaken. 'I've just had a message from Paul. He says not to worry, he's fine, but he's going to spend the night with a friend and go straight to work tomorrow.'

Fern didn't feel any less sick for hearing that. Now he was too angry to stay in the same *town* as her. And he couldn't even bring himself to tell her directly. That was the most hurtful, humiliating part of all. What did that say about the state of their relationship?

Who *was* this friend of his, anyway? A colleague? And how could he be going straight into work if he hadn't taken his suit with him? Paul hadn't taken *anything* with him – he couldn't have done, given the suddenness of his departure. Unless . . . unless he had it all planned out already, with an emergency escape kit tucked away in the back of the car for when Fern finally pushed him over the edge. Or maybe he had fresh underwear and a toothbrush already waiting for him at this so-called friend's house. The thought hit her like a fist to her stomach, just like before, when her paranoia had got the better of her and she let herself imagine that Paul was cheating on her . . .

'Another cup of tea?' asked Tina, interrupting Fern's spiralling train of thoughts. She was studiously avoiding eye contact as if she was embarrassed for her too.

'What? Oh, no thanks.' Fern took a deep breath, trying to pull herself together again. Paul wouldn't have taken on a new house and a bigger mortgage if he was planning on leaving her. And he wasn't a cheater, Fern knew that really. Of course she did. Didn't she? But the message from Paul had broken the spell of her new rapport with Tina. She just wanted to be on her own again now. It didn't occur to her until later that Tina might have needed some company herself. That her no-nonsense mother-in-law might be putting on a brave face for *her* benefit. 'I think I'll get an early night instead,' Fern told her, adding a fake yawn for good measure.

Not that she was faking the tiredness itself. Fern was genuinely exhausted. That's why she was such a mess, most likely – stress and tiredness and that wretched woman. The thought of closing her eyes and letting Marte worm her way back into her dreams didn't exactly appeal, but what choice did she have? Staying awake all night with that face leering down at her from the ceiling? With the pipes wailing in her ears? With Paul's empty side of the bed a gaping reminder of how wrong everything had gone? But wait, maybe there was another option after all. Something to keep the nightmares away for a little longer . . .

The overblown plot of Eddie's *Blood Lovers* was exactly what Fern needed. Pure escapism. At least it would have been if the characters didn't remind her of their new neighbours quite so much. She couldn't help picturing the nurse who lived next door to the murdered au pair as April, while Kerry slipped seamlessly into the role of Esme, the rude, jealous mother, despite being childless in real life. Eddie didn't last long as the suspected villain though, funnily enough. Not once Fern read about his pet red setter. From that point on the anti-hero was Richard as far as she was concerned, just as the dead Scandinavian blonde stopped being the girl on the cover and became Marte instead. Fern was too caught up in the unfolding drama to care by then though.

It was half past three in the morning when she last checked her bedside clock. She had the beginnings of a headache behind her eyes, and a crick in her neck and shoulders from reading in a fixed position for so long. But on the plus side she'd barely thought about Paul spending the night with another woman, or lying smashed and broken in a ditch, that whole time. Or about the sicko targeting their house, already planning out the next stage in their escalating campaign. She'd been too busy following the twists and turns of the murder investigation to agonise over Mrs Rochester's reaction to Marte's name. Too involved in the dangerous romance between Red Setter Richard and the feisty detective to dwell on those five letters dripping down the bathroom window . . . letters that didn't just spell out a name but the end of Paul's patience too. Maybe even the end of Fern's sanity. What was left of it.

She shivered as she got back into bed after her final toilet trip, pulling the duvet up tight around her neck. The bed felt emptier than ever on her return, without Paul snoring there beside her, muttering into his pillow. The whole house felt empty, even though she knew Tina was only a few feet away on the other side of the landing. The bedroom radiator shuddered and clanked like an erratic metal heartbeat, as she lay there listening in the darkness – *da-ba-da-doom, dah da-doom*, while the bathroom pipes geared up for their nightly chorus. They hadn't reached full-on screaming yet; this was more of a soft keening moan. It made her think of Linny, bleeding out on the road, delirious with pain and shock. Fern forced her eyes open, blinking the image away again. It wasn't even true: the coroner said the impact would have rendered her sister unconscious. But as fresh moans came reaching for her through the flimsy wall, Fern had another flash of long blonde hair, matted with congealing blood. She could almost taste the bitter tang of iron on her tongue.

Marte stayed away the rest of that night though, thank goodness. No more bad dreams. Or maybe Fern's altered sleep pattern simply meant she didn't remember them afterwards. Either way, it was almost nine when she woke next morning, roused by the same crackly singing as before – impossible! – to discover things were just as bad in the cold light of day as they'd been the previous evening. Nothing had changed. Paul's side of the bed was still untouched, and whoever had posted that flyer through their door was still out there somewhere. Still watching. Still plotting . . . And Linny? This would be the fourth day without so much as a glimpse of her sister. She and Paul *both* seemed to have abandoned her.

Fern made it as far as the bathroom, topping up her bedside water glass, before struggling back to bed and chapter thirty-seven of *Blood Lovers*. Anything to escape the sorry mess of real life.

'Fern, love?' She nearly jumped out of her skin when Tina knocked on the door a couple of hours later.

'Yes,' she called back, reaching onto the bedside table for a stray Kirby grip to use as a bookmark. *Damn.* Just when the murderer was about to be revealed too. Fern's money was on the Kerry character, Esme, but maybe that was wishful thinking on her part, wanting to see the real Kerry get her comeuppance for being so rude to her. 'Come in.'

Her mother-in-law looked smaller this morning, somehow, taking up less space in the room than Fern remembered.

'Just came to check you were all right,' said Tina. 'I didn't like to wake you but . . .'

'No, no, that's fine, I've been awake for ages. I got caught up in Eddie's book – it's surprisingly addictive.' *Cathartic too*, she realised. A novel about a poor young woman, dead before her time, should have been the last thing Fern wanted to read. But unlike

Linny there was a proper reason for the victim's death, which the detective was on the brink of revealing. And then somehow everything would be right again. Order restored. Whereas Linny's death made no more sense now – no matter how many times Fern turned it round in her head, trying to understand how she could have gone, just gone – than the first time they explained it to her: *Pneumothorax. Rupture of abdominal aorta.*

'I got an emergency locksmith out, first thing, to change the locks,' said Tina. 'I just didn't feel safe after last night, and I've read that you should always get new ones fitted when you move house anyway. And I hope you don't mind but I've arranged for a plumber to come and have a look at the bathroom after lunch. Paul mentioned something about the pipes and water pressure . . .' She sounded uncharacteristically tentative, as if she was worried Fern would be cross at her for interfering. Like that had ever stopped her before.

'Gosh,' said Fern, trying to muster some enthusiasm. 'You *have* been busy.'

'You know me, up with the lark,' said Tina, without her usual smugness. 'Barely slept a wink all night, to be honest, what with Paul and that horrible business with the flyer . . .' She rubbed at an invisible mark on the wall. 'I know you didn't want to ring the police but . . .'

But you went ahead and called them anyway. Fern finished off the sentence in her head, and found she wasn't as annoyed as she might have been. She felt relieved, if anything. The thought of someone targeting the house – targeting *them*, especially with Paul missing in action – made her skin prickle. She was wrong though. That wasn't what Tina was going to say at all.

'. . . the flyer wasn't even there when I went to look for it this morning. I checked all along the gutter as soon as it was light, poking around under the hedges on the other side of the road, but there was nothing there. I mean, plenty of crisp packets and a couple of chewed tennis balls, but no flyer.'

Crap. That was the first thing the police would ask, wasn't it? *And do you still have this political leaflet?*

Tina sighed. 'To be honest, after the amount of rain we had in the night it'd probably be no good as evidence anyway.'

Why hadn't she held on to it? Fern cursed her own stupidity as she manoeuvred herself back out of bed. She needed the loo again, but Tina was still going strong:

'On the plus side, I've been talking to your neighbour about what you told me last night. About this Marte lady. I hope that's okay?' she added, sounding less sure of herself.

'Eddie? I meant to ask him at the party but we were interrupted,' said Fern. 'And then he was out when I called in yesterday.' *Despite telling us he had to finish his rewrites when he popped round with his book.*

'No, your other neighbour,' said Tina, pointing towards the far end of the room as if Fern might be able to spy them through the solid wall.

'Oh, right. I haven't met them yet. I assumed they were away. They weren't at April's thing on Saturday and everyone was out when the delivery guy came yesterday.'

'She's been visiting her daughter in Cornwall and didn't get back until last night,' said Tina, 'which is why she hasn't been round to say hello yet. Her name's Yasmin. She seems very nice . . . very helpful too.'

Helpful? That sounded promising. 'So . . . what did you find out?' Fern asked, torn between the growing pressure on her bladder and her growing need for answers.

'Ah, now then.' Tina lowered herself down onto Paul's side of the bed. 'That's where things get really interesting . . .'

No, it was no good. Fern's bladder trumped her brain every time these days. The story would have to wait. 'Sorry, I won't be a sec,' she apologised, hurrying past her mother-in-law at full-speed waddle.

Chapter 20

If Tina really had got to the bottom of the Marte mystery, that could be an end to it all, Fern thought. No more dreams. No more jumping at her own shadow. No more interrogating everyone she met. Which meant she could focus her energies in more useful directions instead: like rescuing her poor, limping marriage. That's if she still had a marriage to save. Paul and the baby, they were what *really* mattered now. And Dad, of course. And Linny. Even Tina, she thought. Whatever happened now though – whatever it was this Yasmin woman had to say – at least she wasn't on her own anymore. And even though she'd much rather it was Paul fighting her corner than his mother, Tina was still a major improvement on no one. Fern hadn't fully understood until now – until last night – quite how lonely and isolating it had been, keeping her fears bottled up like that.

Back in the bedroom, Tina was leafing through a small, patterned notebook, like a detective on a murder show. She wasn't a patch on Eddie's Detective Rosella Ransom, but Fern still felt surprisingly grateful to have her on her side.

'Now then,' said Tina. She licked the tip of her index finger and turned back to the previous page, clearly relishing her new role as amateur sleuth. 'According to Yasmin, your house has changed hands rather a lot lately. And I mean a *lot*. Five different owners in as many years, she worked it out as, which is pretty unusual round here.'

Fern opened her mouth to agree, to chip in with what Eddie had told her at the party – although he'd said four owners in four years – but Tina barely stopped for breath. She was in her element now, dishing out information like sweets.

'She's been in *her* house eight years next March – and on her own for the last two of those, since her daughter moved out. I think that's right, anyway. Apparently her husband left her for another man not long after they first moved in. Can you imagine?'

Fern didn't want to imagine. She wanted Tina to hurry up and get to the important bit. But she was out of luck on that score.

'Yasmin said it was in a bit of a state when they first moved in. Needed a full rewire and lots of replastering work upstairs.'

Replastering? Why had Tina bothered writing *that* down?

'I've got the names of all the people she used – it's always good to get some local recommendations when it comes to tradesmen, don't you think? That's where I got the plumber's number from too, the one who's coming this afternoon; although Yasmin said the son's taken over the family business now that his dad's retired, so she can't vouch for him personally . . .'

Forget about the sodding plumber and get on with it. Tell me about Marte. Unless there was nothing *to* tell, thought Fern, her new optimism ebbing away again. Maybe the rest of Tina's notes were more of the same: contacts for interior decorating firms and woodworm specialists.

'Anyway,' she went on. 'Yasmin said *your* house used to be one of those multi-occupancy dwellings until about six years ago. Mature students mainly, she said.'

I know. I know. Natural Birth Nicky and her friends.

'And one of them . . .' Tina paused for dramatic effect.

Yes? Spit it out.

'Was Norwegian.'

Huh?

'I know you said you thought Marte was Swedish but it's practically the same thing, isn't it?'

Not if you're Swedish or Norwegian, thought Fern, hoping that wasn't the full revelation. She'd only been guessing, after all, because of the accent. Because of the blue eyes and blonde hair combo. It could probably just as easily have been a Norwegian accent, now she came to think about it. Danish even. Her own expertise on all things Scandinavian was pretty much limited to crime dramas, and she hadn't watched one of those in a long time. Not since Linny . . . And now Eddie's book, of course, with the poor Norwegian girl buried in the woods. Yes, 'limited' was probably the right word.

'And Yasmin said this Norwegian lady had long blonde hair, like this Marte of yours, *and* that she was pregnant while she lived here. She didn't know her name though, unfortunately. It *could* have been Marte, but she really wasn't sure. She didn't have much to do with them.'

What was it about this woman? Marte, not Yasmin. How come *no one* could tell them who she was?

Tina wasn't even looking at her notes anymore. She must have committed the rest of the story to memory: 'It was Yasmin's daughter, who was still living at home back then, who got chatting about revision or something with the Norwegian lady at the bus stop one day. *That's* how they knew she was pregnant, because she didn't have much of a bump. The lady said she'd been struggling with morning sickness and couldn't concentrate on her studies . . .'

'Would her daughter remember what she was called, do you think? If Yasmin were to give her a ring and ask?'

It was a stupid question. How was Tina supposed to know that? And besides, they already knew the answer, didn't they? It couldn't be Marte if all this happened six years ago.

Tina pushed her lips to one side, chewing over the idea. 'It's possible, I suppose. I'm not sure her daughter knew her any better than Yasmin from what she was saying though. She just happened to remember that one reported conversation, mainly because she'd been wondering who the father was. A bit of nosiness on her part, she said.'

'But that was all six years ago? And she hasn't seen her since?' Fern tried not to let the disappointment show on her face.

Tina shook her head. 'She didn't say. I'm sorry, it's not much to go on, is it? Only I was thinking, what if this Norwegian lady *did* turn out to be your Marte after all? She might still have a key to the house from when she lived here. And maybe the locks stayed the same . . .'

Oh. Fern hadn't thought of that. Hadn't the midwife mentioned something about a Norwegian lady a few years back? She shivered, remembering the first time she'd mentioned Marte to Paul. How he'd promised to change the locks as soon as they moved in. What if Tina was right? What if the woman was back some six years later and pregnant again? What if she'd been letting herself in and out of their house at will? Leaving messages on the glass and dog turds on the doorstep? Maybe she'd done the same to the Rochesters . . . driving poor Mrs Rochester towards a medical meltdown. And all the other people who'd lived there too – the ones who sold up and moved on with unprecedented haste . . .

No. People didn't do things like that in real life. Or if they did, they didn't get away with it. Someone would have noticed. Someone would have caught her. And besides, what could she possibly have to gain by impersonating Mrs Rochester at a house viewing? It was nice of Tina to try, but they were no closer to finding the answer than before.

Tina was watching her expectantly, waiting for a response. But Fern was spared the need for any feedback by the sound of her phone ringing from the other side of the bed. Paul's ringtone: *This is your husband calling. Answer the phone, dear. This is your husband calling . . .*

Her mother-in-law was on her feet before Fern had a chance to react, racing round the end of the bed to fetch it for her. *Answer the phone, dear. This is your husband calling.*

'It's him,' Tina hissed, passing the still ringing phone over to Fern.

Really? You don't say.

'I'll leave you to it,' she added in a stage whisper, as if Paul might somehow be able to hear her over his own ringtone. She pointed to the doorway for good measure, and then, with a final worried glance, left the room, shutting the door behind her.

This is your husband . . .

'Hi,' said Fern.

'Hi,' Paul answered.

Fern thought she'd feel relieved when he finally called, but she didn't. Maybe she would have done last night, with a head full of dark winding roads, of crushed metal and shattered windscreens, and Paul in other women's beds, but not now. It definitely wasn't relief coursing through her body at the sound of his voice. It was more like anger. Resentment. What did he think he was playing at, scaring her like that? Storming out on her when she needed him more than ever. What if that defaced flyer was just the warm-up act? What if the next thing through the letterbox was a homemade petrol bomb? A Molotov cocktail through the bedroom window? There'd been worse than that on the news lately. Horrible, sick people doing horrible, sick things to each other.

'I'm sorry about last night,' he said, although he didn't sound it. The cold hardness in his voice suggested he was still angry too. 'I shouldn't have left like that. Without telling you where I was going.'

That was his apology, was it? Not 'sorry for shouting at you', 'for abandoning you when you were clearly upset'. Not even 'sorry for storming off like a child.' Fern said nothing, refusing to play along, waiting for him to fill the silence that followed.

'Are you okay?' he asked.

148

No, I'm not okay. This *is not okay. Why are you being such a shit?*
'And the baby. Is he all right?'

She, thought Fern. *Not he.* 'Never better,' she told him flatly, watching the bony point of an elbow drag across the inside of her stomach like some weird alien lifeform. *We're all right, aren't we, sweetheart? No thanks to Daddy.*

'I'm sure Mum's taking excellent care of you.' Paul laughed – a hollow, nervous laugh. 'And driving you round the bend with endless cups of tea and fussing.'

'Not at all,' said Fern, coming to Tina's defence. 'I mean, yes, she is taking good care of me.' *At least someone is.* 'But she's not driving me round the bend. We're getting on really well actually, now it's just the two of us.' She realised, after she'd said it, that she'd given him free ammunition for extending his mother's visit even further. But the idea didn't fill her with as much dread as it might have done before, and Fern didn't even try to remedy the situation, leaving the unspoken implication hanging there in the empty pause that followed. *It's you who's the problem right now. Not your mother.*

Paul didn't rise to the bait though. 'That's good,' he said. 'I'm glad. Because I was thinking I might stay another night with Simon, if that's okay? Give us both a bit of space to get our heads together. I left my laptop and my spare suit at work last week – I was worried about losing track of them in the move – so there's no need to come back home for them.'

What? No need to come back for your suit? How about coming back for me? For your wife? Fern lowered her mobile and stared at it, as if the fault lay with the phone itself rather than this new stranger of a husband. The ten or so inches between the tinny voice and her ear could have been ten miles. Ten counties even. The distance between them had never seemed greater.

'Fern?' Paul squeaked. 'Are you still there?'

'Fern? Say something.'

She pressed the red phone icon and flung the offending mobile at the wall, hating herself for the tears already coursing down her cheeks, but hating him more. Her phone bounced off the textured wallpaper, landing on the carpet with a soft thud, refusing to smash into a thousand tiny pieces. She couldn't even get that right. And then it started ringing all over again: *This is your husband calling. I'm not coming home* . . .

Fern let it ring until her answerphone kicked in. But there was only a brief respite while Paul left his message – at least she guessed that's what he was doing – and then the most irritating ringtone in the world was back again. Those same two sentences, over and over. *This is Bastard calling*, would have been more accurate, she thought. *Pick up the sodding phone* . . . She finally answered, halfway through the fifth cycle, when she couldn't bear to listen to it any longer.

'Fern? Is everything all right?' His voice still sounded wrong: too craven, too cowardly. 'We must have got cut off.'

She shrugged, the exact same shrug that drove her mad when he did it. 'If you say so.'

'Look,' he told her, 'I'll come back tonight if you need me to, you know that.'

Did she know that, given she didn't know he was the sort of man to leave in the first place? Fern had never heard of this Simon either. Who was he? Someone from his old job? His new job? She'd no recollection of Paul even mentioning him before. Although perhaps . . . perhaps she'd been too wrapped up in her own world, since Linny went, to notice. To listen. She felt a faint stirring of guilt, wondering if she was being unfair. Maybe Paul really *was* the injured party here. Maybe she'd driven him away with her endless grief and misery. But then she remembered the look of rage on his face the night before – the way he'd tapped the side of his head to show how crazy she was – and the guilt shrivelled away to nothing.

'No, I don't need you,' she said, ending the sentence there out of spite, although she knew full well it wasn't true. He was all she had left now. Of course she needed him.

Paul pressed on, as if he hadn't heard. 'But I think a bit of space might be a good thing for us right now.'

So you said.

'For both of us. All this stuff with Linny . . . I don't know. I can't seem to . . . Simon says maybe *I* should think about counselling too.'

Oh really? Simon says, does he?

Simon says . . . touch your toes.

Simon says . . . shrug your shoulders.

Simon says . . . leave your wife.

Come home and make it all better . . . Hah! Simon didn't say that one. You're out!

'It's not like you're on your own,' Paul went on. 'You've got Mum there, and I'll be home tomorrow I promise . . . Wednesday at the latest. I just need to get my head together, that's all.'

Had this been his plan all along, Fern wondered? Was that why he was so desperate for Tina to come and stay?

'Please. Say something.'

Like what? You want me to beg, is that it? She should tell him about the poisoned-pen flyer. That would bring him home soon enough. But something held her back from mentioning it. Perhaps it was the thought of her own stupidity in destroying the evidence – she could already imagine what he'd have to say about that. Perhaps she was punishing him for his absence, knowing how guilty he'd feel when he found out afterwards. Or maybe, in pushing him away, she was really punishing herself.

'I love you,' she answered, just in case. Just in case those were the last words she ever said to him. Windscreens shattered every day. Every second. The world was full of thin metal carcasses crumpling in on themselves. Of soft, unprotected bodies flying. Falling. Failing.

That was all she said though – 'I love you'. Then cut him off, dead.

Chapter 21

Monday afternoon found Fern in the bathroom with Barry the plumber, while Tina was out in Westerton on emergency kettle business.

'There, that ought to do it,' said Barry, as the unwanted bubble of air hissed itself out into the world at large. Fern didn't have the heart to bother thinking up a nickname for him. Not with Paul gone. He seemed pleasant enough though. His face wore the same look of concentrated rapture as her father's, she thought, whenever he listened to Tchaikovsky, or that Simon & Garfunkel song that reminded him of their mum. But the only music in the bathroom was the soft sigh of escaping air from the errant radiator. Barry let out a contented sigh of his own as the sound died away. 'Perfect,' he said, retightening whatever it was he'd just loosened. 'You shouldn't have any more problems now.'

Fern's day had been nothing *but* problems so far: work had proved out of the question following Paul's bombshell that morning, despite a nagging voicemail from her agent to spur her on. How could she concentrate after that? And then there was Marte. There was *always* Marte. She'd had such high hopes that Tina's conversation with the neighbour might have got to the bottom of it all at last – that she could finally prove to Paul that Marte wasn't just another figment of her troubled imagination – but the woman remained as elusive as ever. The piano had dropped even further out of tune overnight and Fern's favourite character in Eddie's book – the April character – had turned out to be the murderer after all, leaving 'Kerry' free to terrorise the neighbourhood. And *someone* (Fern suspected Tina) had accidently turned up the temperature on the fridge. It was hard to see how she'd managed it exactly, short of climbing in and nudging it with a misplaced elbow, but there was no disputing the evidence: the sour milk and rotting salad, and the discoloured chicken breasts trying to cook themselves back to life on the bottom shelf. And the kettle, Fern's trusty kettle had turned against her, giving up the ghost after years of faultless service. She'd tried changing the fuse, tried plugging it into a different socket – even tried plugging it into a different room – but the wretched thing still refused to work. They'd have been better off warming water in the over-heated fridge.

Tina had taken off in a state of kettleless panic half an hour before the plumber arrived, already suffering from cuppa withdrawal symptoms, bussing it into Westerton in search of a suitable replacement and some fresh milk. She'd insisted. Which left Fern loitering awkwardly in the bathroom doorway, averting her eyes from the double gape of flesh escaping from Barry's waistband, wondering if it was rude to leave him to it. She'd always hated having workmen in the house. It felt like an invasion of her space.

'And you wanted me to check the water pressure too, while I'm here, is that right?'

Oh crap. She'd forgotten about that. 'Yes please. That would be great.' It wasn't great at all – Fern just wanted him gone. She wanted to be back in bed, catching up on lost sleep, or out in Westerton with Tina, supervising the kettle-buying. Making sure she didn't buy a 'Country Charm' one with chickens or roses round the outside. Vetoing any suggestion of matching tea cosies.

'I don't suppose there's any chance of a coffee, is there?' mused Barry. 'Cheeky of me to ask, I know, but . . .'

Fern waited for the 'but', only it never came. But nothing. 'Could be tricky,' she told him, 'without a kettle or any milk. I could boil up some water on the stove for a black coffee, if that's any good, otherwise it's a glass of water, I'm afraid.'

'Water'll be fine, thanks. Wouldn't say no to a custard cream though, if you've got one.' Fern imagined him winking as he said it.

'I'll see what I can find,' she promised, grateful for the chance to escape, even if it was only down to the kitchen.

She took her time, stopping to sort through the unopened mail Tina had hidden away behind the toaster: a boring bank letter for Paul, a gaudy New Home card from one of his aunts, and what looked like an insurance circular for someone called Mrs Porter – one of the other residents the house had seen off, maybe? But then she spotted a man in the garden and forgot all about the long list of previous owners. Forgot about Barry and his water.

Paul, she thought, the baby kicking its feet against her stomach, as if sensing her excitement. *He's home.* Fern felt an odd mixture of relief and anger. Relief that he was back, that he hadn't left her for good. Relief that he *did* still love her, despite everything. And a fresh wave of anger running underneath it for having walked out on her in the first place.

It wasn't Paul, though. Nothing like him. The hunched figure skulking past the dead roses was a different kind of build altogether, Fern realised. Too short. Too stocky. And the gait was all wrong too. That's when relief and anger gave way to a slow fear. Eddie? No. Nothing like him, either. Besides, what would *he* be doing prowling through the bushes? The plumber then? He must have slipped out the front door and let himself in through the side gate without her noticing. But no, it wasn't Barry, either. Fern could still hear him banging around upstairs, singing to himself.

154

What if it was *him*? The neighbourhood psycho who wanted them gone? Fern thought about the scratches on her car, which didn't seem like kids messing about anymore. She thought about the 'present' on their doorstep and the blacked-out flyer shoved through the letterbox, about the steady escalation from mindless vandalism to targeted threat. What came after that? What if he was out there even now, searching for a rock to smash the glazed panel in the back door? Fern ducked her head, instinctively shielding her stomach with her hands as she moved away from the glass and out of range.

'Shh, it's okay,' she whispered, for her own benefit as much as the baby's.

But it wasn't okay. Now Fern couldn't see the intruder at all, which was even worse. She should have gone back upstairs and got Barry, for safety in numbers and all that. Or shouted for him to come down. But she wasn't thinking straight. Instead she picked up the kitchen phone from its charging cradle, ready to call the police, forgetting, in her breathless panic, that the line wasn't connected yet. And then, armed with nothing more than a dead receiver, Fern crept into the dining room for a better view of her would-be assailant. There he was.

Wait. What was he doing? He was going the wrong way – heading *up* the steps onto the top level. It didn't make any sense. But then he turned, briefly, glancing back towards the house, and Fern stared at him in surprise.

Sean.

'What are *you* doing here?' she called up to him as she hurried outside, her heart still hammering in her chest. Fear had lent her voice a note of unintended aggression. 'You gave me a fright,' she added, as he headed back down the steps to meet her, looking suitably mortified.

'I . . . I'm sorry,' he stammered, blood rushing to his cheeks. 'I didn't mean to scare you. Your mum asked me to come and do a final tidy-up of the garden before winter sets in. I just popped round to see what needs doing.'

'My *mum*?' It took a second or two for Fern's overexcited brain to catch up. 'You mean Tina? That's Paul's mum.'

Sean nodded. 'Yes, Tina, that's right. We got talking this morning and she said there were some brambles at the back that needed getting rid of and a few other bits and pieces to take care of.' He gestured towards the top of the garden. 'Her treat, she said – a housewarming present for you and your husband.'

'Oh.' Fern was the one blushing now. 'I didn't realise. She must have forgotten to mention it.' She must have been in too much of a hurry to get to her conversation with Yasmin.

'I didn't realise there was anyone in,' continued Sean. 'Your car wasn't on the drive.'

'My husband's car,' Fern corrected him.

'I see. Sorry, my mistake. I should have knocked in that case. I got used to letting myself in the side gate when I was working for the previous owners though.'

'No, *I'm* sorry,' said Fern. 'I completely overreacted. I'm a bit jumpy at the moment. Someone scratched my car yesterday and then we had a horrible note through the door last night. I don't suppose you've spotted anyone strange hanging around the place?'

Sean shook his head. 'I'm afraid not. I wouldn't worry though. It's a very safe area round here. Nothing bad ever happens on Crenellation Lane . . .' He paused. 'What *sort* of horrible note? What did it say?'

'*Get out. We don't want you here. Leave now.* It's probably just someone's sick idea of a joke,' said Fern, although it hadn't got any funnier. 'So how's the garden looking?' she asked, changing the subject. 'I'm not sure I'd know where to start.'

'Not too bad,' said Sean. 'I just wanted to check out those brambles along the back wall while I was passing. See if it's going to be a shredder job or not. The Rochesters didn't want them cut back until the birds had finished the berries. *Not* a good idea if you ask me – goodness knows how many new shoots they'll have put down in the top flowerbed in the meantime – but they wouldn't listen.' He clearly took his job very seriously.

'I've not even been up there yet,' Fern admitted. She'd hardly set foot in the garden full stop, she realised. It certainly felt more like Sean's territory than hers, now that they were out there together. As if *she* was the intruder.

'Probably just as well in your condition,' he said, staring pointedly at her stomach. 'Gets a bit slippery on the steps when it's wet. Mrs Rochester was laid up for a good week or so after she turned her ankle coming down,' he told her. 'Lucky I was there.'

'She wasn't very well generally, was she?' asked Fern, thinking she could turn the conversation back round to Marte if she was clever, without Paul trying to rush her off this time. 'Must have needed a fair bit of help round the house too . . .'

'I wouldn't know anything about that,' said Sean, looking at his watch.

'That's why I thought Marte must be their cleaner . . . when I asked you about her the other day?'

His shook his head again. 'Sorry. Like I said, the name doesn't mean anything to me. Was there anything else or am I all right to carry on? Only I've got an order to pick up at the nursery in a bit.'

Fern followed him to the bottom of the steps. 'It's possible she was living here – in this house, I mean – about six years ago. Would you have been doing the garden back then? It was a shared rental house in those days, so you might not have known her by name. She was very striking though . . . long blonde hair and blue eyes . . .' She trailed off, realising how desperate she must sound, hounding the poor man round the garden with her endless questions. No wonder he was so keen to make his escape.

'Sorry,' she said. 'I didn't mean to interrogate you. It's just . . .' She tried to think of an explanation that would make sense. Something that didn't make her sound weirdly obsessed with someone she'd only met once before. 'She reminded me of someone,' she said. 'Of my sister. My *late* sister.' It was true. When she'd first seen Marte at the bottom of the stairs that day, she really had mistaken her for Linny.

'I don't know,' said Sean. 'I'd have to check my books. Six years is a long time.'

'Yes, of course, I'm sorry,' Fern apologised again. He clearly didn't know who she was talking about. 'I er . . . I'll leave you to it.'

'Mrs Croft?' It was Barry, coming to see where his biscuits had got to, most likely. The plumber stood there, framed in the kitchen doorway, holding up a red rag, like a matador.

'I'll be with you in a sec,' Fern told him. But when she turned back to the gardener, to say goodbye, she found he was already gone.

'Something I said?' joked Barry, stepping out to join Fern on the patio.

Fern forced a smile. No, Barry hadn't said anything wrong. Not yet, anyway. Of course if she'd known what he was *about* to say – about to show her – she certainly wouldn't have been smiling. Not even a forced smile. And she'd have made damn sure she was sitting down before he carried on.

'I found a bit of a leak under the bath while I was up there,' said Barry. 'Don't know what made me check, really. A hunch, I guess, or professional nosiness. The panel comes off easily enough, so it's not a biggie, but it might be worth keeping your eye on – don't want the ceiling coming down on you when you're watching telly downstairs.' He scratched behind his ear. 'I've retightened everything for now and that seems to have done the trick. Thought I'd better mention it though . . .'

'Great,' said Fern, only half listening. 'Thank you for that. Sorry, I still haven't got you your water and biscuit, have I? Got a bit side-tracked.'

But Barry wasn't finished yet. 'It's clearly been a problem in the past as well. You've got some serious water staining on your floorboards under there.' There was a slight accusatory edge to his voice, as if Fern had been neglecting her plumbing duties.

158

'I wouldn't know about that,' she told him. 'We've only just moved in.'

'Well, *someone's* had a look at it before, judging by this old thing. Reckon they were using it to soak up the puddles.' He shook out the red material as if he was shaking out a tablecloth, or trying to get his bull back for another charge.

A cold shiver of dread wriggled down Fern's spine as she stared at it in disbelief.

It wasn't a tablecloth. It was a blanket. There were holes in it now – signs of sharp little teeth nibbling at the fibres – and angry rust stains streaked across the middle like dried blood. But it was still recognisable as a blanket. A baby's blanket, with a name lovingly embroidered along the bottom corner in yellowing thread. SOFIA. The name from the window. Marte's baby. The cold shiver spread to the rest of Fern's body, turning her insides to ice.

Chapter 22

All this time Fern had been looking for proof of the woman's existence and now she'd found it. But something was wrong. Very wrong.

'Marte!' Her name caught in Fern's throat as she reeled back, reaching blindly behind her for a wall that didn't seem to be there. She almost thought she saw her – a flash of golden hair spinning out in a dizzying whirl. Marte? Linny? But Fern was the one spinning, twisting away from the blanket as if it was burning her eyes.

Twisting.

Stumbling.

Falling.

'Whoooooaaah there,' came a voice, growlingly deep and slow, words stretched all out of shape. Too long. Too low. Like one of her dad's old vinyl singles on the wrong setting. 'Steady noooow.' Hands snatched at her as she hit the ground, ankles and knees buckling beneath her. And then came the pain – a long shoot of it, hot and red, barrelling up her left leg, bringing everything back into focus. Too much focus. She could see the individual pores on Barry's nose, and the dark hairs straying from the tufted tunnels of his nostrils. She could see the thin line of sweat beading on his upper lip. And his breath. Oh, his breath. Cheese and raw onion, with top notes of coffee halitosis. Fern jerked her face away, wincing as another shaft of pain ricocheted up towards her knee.

'Are you all right?' asked Barry, his voice heavy with concern, but otherwise back to normal. Vowels all operating at the correct speed.

Fern wasn't all right, no. She felt sick and clammy, nausea swimming inside her stomach as she closed her eyes against the sight of the blanket. *Marte's baby blanket.*

'Can you get up or do I need to call someone? Is the baby okay?'

Fern nodded, holding in a squeal as the plumber's fingers wedged themselves under her arms. But then he straightened up, pulling her with him, and she took a long gulp of clear air, collapsing her weight against the stone wall she'd somehow missed on her way down, and breathed into the pain.

No sign of any phantom blondes now. That was all in her head. But the blanket was real enough. It lay in a discarded heap at her feet, the S of 'Sofia' snaking away into a deep fold, taking the other letters with it.

'How long do you think it's been there?' Fern asked. 'The blanket. How old would you say it was?' *Six years?* She shivered as she imagined Marte bent over the red fabric, smiling as she stitched her daughter's name. Where was she now? And Sofia?

Barry kicked at it with his booted toe. 'No idea. It's certainly seen better days though. I take it it's nothing to do with you?'

'No,' she whispered. Not six years. How could it be six years?

'That's old houses for you,' he said. 'Never know *what* you might find. Priceless antiques in the attic? Bodies under the floorboards?'

Don't say that. Stop it. Fern didn't want *that* picture of Marte in her head. But it was too late – it was there now. *She* was there now, all stretched out like the victim in Eddie's book.

'No,' she said again, louder this time, trying to still the trembling that had taken hold of her lower lip. 'No, no, no.' Her head was spinning, trying to find an explanation that made sense. *The baby clothes in the attic . . . The monitor . . . The blanket . . .* Maybe Marte *had* lived there six years ago. Maybe she lost the baby – the one Yasmin and Beverly were talking about – which was why she told Fern she was expecting her first. And maybe she'd chosen the same name both times, trying to patch over the hole that the loss of the first Sofia had made in her heart. It wasn't *such* a morbid idea. Not really. Not so different to Fern choosing 'Linette' in memory of Linny. But it still didn't explain why Marte was there the day she came to look round. *How* she was there that day.

Or maybe Fern had seen the blanket on her first visit to the house, without realising. Maybe it was drying on the bathroom radiator after another leak and her brain had stored the name away for future reference. Add in a healthy pinch of guilt over that stupid martyr comment to Linny and she had all the ingredients she needed for a hallucination spectacular . . . for an entire house viewing that never happened.

Barry let out a nervous laugh. 'Sorry,' he told her, scratching behind the other ear. 'Stupid thing to say. Only an old blanket – that's all! Nothing else. Besides, it's a lovely house, this. All period features and what have you.'

'I wish we'd never come,' said Fern. 'I thought things would be different here. Better.' She stole another glance at the blanket, wondering if it was the same one she'd seen in her dream the day they moved in. Wondering if it was *all* a dream – the whole meeting with Marte. Would that make it any better? Knowing she'd conjured up an entire afternoon in her sleep, dozing off in the sunshine while her unconscious mind looked round the house without her? Would that make her any less mad? 'It's all wrong,' she murmured, shoulders shaking as she turned her face back to the wall, away from the plumber's worried gaze. 'Everything's wrong.'

Poor Barry. He didn't know what to do with himself. Or rather he didn't know what to do with her. What to say.

'There now,' he murmured, laying a tentative hand on her arm, then thinking better of it and snatching it away again. 'Don't cry, love. It erm . . . well, it erm . . . always takes a while to settle in, doesn't it? Just a bit of water underneath the bath, that's all. And I've sorted that now.'

If only it *was* just a matter of water under the bath. There could be a whole swimming pool under there for all Fern cared. But she *did* feel like she was drowning. Marte. Paul. The neighbourhood creep. Linny. Where *was* Linny? It was four whole days since Fern had last seen her, disappearing under the removal lorry. Why had she chosen *now* to stay dead though? Was it something about the new house? Had she taken one look at it on moving day and killed herself all over again?

'Are you all right to walk?' asked Barry, when Fern didn't respond. 'Why don't I help you inside and get you a chair? You'll feel better then, I'm sure. Cup of tea and you'll be right as rain.'

'Okay,' Fern agreed, forgetting for a moment, as Barry clearly had, that they were still kettleless. Still milkless. But she leaned into him when he offered his arm and started the slow limp inside, grateful for his gruff concern. Glad that there was someone there, someone real and solid.

'Tricky time when you're pregnant, isn't it?' said Barry. 'My wife was just the same. Emotions all over the place. Hormones and what have you.'

Ah yes. Good old pregnancy hormones. It was all their fault. Disguising themselves as expectant mothers and scrawling all over your mirrors and windows when you weren't looking. Gate-crashing your dreams every night . . .

'Maybe I can ring someone for you? Where does your husband work? Is he local?'

Fern shook her head, wiping her eyes on the back of her cuff. 'No, I'll be fine, thank you. My mother-in-law will be back soon . . .'

'At least let me get you some ice or something to put on that ankle. It looks swollen.'

But there was no ice. The freezer seemed to have turned itself off in sympathy with the overheating fridge. Fern slumped her head down on the table when Barry broke the news, and wept all over again. Wept and wept and wept. Even the electrics had turned against her now.

Barry was a star. There were no two ways about it. Fern felt bad for not giving him his custard creams. He kept up a steady stream of chatter as he bustled about the kitchen, sorting out the errant freezer, fetching *her* a glass of water and the long-awaited biscuits, and tearing off a ready supply of kitchen roll sheets in lieu of tissues. Extra strong when it came to mopping up tears, he joked. He fetched her mobile for her too, hunting all over the house until he found it, waiting patiently while she rang Tina. He'd have waited longer too – waited until Tina got home, or taken her to the doctor's himself – if Fern hadn't insisted.

'No, honestly, you've done more than enough. I'm sure you've got other jobs to get to.'

'Only if you're sure . . .'

'Really. I'm fine. Much better.' Her tears had dried now and the initial wave of shock and nausea had passed, settling into a more general, gut-tightening worry in the pit of her stomach. 'The cavalry will be here soon. Thank you, though. For everything.'

The cavalry cheated a little, as it turned out, galloping home in a taxi for extra speed. But the wait felt long enough, even then. It was embarrassing – excruciatingly embarrassing – having Tina walk her to the toilet and help her down onto the seat but Fern didn't really have a choice. Her ankle was a ball of fire, even without any weight on it, and walking wasn't an option. Try telling that to her bladder though. Or the baby, pressing down on it like a ten-tonne weight.

'All done?' came the call, the second Fern finished. Before she'd even begun the battle with her underwear, trying to wriggle it

164

back into place. Tina must have been camped outside the door, listening. *Perfect.*

'No,' Fern called back. 'Give me a minute.'

'All right, love. Just shout when you're ready. And then we're going straight down to A&E to get you checked out, okay? I'll ring Paul now and tell him to meet us there . . .'

'No,' Fern called a second time. 'Don't do that.'

It took all her powers of persuasion to convince Tina not to ring him. 'Really, there's no need.' No need to disturb him at work. No need to panic him with talk of hospitals. It wasn't really out of consideration for Paul though. Not if she was honest. Fern wanted him home because he couldn't stay away – because he loved and missed her and wanted to make amends – not out of a sense of duty. Not because she'd been invalided out of action and needed someone to help her to the toilet every five minutes.

Besides, A&E was the last place she wanted to be right now. Even though Linny was pronounced dead on arrival – even though it was all over before they got there – Fern still felt sick whenever she thought about the place. They'd known it was bad, of course, really bad, but until they reached the hospital there was still a glimmer of hope. A chance. And then . . . the chance was gone and both their lives were over, just like that – hers *and* Linny's – and nothing the doctor, or Paul, or anyone else had to say could change that. It would be a different hospital, but that hardly mattered. In Fern's head, it was the same one. The same waiting room full of people, with their stupid little injuries that meant nothing – swollen ankles, for example – stewing in their petty oblivions while the world imploded. *Her* world. No need to relive any of that again, surely? As if she hadn't relived it a hundred times already. A thousand times.

'I think the swelling's gone down a bit,' she lied. 'Definitely less painful than it was.'

Tina looked doubtful.

'Honestly,' said Fern. 'It's just where I twisted it last night in the bathroom. I must have aggravated it again when I fell.

Look, April's only up the road – the nurse whose party I went to on Saturday – why don't we ask her to have a look at it first? See if *she* thinks it's a hospital job or not. She did say to pop over whenever.'

But April was definitely out this time, judging by her empty drive when Tina went to check, which meant waiting for another taxi to take them to the surgery, or asking one of the neighbours for a lift. In retrospect, they should have held on to Tina's cab while the going was good, because the wait was anything up to forty-five minutes now. All the company's free cars were down at Blatchford Station, waiting for the London train. Which, as far as Tina was concerned, only left one option: the neighbours.

She returned from Yasmin's a few minutes later, with a welcome bag of frozen peas – some small relief from the throbbing pain anyway – and the rather less welcome news that her car was in the garage that afternoon having its brakes checked. 'Bit of a nasty scare at a roundabout coming back from her daughter's,' Tina reported. 'I'll have to try Eddie.'

'No, he'll be working,' said Fern. She didn't want him to see her like this – useless and incapacitated – although she couldn't have said why, exactly. 'I don't want to interrupt him.'

But Tina batted her objections away like flies. 'Nonsense. He'll be only too happy to help. At least he will be once we explain the situation. And the sooner we get you looked at, the better, quite frankly. I mean, you can't even go to the loo on your own . . .'

Good point. That sealed it for Fern. And Tina was right as it turned out. Eddie was all smiles and flirtatious neighbourly concern when they arrived back together, eager to play the part of medical chauffeur for an hour.

'Beats working on my synopsis,' he assured them, although Fern had met enough writers during the course of her career to realise how little that meant. Pretty much *anything* was better than synopsis-writing. But Eddie's cheerful attentiveness seemed genuine enough. He'd even dug out a pair of crutches from somewhere. 'Stolen props for research purposes,' he told her as he handed them over, grinning like a naughty schoolboy. 'I was trying to work out if one of these would make a good murder weapon. Not a very sexy way to go though. I think that's why I decided against it in the end. Don't tell April where you got them . . .'

Fern found herself wondering about the two of them again – April and Eddie – and the closeness of their relationship.

'Don't worry. Your secret's safe with us,' said Tina. She was all smiles too, concern for Fern's ankle taking second place to her obvious pleasure in Eddie's company. 'Isn't that a bit of luck, eh, Fern? Just what we needed.'

Fern nodded, wincing as she hauled herself up onto her good foot, almost toppling over as her arms fought to take the extra weight. She might well have done if Eddie hadn't been there to steady her.

'Easy does it,' he said. 'Otherwise your lovely mother-in-law and I will have to carry you! What do you think, Tina? Bagsy I get her arms . . .'

Fern gritted her teeth against the suggestion, pushing off with renewed determination, studiously avoiding the back door as she lumbered past. The blanket must still be out there on the patio where Barry had kicked it, hugging the baby's name into its hidden creases. Lying in wait. The thought of it made her feel sick again, dredging up half-remembered fragments from her dreams: that poor screaming baby locked in the attic cupboard; a tongueless, toothless Marte spelling out her daughter's name on the remote control before the explosion; Fern's own baby dripping away through the floor in a pool of red . . . But she forced the images away again, focusing her energy on getting across the kitchen and out through the front door.

The crutches took a bit of getting used to, balance-wise, but they were more dignified than clinging on to Eddie like a human limpet, and made the short trip to his car slightly less of a marathon. It was enough of an ordeal as it was, having to listen to him flirting with Tina. But Fern soon had more pressing things to worry about than flirtatious banter, like not passing out from the pain when they took the speedbump too fast, sending a stray water bottle crashing into her ankle. Eddie didn't even seem to notice. He was too busy talking.

He kept up his steady stream of chatter all the way to the surgery, with tales of boyhood broken limbs and various head injuries he'd acquired along the way. And then he moved on to his synopsis, the near-impossibility of condensing an entire novel down to a few measly paragraphs. 'Especially with this latest book. Too many interwoven story strands to pick apart, that's the problem. It's got more red herrings than a Swedish fish-smoker!'

The joke was somewhat wasted on Fern, not fully understanding the reference, but her ears pricked up at the word 'Swedish'. If she wasn't in so much pain she might have asked him about Marte there and then, still clinging to the hope of a rational explanation. *Tell me what she was doing there that day. Tell me I'm not going crazy.* But even if she *had* felt strong enough, collected enough, to try again, Eddie was already swinging into the car park with a flamboyant scattering of gravel, congratulating himself on nabbing the last available parking spot: a disabled space directly outside the surgery door.

'Don't you need a blue badge to use this one?' fussed Tina, as if she'd be happier parking down the road and letting Fern crawl the extra two hundred yards.

Eddie grinned. 'I think we'll be all right. The main receptionist's got a bit of a soft spot for me. Besides, Fern's more disabled than abled at the moment, isn't she?'

Tina still looked unsure. She had very firm views on the abuse of allocated parking spaces, just like she had very firm views on most things. But a promise from Eddie to move the moment a blue-badged car appeared (coupled with his resourceful procurement of a fold-out wheelchair from the soft-spotted receptionist) seemed to do the trick, and she had nothing but praise for him as they sat in the waiting room.

'Such a nice man,' Tina announced, leaning down to adjust the bag of peas on Fern's foot.

Fern flushed with embarrassment, with the delayed humiliation of being wheeled in by her mother-in-law, covered in half-defrosted vegetables. The paracetamols Tina had given her were finally starting to kick in, taking the edge off her pain and allowing her to focus more fully on the awkwardness of the situation. But she nodded her agreement nonetheless. Eddie *was* nice. A bit full-on, maybe, but good company, and chivalrous to a fault in her hour of need.

'And clearly very talented,' Tina gushed. 'All those books! Genuinely funny too. I can't believe he's all on his own. You'd think there'd be women queueing up for a man like that.'

They *were* queueing up though, weren't they? thought Fern. The 'Casanova of Crenellation Lane', that's what April called him. She'd said it so warmly though, so affectionately that Fern found herself wondering, yet again, about the true nature of her feelings for Eddie. But that was an idle thought for another day. What she needed to know now was whether *Marte* had ever been a member of the Eddie Gumley fan club. If their paths had crossed six years ago? Or now? He must have flirted with her, at the very least, given that he clearly flirted with everyone. And what if it was more than flirting? What if *he* was the one with the spare key to the Rochesters' house and they'd both been there that day, playing out some strange fantasy in one of the bedrooms while his neighbours were out? Maybe that's how he got his kicks, or maybe it was research for one of his books, like the crutches had been . . . or maybe it was Marte's idea. Maybe there was nothing sexual about it at all. Perhaps she just wanted to revisit her old student digs. Lay some ghosts to rest now that she was pregnant again. And then Eddie managed to sneak out the back when Fern and Gemma turned up but she hadn't been as quick . . .

Fern didn't know which was more plausible – the notion of her neighbour sneaking out the back door after some strange tryst, or the idea that she'd somehow imagined the whole thing. For a while there, after the business with Barry and the blanket, she'd given in to the idea that she really *might* have dreamed it all. But how could she have done? The messages on the mirror and window were one thing. Maybe they *were* just tricks of the light, or her overwrought mind playing pranks on her. But the house viewing was different. *I spoke to her. And so did Gemma. How could I have made the whole thing up?* Either there was a rational explanation to all of this, or Paul was right – she really did need help. And sitting there in the waiting room, going over it all again, the Eddie theory was the closest to a rational explanation Fern could come up with. It was time she had a proper talk with him about Marte – no interruptions this time and no excuses – and found out exactly what he knew.

Chapter 23

'Mrs Croft? The nurse is ready for you now, if you'd like to go through.'

Fern felt oddly shy as Tina wheeled her into the examination room. A couple of days ago she and April had been talking like friends – potential friends, at least – and now here Fern was playing the patient again – the ditzy, pregnant patient, lurching from one ridiculous drama to another. She didn't quite know how to act. Didn't know what to say.

She needn't have worried on that last score because her mother-in-law was already off, filling April in on the full story of the injury in typical Tina fashion: 'You should have seen her when I got back, poor thing. Couldn't even go to the toilet on her own. Good job I arrived when I did!'

Fern rolled her eyes, as if to say, *Mothers-in-law, eh? What can you do?* But April didn't miss a beat – professional to the point of indifference. They'd really hit it off on Saturday – Fern was sure they had – but now? April was like a different person. Like Kerry. No, that was unfair. She wasn't *openly* hostile and unfriendly. She wasn't even unsympathetic, making the right noises in the right places and saying all the right things. But the warmth and spark – the very things that had drawn Fern to her in the first place – were missing today.

'Is everything all right?' asked Fern, after April had finished with her questions and examination. 'You seem a little . . .' *Reserved? Aloof? Cold and standoffish?* She let the end of the sentence hang there, unfinished. 'I popped round to see you yesterday afternoon, but you didn't answer. I guess you must have been out.'

April's cheeks coloured slightly. 'Probably,' she said, but she didn't elaborate.

'It wasn't anything important,' Fern lied. 'I just happened to be passing. I wanted to say thank you again for Saturday. It was lovely to meet you properly . . . and good to meet everyone else too.'

'Apart from Richard, of course,' said April. 'And Kerry. You'd already met them.'

That wasn't strictly true. Fern hadn't met Richard before the party – she'd only heard him in the hallway talking to Paul. But she didn't bother correcting her. 'And I meant to say that you're welcome to pop over to ours for a cuppa anytime too,' she said instead.

'Thank you,' said April. But that was *all* she said. No 'that would be lovely' or 'I look forward to it', just a plain 'thank you'. Maybe she liked to keep her personal and professional lives separate during work hours. Or maybe she really *had* been in when Fern had called round the previous day and it was embarrassment driving her cold behaviour. Embarrassment at being caught out with Eddie?

'So there's no need for an X-ray or anything?' asked Tina turning the conversation back to more medical concerns. She almost sounded disappointed it was only a sprain, and that the drama was all over.

'I don't think so,' said April. 'You've just got to take it easy and let it mend on its own. RICE is what we recommend for sprains: Rest, Ice, Compression, Elevation. And try to avoid any HARM. That's Heat, Alcohol, Running, Massage.'

'What? No alcohol or running?' Fern joked. 'Anyone would think I was pregnant.'

April didn't even break a smile. 'And no ibuprofen, obviously. Have to be especially careful in the last trimester.'

'What about driving?' asked Tina. 'My son works long hours and I don't have my car down here. If Fern can't drive that leaves us a bit stranded when it comes to appointments and things.'

Paul. Fern's eyes stung at the thought of telling Tina what he'd *really* said when he rang earlier. How he'd decided to stay away another night rather than come home to her. Or maybe it was the coldness of April's response that made her feel like crying.

Well, you know where I am if you need a lift. That's what the old April would have said. Saturday's April. *Always happy to help. Just give me a shout . . .* But it was very much the nurse who answered, not the neighbour: 'I'm afraid not. Like I said, her ankle needs rest. That's the main order of the day. Especially with a little one on the way.' Even as she said it, she was heading for the door, ready to show them out. To *shoo* them out.

'Yes, of course. I'm sure we'll manage somehow. Thank you,' said Fern, taking the hint. 'And as I say, do feel free to pop round for a cuppa anytime . . . especially once I'm back on my feet.' There. One last try at breaking the ice, cutting through the strange chill between them.

'Mind how you go on the ramp with the wheelchair,' April told Tina, as if Fern hadn't spoken. 'Bit of a sharp turn at the bottom, which catches people out sometimes.'

But Tina refused to be hurried. 'One last thing before we go,' she said, reaching into her handbag for her notebook. 'You don't know anything about the students who used to live at Fern and Paul's, do you? About six years ago? We're trying to track down a lady called Marte.'

'What? Sorry, I mean, who?' April's mask of professionalism slipped for a moment, as if she'd been caught on the hop by such a left-field question.

'Her name's Marte,' Tina repeated. 'And er . . . well, it's a bit confusing really. We think she used to live in the house. And now we think she might be back again. In the area, I mean.'

Tina was right: it *was* confusing. Which made her uncharacteristic tact on the subject – no mention of mysterious messages or Paul's departure – even more impressive. Fern twisted round in the wheelchair to study the nurse's face better.

'Six years ago?' repeated April. 'We must have only just moved in ourselves. Didn't really know anyone very well back then, apart from through work. And not sure we'd have had much to do with students . . .'

'Mature students,' said Tina, as if that made all the difference.

April pressed her lips together and shook her head. If she *did* know something she clearly wasn't saying.

'What about her name, though? It's quite an unusual one. That doesn't ring any bells?' But Tina didn't even wait for an answer, ploughing straight on to the next question in her eagerness to cover all the bases. 'And you haven't seen a pregnant blonde lady hanging around the road lately? Present company excluded, of course,' she said, patting Fern's arm. 'We think she might be something to do with the Rochesters, maybe . . .'

'Sorry,' April told her. 'You should try Eddie. He sees most of the comings and goings on the street as he works from home. Especially if they're young and pretty,' she added with a note of something else in her voice. What was it? Amusement? Bitterness? Jealousy? Fern couldn't quite tell.

Tina bristled, as if she didn't like what April was implying. As if she thought Eddie was above such low considerations. 'Yes, I fully intend to ask him too. I just thought while we were here . . .' She slipped the notebook back into her bag and stood up. 'Sorry to have taken up so much of your time.'

They were barely through the door when Tina let out a weighty sigh of exasperation. 'Well,' she said. 'I don't know what *her* problem is. Anyone would think you were perfect strangers the way she talked to you. Got a right stick up her arse, that one.'

Fern had been hoping it was all in her head for once. Hoping she'd imagined April's coldness towards her. But no, even Tina had noticed. 'Come on,' said her mother-in-law, pushing her towards the exit. 'Let's get you back to the car. Eddie will be wondering where we've got to.'

She was wrong. Eddie *wasn't* wondering where they'd got to at all. He was asleep, dozing open-mouthed behind the wheel like an old man, head thrown back, tongue lolling limp over his bottom teeth. Tina rapped on his window with her knuckles, sending his entire body shooting forwards in surprise.

'Caught in the act,' he admitted, grinning sheepishly as he came round to collect the wheelchair. 'One minute I was plotting out a new novel idea in my head and the next . . .' He made a snoring, snorting noise like a pig.

'Speaking of novels,' said Fern, when he got back to the car, 'I finished yours this morning.' She needed to work her way round to Marte carefully, without scaring him off like she had with Sean, and *Blood Lovers* seemed like the perfect way in. The need for answers was growing more urgent all the time. Fern needed answers and she needed proof, something more than messages on glass and a ratty old blanket this time. Proof that she *wasn't* crazy. Proof that Paul was wrong to walk out on her like that, before the rift between them grew too wide and too deep to cross back and find each other again.

Marte was the one pushing them apart now, not Linny. Not anymore. It was Marte who'd been at the heart of everything that had gone wrong since they first arrived on Crenellation Lane: Paul storming off into the night; the terrible dreams that still haunted Fern during the day; even her sprained ankle . . . they all came down to Marte in the end. Maybe she was the one behind the horrible leaflet as well, and the scratches on her car. And maybe, just maybe, Eddie was the key.

'*Blood Lovers?*' he said. 'What did you think of it?'

Fern nodded. 'It was a good read. Really good. I was totally gripped.'

Eddie let out a puff of air – *pah, that old thing?* – waving the compliment away with his hand. But it was false modesty. Fern could see it in his eyes, the way they lit up when she said it, in the subtle straightening of his shoulders and forward thrust of his chest. She pressed home her advantage.

'It kept me up half the night, which is probably why I'm such a mess today.'

'Really?' he said. 'You didn't think it was "a passionless crime of passion, with a two-dimensional cast of characters and a boringly predictable twist"? Not that I've committed that gem of a review to memory. Not that I still wake up in the night, grinding my teeth over the injustice of it all . . .' He pulled a mock-angry face with a bubble of laughter lurking behind it. 'Not that I daydream about committing a passionless crime of my own on the lovely reviewer who penned it, either. Oh no. I would *never* do that.'

Fern laughed. 'Well, you kept *me* guessing right to the end. My money was on Kerry as the killer.'

'Kerry? I don't even remember a Kerry. Are you sure it was *my* book?'

'Oh, no, sorry,' said Fern, worried he'd think she hadn't read it properly. 'I meant the mother. Esme. For some reason I pictured her as Kerry Brantley when I was reading it. Richard's wife.'

'Ah yes, your good friend Kerry. I guess I can see that . . . Who knows? Maybe I was channelling her subconsciously . . . What about my wicked anti-hero, Patrick, then?' he asked, turning to Fern with a playful glint in his eye. 'Who does *he* remind you of?'

Eddie probably thought it was him: dashing and debonair – the Casanova of Crenellation Lane. He certainly seemed surprised by her answer.

'*Richard*?' he repeated, looking slightly put out. 'Really? Can I ask why?' *What's he got that I haven't?*

'It's mainly to do with his dog,' explained Fern. 'He mentioned that he used to have a red setter too . . . and I couldn't help picturing the victim, the au pair, as the lady who showed me round our house on the second viewing,' she added, steering the conversation towards Marte.

But Eddie was still fully focused on Richard. 'I'll be looking at him in a whole new light now you've said that,' he laughed. 'Seducing young ladies left, right and centre. No *wonder* Kerry's such a misery these days!'

It did sound a bit of a leap from the dashing fictional Patrick to real-life Richard, put like that. It was certainly hard to imagine him as a serial womaniser; although Fern had no problem picturing Kerry as the wronged wife, nursing a grudge against the whole of womankind.

'Mind you,' said Eddie, more thoughtful suddenly. 'There *was* that woman in the city a while back. Quite besotted with her, he was . . .' He signalled the turn into Crenellation Lane, frowning to himself as he did so.

They seemed to have got back in no time at all, before Fern had got her answers. Where was a traffic jam when you needed one?

'Of course he told me all that in the strictest confidence,' Eddie went on. '*Drunken* strictest confidence, which is the most sacred form of all. You know, what happens in the pub stays in the pub . . .'

'Don't worry,' Fern assured him. 'There's no danger of *me* blabbing it to Kerry over coffee. Besides, it's none of my business.' There was a small part of her though – a mean, petty part of her – that was grateful for the information. Pleased by the sense of secret power it gave her over the poor woman, like a hidden defence against future rudeness. 'And anyway,' she said, 'it's the au pair character I'm more interested in. Marte. *That's* who the dead woman reminds me of.'

Eddie fell quiet, an odd look passing over his face.

'Marte,' Fern repeated. *Here we go again.* 'Do you see much of her these days?' she added casually. By which she meant, *WHO IS SHE, FOR CRYING OUT LOUD? WHY WON'T ANYONE TELL ME?*

Tina was so far forward in her seat now that Fern could feel her breath on the back of her neck.

'Marte Hortlassen?' Eddie said at last. 'Who used to live at your house?'

'Yes,' agreed Fern, swallowing down a wild rush of giddiness. Finally – *finally* – someone knew who she was talking about. Someone who could prove she hadn't imagined the whole thing. 'That's her.' It had to be. She repeated it in her head – Hortlassen, Hortlassen, Marte Hortlassen – not wanting it to escape. There was an odd comfort in the name too. 'Marte' on its own had become synonymous with dead babies and nightmares, with Fern's tenuous hold on her own sanity, but 'Marte Hortlassen' sounded perfectly normal and business-like. A surname would also make it a damn sight easier to find out who the woman really was.

Eddie's smile was back, but it didn't quite reach his eyes this time.

'Marte Hortlassen,' he said again. 'Now *there's* a blast from the past. What's she doing with herself nowadays?'

Was he playing it cool to cover his tracks – *me and Marte, breaking into someone else's house? Whatever gave you that idea?* – or did he genuinely not know?

'I've only met her the once, to be honest,' said Fern. 'But someone mentioned *you* knew her quite well.' That was a lie, of course. No one had told her anything of the sort. It was a good call though, judging by Eddie's reaction.

'Who?' he demanded. 'Who said that? What did they tell you?'

Fern shrank back into her seat, shocked by the aggression in his voice. 'Oh . . .' she stammered. 'I erm . . . I'm not sure I can remember actually. There've been so many new faces over the last few days . . .'

But Eddie didn't seem interested in her answer anyway. 'It's Sean,' he said, speaking over the top of her. 'Not me. Sean's the one you should be talking to. I barely knew her.'

178

Sean? He'd never even heard of Marte. Or so he said. Was Eddie just trying to deflect attention away from himself? He certainly seemed rattled. Or was it Sean who'd been lying? Was Sean the one who'd been sneaking round with her that day – making the most of the empty house – not realising there was a viewing booked in for the afternoon? Was Sean the one who'd crept out the back, leaving Marte to deal with Gemma and Fern? It was hard to imagine the gardener involved in that kind of romantic intrigue but perhaps there was something to it. Perhaps the Rochesters had entrusted Sean with a key for his gardening work, to allow him access to a plug socket and the toilet. Was that the sort of thing people did?

They were coming up to the house now, pulling into the kerb in front of Fern's car, affording a clear view of the scratches along her paintwork. She shuddered. Was that really only yesterday? And then the rain started – nothing too dramatic, just a light drizzle – and the scratches disappeared again behind the clouding glass.

Eddie switched off the engine and sat staring blindly through the steamed-up windscreen. He looked pale and shaken. But then he turned back to Fern with his easy grin, regular service resumed.

'We should have stolen that wheelchair while we were at it,' he laughed. 'Missed a trick there, didn't we?' He leaned over, unclipping Fern's seatbelt for her. 'So Marte's back again, is she? Well I never. Must be years . . .'

'Six,' piped up Tina from behind.

'Gosh. As long as that?' Eddie shook his head, as if he could hardly believe it. 'Her little one must be at school by now then. Imagine that.'

But Fern couldn't imagine it. Either Eddie was wrong – perhaps he didn't realise she'd lost the baby? Perhaps she'd already moved away by then? – or Marte had lied to her that day.

My first. Sofia. That's what she'd said, standing there in front of the hall mirror, her hands cradling her belly. *My first.*

Chapter 24

Marte Hortlassen. Fern typed the name into her mobile search engine as soon as they walked in the door, her heart pounding. This was it. This was when she finally got to find out who the mysterious woman was. So far, it felt like she'd been groping round in the dark, not knowing who or what to ask. But that was all about to change. Fern clicked on the search button and waited . . .

No results found for Marte Hortlassen. Ensure words are spelled correctly.

Fern tried Marte Hørtlassen, Marte Hawtlassen and Marte Håtlassen, trying every phonetic alternative she could think of. They brought up plenty of other Martes (and Martins), a balcony glazing company, an article on mycotoxins in Norwegian cereal grain, and a dubious-looking link for a site promising to make people look ten years younger. But there was nothing about Norwegian ex-students formerly residing in Crenellation Lane, Westerton. There were no social media links for *her* Marte with any one of the spellings Fern tried. No Facebook or LinkedIn profiles. No Twitter handles. Nothing. It was as if the woman didn't exist. Had never existed. *But Eddie knew her. Sean knew her. And I'm pretty sure the Rochesters knew her too.* The pounding in Fern's chest eased as her initial excitement gave way to bewilderment. Did that mean Marte Hortlassen wasn't her real name after all? Had Eddie simply misremembered – six years was a long time – or had Marte been hiding under a fake name? Hiding from who, though?

'Well,' said Tina, after she'd shown Eddie to the door, shouting another round of 'thank yous' down the path after him. 'What do we make of *that*?'

It was 'we' now, Fern noticed. Not 'you'.

'If I had to pick one word to describe Eddie's reaction, it would be "rattled",' Tina went on, without waiting for an answer.

The one-word game. Memories flooded into Fern's head. That had been a favourite of hers and Linny's when they were younger. They used to play it in bed, after Dad kissed them goodnight, whispering together in the darkness. Giggling and bickering in equal measures as they reduced the people around them to a single word:

Okay, I've got a good one. That new dinner lady, Mrs Broomer.

That's easy: Fat.

You can't have fat. That's just what she looks like on the outside.

All right then . . . Strict.

Power-hungry's better. I win. That had been Linny's favourite for a while: *Power-hungry.* She liked long words. Liked showing off with them.

But that's cheating. That's two words.

Not if they're hyphenated. Another long word. *That's allowed.* It was Linny's game really: Linny's game, Linny's rules. They always were. Maybe that's why she used to 'win' all the time, or maybe she was just better. After all, Mrs Broomer *was* power-hungry. And somehow the 'hungry' part captured the way she shovelled in endless packets of crisps and chocolate bars as she patrolled the upper playground, spitting crumbs and barking out orders. Fern could still see her now, power-hungry Mrs Broomer. Two words. One hyphen.

The game worked almost as well with boys, their classroom crushes. She and Linny were older by then, but Fern remembered

181

the one-word labels long after their owners' faces had faded: Ben Sampson: clever. Adam Sharp: funny. Robert Manser: passionate. Although Linny had changed her mind about Robert after a clumsy encounter behind the school tennis courts, downgrading him from 'passionate' to 'pathetic' and taking her affection elsewhere. Linny's affections were constantly shifting but the game always stayed the same.

'So, Paul,' she'd teased Fern years later after their first official date. After the film she'd hardly watched and the dinner she'd barely tasted. 'Go on – one word. Hit me.'

Where to start? Fern had thought. *Sensitive. Witty. Handsome.* Only it hadn't proved that hard after all: *Perfect.*

But Linny had refused to play when Fern turned the game back on her with her last boyfriend – the one she insisted on keeping to herself. She'd refused to enter into the spirit of the game, just like she'd refused to allow Fern into their relationship.

'Well, if I'm not allowed to meet him, at least tell me something about him,' Fern had begged, trying not to sound as hurt as she felt. 'Come on. One word.'

Linny *had* answered, but it wasn't a proper answer, hiding her real feelings behind something shallow and meaningless that told Fern nothing. *Well-off.* Was that it? Two words, one hyphen? No, that really *was* two separate words. Perhaps it was *loaded* then. Or *wealthy.* Something so unlike Linny, who'd never given a stuff about money or status, that Fern had dismissed it as nonsense. Hurtful nonsense, but nonsense nonetheless. It was clearly Linny's way of telling her to back off; that this so-called relationship of hers – how could it be a proper relationship if Fern wasn't included? – was out of bounds. Was it any wonder she'd let her imagination get the better of her during that last terrible night?

'Rattled,' Fern repeated, dragging her mind out of the past, into the present. To Eddie's shaken reaction to the news that Marte was back, whatever that meant. Back from where? Norway?

That would certainly tie in with what Beverly had said at her antenatal appointment. And where was she now? *Who* was she now, come to that? Because how could anyone, in this day and age, not have some sort of online presence? 'Yes,' she agreed. 'I thought Eddie seemed rattled too . . . and very keen to deflect attention back onto Sean. But I was talking to Sean before I fell. He still claimed not to know anything about Marte. Said he'd never heard of her.' Maybe *everyone* was lying. Maybe there was some street-wide conspiracy of silence surrounding the woman. A worldwide conspiracy. 'And I just looked her up on my phone now, and I can't find a single record of her anywhere. It doesn't look like Marte Hortlassen is her real name after all.'

Tina raised her eyebrows. '*Interesting*. The plot thickens,' she said, clearly enjoying herself. Perhaps it was all a game to her, like that awful murder mystery party she'd hosted when Paul and Fern came for Christmas, the year they were married. But *Tina's* sanity wasn't in any doubt, was it? She wasn't the one plagued by nightmares and imaginary letters dripping down the window like a . . . like a what? A warning? *My baby. Not yours. Mine.* And she didn't know about the blanket yet, either, calling from underneath the bath, begging to be found.

The patterned notebook was out again already, pen poised for a fresh round of notes. For a fresh round of *Let's Humour Little Miss Crazy-Croft*. But once again it seemed Fern had underestimated her mother-in-law.

'Look,' Tina said. 'Promise you'll say something if I'm overstepping the mark here, but it seems like you're not going to rest easy, not going to be happy, 'til you get to the bottom of all this. And neither is Paul.'

'Paul? He's the one who convinced me she was the Rochesters' cleaner in the first place. He was the one telling me not to worry.' That all seemed like such a long time ago. 'But yes, he probably thinks she's all in my head, like Linny. You saw what he was like. He thinks I've lost it.' It was Paul who was wrong though, and

Tina had heard the evidence with her own ears. There really was a woman calling herself Marte. Fern hadn't invented *that*.

'Exactly,' said Tina. 'Which is precisely why this Marte's been driving such a wedge between the two of you. She's driving out all the trust. And once that's gone . . .' She didn't need to finish the sentence; they both knew exactly what she meant. Paul's parting words hadn't left much room for doubt: *We need more than a sodding cup of tea to fix this one . . . I give up. I can't do this anymore . . .*

'So,' Tina went on, 'the way I see it, the sooner you get to the bottom of what's been going on, the better. Then you and Paul can finally clear the air and put it all behind you, once and for all. Go back to how things used to be.'

'Yes,' agreed Fern. That's all she wanted. To have Paul back. To have Linny back. And Marte gone. 'That's why I need to find out who she is. That's why I'm *going* to find out who she is,' she corrected herself. 'She might not exist online but she's out there somewhere. She has to be.'

'It's going to be tricky though, with your ankle,' said Tina. 'You're going to need some help.' She blushed. 'Look, I know you think I'm an interfering old so-and-so . . .'

Fern opened her mouth to protest – *that's not true, not completely true, anyway* – but Tina didn't give her a chance.

'It's fine,' she said. 'I used to think exactly the same about Graham's mother. Mind you, she really *is* an interfering old so-and-so. But even if I go about things in the wrong way some-times – taking over – it's only because I want to help. That's all I've *ever* wanted.'

'I know that,' said Fern. And she did, really. 'It's me, as well. I guess I'm not used to having a mum around.'

Tina's cheeks grew redder still, but she couldn't have looked more pleased. 'Oh, love,' she said, putting down the notebook and pen, and wrapping a motherly arm round Fern's shoulder. 'You haven't had it easy, have you? So much sadness . . . so much loss . . . and now all *this* to deal with too. But we'll sort it out, don't you worry. We'll crack the case together. You and me. The Cagney and Lacey of Crenellation Lane.'

Fern knew the names – Eighties American detectives, weren't they? – but couldn't picture them. 'More like the Laurel and Hardy of Crenellation Lane,' she teased, clutching her big round belly. 'But yes. Thank you,' she added. 'I'd like that.'

The pair of them got straight to work, drawing up a hit list in Tina's notebook of who to talk to next. What questions to ask. Sean was right up there at number one, obviously, after what Eddie had told them. 'Maybe you could tackle him this time?' suggested Fern. 'See if you have more luck getting any information out of him than I did. Ask him about Marte obviously, and also if the Rochesters gave him a spare key. It could be that they were sneaking around together while the house was empty. Maybe that's how they got their kicks.'

Tina's eyes widened. She looked scandalised at the very suggestion.

'It would certainly explain why he lied about knowing her,' said Fern. 'I mean, nobody would want to hire him if *that* got out, would they? Oh and we need to talk to Richard,' she added. 'I haven't tried him yet. And the dreaded Kerry. It's a pity I didn't get the right number for the lady I met at the doctor's on Friday. Nicky, who used to be a student here . . .' She thought for a moment. 'Although I think I know where we can find her. The midwife was telling us about a social group they run every other Tuesday, out at one of the local pubs. This lady's *exactly* the sort of person who'd go. And I'm pretty sure the next one's tomorrow night.'

'Excellent,' said Tina. 'Once you've sorted out the car insurance, I can drive us there. And maybe we should have another chat with your Mrs Rochester? She could be the key to the whole thing.'

'Her husband told me not to call them again,' said Fern, remembering the anger in his voice.

'Ah yes, but he didn't tell *me* not to call, did he?' Tina grinned. 'If you give me the number I'll try her now, while the kettle's boiling. I don't know about you, but I could murder a cup of tea.'

Fern nodded gratefully. 'Thank goodness for the new kettle!' And thank goodness for Tina. Sometimes, just sometimes, it was nice to have her telling her what to do. Deciding for her.

Tina headed out into the garden where the reception was better and Fern carried on with her fruitless search for Marte online. It felt better to be doing something, even if that something was proving every bit as useless as before. But then she caught sight of Kerry in a pink rain mac, staring over the garden wall as she stopped to do up her shoelace, and Fern tossed her phone aside again. This could be her ideal chance to quiz her about Marte, and maybe try and clear the air at the same time. She picked up her crutches and hobbled to the front door.

Too late. By the time she'd finally managed to wrench it open with only one hand, Kerry was gone again. Long gone. Fern cursed her own slowness and incapacity, staring down the street at the retreating pink coat in frustration. She shut the door and turned to begin the slow hobble back to the sofa, only to find a bedraggled Tina waiting for her in the hall.

Fern knew it was bad news the moment she saw her mother-in-law's pale face. Tina couldn't even speak at first. She just stood there shaking her head.

It must be Marte, thought Fern. It had to be. The curse of Marte stretching all the way across the Atlantic and back again, to render her mother-in-law speechless.

'What happened?' she asked, as a trembling dread took hold of her. 'What did she say?'

Chapter 25

'I didn't get to talk to Mrs Rochester,' said Tina. 'I tried, but . . .'

Oh, thought Fern. Was that all? She'd been expecting something a little more dramatic than that. A little more world-ending: *Oh yes, she knew all about Marte. In fact, Marte's the reason Mrs Rochester got so ill in the first place. The poor woman didn't sleep for an entire year . . . She said it wasn't too bad to start with, just the odd nightmare here and there. But then the messages started appearing . . . That's* what Fern had been expecting.

'Oh well, at least you tried,' she said out loud. Tina had looked so ashen when she first came in, so stricken, that it was a genuine relief to discover the conversation hadn't even happened. No stories of dead babies locked away in attic cupboards. No tales of cursed blankets buried under the bathroom floorboards to keep them awake at night. It must have been the wintry rain draining her mother-in-law's cheeks of colour, that's all, rendering her too cold and numb to speak.

But Tina shook her head again. 'No,' she said. 'I didn't get to talk to her because she's gone. Passed away during the early hours.'

That's when the numbness came for Fern, too – an icy nothing creeping through her body, through her brain, freezing the words on her tongue. *No*, that was all she could think. *No. No. No.*

'I'm not sure who it was I spoke to,' said Tina. 'A neighbour maybe? She didn't seem to know Caroline very well. That's what she called her – Caroline. I had to double-check we were talking about the same person, which was a bit awkward. She said it happened at four o'clock this morning. Their time, obviously. I don't know what that would be for us.'

Nine o'clock. Fern got there eventually, driving through the frozen fog of her brain to find the answer. Not that it made the slightest bit of difference. Mrs Rochester was dead. *Marte found her all the way over there. She* still *found her.* That was Fern's next thought, but she knew, even as she was shivering inside at the drama of it all, that she was being ridiculous. It was just shock talking, that's all. Shock and fear and an overwrought imagination. It was Barry and his tales of bodies under the floorboards. It was staying up too late reading about corpses in the woods. And it was Fern herself, looking everywhere for Linny, and finding Marte instead.

'What was it?' she made herself ask. 'What killed her?' *Or should that be 'Who killed her?'?* 'Did they say? Do they know yet?' She imagined the woman she'd met outside the bakery in the grip of a life-ending nightmare. Imagined her clutching at her chest in the darkness, fighting for breath. No, that was crazy. *Dreams* couldn't kill people, could they?

'I didn't like to ask,' said Tina. 'Sorry,' she added, as if she'd let Fern down. 'She just said "I'm afraid Caroline passed away at four o'clock this morning" – she was very definite on the time – "and Geoff's not really in a fit state to talk at the moment." She did offer to take a message but I made my excuses and went. Never even said who I was.'

'It's probably for the best,' Fern agreed. 'I'm sorry to have put you in that position in the first place. I had no idea.' A coincidence, she told herself firmly, trying to get a grip on her imaginings. That's all it was, a horrible coincidence. Mrs Rochester was clearly ill and had been for a while. Some kind of underlying condition.

'There's no way you could have known,' said Tina, looking more herself already, the colour seeping back into her cheeks. 'Poor woman,' she added softly. 'Poor *man* come to that. I wonder what he'll do now? Whether he'll stay out there or come back to this country?'

Fern didn't want to think about it anymore. Didn't want to picture Mr Rochester waking up to his wife's last breaths, holding her through the final spasms. Willing her back into the sudden stillness of her body, begging her to stay. 'Do you know what?' she said. 'I could really do with that cup of tea you promised me. And then I guess we should start thinking about dinner,' she added, although it was hard to summon up any enthusiasm. 'Why don't we order in pizza or something, and see what's on telly? Something trashy and silly for light relief?'

'Sounds good to me,' said Tina. 'But what about Paul? Shouldn't we wait for him? What time do you think he'll be back?'

Oh yes. Paul. Tina still didn't know, did she? Fern had been too embarrassed and angry to tell her earlier. Too hurt. 'Oh, that's okay,' she said, aiming for an air of cheerful indifference. 'He's going to stay on at his friend's for another night. I'm sorry, I meant to tell you before . . .'

Tina gave her a long, hard look. 'And are you all right with that?'

'Mm-hmm.' Fern nodded.

'Really?'

No. Of course she wasn't. She was about as far from all right with it as it was possible to get. But that's how it was – that's how Paul wanted to play this – and Fern was damned if she was going to sit at home weeping about it.

Five seconds. That's how long she managed to keep up the fake smile for. How long it took for the tears to start again. *Bloody pregnancy hormones.* And then there she was, sitting at home, weeping about it, spilling out the whole sorry mess to his mother.

'Just like his father,' Tina said. 'Can't cope with things he can't understand.'

189

But that only made Fern cry harder. What if Paul was like Graham in *every* respect? She hadn't thought of that before, but suddenly it was all she *could* think about. That or Mrs Rochester, dead in her bed, which wasn't much of a choice. What if Paul decided to trade *his* wife in for a better, saner model too? Or what if he already had? What if she'd driven him away with her grief and coldness, straight into someone else's arms? Maybe that's where he was, even now. Not with a Simon at all. With a Simone.

Simone says . . . Your wife doesn't understand you.

Simone says . . . Choose me, instead.

Choose me.

Touch me.

Simone says . . . Nothing. She's too busy kissing you . . .

It was like the night of their wedding anniversary all over again. The same poisonous doubts mushrooming out of nowhere. But what if Fern was right this time?

'What if he leaves me,' she blurted, 'like Graham left you?'

Tina's face fell.

'I'm sorry, I didn't mean . . . But what if he finds someone better?' she asked. 'Without all this baggage? Someone who can make him happy? What if he already has?' She didn't realise she was shaking until Tina anchored her tight in her arms, resting her chin in Fern's hair, shushing her back to stillness.

'Shhhh, there now. Shh come on, it's all right. Paul's not going anywhere. He loves you too much for that.'

'But . . .'

'But nothing. He might take after his dad in every other way, but not that. Never that. I'm not excusing him for running away when you needed him – there's *no* excuse for that – but you've got to understand, it's only because he's scared. You're his whole world, Fern – you and the baby – and he's terrified of losing you.'

But I'm still here. I haven't gone anywhere. What kind of a back-to-front answer was that?

'I've never seen him look at anyone the way he looks at you,' Tina went on, stroking the back of Fern's hair. It should have been annoying, an invasion of her personal space, but it wasn't. It felt nice. Comforting. 'And it's the same look in his eyes now as it was back then, when you first met. Smitten. That's the word . . . Besotted.'

Besotted? Really? That's what Eddie said about Richard, Fern remembered. Besotted with his mystery woman, his city bit on the side. What if *Richard* was the one seeing Marte, and Eddie was covering for him? Trying to throw Fern off the scent by mentioning Sean? What if Richard had set her up in a city love nest after she left Crenellation Lane, only to break it off years later when the guilt finally got too much for him? Maybe Kerry had started to get suspicious. And then Marte had come back to the house that day to . . . to what? Spy on him across the road? Plot her revenge? Show a complete stranger around the property while no one was looking? No. That didn't work either. It still didn't explain what Marte was doing there that day. Fern closed her eyes against the tangle of theories battling it out in her head, abandoning herself to the soft rhythmic pressure of Tina's hand and the solace of her words.

'I still remember the first time he told me about you: *I'm not sure I'm going to make it up next weekend after all, Mum.* That's what he said, all shy and sheepish. *The thing is, I've er . . . I've met someone. Fern.* I was a bit put out to be honest, maybe even a bit jealous. Didn't see why that meant changing his plans. But when I saw the two of you together, saw the way he looked at you, suddenly it all made sense.'

If only they could go back to how it used to be, thought Fern. To how *they* used to be. Those first heady days.

'Love at first sight,' mused Tina. 'That's what he said afterwards. And you know Paul, he's not exactly given to that sort of thing. To soppiness. *She's the one, Mum – I knew it the moment I saw her. The moment she smiled. The first time she spoke . . .*'

Technically speaking it was Linny at first sight, not Fern. Linny who'd locked eyes with him across the crowded bar that night. Who'd dragged him onto the dance floor away from his friends, coaxing him into a laughing shuffle, despite himself. It was Linny who'd brought him back to the table afterwards as a present for Fern, like a cat with a still-wriggling mouse trapped between its jaws. And for a moment, Fern had hated her for it, misunderstanding the true nature of her gift.

Fern had been watching him for a while, eyes seeking him out whenever she looked up from her drink. Whenever she'd turned her attention away from Linny, and whoever else was there that night. There was something about the tall, unassuming stranger that pulled her back time and time again. The steady stillness of him in a sea of jostling bodies. The way his head tipped back when he laughed and the slender curve of his fingers round his bottle of beer. Fingers she'd already imagined against her lips. Her skin. Was that love at first sight, or just lust?

And then Linny, being Linny, had dived on in and snatched him for herself, blind to the secret glances Fern had been throwing him all night. Failing, for once, to read her sister's mind. Only it wasn't like that at all. Linny knew her better than she knew herself.

'Here she is,' Linny told Paul, practically pushing him down onto the seat beside Fern. 'My infinitely more beautiful sister.' It was a naff line, no two ways about it – identical twin humour at its lamest. But Paul had laughed, tipping back his head, as if it was a proper joke. And yet there was something in the way he held Fern's gaze – something intangible passing between them – that suggested it was more than that too. That she really *was* beautiful. That she really *was* the one he'd come to meet. No one else had ever made her feel like that. Picked her over Linny.

Later that night when Fern played it all back in her head, from opening words to last kiss, she wondered if that was the real attraction. The idea of *her* being the special one. But then their first proper date a few days later – the film she didn't watch and the meal she didn't taste – had done away with any such doubts.

So, Paul . . .? Go on – one word. Hit me.

Sensitive. Witty. Handsome . . . He'd been all those things and more. So much more. *Perfect.*

And now? *Oversensitive*, thought Fern miserably. *Humourless. Angry.* And it was all her fault. Hers and Marte's.

Chapter 26

Marte. She was back with a vengeance that Monday night. One dream after another, that's what it felt like to Fern. When she wasn't strangling Mrs Rochester in her sleep, standing over her like some woolly-jumpered angel of death, she was holding the red baby blanket down over Tina's face instead, smiling as she squeezed the last choking breath out of her. And afterwards, when Tina finally fell still, when the violent twitches in her limbs died away, Marte shook the blanket out like a picnic rug or tablecloth and draped it shroud-like over the body. TINA, it said in the corner, in looping yellow letters, as if it had been waiting for her all this time. Except that with all the nonsensical logic of dreams, it was somehow Paul under the blanket then – sleeping, not dead, because he was still snoring – and Fern was trapped in the bath, watching, helpless, as Barry peeled up sodden floorboards ready to bury him alive in a damp bathroom grave. And no sooner would Fern pull herself up to try and stop it – to shake Paul back to consciousness before it was too late – than the water would suck her back under again, filling her mouth and lungs, drowning her screams. It was a relief when the pipes started up *their* screaming (so much for Barry solving that problem), dragging Fern back from the water into wakefulness, spitting her out onto sweat-drenched sheets.

And then, sometime after four – after her third limping toilet trip of the night, crutches catching on every jut of doorframe – Marte came for *her*. For the baby. She leaned in over the bed, unzipping the envelope of Fern's belly as she lay there, peeling it back like a flapping fruit skin, ready to scoop out the kicking flesh inside.

'*My* baby,' Marte whispered as she reached in to swap one bloodied bundle of arms and legs for another. 'Not yours.'

'Fern?' Someone was calling her from the other side of the bed. 'What's happening? Is it the baby?'

'Please,' Fern moaned, fighting a path through the slippery panic of limbs and duvet towards the calm safety of the voice. *Please don't let her take my girl.*

'Shh, it's okay, I'm here now. Where does it hurt? Are you having contractions?'

What? It wasn't Marte standing over the bed in her blood-stained jumper when Fern opened her eyes; it was Tina, in a coffee-stained dressing gown, with the soft light from the bedside lamp haloed behind her head.

'It's okay, love.' Tina reached a hand down to Fern's forehead, stroking sweat-drenched hair from her eyes. 'It's too early to be proper labour ones, I'd have thought. Braxton Hicks, that's what they call practice contractions, isn't it? I was reading all about them at the doctor's last week. A chance to work on your breathing techniques ahead of labour. That's what the article said.'

But Fern could barely breathe at all, as if Marte had sucked the very air out of her, along with her unborn child.

'No, it's not contractions. It's *her*. Where is she? What's she done with my baby?'

That's when Fern spotted the face on the ceiling. It wasn't just yawning anymore. It was screaming, its yellow-brown mouth stretched wide with terror. She yanked herself up into a sitting position – too quick, much too quick – darkness swimming behind her eyes as she swatted Tina's hand away.

'Let me go. I have to find my little girl, before she . . . before she . . .' Before what?

'Hey, hey, calm down now,' said Tina, reaching for her again, stilling Fern's trembling shoulders in her tight grip, pressing through the damp cotton of her nightie. 'No one's taken your baby. It's just a dream, that's all. Just a bad dream.'

'But . . .' Fern touched her hands to the hardness of her belly, feeling with her fingers for the tell-tale flap of skin, and finding nothing. Holding them up to her face afterwards to examine the blood . . . blood that wasn't there.

'See? Your baby's fine, isn't she? Still tucked up safe inside you.'

'But . . .' How would Tina know? thought Fern irrationally. How would she know *whose* baby was in there now? How would anyone know?

Tina drew back and switched on the main light, scorching Fern's eyes with the sudden brightness. 'Come on, let's get you out of there, shall we? Look at you, you're soaked through.'

A fresh panic settled on Fern as the dream receded and reality kicked back in. Had she wet herself in her sleep? Was it her waters? Had they broken?

'Dripping buckets by the looks of it,' said Tina, with her usual delicate turn of phrase. 'I was the same when I woke up earlier. Sweating like a pig. I think the plumber must have knocked the thermostat or something. Mind you,' she added, tugging the edges of her dressing gown tighter over her stomach. 'It's cold in here now.'

Hot? Cold? Fern didn't even know *what* she was. Both at the same time. Burning up and shivering.

'Why don't you pop into the bathroom and flannel yourself down while I change these sheets for you?' Tina suggested, as if Fern was a little girl again. As if she really *had* wet herself and needed her patient mother to magic away the soggy humiliation of it all. The same role Fern's dad had played for months after their real mother died. But Tina lacked his gentle patience and understanding of other people's shyness, already tugging at the duvet, even as she said it. 'Wash away that horrible dream,' she added. 'You'll feel much better then.'

But Fern *wasn't* a little girl in need of wiping down, and the bathroom was the last place she wanted to be. Not with Paul so recently buried under the floorboards, still snoring under his blanket shroud as Barry hammered the final nails back into place. Besides, 'flannelling herself down' would be nigh on impossible with a swollen belly and sprained ankle to contend with. And the last thing Fern wanted was Tina coming to help with *that*.

'If you could just watch me on the stairs,' she said, changing the subject, not quite trusting herself, or her crutches, to carry her safely down in one piece. 'I might set up camp on the sofa instead. It'll be cooler down there.' *Away from the dreams. Away from* her. *Because we all know how well that worked out for Mrs Rochester . . .*

Tina gave her a long look, as if Fern was a puzzle in need of solving, and then nodded. 'Of course, love. Wherever you'll be most comfortable. And you're sure you don't want me to ring Paul? He'd be back in a flash; I know he would.'

Fern sighed. They'd been through all this twice already. Once when talking about the horrible flyer business over cardboard pizza that neither of them quite had the stomach for, jumping at every little sound from outside, and then again, just before bed, with Fern's reluctance to tell Paul still a bone of contention between the two of them. Tina had, eventually, promised to support her decision, but Fern knew what she was really thinking: *Surely he deserves to know what's happening? Deserves another chance?* To give Tina her due though, she never said as much out loud.

'No one's going to try anything at this time of night, anyway,' said Fern, with more certainty than she felt. It was a toss-up really: stay upstairs and be haunted by horrible dreams, or wait out the rest of the night on the sofa, worrying about some local weirdo

197

targeting their house. She probably *would* feel safer with Paul there beside her, but she was nothing if not stubborn. It had to be *his* choice, otherwise having him home again counted for nothing. 'Seriously, Tina, please don't call him. He'll be asleep anyway,' she added, hoping he wasn't. Hoping he was tossing and turning in some lumpy spare bed – on his own, obviously – racked with guilt for having stayed away another night. Hoping that he was missing her too much, too hard, to even *think* about sleep. But no sooner had Tina finished her fussing – 'Another blanket? Glass of water?' – and retreated back upstairs with strict instructions to wake her at the slightest sign of trouble, than Fern weakened, reaching for her phone to text him.

I can't sleep, she typed, the light from her screen dazzling against the low energy glow of the table lamp beside her. *Are you awake too?* There *was* a time he'd have been up texting half the night if they were apart. He was a whole lot soppier in those days than Tina gave him credit for. Proper long love letter texts they were too, hundreds of the things waiting for her on her phone when she woke up next morning.

I can't sleep without you there beside me: that's what he'd told her when he got back from that first overseas trip without her. Paris, wasn't it? Or Berlin . . . Some conference, anyway. *That's why I'm so shattered*, he'd whispered, lips nuzzling into the back of her neck, fingers already tracing a fresh pattern up her thighs. Pushing on through his alleged exhaustion with renewed commitment to the cause, while the Welcome Home dinner she'd slaved over all afternoon fossilized in the oven downstairs. *I'd be lost without you, Fern*, he murmured, even as he found her again . . .

The text took forever to go – the circular 'sending' icon whirling round and round on a seemingly endless loop. Long enough for Fern to change her mind again, anyway. To wonder if there was any way of *un*sending a text once the button had been pressed. But by then it was too late. Message delivered.

She pushed her phone aside, out of her eyeline, pretending she didn't care whether Paul replied or not. Pretending she wasn't scared, or lonely, or missing him so much it hurt. She must have managed the best part of a minute before fetching it back to make sure the volume was on.

Nothing.

Five minutes later she checked again, half-thinking she'd felt it vibrating (and that she'd somehow missed the 'ping'), tiny reverberations rippling along the sofa to find her.

Still nothing.

Screw you then, she whispered, reaching for the TV remote control instead. She switched it on, to fill the gap where his reply should have been, proving she had better things to do than wait around for him. Because sleeping definitely *wasn't* one of those better things, not with branches batting against the sitting-room window like knocking fingers. Not with the wind grinding something against the gate like the sound of slicing blades coming for her in the darkness. Not with that last dream still lying in wait . . . with Marte waiting there to finish what she'd started. And the fact that it was impossible, that there was no earthly way she really *could* swap her baby for Fern's – Sofia for Linette – made no difference at all. Everything about the woman was impossible.

Fern's hands went back to her belly as the TV flickered into life, to make sure the baby was all right. Still alive. Still kicking.

'Still you,' she whispered. 'Tell me it's still you in there.'

And then, without any warning, she was shaking again. Crying, and shaking, exactly like before. Only Tina wasn't there to hold her and make it better this time. And the longer Fern sat there, shaking and sobbing under her blankets, the darker the room seemed to get, despite the telly chattering softly to itself in the corner. Darker. Colder. Lonelier.

All she had to do was call for her; Fern knew that. Just one shout and Tina would be there, bustling round with tea and common sense, with wet flannels or extra pillows. With tablets for the fiery throb in Fern's ankle, reawakened by the awkward climb downstairs. But she didn't want Tina, she realised. She wanted Paul. She wanted him to need her, like she needed him. Two nights and one day – that's all it had been. Two nights. One day. Half a lifetime.

I can't sleep without you here beside me. That's why I'm so shattered. I'm lost without you Paul.

She'd never *been* so lost, with no chance of finding her way home because she didn't even know where that was anymore. *Please let's forget about Marte. Forget about Linny. Let's go back to you and me. You, me and the baby*, she corrected herself. If only they could. Even as another wave of anger rose up inside her – a fresh burst of hurt and resentment towards him for abandoning her when she needed him most – Fern would still have given anything to do just that. To forget about Marte and the nightmares, and the Linny-shaped hole inside her that refused to heal, and go back to how things used to be. Her and Paul together like a proper family.

Fern's finger hovered over the send button for a full ten seconds before her anger won out over her loneliness and she hit the backspace, deleting the lot.

Chapter 27

Tuesday was another late morning. Another groggy haze of confusion to blink away, while Fern worked out where she was and how she'd got there. For a moment she could have sworn she heard the baby monitor again – that same crackled singing as before – but no sooner had the thought lodged itself in her mind, than the singing stopped. *It must have been the TV*, she told herself. But when she turned her head to look, she realised it wasn't on anymore. Maybe Tina had crept in and turned it off while she was dozing.

Yesterday's ankle pain had given way to a numb heaviness, which felt like progress of sorts. That was until Fern tried to pull herself up or put any weight on it. The pain came shooting back quick enough then, to remind her how helpless she was. How trapped. But the baby was kicking away like a good'un and for a while that was enough. They'd made it through another night together, safe and sound, despite the nightmares. Despite everything.

And today? Today was the day Fern started fighting back. No more pussyfooting around the neighbours, hoping to steer the conversation towards Marte. Today was a day for answers. *Someone* must know where the woman was, or at least be able to explain what she'd been doing in their house that day . . .

Someone must be able to tell her *something* that would make sense of the blanket under the bath and the two 'first' babies, both with the same name yet somehow six years apart. And maybe that would be enough to finally break the woman's strange hold over Fern's imagination – and the house itself – putting an end to the nightmares. Then all she had to worry about was the vandalism and the business with the anonymous flyer . . .

Fern reached for her crutches and dragged herself up onto her feet to check whether the baby monitor was still in the bin, and saw that Tina had already started the day's quest for answers without her. Through a gap in the curtains, she could see her deep in conversation with Sean in the front garden. Hopefully Tina was doing a better job of quizzing him than Fern had managed the day before. If anyone could talk him into revealing secrets, it was her mother-in-law. *All right, all right. I'll tell you what you want to know. I'll tell you anything as long as you stop talking.*

Fern smiled to herself at the thought. Tina was in full flow already by the looks of it. There certainly seemed to be a fair bit of arm-flapping going on. And now Sean was . . . wait, where was he going? He was walking away from her, turning his back on her wild gesticulations. And then . . . well, Fern couldn't really tell what was happening after that – could only guess at what they were saying – but it wasn't long until Sean was on the move again. Back down the drive this time, in a hurry.

Damn! He was doing it again, wasn't he? Running away from their questions. Refusing to answer. Fern clenched her hands into helpless fists as she stood there, watching him go. She half expected to see Tina chasing after him, rugby-tackling him to the ground as he reached the pavement, pinning him down with thick cardiganed arms. Was that what Cagney and Lacey would have done, or would they have had guns? *Stay right there, Sean. You're not going anywhere. One false move and* . . . No, Fern couldn't quite see her mother-in-law with a revolver somehow. But Tina must have admitted defeat – Fern could hear her coming back in.

'Any luck getting to the bottom of it?' she asked, as her mother-in-law peeked round the sitting-room door to check on her.

'No,' said Tina. 'It could have been anybody.'

'What do you mean? It could be anybody with a spare key? Or it could have been anybody sneaking round with Marte?'

Confusion flickered across Tina's face. 'What? Oh, no, sorry, I didn't even get to *ask* him about Marte. And now he's had to rush off home to deal with his mum . . . Some crisis or other. He's her main carer, apparently so . . .'

Fern hadn't realised that – didn't even know he lived with his mum – but then why would she? Other than his occupation, his dog, and his unerring ability to be both pushy and reticent at the same time, she didn't know the first thing about the man. 'So what *were* you talking about?' she said, swallowing back her disappointment. So much for today being the day they finally found out the truth.

'Of course, you won't have seen it yet,' came the reply. 'Someone's gone and hacked off all the flowers in the front garden. That lovely *Camellia sasanqua* I was admiring at the weekend – I was even thinking of taking some late cuttings – *and* the cyclamen. Sean spotted it on his walk this morning and called round to let us know.'

'Oh, that was good of him,' said Fern. 'I didn't hear the door. But I *did* hear something in the night,' she said, remembering the metallic slicing sound. 'I assumed it was something catching on the gate.' If she'd thought to look out the window she might have caught them in the act. And by 'them' Fern meant some peculiar amalgamation of Marte and a sinister stranger in a black balaclava. Her imagination kept veering from one to the other, depending on her state of mind.

'I think we should call the police,' said Tina. 'Now that we've got some proper evidence to show them. I'll tell them about the flyer and the dog mess on the doorstep and *this*, and see what they have to say.' She shivered. 'I'm glad we got the locks changed when we did, otherwise . . .'

No, Fern didn't want to think about that otherwise. The idea made her feel sick and shaky. She closed her eyes as a wave of dizziness came for her, but things were just as bad when she opened them again.

'Hey,' said Tina, forcing her mouth up into a smile as she reached out a steadying hand. 'It's going to be all right. The police will know what to do. Then we can stop worrying, can't we?'

Can we?

'I mean it, Fern,' said Tina, giving her cheek a gentle squeeze. 'No more worrying, okay? It's not good for the baby. You sit yourself back down on the sofa and think about something nice instead. Think what you'd like for breakfast while I go and put the kettle on.' And with that she was gone, leaving Fern alone with nothing *but* worries.

Mindless vandalism, that was all. Local kids mucking around . . . nothing more than pranks and dares. That's what the police seemed to think anyway – as if teenagers were always carrying around a pair of secateurs – although they'd promised to send someone round at some point to file a report. Or maybe it wasn't secateurs. Maybe it was a knife. That was even worse though. Fern still felt cold and shivery inside at the thought of strange feet planted in the darkness outside her window, slicing away at those fragile stems, but Tina seemed reassured. For now, anyway. She was back to her usual chatty self afterwards, keeping up a steady stream of conversation over a belated breakfast of burned toast and jam.

'I almost forgot,' said Tina. 'I met Kerry, the lady from number six, when I popped back out to take garden photos for the police, in case they wanted to see them. I think it must have been when you were in the bathroom.'

'And?' asked Fern, wondering if she'd been equally as cold and unfriendly to Tina.

'And I asked her if she'd seen anyone suspicious lurking around our house in the dark last night, but she said she had an early night and slept straight through. Then I asked about Marte, but no luck there either.'

'And did you believe her?'

Tina thought for a moment. 'Hmm, I don't know,' she said. 'She seemed kind of cagey now I come to think about it. Pretty keen to get away, too. But maybe she was running late for work. She disappeared off at quite a lick when Yasmin came out to say hello . . . speaking of Yasmin, I asked her about piano tuners while we were talking and she knew just the chap. I'll give him a ring as soon as we're done here. And yes, before you ask, I *did* talk to Yasmin about her daughter,' Tina added. 'About seeing what else she might remember.'

Fern was waiting for the inevitable hitch. *But sadly she's on a three-month expedition to the North Pole. Unfortunately she's just joined a closed order of nuns and taken a vow of silence.*

'She said they normally have a phone catch-up over the weekend so she's going to ask her about Marte then,' continued Tina. 'I didn't really impress on her any sense of urgency, I'm afraid, because . . . well, I didn't want her to think I was weird. Or that *you* were weird, come to that, given you haven't even met her yet.'

'She probably thinks I'm unhinged already,' said Fern. 'I'm sure *someone's* filled her in on my moving-day meltdown by now.' Five days ago, that's all it was. Hard to believe, really. Which meant it had been five days since she'd last seen Linny as well. Five entire days. But the real shocker – the thing that hit Fern like an iron fist to her throat – was the jolting realisation that she'd stopped looking. She'd been so busy concentrating on Marte these last twenty-four hours or so – searching for signs of her wherever she went – that she'd shut her eyes to her own sister.

Oh, Linny, I'm sorry.

Please don't go.

Not yet.

'Are you all right?' asked Tina. 'You've gone awfully pale. You're not still worried about those pesky vandals, are you? You heard what the police said . . .'

Fern shook her head. Tina's conversation with the police hadn't exactly put her mind to rest. Someone could still get in through a window if they were *that* determined. Those single-glazed sashes didn't look like they'd offer much resistance. But that wasn't the issue. It was Linny. It was the empty space where Linny should have been.

'Is it your ankle again, love?'

'Yes,' Fern lied, too ashamed to admit the truth – that she'd forgotten her own sister. Even though that was exactly what everyone wanted her to do: Paul, Dr Earnshaw, and Tina too, most likely. They all wanted her to put Linny to rest and start moving on with her life. Start living again. But not like this, surely? Obsessing over a stranger, in a bid to prove her own sanity, wasn't living, was it? Chasing down one dead end after another in her growing desperation for answers – that didn't feel like much of a life either. As for snivelling through the night on the sofa because her husband refused to come home . . . surely that was the very opposite of living? It certainly wasn't Fern's idea of moving on. Moving backwards, more like.

One step forward,
two steps back,
the Bogeyman will get you
if your feet touch the crack.

'You poor thing,' said Tina. 'Never rains but it pours, eh?'

Hard enough to drown, thought Fern.

'I'll fetch you some more paracetamol, shall I? And maybe a fresh cup of tea to wash them down with?'

'Yes please.' *Might as well drown in tea as anything else.* 'I'll have the full caffeine version though this time, if that's okay,' said Fern. 'The stronger the better after last night.'

She waited for the soft tut of disapproval, the mini lecture. But they never came.

Tina turned back to her with a wink. 'Shame you're not allowed to drink in your condition. You look like you could do with a drop of the hard stuff.'

An entire bottle, thought Fern, miserably. She jumped as her phone vibrated in her dressing-gown pocket. It was a reply from Paul. *Finally.*

Sorry. Just seen your message now. Hope all OK. Talk soon x

She wasn't sure what to read into that – if there *was* anything to read into such a short, sterile reply – but it certainly didn't do anything to lift her mood. She felt cheated somehow, brushed-off and silly. And then she felt angry again.

That sealed it, Fern decided, pushing away the last few bites of blackened bread. Linny – that's who she needed now, whether Paul liked it or not.

'Aren't you going to eat that?' fussed Tina, coming back with a packet of paracetamol. 'Is it too burned? I'm sure I had it on the lowest setting.' *The curse of the Crenellation kitchen strikes again.* 'Do you want me to make some more?'

'No, really,' said Fern. 'I'm all done, thanks.' It wasn't just that it tasted of soggy charcoal, or that she'd lost her appetite stewing over Linny's continued absence. It wasn't even the thought of some stranger sneaking round the house. There simply wasn't enough room in her stomach for any more. That's what it felt like anyway. It was all baby down there now. A big fat healthy baby, despite everything.

'But I do have another favour to ask you,' she added. Linny might have been keeping her distance from *her* these last few days, but maybe Fern wasn't the only one she visited. She was thinking about her dad again, about what he'd told Anne and the other care-workers. *I've seen my girl . . . My lovely girl.* What if it really *was* Linny? There'd been no other visitors in the visitor book when Fern had checked last time. And what about poor confused Maisie, accusing Fern of bringing 'them all' with her.

207

Could *she* have been talking about Linny too?

'If I stick some clothes on,' said Fern, 'do you think you'd be able to drive me over to the care home? It's not far, and we can always go the back way while you're getting used to my car. You don't even have to come in, unless you want to.' It was a grim place at the best of times, although the staff did everything they could. And the chances of Dad knowing who Tina was – even after repeated introductions – were slim to non-existent. 'There are some nice shops nearby.'

'Of *course* I'll take you,' said her mother-in-law, with what sounded like genuine enthusiasm. Perhaps she was just glad to help, like she'd said the day before. *That's all I've ever wanted.* And maybe, for all Tina's jolly bravado, she still didn't feel a hundred per cent safe in the house either. 'A lovely man, your dad. Such a generous spirit. And that speech he made at your wedding . . . my goodness. Half the room was in tears by the time he'd finished. Me included.' She reached over the pot of jam and squeezed Fern's hand. 'I only wish I could have got to know him a bit better before . . . well, you know . . .'

Yes. Fern knew *exactly* what she meant.

'Such a cruel disease.'

Yes, Fern knew that too. Better than most. There was still the odd teasing glimpse of the man he'd been – the same warm, clever man who'd reduced a roomful of semi-strangers to tears – but those were few and far between now. He seemed to slip away a little further every time she saw him, until he felt like a semi-stranger himself – a muddled interloper who'd set up camp in the ravaged shell of her former father. But maybe today would be one of the good days. Maybe today he'd tell her about Linny. About how she still came to see him. Who knew, Fern thought with a glimmer of excitement, maybe Linny would be there too?

Chapter 28

The first person they saw in the care home lounge was Maisie, fully clothed this time, but no less agitated than before.

'It's you,' she hissed, staring up at Fern as they approached. 'Why do you keep coming here? And what's *she* doing with you?'

Fern froze. Did she mean Tina or someone else? Could it really be Linny?

'Who is it, Maisie? Who do you mean? Does she look like me?'

Maisie shook her head, her lower lip trembling. 'Why can't they just leave us alone? Why do they keep laughing? I don't like it when they laugh.'

'Hello there,' said Tina, crouching down beside her chair, seemingly unfazed by the peculiar exchange and the way the poor woman kept plucking at her own clothes. 'I'm Tina. I'm so sorry if we disturbed you. There's no one else with us though. No one's laughing. You're quite safe here.'

Maisie stopped her plucking and nodded solemnly, her pale grey eyes fixed on Tina's face.

'Bye for now,' said Tina, steering Fern on with cheerful calmness. But the smiles were all for show. 'It breaks your heart, doesn't it?' she murmured under her breath afterwards.

Speaking of which . . . thought Fern, catching sight of her dad across the room.

'Hello, sweetheart, this is a nice surprise,' he said, getting out of his armchair to fold her into a hug.

And so's this. Fern savoured the rare feel of his arms around her, trying to commit the sensation to memory, even as she was basking in it. As if she could save it up for a rainy day.

But today was all lucid sunshine, relatively speaking anyway, and brightness. Almost like old times, in fact. He didn't have a clue who Tina was, of course (she'd insisted on popping in, just to say 'hello'), but that didn't stop the pair of them chatting happily together about the daytime quiz show playing to itself at the other end of the lounge, once he'd satisfied himself that Fern's crutches weren't a sign of more serious injury. And once he'd got over the delayed shock of her belly – *I knew there was something different about you today!* – with the accompanying shock of his own impending grandfatherhood. *I'll never forget the day you girls were born . . .*

'Well, it's been lovely to see you again, William,' said Tina at last. 'I'll leave you two to catch up while I do some shopping.'

'Yes. You too, er . . .' He frowned. 'You'll have to excuse me, my mind's gone blank. It does that rather a lot, I'm afraid,' he added, ruefully.

'It's Tina, Dad,' Fern reminded him, trying to keep the heartache out of her voice. It was even harder to bear when he knew it himself, when he understood what it was he'd lost. 'Paul's mum.'

'Yes, of course. Paul's mum. That's right. Paul's mum,' he repeated, as if to anchor it down in his brain. 'And how is Paul?'

Tina hesitated for a moment, studiously avoiding Fern's eye. 'He's very well, thanks. Busy with work, you know how it is, but looking forward to becoming a dad. Not long now!'

'A dad? You mean . . .?' His eyes lit up with excitement all over again. 'You didn't tell me you were expecting. Wait 'til your mum hears about *this*,' he said, as Tina waved a discreet 'goodbye' to Fern, heading for the door.

'Mum's gone, Dad, remember? She's been gone a long time now.'

'Yes, yes, I know that, but . . .' He dropped down to a loud whisper, the leakproof pad on his chair creaking as he leaned forwards to share his secret. 'She still comes to see me. My girl.' He tapped the side of his head. 'In here, I mean. And here,' he added, touching his hand to his chest.

Oh. So his 'girl' wasn't Linny at all. But then Fern felt bad for being disappointed, for dismissing such a sweet revelation out of hand. 'Your girl?' she repeated, playing along. And yes, playing dumb too, in the selfish hope that she'd misunderstood and he *did* mean her sister.

'Maggie,' he said, with a shy smile. 'Your mum. She loved you girls so much, you know. Still, at least they're together now, that's something isn't it?'

Mum and Linny together. Fern wished she could believe in that too, as a good thing, as a source of comfort, rather than another reminder of her own abandonment.

'And Linny?' she insisted, just in case. 'Do you see her too?'

Her father looked hopeful for a moment.

'Not up here,' she said, tapping the side of her own head, mirroring his gesture. It made her think of Paul and their fateful showdown in the bathroom. She could still hear the fury and frustration in his voice as he drummed his fingers against his skull to show how crazy she'd become.

'No, not up here,' she said again, shaking the memory away. 'I'm not talking about that. I mean outside . . . in real life.'

Her father's face fell. 'Oh, my poor girl, I thought you knew. Didn't they tell you? Linny's . . . she's . . . oh, Fern. There's been an accident, my love. Your sister . . .' His eyes were already wet, fingers clenching into fists as he tried to find the words.

What had she done?

'No, no, it's all right,' Fern said, levering herself back out of her seat to comfort him, forgetting about her ankle in the heat

211

of the moment. The pain brought her up short with a reminder all of its own, her voice jumping the best part of an octave as the sharp spasms reclaimed her.

'Please, don't go upsetting yourself,' she squeaked, catching at the back of his chair for support, easing the weight off her offending foot. *Ahhh. That was better.* 'It's okay, honestly. Everything's going to be okay.' *Lies, lies and more lies.*

But her *real* dad had vanished, spirited away again before her eyes: 'Don't go *upsetting* myself?' he snapped, pity shifting to anger with alarming speed, as a switch flicked inside his brain, balled fists thumping, now, against his thighs. 'My little girl's gone, you heartless bitch. So don't you *dare* tell me it's okay, do you understand? My baby girl's gone and I wasn't there to save her. That might be okay where *you* come from but . . .'

And then, just like that, the switch flicked the other way again, the menace in his voice draining back to grief. It was a raw, fresh grief, utterly untouched by the passing months. 'I promised their mother I'd look after them. I *promised* her . . . and . . . and what about her sister?' he stammered. 'Like peas in a pod, they were. What will I tell her sister?'

It wasn't much of a hug – a lopsided one-armed effort was the best she could manage at that angle, but Fern squeezed the jutting bone of his shoulder tight, resting her lips on the top of his head. 'Shh, it's me, Dad – it's Fern. I'm right here.'

'Fern,' he said. 'Of course it is. My little Fern.' His fists unfurled, fingers reaching up to find her. 'I'm sorry, love. I was just thinking about Linny. She's not here anymore though, is she?'

'Linny?' It was hard to keep up with such dizzying changes of mood and cognizance. It was her own fault though. She shouldn't have said anything in the first place. All she'd done was upset him, and for what? Poor old Linny could have cartwheeled round the lounge to a full bagpipe rendition of 'Sister Midnight' and there was no guarantee he'd remember it ten minutes later. 'No, that's right. Linny's not here, Dad.' She probably never was, either. It was merely wishful thinking on Fern's part, clutching at straws to atone for the sin of forgetting. Of giving too much space in her head to Marte, and not enough to her beloved twin.

The squeeze of his fingers on hers became more insistent. 'Have you seen her?' he asked. 'Your sister? I don't like to think of her all alone out there, with no one to talk to.'

'At the cemetery, you mean?' Fern held her breath, wishing she could take back the question as soon as she'd uttered it. At the rate he was going today, he'd probably have forgotten again already: *What do you mean, the cemetery? What's happened to my Linny?*

But he hadn't forgotten at all. He nodded – a heavy sombre nod – as if he couldn't quite bring himself to answer with words.

The truth was Fern hadn't been back to her sister's grave since the day of the funeral. She'd never needed a headstone to weep at and couldn't bear to think of her other half, her better half, lying there under the soil, in the cold and the damp and the darkness. And why would she, anyway, when she still saw Linny every day? In the flat; on the street; even in Dr Earnshaw's office that one time, although she'd kept that particular sighting to herself. Only now it had been five whole days without so much as a glimpse.

'I'll go tomorrow,' Fern promised. It might not be so bad, so bleak, now that the ground had settled . . . though even the *thought* of the soil searching out its new level round the sides of her sister's coffin, was enough to make her retch.

'And take her some tulips from me.' Her dad nodded to himself at some unspoken memory. 'She always did love tulips, didn't she? Make sure they're red ones though – they're her favourite.'

'Yes, Dad,' Fern said, even though it was entirely the wrong season for tulips, red or otherwise. Even though they'd been their mum's favourite flower, not Linny's. *She* preferred roses. (Right colour, wrong bloom.) 'Two bunches,' she told him, steeling herself to see it through, to make up for her recent neglect. 'One from you and one from me.' She should have made herself go before now. Should have taken some flowers, at the very least, a soft red pillow to keep her sister's head warm.

'And tell Linnaea I'm thinking of her,' he begged. 'Be sure to tell her that. Tell her I'll be there just as soon as I can . . . as soon as I get out of here.' He let go of Fern's hand, pointing back towards his own chest, but she pretended not to see. She pretended he was talking about the care home instead – a plea for day release, that was all, not *life* release. It was selfish of her, Fern knew that, but she wasn't ready to let him go. Not yet. Even though in many ways, he'd already gone.

Chapter 29

Paul might still be missing in action, but the house seemed full of men all the same that afternoon: a piano tuner – thanks to a last-minute cancellation – and an engineer to set up the phone line and Wi-Fi. Two for the price of one.

Tina had bustled off into the kitchen with coffee orders, leaving Fern to field any questions from the ankle-elevated comfort of the sofa. Not that there *were* any questions, which was just as well given the engineer had already left by the time she woke up from her impromptu nap.

It must have been the sound of his shouted 'cheerio' and the door shutting behind him that roused her, but not for long. Fern hadn't felt remotely sleepy before, that was the funny thing, but *now*, after a power nap taster, she felt positively drugged with tiredness. She listened for a moment to the sound of the piano moving through its octaves; to Tina's voice rising and falling alongside it; to the faint crackle of a baby monitor, and then shut her eyes a second time, powerless to resist.

Satie's 'Gympnopédie, No.1' drifted through her dreams, but that was all: a muted soundtrack playing somewhere in the distance – the piano tuner, in the dining room maybe, or her and Linny back in Mrs Jackson's lounge – but no images to tie the music to. At least, nothing she remembered when she yawned and stretched some two hours later to find half the afternoon gone.

'There now,' said Tina, already on hand, somehow, with steaming cups of tea. 'Don't you look better for a bit of shut eye?'

'I *feel* better,' Fern told her. She might not have caught up on *all* the hours she'd missed lately, but it was a good start and a proper Marte-free rest.

Tina put their mugs down on some hideous butterfly coasters that had somehow found their way to the new house. Fern could have sworn she'd put them in the charity box along with the other unwanted stowaways, but Tina must have rescued them when no one was looking. For some reason the sight of them made her smile now though. Their very naffness felt like a protection of sorts against the dark thoughts jostling for her attention. *Begone foul spirits of the night or ye shall feel the full force of my scallop-edged coaster set . . .*

'Paul rang a little while ago to check whether we were all connected now,' said Tina, perching on the far arm of the sofa. 'Which we were, obviously, otherwise he wouldn't have been able to get through. And to apologise for not passing the message on about the engineer coming. He was in a meeting when he got the text yesterday, apparently' – she rolled her eyes, on cue – 'and it slipped his mind. Though I rather suspect he was ringing for some advice as well.'

'About me?' *What do you think, Mum? Should I stay or should I go? Will I still have a shot at custody if I leave her now?*

'About this evening,' Tina said. 'He's decided to stay another night with this friend of his – Simon – as he's got an early client meeting in that neck of the woods scheduled for tomorrow. Apparently Simon's booked them in for some evening retreat whatsit at the local church – combatting the stresses of modern life through silent contemplation and prayer, I think he said – but Paul had forgotten about the antenatal group at this pub. He wanted to know if he should cancel on Simon and come home instead.'

Fern frowned. Were they talking about the same Paul? The Paul who'd turned down the role of godfather to his oldest friend's son because he'd have felt like a fraud when it came to the religious promises? The same Paul who'd pretty much insisted on a civil service rather than a church wedding because religious vows felt too much like hypocrisy?

'Do you believe him?' she asked.

Tina looked at her in surprise. 'What do you mean?'

'Do you buy that story about the church meeting? Or do you think it's something else keeping him away? *Someone* else?' Fern felt physically sick as an image of Paul with his arms wrapped round another woman nudged its way into her brain.

'No, no, Fern, you mustn't think that. Paul loves you; I know he does. He's just a little lost at the moment, that's all. Who knows, maybe this stress workshop thing is just what he needs.'

What he *needs?* thought Fern, bitterly. She was the one dealing with all the stress. She was the one trapped in the house, in the pain and clumsiness of her own body, with only Tina and the Demon Flower-Cutter of Crenellation Lane for company. She was the one doing battle with cursed electrics and nightly terrors in a place she was rapidly coming to hate, with half the street giving her the cold shoulder and the other half lying to her face, while Paul was . . . well, who knew what *he* was doing?

'He loves you,' Tina said again, as if repeating it would make it true. 'And once we've got to the bottom of this Marte business there'll be no reason for him to stay away, will there? Everything can go back to normal.'

'I suppose so,' agreed Fern, praying that she was right. Praying that it wasn't already too late. 'So what did you tell him?'

'I told him to go ahead with his retreat because we'd already got the antenatal thing sorted.' Tina looked worried for a moment. 'That *was* right, wasn't it?'

'Yes,' said Fern. As furious as she was with him for staying away, it would be a whole lot trickier pumping Nicky for Marte information with Paul in tow. 'You didn't mention anything about my ankle then?' *Or the flowers? Or the flyer?*

'Nope. Not a word about that, just like you asked. Although I might have mentioned something about getting his bloody act together sooner rather than later if he knows what's good for him. In my very best telling-off voice, naturally.'

Fern grinned, despite herself. Despite everything. 'And he was suitably scared, I take it?'

'Terrified,' Tina said, grinning back at her. 'I've still got it, you know. Once a mum, *always* a mum. He'll be back home on that naughty step before you know it.'

Fern threw herself back into the investigation, towards the end of the afternoon, in an effort to take her mind off her failing marriage. In an effort to *save* her failing marriage. She sent Tina off on a door-to-door interrogation of the neighbours at the top end of the street, while she hobbled her way around the remaining houses down at their end. Divide and conquer. That was the way to do it.

The elderly lady at number one remembered *someone* matching Marte's description from a few years back, but her eyesight had deteriorated so much since then that she probably wouldn't recognise her anymore. The owner of number three turned out to be the hospital porter Fern had met at April's party – the one who worked night shifts, whose name she still couldn't remember – and there was no one in over the road at number two. But Fern struck gold at number four, with Callie, a round-faced woman with dyed red hair that was starting to grow out and an impressive array of old-fashioned bangles. She'd only been living in the street for a year herself, after a lottery win that allowed her to give up work and relocate to be nearer her children, but she *had* seen Marte, she was sure of it. At least, she'd seen a thirty-something lady with long blonde hair and blue eyes – 'just like you,' she said – but it wasn't on Crenellation Lane. It was at a swanky bar in the city where Callie had arranged to meet her blind date. The reason she remembered it so clearly wasn't because of the date though; it was because of who the blonde lady was there with. . . .

Fern held her breath as Callie leaned towards her with a conspiratorial whisper. 'Richard,' she said. 'Richard Brantley from up the road. I hadn't met his wife back then, but I'd seen her on the street. And I knew she didn't look like that.'

'Richard?' Fern repeated, feeling strangely giddy at the revelation. So Eddie had been right about the secret woman in the city. It had to be Marte. *She* was the one Richard was besotted with.

Callie nodded. 'They clearly weren't there on a business meeting either.'

'And did you say anything?' asked Fern, still reeling from this new information.

'Not to him, no,' said Callie. 'He hadn't seen me, and I wanted to keep it that way. As for Kerry – that's his wife – I didn't know what to do for the best. As I say, I'd never even met her before. But if it was *me*, I'd want to know. My ex-husband was a two-timing rat as well,' she added, with a bitter laugh. 'In the end I took the coward's way out and popped an anonymous note through the door after he'd left for work.'

Another anonymous note. Was that how things worked on Crenellation Lane?

'And did she confront him about it, do you know?' Fern knew how nosy she sounded but she didn't care. The answers to the Marte mystery were in touching distance now and she'd take whatever information she could find.

Callie shook her head. 'I've no idea. They're still together, so who knows. You won't say anything though, will you?' she checked, as if she'd suddenly realised how indiscreet she'd been. 'I wouldn't want them knowing it was me who sent that note. It's a bit awkward when you live on the same street.'

'Of course not,' said Fern. 'That's been really helpful, thank you. It was good to meet you.'

Fern's body was crying out for a rest as she hobbled back down the path. The pain in her ankle had flared up again, and her arms and back – all of her – ached from the crutches. But she pushed through her discomfort and hobbled on up the road to number six, Richard and Kerry's house. The sooner she talked to Richard, the sooner she'd get to the bottom of it all.

There was no red Audi on the drive when she got there. He'd still be at work, wouldn't he? *Curses.* Fern toyed with knocking anyway and asking Kerry when he'd be back – she even got as far as the front door – but then her courage failed her. Maybe she should wait until she'd talked it through with Tina. Until she'd worked out exactly what she was going to say.

'Hello. Can I help you?'

Fern turned her head to see Kerry coming up the drive behind her, looking as unfriendly as ever.

'Oh,' Fern stammered. 'Er, yes, hello again. I was just wondering when Richard was due back. I wanted to ask him about . . .' Her mind had gone blank. All she could think about was Richard and Marte canoodling in some fancy bar. 'About . . . electricians. He mentioned something about a good one to Paul when he was round the other day, but he forgot to write it down.'

'An electrician?' Kerry's mouth curled up in a sneer. 'I see. Well, I'll be sure to pass the message on.'

'Right,' said Fern, anxious to be gone. After everything she'd heard about Kerry – about her problems conceiving and her cheating husband – she ought to feel sorry for the woman. But her open unpleasantness made it hard. 'Thank you. That would be great.'

Tina's investigations hadn't turned up anything very useful. No one at the top end of the street seemed to have any idea who Marte was, no one except for Sean's ailing mum. But Sean had arrived home from a gardening job just as Tina had finally worked the conversation round to Norwegian girlfriends, and he was having none of it, sending Tina packing with a huffy lecture about a lack of consideration for his mum's health. The episode had rather taken the wind out of Tina's sails and she wasn't nearly as excited by the news of Richard's marital indiscretion as Fern had hoped.

'It might *not* have been her though,' Tina pointed out, through a mouthful of Spanish omelette. Any talk of Marte had been pushed back to dinner, to make sure Fern got some rest after her investigative exploits. 'Long blonde hair and blue eyes could describe any number of women.'

'I suppose so,' Fern said, feeling deflated. 'I just thought . . .' *I thought I might finally be able to put this mess behind me. I thought this was my chance to put an end to the nightmares and the weirdness, and get my marriage back on track.* Even now she could feel the familiar nightly dread creeping back as darkness took hold outside. She could feel Marte waiting in the shadows to reclaim her rightful place in her dreams.

'Don't get me wrong,' said Tina, reaching across the table and squeezing her arm. 'It's a good lead. A *really* good lead. But I don't think we should get ahead of ourselves just yet. Not until we've had a chance to talk to Richard. We need to think of a way to get him on his own. It's not a conversation we can have with Kerry there.' A fleck of eggy potato flew across the table as she attempted to talk and chew at the same time. What little appetite Fern might have had fizzled away to nothing at the sight of a glistening speck centimetres from her water glass. She put down her knife and fork and tried not to look as queasy as she felt.

'And in the meantime,' said Tina, shovelling in another mouthful, 'we should go to this antenatal thing and try and track down this Nicky of yours. Richard will still be there tomorrow, but you might not get the chance to talk to *her* for another fortnight. It might be too late by then.'

Too late? Was Tina referring to Paul? Was that how long she thought their marriage had left to run?

'She might have had the baby by then,' Tina finished.

Her baby. Yes, of course.

'And I'm not sure your nerves will manage another fortnight either.'

'No,' agreed Fern, pushing her plate away. The thought of still being in the same situation in two weeks' time filled her with genuine panic. She'd practically be due by then. Coming up to thirty-eight weeks anyway, which, as Fern knew all too well, was when *her* mum had gone into labour. *I'll never forget the day you girls were born ....*

What kind of state would she be in by then if the nightmares continued? If they carried on escalating? Two more weeks without proper sleep? Fern needed answers now. She needed to break Marte's hold on her imagination once and for all if she wanted to stop those cold, cold hands reaching back into her open stomach for her baby.

Chapter 30

They were late getting to the pub, thanks to the shocking discovery of a red-painted STAY OUT message scrawled up the side of the house, plus another phone call to the police. Fern had mistaken the paint for blood at first – like a supernatural warning from some kitschy horror film and was relieved to realise it must have been someone creeping round outside their house in the early evening darkness instead. Someone who wanted them gone so badly that they couldn't even wait until the middle of the night to carry out the next stage of their campaign. Who'd risk detection just to show Fern how much they wanted them gone. The relief, when she thought it through like that, had been pretty short-lived. Tina was clearly shaken too but insisted that they went along to the antenatal group as planned. She refused to be intimidated, she said, but Fern suspected it had more to do with putting some distance between them and the house than anything else.

Someone had parked them in over the course of the afternoon, which didn't help matters either. Tina wasn't the best at getting out of tight spaces, especially not with her nerves in such a fragile state. She was used to her own little car, she kept saying, as they inched forwards and backwards, forwards and backwards, to little discernible effect. Eddie had taken pity on them in the end – he must have been watching them from his window – and came out in his slippers to oversee the manoeuvre.

He hadn't seen any sign of paint-wielding vandals through the window though, which made Fern wonder if *he* was behind the message. Maybe his story that he was eating dinner at the time was just that: a story. But then she felt bad for thinking ill of him while he was out there in his slippers acting the good neighbour. Whoever was behind it all was certainly doing a good job of making her paranoid. It wasn't enough that she suspected everyone she met of lying about Marte. Now she'd started suspecting them all of targeting the house as well. But maybe that's because the two were connected. STAY OUT – that's what the message had said, not GET OUT . . . as in *STAY OUT OF IT*? Perhaps the perpetrator *had* been disturbed, before they could finish painting their warning. Maybe it was Fern's questions about Marte that had kicked off the attacks on the house, and now, after an afternoon of door-to-door questioning, their attacker had taken it up a gear. There was no time to dwell on that now though – Tina was a woman on a mission. No sooner were they out of the parking space than she was off, speeding away down the lane with a hurried wave of thanks to Eddie, almost colliding with Richard at the end of the road.

'Sorry,' Tina mouthed at him through the windscreen. 'Still getting used to the steering in this thing.' It wasn't her fault though. At least it didn't seem like it from where Fern was sitting. Richard was the one swerving onto the wrong side of the road, looking pale-faced and shocked in the sudden glare of their lights, as if he'd given himself a bit of a turn. He put up his hand by way of an apology and the two cars edged past each other without further incident. It hardly delayed them by much – not compared to the paint and the parking space – but Fern couldn't help wondering, as they drove off, if it was a sign. A sign that they should have struck while the iron was hot – pulled over and tackled him straight away, before he got home – and found out the truth about him and Marte, regardless of what dangerous feathers it might ruffle. But by the time they were back on the main road, it was too late. As far as that night's quest for answers went, it was Nicky or bust . . .

Bust.

She wasn't there. Fern sensed her absence the moment they walked in, and a quick scan of the room only confirmed it.

Crap, crap, and double crap.

It all looked cosy enough if you liked that kind of thing, but it wasn't Fern's cup of tea. Intimate baby talk with people she'd never met was the last thing she felt like. The last thing she felt capable of, with so much else on her mind. *So you'd recommend chilled cabbage leaves for painful breasts, would you? Interesting. And what about non-existent Norwegians unzipping your stomach while you're asleep? Got any hot tips for that?*

'We were just discussing the merits of controlled crying,' said a round-faced lady, as Fern and Tina took their seats at one of the tables. 'My sister swore by it with her two.'

It was all Fern could do to control her *own* crying. To keep from bursting into tears in front of a room full of strangers. Why did she let Tina talk her into this? And why wasn't Nicky there?

Tina was in her element though: 'Oh yes,' she said. 'I read a really interesting article about that the other day . . .'

Fern must have switched off not long afterwards, lost in her own gloomy thoughts. Thinking of all the questions she *would* have asked Nicky if she'd actually turned up: questions about the embroidered blanket under the bath and the missing baby, Marte's *other* first baby. The other Sofia. She didn't notice the latest arrivals, clattering in with their shiny new car seat and oversized changing bag. She didn't even look up until the baby started crying. But suddenly there she was, Natural Birth Nicky herself, looking smug and exhausted in equal measure, with her proud partner in tow and an angry little bundle in a yellow Babygro, who seemed about as pleased to be there as Fern. Until now, that was. Now Fern couldn't have been more pleased if she tried. And when the rest of the room erupted in a spontaneous round of applause – *well done, you squeezed out an entire person and you're still able to walk!* – which only made the baby cry louder, Fern clapped so hard she sent both crutches flying.

There was an air of weariness about Nicky's husband when he finally shook hands with Fern, as if the sleepless nights were proving too much for him already. Or maybe it was all the cooing and back-slapping he'd had to contend with that evening, as he and Nicky worked their way round the rest of the group, showing off baby Bruges (what a name!) and imparting parental wisdom from The Other Side. Perhaps he was simply exhausted by the sheer effort of maintaining a smile through endless accounts of his wife's labour, which seemed to grow louder and more graphic with every retelling. By the time the couple reached Fern, she was more intimately acquainted with the dilatory progress of Nicky's cervix than she'd have previously thought possible. She could probably have given a passable academic paper on the contents of the woman's bowels as well, with particular reference to what did or didn't float in the birthing pool. And on what her husband did or didn't manage to scoop out with the net provided . . .

'Hi Fern, good to meet you,' he said, smiling on bravely. 'I'm Ant. And you're the proud new owner of number seven, Crenellation Lane, I believe? Small world, eh? That's how Nicky and I met. I expect she told you.'

'Yes,' said Fern, although 'proud' wasn't *quite* the word she'd have chosen. *Try 'scared'*, she thought. *Try 'miserable'*. 'Small world indeed. Tina and I have been trying to track down one of Nicky's other housemates from that time. Marte Hortlassen? Do you remember her?'

'Marte . . . hmm . . . the name sounds familiar . . .'

'Yes, *you* know,' cut in Nicky. 'That Norwegian lady in the funny attic room upstairs. Sorry, no offence,' she added, turning to Fern. 'I'm sure it's lovely up there now.'

Fern realised she'd been holding everything in – breath; muscles; hope against desperate hope of getting some answers – and forced the air back out of her lungs as she replied. 'No, no, none taken. To be honest, it's just a normal attic now.' *Marte's attic.*

'Oh wait,' said Ant. 'Yes, I *do* know who you mean. She's the one who did a bunk when everyone else was out for the night, isn't she? Ran off back to Norway without paying her share of the bills. Owed a full month's rent as well.'

'She certainly did.' Nicky still sounded put out about it some six years later. 'Had us all thinking she was the perfect housemate up 'til then. Bit quiet, maybe, tended to keep herself to herself, but that's not a bad thing when you're sharing with people you don't know, and she was good company once she warmed up . . .'

Fern nodded along encouragingly. *This* was what they'd been waiting for: someone who'd not only known Marte but was willing to talk about her. Tina was all ears too, her face a perfect picture of concentration. Mentally jotting it all down in her notebook, most likely.

'. . . Had a nice couple of chats with her over a bottle of wine,' Nicky reminisced. 'You know, proper heart-to-hearts. Though I might have imagined the wine bit, now I come to think of it, given she was pregnant.'

Eddie was right, then. And Yasmin's daughter. Marte had definitely been pregnant six years ago. Which presumably meant that Fern had been right too. Something must have happened . . . something that didn't bear thinking about. That baby *couldn't* have survived if Marte was expecting her first child when she showed her around the house.

Fern touched her hands to her own stomach, feeling a sudden surge of pity for the woman who'd been making her nights such a misery. But the Marte she was hearing about now wasn't the

227

Marte of her dreams, the one who unzipped people's stomachs as they lay sleeping. No, this was the Marte she'd met at the house that day, the unassuming mother-to-be with the low clipped voice and the smile reflected in the hall mirror.

Imagine going through that on your own, Fern thought, coping with that kind of loss all alone in a foreign country. Maybe that explained her sudden disappearance, leaving Nicky and her fellow housemates in the lurch. She must have gone back home to be with her family, to grieve in her own language, amongst her own people. What it *still* didn't explain was what Marte was doing back in the house six years later.

'Do you know what happened to it?' Fern said, lowering her voice. It wasn't an ideal question to be asking in a roomful of expectant mothers. 'The baby, I mean.'

Nicky looked suitably aghast. 'What? It was a perfectly normal pregnancy as far I know. A few issues with the father, from what I gathered, but the baby was fine. It was certainly all going smoothly when *I* last saw her . . .'

'Oh no,' said Fern, quickly, 'I didn't mean anything *bad*.' That was a lie of course, but given that Nicky seemed as much in the dark as anyone about Sofia's real fate, it seemed better to keep the conversation light and let her chatter on.

The other woman thought for a moment. 'She must have been about five months by then, I suppose. She'd certainly started buying baby clothes – little dresses and things – and someone she knew had given her a second-hand monitor. I helped her test it out, seeing if it could pick up the signal from two floors away. Oh, and that blanket she was making. That's right. It's all coming back to me now. Really sweet it was: a little red blanket with the baby's name embroidered in the corner . . . something pretty and girly . . . Sarah, was it? Sophie?'

'Sofia,' said Fern, a chill running through her at the memory of the filthy, ragged version Barry had found under the bath. At the thought of the baby monitor Paul had discovered in the attic.

Could it really be the same one? Still playing to itself six years later? No. That was crazy.

'Yes, of course, Sofia.' Nicky flashed her a quick smile of satisfaction, and then her expression darkened again, a defensive edge creeping into her voice. 'I did *try* contacting her after she left, and not just about the unpaid bills, either. I wanted to make sure everything was okay. Goodness knows how many messages I left on her mobile, and she never replied to any of them. I even rang the number I had for her in Norway . . .'

'You don't still have her number now by any chance, do you?' Tina cut in. 'Only there's a box of stuff in the attic we're pretty sure belongs to her, some of it quite personal . . . Or a contact for the father, maybe? Is he still around, do you know?'

Smoothly done, thought Fern, genuinely impressed. Who would have guessed her blunt, forthright mother-in-law possessed such tactful detective skills? *Eat your heart out, Miss Marple.*

'I might do, actually,' said Nicky. 'I tend to copy everything over when I get a new phone.' She handed the baby to Ant, kissing the top of his head as he left her arms. 'There we go, sweetheart, you have a nice cuddle with Daddy while Mummy finds her phone . . . So much stuff,' she mused, emptying her bag out onto the table. A fold-out changing mat. Wipes. Nappies. Nappy sacks. Breast pads. Lots of breast pads. A tub of something advertising itself as Baby Bottom Balm. An empty-looking tube of calendula cream. 'A total lifesaver once you start breastfeeding,' she assured Fern. 'I'd stock up on some ready if I were you.' Another tube of calendula cream, fuller this time. 'Trust me, your nipples will thank you for it. Ah, here we are. Right at the bottom, naturally.' She pulled out a leather-cased phone and scrolled down through an impressively long contact list. Fern wasn't sure she'd *ever* known that many people. 'Let's see . . . M . . . yes, here we go. Looks like we're in luck – a mobile number *and* a home one. Have you got something to write with? Or I can text them to you if that's easier.'

Tina was on it before Fern could reply, pulling out her

notebook and pen in record speed. 'I always carry a little pad in my handbag,' she explained. 'Never know when I might need it.' She copied the two numbers down carefully, reading them back afterwards to make doubly sure. 'And the father,' she prompted. 'What did you say his name was again? Just in case . . .'

Nicky looked doubtful all of a sudden. Suspicious even. But Tina, it seemed, knew exactly how to play it, diverting attention away from the oddness of the question by turning it on Ant instead. 'Did you know him too?' she said. 'One of the other students, I presume?'

And that was all it took – Nicky couldn't resist. 'It's no good asking *him*,' she laughed. 'He used to run away at the first sign of girl talk. He'd come into the kitchen to get some food or a drink, whatever it was, only to scurry away again, empty-handed.'

Ant laughed too, bouncing on the balls of his feet in a gentle rocking motion as his son began to wriggle. 'Just trying to respect your privacy, that's all. Like the true gentleman I was.' Bruges sniffled and moaned, an odd mewing sort of noise, like a baby animal. 'Anyway, I *do* know who the father was. That funny bloke who was always hanging around the place . . . the one who gave her the old map of Westerton that used to hang in the dining room. The one who did the lawn.'

Fern blinked. Not the same old map she'd bought in the charity shop for Paul? The one hanging on the dining-room wall even now? Just a coincidence, surely. Except somehow she knew it wasn't. She could feel it in the pit of her stomach, beneath the baby's sudden flurry of kicks. There was something about the way it had called to her from the charity shop window. The way it sat in the space above the fireplace as if it had always belonged there. It must have stayed with the house from one owner to the next, becoming as much a part of the fabric of the place as the carpets or the built-in shelves in the sitting room. But then all thoughts of maps were forgotten again when she realised who Ant was talking about.

The one who did the lawn . . .

No. It couldn't be. Could it?

Ant nodded. 'Shane,' he announced triumphantly. 'You see, I even remembered his name.'

'Sean,' corrected Nicky. 'His name was Sean . . .'

So Eddie was right about that too. Did that mean Richard was just a red herring? Or were they all mixed up in this together?

'. . . And he wasn't really the father as it turned out.'

Fern stared at Nicky, trying to process the new pieces of the puzzle. Trying to make sense of everything. So the father wasn't Sean after all? Did that put Richard back in the frame then? But if Sean was the one who'd bought Marte that map, why did he insist he'd never heard of her? And why would Marte have come back, six years later, to the house where she'd lost her baby? Something wasn't right. Fern could feel it in her bones. In the sudden stillness of her own baby – little Linette – lying like a weight inside of her.

Chapter 31

The room dropped quiet, baby yoga and raspberry leaf tea conversations all petering out at the same time. It felt as if *everyone* was waiting to hear who the father was, the entire expectant parent population of Westerton holding its collective breath. Until baby Bruges broke the silence with a series of sobs, crescendo-ing into a red-faced wail.

'So, who was it then?' asked Fern, raising her voice in an effort to compete. But Nicky had already lost interest in the conversation, switching back into full-on mother-mode at the first whimper. She was reaching out to take the baby, muttering something under her breath about bath times and car seats.

Please. Keep going. You can't stop there.

'Come on now, Mummy's got you. Shh, that's it, you've done so well . . . all these strange people, eh?' The wailing subsided as the baby nuzzled into her chest, sniffling and rooting round like a blind puppy. 'We should probably think about getting you home.'

No, not yet. Not 'til you tell us the father's name. Was it Richard or not?

'Who was the father then? Someone on the street?' Fern prompted, thinking of Richard's pale face staring back at them through the windscreen of his car. But then again, they were talking about something that had happened six years ago now, and Callie's sighting of Richard playing away in the city was only in the last twelve months. Even if it *had* been Marte who Callie had seen him with that day, it didn't necessarily mean they'd been together all those years before. The father might still turn out to be someone else altogether. Maybe Casanova Eddie himself. 'Was it someone on Crenellation Lane?' she asked again, willing baby Bruges to fall asleep in his mother's arms and let Nicky carry on where she'd left off.

'What?' Nicky looked up in surprise, as if she'd forgotten they were there. 'Oh, no, I don't know who it was, sorry. Marte never mentioned anything about him. Some guy she met in the city, I assume. She used to commute in a couple of days a week for her course.'

Fern bit back her disappointment. It certainly didn't rule Richard out, given what Callie had seen, but she'd been hoping for something more concrete to go on.

'All I know is Sean wanted her to move in with him and his mum – wanted them all to play happy families – and she couldn't go through with it. Said she was going to tell him the truth – that the baby wasn't his.' Nicky scooped bottom balm and wipes back into her bag, one-handed, as she finished talking, already something of a pro at motherly multi-tasking.

'And did she?' asked Tina, reaching over the table to help her.

'I guess so, given what happened afterwards,' said Nicky with the tiniest of glances towards Ant, as if she was weighing up whether she should say any more.

What? What happened afterwards?

'And the next thing anyone knew she was gone,' Nicky finished, 'leaving us to cover all the bills.'

Ant cleared the repacked changing bag off the table and put the car seat down in its place, holding back the cushioned straps while Nicky lowered the baby in. Bruges was already grizzling again.

Oh crap. They really *were* going, weren't they?

Fern touched her hand to Nicky's arm. 'And Sean? Did you see *him* afterwards? Where did *he* say she'd gone?' *Come on, come on. Just a few more questions . . .*

Nicky didn't seem to have heard, at first, ignoring the press of Fern's fingers on her sleeve. She clicked the straps into the buckle, leaning into the car seat to plant a kiss on Bruges' snub little nose. 'There now. All safe and snug.' And when she finally did answer, she was still in full singsong baby-speak mode. 'He said she'd gone back to Norway to be with her family, didn't he, Brugey-Wugey? Yes, he did.'

And . . . and . . .

But there was no 'and'.

'Come on then,' said Ant. 'Let's get this little feller home for his bedtime bath and massage. Nice to meet you.'

'Yes,' said Nicky, straightening back up. 'Good to see you again. Best of luck with it all . . .'

It took Fern a moment to realise what she meant. *Ah yes, of course.* She was talking about the birth, wasn't she? The mere act of pushing out a fully formed human being. Not about Marte.

'Maybe we could pop round for that coffee sometime in the new year? It'd be nice to see the old place again.'

'Yes,' said Fern, swallowing down her frustration. Swallowing down the questions she never got to ask: *And did you believe Sean when he said that? What about when you rang that number in Norway? Did you get to speak to her family? What did they say?* 'Of course,' she agreed. 'That would be lovely.'

Fern and Tina sat in the car, watching the other mums-to-be waddling out into the night, dutiful husbands and partners pinned to their sides. A few shouted goodbyes across the pub car park and then they were off, driving back to their nice stalker-free houses, to carry on their nice, cosy countdowns to the big day.

'We haven't even bought a pram yet,' said Fern. 'Or a car seat. We must be the least prepared parents ever.'

'Don't be silly,' Tina told her. 'Everyone would be the same in your boat. No sense filling the flat with extra stuff when you're trying to move, is there? Besides, there's still plenty of time for all that. You can probably order most things online now. I bet they even do next-day delivery.'

'I suppose.' But it wasn't only about changing tables and travel systems, was it? Fern wasn't mentally prepared for her baby yet either. How could she be? All those months where she'd thought of nothing but Linny . . . then the move . . . and now Marte. There wasn't enough room in her head for the sort of baby chatter everyone else seemed so concerned with. Or maybe her brain wasn't tuned to the right frequency yet: Expectant Mother FM. Maybe that was the problem, too much interference.

'So, what next then, Lacey?' Tina asked. 'Unless you'd rather be Cagney?'

Fern forced a smile. 'Whoever does the least running. I'll be that one.' Her smile faded again. 'I think we should try ringing those numbers we got from Nicky. I'm not sure I can wait until we get home.' *I'm not even sure I want to go home*, she added silently, thinking about the painted message on the wall. But if the Marte mystery and the vandalism really *were* linked, then getting to the bottom of it all was more urgent than ever.

'I agree.' Tina switched on the overhead light and pulled out her notebook, leafing through it until she found the right page. 'Are you going to do the honours or do you want me to?'

'I'll do it,' said Fern, sounding more certain than she felt. 'I need to see this thing through to the end.' She took a deep breath in and out, trying to psyche herself up for another awkward phone call. Trying to work out what she'd say if she actually got to speak to Marte. *Just tell me what you were doing there that day and get the hell out of my head.* 'No time like the present,' she added before she could change her mind, reaching into her coat pocket for her phone. The sooner she got some answers that actually made sense – something to prove her sanity and convince Paul to come back, and allow her to work out who was behind the intimidation campaign – the sooner Fern could turn her energies towards that new little life wriggling away inside her. The sooner she could start filling her days with baby catalogues and birthing forums and all the proper excitement, the normal fears, that came with impending motherhood.

'Okay, I'm ready,' Fern said, feeling sick. 'Do you want to give me the mobile number first? Bit of a long shot after all this time but you never know . . .'

She typed in the numbers as Tina read them out, fingers already shaking with the cold. That's all it was though. *Not nerves*, she told herself firmly, as she held the mobile up to her ear. *Just the cold.* 'Right. Here goes nothing.'

'Nothing' was about right. It didn't even ring. The call went straight through to the disconnected tone and then a message telling her the number didn't exist. Fern knew she ought to be disappointed, that the quickest way to sort this whole crazy Marte mess out would have been to speak to the woman herself. But the rush of relief flooding through her body told a different story. *Thank goodness.* That's all she could think. *Thank goodness for that.*

Chapter 32

One down, one to go. Fern typed in the second number and tried again.

It rang properly this time. Rang and rang. She kept expecting an answerphone message to click in, but it never did. Fern shook her head at Tina – *it's no good, there's no one there* – and got ready to end the call. Five more rings, she told herself and then I'll admit defeat. Four more. Three more. Two more . . .

'Hallo?' came a man's voice, just as she was lowering the phone away from her ear. '*Hvem er det som ringer?*'

'Oh, sorry. Hello.' Fern was thrown by the last-minute response and couldn't think how to begin. 'Er . . . do you speak English?' Yes. That was probably the best place to start. It would be a pretty short conversation if he didn't.

'Of course. I am a little out of practice,' said the man, with impeccable pronunciation – did he sound like Marte? It was hard to tell – 'but I shall do my best. Who is ringing, please? How can I help?'

'I er . . . my name's Fern,' she said, trying to ignore Tina, who'd chosen that exact moment to huff and wriggle herself out from behind the wheel, craning her head to listen. 'I'm trying to get hold of a woman called Marte Hortlassen. Someone suggested I might be able to reach her on this number?' Tina wriggled closer still, until she was practically sitting in Fern's lap.

'Marte?' repeated the man. 'Did you say Marte?'

'Yes,' said Fern. 'That's right. I'm trying to organise a . . .' A reunion was what she was going to say. But the man wasn't listening anymore. He was talking to someone else at the other end, jabbering away in a long rush of Norwegian. Fern couldn't understand a word (apart from 'Marte' and 'England') but the agitation in his voice, the urgency, didn't need any translation. And then a woman was saying something back to him, equally agitated, equally urgent, followed by a soft clunking sound which must have been the phone changing hands.

'Hello?' It was the woman talking now. 'I am Marte's grandmother. Tell me, is she a friend of yours? Have you heard from her? Do you know where she is?' The questions kept on coming. 'When did you last see her? Is she okay?'

'I'm sorry,' said Fern. 'I don't know *where* she is.' Something held her back from mentioning the house viewing. Some strange sixth sense, warning her to keep that to herself until she knew what she was dealing with. 'I was hoping you might be able to tell *me*.'

There was a long silence, as if the woman was fighting her emotions, and then a sigh of resignation. 'No,' she said at last. 'We have not heard from her in years. Not since . . . not since she told us about the baby. She refuses all contact since then. We do not even have a number for her anymore. No address. Nothing. We just want to know she is all right . . .' Another long pause. '*Og babyen*,' the woman added, her voice cracking as she slipped back into Norwegian. 'We just . . . we just want to know they are well . . . and healthy . . . And happy . . .'

'I'm sorry, I didn't mean to upset you,' said Fern, torn between guilt and disappointment, between thoughts for the poor woman at the other end of the line – *please, don't get upset, I have seen her really. She's fine* – and a need to process this new information. Did that mean Marte had lied to Sean about going back to Norway? Or was Sean the one who'd lied?

'We were never judging her,' said Marte's grandmother, 'you have to understand that. We would love her no matter what . . .'

'Of course.' Fern's arm was starting to go numb where Tina was leaning on her.

'But after everything she went through when she was little . . . after her mother died . . . We wanted to see her settled, that was all. Secure. A better start for *her* baby, than she had in life.'

The baby? Fern swallowed. *I don't think the baby got any start at all. That's why the blanket is still in our house. And a baby monitor that refuses to die . . .* But she didn't tell the woman that either.

'Perhaps we scared her with all our talk of marriage and proper families,' her grandmother went on. 'Maybe we should have tongue-bitten ourselves. Is that the word? But to cut us off like that. To refuse all further contact. No. That is *not* our Marte. He has poisoned her against us, somehow. I know it.'

'Who?' said Fern, struggling to keep up. Sean? Richard? Some unidentified man in the city?

'This *father*.' She almost spat the word. So much hurt and hatred squeezed into two short syllables. 'I always thought he must be married. That's why she would not talk about him. But in her last email she says she does not need us judging her and we are not to contact her anymore. We understood she wanted to stay in England to be near her mother. To explore her English roots. But to cut us off altogether?'

Her mother's dead though, isn't she? Isn't that what you said? Perhaps she meant her mother's grave. For a moment, Fern was back at the cemetery visiting her own mother, watching and waiting for another sign. For wind-blown kisses in the tulip leaves. For the soft brush of fingers in the grazing wings of a butterfly. That was before the child psychologist. Before some well-meaning colleague of her father's suggested there were healthier places for

239

the family to spend their Saturday mornings . . . And now look at her, too scared to visit her own sister's grave.

But this wasn't about *her* broken family, was it? It was about Marte's. And if Marte's mother was English then the couple on the other end of the line must be her paternal grandparents. And after her mother died, Marte was sent back to Norway to live with them. Was that right? Goodness only knew where *her* father fitted into it all. Another loss no doubt. Another sadness. How did some people make it through an entire lifetime with their family intact while others suffered one tragedy after another?

Marte's grandmother lowered her voice, as if someone might be listening to their conversation. 'Every time I reread that message it sounds less like Marte. What if he *made* her write it to keep us out of her life? How would we ever know? What if he wrote it himself?'

There was a sharp intake of breath from Tina in Fern's other ear.

'And still no one will tell us where she is,' her grandmother said. 'Not her old friends. Not her university. She does not even have a Facebook account anymore. It is like she has vanished off the face of the earth.'

Don't worry. I've seen her. She's fine. The words were right there in Fern's mouth but still she held back, the sense that something was wrong getting stronger all the time. What was it? What was she missing?

'I'm sorry,' she said again. Was her grandmother right? Had Marte been in some kind of trouble? Had something or someone pushed her into hiding, writing that email to throw her family off the scent? But then why hadn't she made contact again now that she was back? Something nagged at the corner of Fern's brain. Something to do with the blanket under the bath and the baby clothes she'd seen in the charity shop. With the imaginary messages on the mirror and window. *Had* she imagined them?

'How was she when you last saw her?' asked her grandmother. There was a new hunger to her voice now, a need for details, for something positive to hold on to. 'Did she seem happy?'

Demonic. That was Fern's last impression of Marte. Cold hands reaching into her stomach. *My baby. Not yours.* But she didn't tell the woman that. She described Marte as she'd seen her that day at the house: thoughtful and poised, cradling her bump through the thick wool of her jumper. She said how much she'd been looking forward to being a mother, mixing up the Marte of six years ago with the Marte who'd shown her round in an effort to bring the woman some comfort. She told her how Marte had already picked out baby clothes. How she'd embroidered a blanket with her daughter's name: Sofia.

There was a swallowed sob on the other end of the line. 'Yes,' said her grandmother. 'Of course. Sofia was her mother's name. But you have not seen her since then? You have not heard from her again in all this time?'

I saw her a few months ago, and she seemed fine. That's all Fern needed to say to end the woman's misery. Why couldn't she do it? *Five months pregnant again, just like when she disappeared.* 'I'm afraid not. Sorry again if I've upset you. That wasn't my intention.' Exactly *like when she disappeared.*

'No. It is nice to hear the baby was bringing her happiness. That is how I would like to think of her. And Sofia. Little baby Sofia. Yes. That was good to know also. But you have our number now. If you *do* manage to find her. If you hear anything, anything at all, you must let us know. Promise me that, yes?'

'Of course,' Fern assured her, mentally crossing her fingers behind her back. The overhead light clicked off, plunging the car into semi-darkness.

'It is the not knowing that is so hard. Not knowing if she is alive or dead.'

Alive or dead . . . Five months pregnant . . . exactly like before . . . Alive . . .

Or dead.

And there it was, finally. The answer Fern's mind had been skirting round all the time they'd been talking. *Marte didn't disappear, she died.* That's *why she left the baby clothes and blanket behind.* That's *why no one knows where she went. Why she's been haunting my dreams. The woman I saw at the house that day wasn't her. Not really. Just an echo from six years ago. A ghost.*

Of all her theories that had to be the craziest one yet. But sitting there in the empty car park afterwards, listening to the dead air on the other end of the line, it seemed to Fern like the only one that made sense. The writing on the mirror. The name on the window. The peculiar draughts. The long line of house owners who never stayed. What if her grandmother was right to be suspicious? What if it wasn't Marte who sent that final email, cutting off all contact and shutting down her Facebook account? What if it was someone else, trying to throw people off the scent?

'Look at you,' said Tina, cutting through her spiralling thoughts. 'You're shivering like mad. Let's get that heater on before you catch a chill.' She wriggled back into the driver's seat and turned the key in the ignition. The car's sound system blared into life, uninvited. Never mind that they'd been halfway through Paul's relaxing piano playlist on Spotify before. Satie and Debussy were out, and Kate Bush's 'Wuthering Heights' warblings were in.

'Turn it off,' snapped Fern, lunging for the volume knob. She'd always liked that song – she and Linny had played it endlessly the year Dad took them to Dartmoor, inspired by the rugged landscape and the black-and-white Laurence Olivier film they'd watched that first rainy afternoon – but now? A song about a dead woman lurking at the window was the last thing she wanted to hear. And suddenly the car was nothing *but* windows. Steamed-up windows waiting for invisible fingers . . .

The ghostly song disappeared back into the ether as the music clicked off, but it was too late by then. It kept on playing in Fern's head, reminding her how dark it was on the other side. How lonely.

She opened her own window to clear the steam quicker, shivering harder than ever.

'What's wrong?' said Tina.

'Nothing.' *Everything.* 'Old memories, that's all,' said Fern. 'We used to play Mum's copy of "The Kick Inside" a lot when we were younger. Until Linny high-kicked it off the record player and sent it flying.' And now Linny was the one out there on the other side. And Marte too . . . lost and lonely and looking for a way back. *The mirror. The window. The dreams.* 'Sorry. I didn't mean to snap.' *The same crackled song playing in the attic . . .*

'Perhaps we should get you home,' said Tina. 'It's been a long day. A lot to take in.'

Home? That was the last place Fern wanted to be. 'Good thinking, Batman,' she said anyway, trying to lighten the atmosphere. Trying to kid herself it was still just a game the two of them were playing. Cagney and Lacey. Laurel and Hardy. Ghostbusters.

'Nope, you're in charge,' said Tina grabbing hold of the forced banter baton with both hands and running with it. 'Which makes you Batman and me Robin.' She nudged Fern with her elbow, winking in the gloom. 'I *knew* I should have gone for green pants today, but I was worried the lace might rub. I bet Robin never had to contend with *that.*'

Well, that certainly did the trick. Kate Bush's forlorn ghost couldn't get out of Fern's head fast enough after that, leaving a picture of a caped Tina complete with rubbing underwear, in its place. Green lacy knickers. Who knew? And was there any way of *un*-knowing it again? That was the real question. But Fern smiled gratefully at her mother-in-law and gave into the image. Compared to dead women lurking in the darkness outside the window, it was a winner.

'That poor woman,' said Tina, as they turned back off the main road. 'That's the bit I can't get over. Imagine not knowing where her granddaughter was for all those years. Whether she was safe or not. What a price to pay for a few misguided words . . . and I'm sure she meant well. I'm sure she only wanted what was best for her.' Tina shook her head, as if to drive away the very thought of it. The very chance of it ever happening to her.

243

'I'm sure,' agreed Fern, dutifully.

'I mean, she didn't say how long it had been *exactly* since she last saw her, did she? Since that last email. But I'm guessing it's been six years. It seems like *no one's* seen her in the last six years, apart from you. The one and only sighting.' She made Marte sound like an endangered animal. 'It's like *Doctor Who*, or something,' Tina mused. 'Only without the Tardis. Almost as if time slipped back six years when you came to look round the house, and jumped forwards again afterwards.'

I didn't know you watched Doctor Who, Fern was thinking. Tina was right though. That's *exactly* what it was like. Or the other way round, with Marte trapped at the same fixed point in time while life flowed on without her. A point in time six years ago, before something happened, something bad, which meant she never got to have her baby. Never got to leave the house . . . Which brought Fern right back to ghosts and ghouls and things that went baby-stealing bump in the night.

'I have this horrible feeling she's gone,' she told Tina, unable to keep it to herself any longer. 'Permanently gone, I mean.' *And in a decidedly unnatural way at that, otherwise her grandparents would have been informed, wouldn't they?* 'This gut sense that the Marte I met was just a . . .' She paused, choosing her words carefully. 'Just an echo,' she finished. 'I know that sounds crazy but—'

'But it's the only explanation that makes any sense,' Tina finished for her. 'I'm glad it's not just me. I don't really believe in that sort of stuff but . . . well, maybe I should. Was there anything that struck you as unusual that day? Anything else you can remember?'

Fern retraced her steps from room to room, replaying what she could recall of their conversation, trying to dredge up any other clues or signs she might have missed. Not that she even knew what those signs would be, with nothing but half-forgotten novels and films to go on, and childish images of sheeted figures that walked through walls. She'd certainly have noticed if Marte had done *that*.

244

No need to rush, that's what she'd said when she offered to show Fern round. *I've all the time in the world.* It hadn't rung any alarm bells at the time, and why would it? But now? And then when they were up in the nursery and Fern asked her if she was tempted to stay: *No. It's time I moved on.* She turned the heating up higher to try and warm away the shivers down her back. It was funny how sinister those same innocent phrases sounded now. Except it wasn't funny. Far from it.

Fern tried to think if there'd been any physical contact between them that day, but she couldn't even remember shaking hands. No, they hadn't – the more she thought about it the more certain she became. And Gemma hadn't shaken hands with Marte either – she remembered that – because her phone started ringing. What she *couldn't* remember was Marte opening or closing any doors. She'd always been a few steps behind, letting Fern explore the house for herself. Even at the end, when they'd said their goodbyes, it was Fern who'd opened the front door, leaving Marte standing in the hallway, watching her go.

There was nothing. Nothing to prove the Marte *she'd* met was proper flesh and blood. But if she wasn't, if she was only an echo, a vibration in time, then why had she reappeared that day in particular? *I didn't know I'd be here either.* That's what she'd said when Gemma expressed surprise at seeing her, mistakenly assuming she was Mrs Rochester. If only Fern could get hold of the estate agent to compare notes. To see if Gemma's recollection of the meeting matched her own. *I didn't know I'd be here . . .* What did that even mean? Was it something about Fern herself that had summoned Marte? Because of Linny, maybe. Because Fern was still searching for blonde-haired, blue-eyed women wherever she went. Or perhaps it was the baby, and the fact that their pregnancies seemed to match in every way. She remembered how the baby had kicked at the sound of Marte's words: *Your beautiful baby girl . . .* But Fern hadn't even mentioned the baby's gender, had she? No, the more she thought about it, the more certain she was. Marte had already known.

'If Marte really is gone . . .' said Tina, breaking the silence. 'If she's been gone all this time . . . then it can't have been her who Callie saw with Richard that day.'

'Pardon?' said Fern. Her mind was still back in the nursery with Marte. *She* knew *I was having a girl. She* knew *we were the same . . .*

'I said it can't have been Marte who Callie saw Richard with that day. Just someone who looked like her. But that doesn't mean he wasn't seeing her six years ago. It doesn't rule him out as the baby's father. Maybe he's got a secret thing for blondes in general.' Tina flicked on the indicator, the *tck, tck, tck* echoing round the car like a ticking clock. Like a countdown.

'It doesn't rule *anyone* out as the baby's father,' said Fern. 'Apart from Sean.'

'No,' agreed Tina, as they turned into Crenellation Lane. 'But I keep coming back to what Eddie was saying on the way home from the surgery, yesterday. About how Richard was in love with that woman in the city . . . He didn't actually say when that was, did he? What if that was six years ago? What if Richard was commuting into the city for work, and Marte was commuting in too? And what if Kerry—'

She broke off, suddenly, slamming Fern forwards in her seat as she hit the brake pedal. 'Get out of the road, you idiot!'

A figure turned briefly in the glare of the headlights – like a startled hare – and then scuttled away into the darkness. Back towards number six.

'Sorry,' gasped Tina, breathless with shock, or indignation. 'Are you all right? *Idiot*,' she repeated.

'I think so.' Fern eased the seatbelt out where it had snapped against her body. Nothing seemed to hurt. Nothing new, anyway. For a second there it had felt like moving day all over again, only it wasn't Linny in the middle of the road this time. It was Kerry. How odd to see her looming out of the darkness at the merest mention of her name. What had she been doing, standing there, staring up at Fern's house like that? Like an omen, or a warning. Maybe that's what *Linny* had been doing there that day. Trying to warn her about Marte. But no, that didn't make any sense. Her sister had been looking the other way . . .

The other way! Of course, why hadn't Fern thought of that before? Linny hadn't been looking at the new house, she'd been staring at the car reversing onto the opposite drive, hadn't she? Richard's car. *That's* who she was warning her about. Or Kerry. One of the two. Fern peered past Tina's head at the coated figure retreating up the opposite drive, illuminated once more as she triggered the light sensor by her own front door.

Perhaps Kerry was the one behind the blacked-out flyer and the painted warning on the wall . . . and the cyclamen and camellia massacre, that must have been her too. Fern remembered now. Remembered seeing a pink-raincoated Kerry through the window, staring into their front garden as she tied up her shoelace . . . or pretended to tie it. Perhaps she'd been sizing up all the various plants, planning out the next stage in her hate campaign. Perhaps she'd crept back over the road with her secateurs later that night, not realising Fern was only a few feet away on the sofa. And the scratched car and the turd on their doorstep could just as easily have been Kerry too. She certainly had access to a dog, because Fern had seen Richard walking it in the woods on Sunday.

Tina had clearly come to the same conclusion. 'Well,' she said, as she lined the car up alongside the space she'd struggled to get out of earlier. 'I think we can guess who's behind all the mischief that's been going on round here, can't we? She was probably making sure we were out before she delivered her next "present". I wonder what she was planning this time . . .'

Fern didn't like to think.

A brick through the window?

A severed head on her pillow?

'Why don't you put the car on the drive?' she said, adding, in an undertone, 'It's not like Paul's coming back anytime soon.'

'It all kicked off *after* you started asking questions, didn't it?' mused Tina. '*After* you began asking people about Marte. Do you think Kerry might have overheard you at April's party?'

'She could have done,' said Fern.

'I'm probably getting ahead of myself here, but I can't help wondering if there's a connection. If you looking into Marte is what triggered this campaign against you.'

'I'd been thinking the same thing,' said Fern.

'And maybe,' continued Tina, dropping her voice to a whisper as if the perpetrator might be listening in at that very moment, 'there's something Kerry doesn't want you to find out . . .'

'You mean . . .?' Fern wasn't sure *what* she meant.

'I mean what if Kerry had something to do with Marte's death? Or what if it was Richard come to that, trying to silence her about the baby – about *his* baby – and Kerry's covering his tracks?' Tina twisted round in her seat, staring back at number six.

Fern imagined Richard's hands tightening round Marte's neck as she struggled for air . . . as she begged him to stop for the sake of the baby. *Their* baby. It was like something out of Eddie's book.

'Maybe they're both in on it together,' Tina murmured.

Fern's hands went back to her own baby as she sat there in the darkness, remembering the strange, hungry look in Marte's eyes as she'd gazed at Fern's belly during the viewing. She remembered the woman's whispering voice in her dream: *My baby, my baby.* If Tina was right, if there was any truth to her mother-in-law's theory, Marte would have kept on begging, kept on fighting, right 'til the end. Fern swallowed, her own throat tightening in sympathy. And the baby . . . the baby was kicking back against her hands now as if she could sense the violent thoughts crowding her mother's mind.

My baby, my baby.

Chapter 33

Fern hadn't realised quite how shattered she was until she kicked off Paul's old beach shoes – the only things that would fit over her puffed-up pregnancy feet without digging into her ankle – and collapsed onto the sofa. What an evening. All that new information and emotion jostling for her attention. Her poor sleep-deprived brain felt wrung out with the sheer effort of taking it in, let alone trying to make sense of what they'd discovered. And the Kerry bombshell wasn't even the last of it as it turned out. There was still one final surprise to come.

Tina had gone straight through to the kitchen when they came in, turning all the lights on and heading for the kettle, to steady her nerves with a hot drink. But the curse of Crenellation Lane had struck again, with the brand-new Rapid Boil 750 rebelling against its mistress in a daring display of unstoppable steam. The thing refused to turn off, even after Tina pulled the plug out of the wall. It kept on boiling and boiling, sending great billowing steam clouds through the entire house.

The first Fern knew about it was the angry wail of the smoke alarm, rousing her from nervous exhaustion to full-on panic in a few short blasts. Had Kerry and Richard moved onto arson?

'It's not a fire, don't worry,' Tina yelled as Fern fumbled for her crutches, hobbling out to see what was happening. 'It's that blinking kettle . . .'

The hallway was doing a remarkably good impression of a sauna, albeit a sauna with deafening beeps coming from the ceiling. Fern could just make out the misted outline of her mother-in-law's backside sticking out of the cubby hole under the stairs.

'Which one's the fuse for the kitchen sockets?' Tina shouted over the smoke alarm, as if that would have made any difference once the plug was disconnected.

Fern didn't have a clue. She hadn't set foot in the cupboard since they'd moved in and wasn't entirely sure she'd fit through the door if she tried.

'Need a ruddy torch under here,' Tina added, before plunging the entire downstairs into darkness. Silent, steamy darkness. At least the alarm had stopped though. 'Oops, not that one.'

Yes, thought Fern, still wondering what on earth was going on. *A torch would have been good.*

'Don't panic,' Tina called. Fern could hear her flicking levers, one after the other. 'I've got this.'

The upstairs smoke alarm let out a long beep of annoyance, as if it was sorry to have missed all the action, and a clock radio blared into life halfway through 'Spirit in the Sky' before dying all over again.

'There!' came a triumphant cry as the lights finally flicked back on. Tina re-emerged, red-faced and sweating, muttering something under her breath about dodgy electrics and houses burning down as she hurried off into the kitchen. Fern followed behind to find her mother-in-law glaring at the offending kettle. 'Well,' said Tina, 'it's definitely off now. Burned itself out completely by the looks of it. That'll be going straight back tomorr—'

She stopped mid-word, staring through the thinning cloud at the kitchen window and the garden beyond, her mouth a perfect cartoon 'O' of surprise.

'Look,' she hissed. 'Look at the grass.'

Fern joined her at the window and stared out at the sloping lower lawn . . . at the pale words picked out in the bright glare of the outside security light. Four words pressed into the very grass itself:

MY BABY

MY BABY

And then the outside light clicked off again and the message was lost to darkness.

'It must be *her*,' whispered Tina, shaking all over. 'Marte. She's back.' She clutched at her daughter-in-law's arm like a frightened child. But Fern felt surprisingly calm for once. She wasn't the only one. Tina had seen it too, this time. *I didn't imagine it. The mirror and the window . . . and now this. It was all real.* Paul would *have* to believe her now.

Fern was asleep on the sofa when Paul's text came through that night. The drama with the kettle and the lawn had proved too much for Tina, who flat-out refused to talk about Marte anymore. Or Kerry, or Richard. She'd made a point of double-checking all the locks – doors *and* windows – before settling down with her saucepan-boiled cup of tea, but that was her only concession to the events of the night. Other than that, she seemed determined to carry on as if nothing had happened. As if it were a perfectly normal evening in a normal house on a normal street. And even though Fern knew it was just her way of coping, that hadn't made it any less frustrating, with so much new information to process and yet another Marte-filled night looming. All Tina had wanted to talk about was kettle warranties, and the best time, traffic-wise, to set off for the cemetery the following day, 'like you promised your dad this morning.'

Fern had been thrown for a moment. She remembered telling Tina about it on the way back from the care home but couldn't believe it had only been that morning. So much had happened since then. Marte had still been alive for one thing, as far as Fern had known. And now . . .

251

'You promised him you'd see Linny tomorrow,' Tina had insisted, making it impossible for Fern to argue. How could she choose Marte over her own sister?

Fern hadn't actually planned to spend the *whole* night downstairs, just long enough to make sure Kerry wasn't coming back, or Richard himself, planning to silence them for good like he silenced Marte. It was an outlandish theory by any standards – not the sort of thing they could take to the police without some more evidence – but once Tina had planted the idea in her head, it was hard to ignore. What if she was right? They'd certainly have to tread a lot more carefully with their questioning from now on. And what if Richard *had* been at home when Fern called round after talking to Callie? What if Fern had blundered in with her questions about Marte and Richard had decided to finish her off there and then?

The longer Fern kept up her vigil, the less time there'd be for nightmares, and that could only be a good thing. Not for Tina though – sleep was undoubtedly the best remedy for *her* after her traumatic night, and Fern needed her fresh for the morning if they were driving out to the cemetery. But there'd been no telling her. She'd refused to turn in until Fern did, despite her heavy head and drooping eyelids, leaving her daughter-in-law with no other option than to close her own eyes and pretend.

It worked. Fern had felt a gentle tug on her shoulder a few minutes later, as Tina tried to rouse her, with the hushed suggestion that she'd be more comfortable in bed. But she'd merely deepened her breathing by way of a response, snuggling her cheek even further into the sofa cushion, until Tina had finally admitted defeat, fetching Fern's duvet down from upstairs and tucking her in like a child.

Sleep well, sweetheart, she'd whispered, as she'd adjusted the covers under Fern's chin. *Pleasant dreams.* Fern remembered that much – remembered smiling inside at such maternal endearments – but that was all. Exhaustion must have won out over fear, despite everything. She must have faked sleep so successfully that she somehow slipped into the real thing, because there was nothing after that until the vibrating buzz of her mobile stung her back into consciousness.

Are you awake? I need to talk to you. I need to tell you how sorry I am.

At last. Fern could have wept with happiness and relief. But she didn't. She was too busy texting Paul back – *Yes I'm here. Ring me* – too busy staring at the lit screen, waiting for it to buzz a second time.

'Hi,' she whispered when the call finally came. *Thank goodness*, she'd imagined herself saying. *I've been going out of my mind here. Why didn't you call sooner? I miss you so much it hurts.* But she didn't say any of that. Didn't tell him how lost she'd been without him; how angry; how crushed; how suspicious. She hid the whole messy tangle of feelings behind a whispered 'hi' and waited for him to make the first move instead.

'How are you?' he asked.

'All right.' *Apart from the ankle and the nightmares and a potential murderer's psycho wife trying to hound me out of my own home.*

'And Mum?'

'Yes, she's fine too.' *She was until tonight, anyway.*

'Good. Good.'

'You?' said Fern. None of this sounded much like an apology to her. Not so far.

'Not bad.' There was a long pause. 'Actually no, that's not true. I feel like shit.'

Fern swallowed down her annoyance. *What was this, a man-flu sympathy call?*

'*I've* been a shit,' said Paul. '*That's* what I'm trying to say. Oh, Fern, I'm so sorry. I should never have walked out on you like that. I don't know what I was thinking.'

'Well, I guess it was—' she started, but he cut her off short.

'No, please, let me say this. I *need* to say it. I've written down notes and everything.' There was a soft rustle of paper at the other end of the line and then it all came tumbling out in a long un-Paul-like speech. 'I know it's been hard going these last few months – since Linny, really – but I honestly thought I was doing the best for us. With the move and everything, I mean. Only I realised tonight, when I was talking to this vicar chap at Simon's church, that I shouldn't have pushed you into it before you were ready. All that stuff with the lorry on Thursday, and the message on the window . . . I can't even pretend to understand any of that, but I think I know where it's coming from now, at least. It's because you never wanted to be there in the first place, isn't it?'

He carried on talking without waiting for an answer, barely even pausing for breath.

'I took you away from the last place you were happy, away from all your memories, kidding myself that it would somehow make you better. Make *us* better. But all I did was make things worse, and then run away like a coward. And I know it's too late now – I can't undo what's been done – but I *am* sorry. Truly, truly sorry. And I'm going to do everything in my power to make it up to you. Whatever it takes, Fern. I mean it. I love you. These last few days have been . . . well, I don't think I've ever been so miserable. When I say "talking" to the vicar, I mean crying . . . Sobbing like a baby.'

His voice was breaking again now, even as he finished speaking. Fern wanted to reach her arms down the phone and wrap him up tight. 'Why didn't you talk to *me*?' she said. 'I was worried you weren't coming back. I've been thinking all sorts of crazy things.'

'Oh, sweetheart, I'm so sorry. I just didn't know what to . . . how to . . . I've gone and made everything ten times worse, haven't I?'

'No,' said Fern, wiping her cheeks on the back of her hand. 'Not *ten* times. More like seven or eight, I'd say. Nine, tops.'

'Only nine? That's not *so* bad then.' Paul was half-laughing now, half-crying. 'Does that mean I can come home again?'

Yes. Yes. Yes. All her anger was gone now. Melted away into insignificance, along with Marte and Kerry and everything else that had been going on. For a moment or two there was nothing but her and Paul reaching back to each other through the darkness. 'Of course you can come home. Come now!'

'Better not,' he said. 'I had rather a strong whisky earlier. Two or three rather strong whiskies, if I'm honest. But I'll be back tomorrow, straight after my last meeting. Maybe we could go out for dinner in Westerton if it's not too late? If you're up to it? Just you and me, I mean. I'm sure Mum can fend for herself.'

'We'll see,' said Fern, knowing they couldn't leave Tina alone in the house after dark even if they wanted to, with everything that had been going on. Her heart sank again at the thought of all the other things she still needed to tell him. 'I'm er . . . I'm not amazingly mobile at the moment. I had a bit of an accident . . .' *Start with the easy one*, she thought, *and work up to the rest.* 'Just a sprain, that's all,' she added quickly, before his imagination had a chance to dream up something worse. 'But I'm reliant on crutches for a bit.'

Paul still sounded scared though, panicked even, as if 'accident' was the only word he'd heard. There was a sharp intake of breath, a murmured string of expletives, and then came the questions. 'A fall? Why didn't you ring me? Why didn't *Mum* ring me? How did you get to the hospital if you couldn't drive? And what about the baby? Are you sure the baby's okay?'

Fern filled in *some* of the details, doing her best to smooth away his worries. She didn't mention the blanket though. Didn't mention how on edge she'd been when it happened, after finding a man creeping through the garden. The last thing she wanted was Paul tearing home through the night to protect them. Not if he'd been drinking. So when he still seemed upset – hurt too, probably – at the thought of not having been there, Fern changed the subject entirely. She told him how Tina was driving her out to the cemetery the next day. 'I thought it was time I went to see my sister,' she said. 'Her grave, I mean.'

'Really? That's a positive step,' said Paul, distracted into thinking about Linny now instead of Fern's ankle. 'I'm just sorry I can't be there with you. Next time, though. Any time you want, you know that.'

'Yes,' she agreed. 'I know.'

'We *are* going to get through this,' he promised. 'And we're going to come out stronger than ever, just you wait and see. You, me, and the baby.'

'Yes,' Fern said again, wanting so badly to believe him. 'I know that too.' *You, me, and the baby.* And for once – for the first time ever, maybe – she didn't automatically add her sister to the list. But yes, Linny too. Of course. If she was still there . . .

There was something different about Marte when the dreams came that night. She still found Fern downstairs on the sofa, but she seemed more frighten*ed* than frighten*ing*. Fern was in a smoke-swirled graveyard looking for Linny's grave. It was a proper gothic job, straight out of Beginner's Horror 101, with dark sloping headstones and cracked angels gazing down on her as she stumbled past. The grass under her feet was wet and marshy and the ground kept trying to suck her down. And Marte was there too, running through the graves beside her, screaming into her baby monitor for Sofia, as the dark, shadowed figure of a man bore down on them . . . Red Setter Richard, coming to steal his baby.

My baby, not yours.

But when he looked up at Fern, laughing, it wasn't Richard anymore. It was Paul.

Chapter 34

Another disturbed night saw Fern sleeping late on Wednesday morning. It was Tina coming in that woke her this time, the sound of the front door closing behind her.

'Forgot the ruddy receipt,' she said, when Fern joined her in the kitchen, shaking the boxed-up kettle for extra emphasis. 'Went all the way into Westerton to take the thing back and managed to leave the receipt behind. I can't even *find* it now though.'

'Oh dear,' murmured Fern. She could have done with a cup of tea. There was no sign of the writing on the grass this morning, at least. That was something. Whatever strange trick of the light Marte had wrought on the lawn the night before was nothing more than a disturbing memory now.

'The man offered to do a straight swap for me, but I said I didn't want *another* one. *That kettle's a blinking liability*, I told him. *Lucky it didn't burn the whole house down.* He didn't take too kindly to that though, what with a queue of other customers listening in. I'll have to try again later. It must be round here somewhere. Sorry, morning, by the way. How did you sleep?'

'Not too bad. I spoke to Paul. He's coming home tonight.' For a moment Fern was back in her dream, watching him chase after Marte, but she forced the memory away, thinking of his last whispered words to her instead. *That* was the real Paul. The Paul who loved her – had always loved her – and was coming home to make things right. She realised, too late, that she'd forgotten to warn him about the new locks, but he'd find that out for himself soon enough. They'd just have to make sure they were in when he got back.

Tina put the kettle down and swept her up in an impromptu hug. 'There, what did I tell you? About time too. I know he's my son but he's a silly bugger sometimes.'

Fern's phone vibrated between them (she'd taken to carrying it round in a pocket now, in case of another emergency) and Tina let out a little squeal of surprise, laughing as she let her go. It was Paul, right on cue, with another text. Tina headed for the other side of the kitchen, ostensibly to carry on her hunt for the kettle receipt, but Fern suspected it was to give her some privacy. Her mother-in-law's newfound powers of discretion knew no bounds, it seemed.

It wasn't a very long text – *Hope the ankle's OK this morning. I can't wait to see you xxx* – but Fern could feel herself grinning like an idiot as she sent kisses of her own back. It *was* going to be okay, wasn't it? Not just her ankle but everything. Paul would believe her this time – he *had* to now that Tina had witnessed Marte's handiwork too, written out across the lawn – and that would be half the battle won already. Knowing Paul, he'd probably have an idea how to fix it too. Some simple, practical solution that would make everything right again. Perhaps he could get that new vicar friend of his to perform some sort of exorcism for them. Security cameras would be good too and a restraining order for Kerry. As for Richard . . . No, the thought of Paul questioning Richard about Marte was just as scary. Who knew what he'd be capable of if he really *was* a killer? Perhaps they should cut their losses and get out, like all the other owners before them. A fresh start somewhere else . . .

'Oh,' said Tina, 'I almost forgot. I called in on Mrs Hoskins again this morning.'

Fern couldn't think who she meant at first. 'Yasmin?'

'No, Sean's mum.'

Tina must have recovered from her shock of the previous night, if she'd been out Miss Marpling again already. 'What happened?' said Fern. 'Did you ask her about him and Marte?'

'It was Sean I'd gone to see, actually, to ask him about the writing on the lawn. To see if he'd ever spotted anything like that when he was here doing the garden. But it seemed a shame to leave without doing a *little* bit of digging around, while I was there. Especially after what Nicky and Ant told us yesterday . . . I don't *think* it'll get back to Kerry,' she added, sounding less certain of herself suddenly.

'And? What happened? What did you find out?'

'Well, that's where it gets interesting. She insisted I come in for a cup of tea even though Sean had already left. What could I say? Particularly given that we're kettleless again . . . it would have been rude not to. Sean always brews her up a big thermos before he leaves, apparently, to get her through the morning, but I made us a fresh pot anyway. Much nicer.'

That wasn't the interesting bit. Surely?

'And then we got talking about the house and the garden and she told me we've got twin roses – one at their place, I mean, and one here – to remember her little grandson, or granddaughter.' Tina raised her eyebrows to indicate that *this* was the interesting bit coming up now. 'The one who died six years ago. The one whose wicked Norwegian mother ran off after she lost the baby, breaking poor Sean's heart twice over. He planted one outside their sitting-room window for himself, and one here for Marte – up at the top by the folly – although she didn't stick around long enough to appreciate it. He's carried on looking after it all these years anyway, while he's been here doing his official gardening work. Which might go some way to explaining why he's so keen for us to take him on too . . .'

'I guess so,' Fern said, although Mrs Hoskins' version of events

259

seemed just as flawed as everyone else's. If Sean was busy planting memorial roses in the back garden, why did Nicky and Ant think Marte was still pregnant when she left?

'And Sean must still believe the baby was his, even now,' Tina continued, 'otherwise why would he bother with the roses? Maybe Marte lost it before she got the chance to tell him . . . and then, well, what would she gain by telling him afterwards?'

'Maybe,' said Fern. Or maybe Nicky was the one who had it wrong. Maybe Sean really *was* the father. But where did that leave Richard? The more information they uncovered, the more confusing it all got.

'Perhaps that's why she's still here.' Tina cast a furtive glance over her shoulder, as if Marte might be listening in. 'Because she feels bad about lying to Sean. Because she doesn't want him grieving anymore for a child that was never his to start with.'

My baby. Not yours.

'Or maybe Nicky got confused and Sean really *was* the father,' said Tina, echoing Fern's own thoughts. 'Maybe it was Richard, her secret lover in the city, who Marte had been lying to. Maybe he *wanted* the baby – didn't you say he and Kerry had been having problems conceiving? – and when he found out it wasn't his, it tipped him over the edge.' Tina shivered. 'I don't know. Anyway, that's not the real reason I brought it up. Today's not about Marte, it's about you. You and your sister. But talking about the roses gave me an idea – I thought it might be nice for you to have matching flowers too. One here and one with Linny, so you'll feel connected to her every time you look out into the garden . . .' She wrinkled up her nose. 'It's a silly idea, isn't it? You hate it, I can tell.'

'No,' said Fern, who didn't know *what* she thought about it. She was still thinking about Marte and her baby. About all the different things they'd been told, and still no way of knowing which ones were true. But Tina was right. They should be thinking about Linny. Everything else would have to wait until after the cemetery. Until Paul got home. 'It's a lovely idea,' she said. 'We should do it. Definitely.'

'Really? Oh, I am glad you said that.' Tina looked genuinely relieved. 'I've already been and bought a couple of miniature roses while I was in town. They're out in the boot now. I was after twin-flowers really – *Linnaea Borealis* that's what it said on my phone when I looked it up – but the man in the little garden centre had never even heard of them. So I got red rose bushes instead. I know you said they were her favourite. Oh, and some red tulip bulbs for your dad. That was the closest I could get, I'm afraid.'

Fern was touched. Her mother-in-law had barely known Linny – had only met her the once at their wedding – but she'd clearly put a lot of thought into this visit. Into making it special for Fern's sake.

'I thought we could take Linny's rose with us today,' Tina was saying. 'I managed to find one with a couple of late buds on it. And then plant yours out there where you'll be able to see it from the kitchen window . . . If you'd like to, that is.'

'That sounds perfect. Thank you. I honestly don't know what I'd have done without you these last few days.' It was true.

'It's been my pleasure,' said Tina, blushing furiously, twin red roses of her own blooming across each cheek. 'My absolute pleasure.' She picked at a piece of imaginary fluff on her skirt. 'Did you want to have a bath or anything this morning, before we go? I can give you a hand getting in and out with your ankle . . .'

And just like that the moment was broken again. Fern was blushing too now at the very thought.

'No, no, it's fine, really,' she said quickly. 'I'll wait 'til Paul gets back.' She glanced down at her slept-in maternity leggings and crumpled top, wondering if she smelled. Sunday's ill-fated bath seemed forever ago now. 'But maybe you could bring me down a clean set of clothes to save me crawling up the stairs?'

'Of course,' said Tina. 'And then I'll rustle us up a spot of

261

breakfast while you're getting ready. What about bacon sandwiches? Bit of a treat to set us up for the day?'

Fern nodded. She would rather have had cereal. Rather have had nothing. Not that it mattered. She'd feel sick enough once they got there, regardless. She felt sick already, just thinking about stepping out of the car. And then hobbling back down that path through the clipped green grass, like a golf course, with headstones instead of flags to show where the holes were. So many holes.

And Linny.

Oh, Linny.

Chapter 35

Richard's car was still on his drive as Fern and Tina pulled out onto the road.

'He hasn't gone to work today then,' said Tina.

'Maybe he's ill,' suggested Fern. 'He looked very pale when we saw him yesterday, when he almost drove into us. Maybe he was having some kind of funny turn . . . or maybe it was the guilt finally catching up with him.' But even as she was saying it, she caught sight of him in the passenger mirror, hurrying out of his front door in what looked like jogging bottoms and a jumper, closely followed by Kerry in her dressing gown. 'Speak of the devil.'

She watched as Richard headed for his car, shouting something over his shoulder. And then he opened his car door and climbed in before winding down the window and shouting some more. He was looking back towards his own house though, not at them.

Fern remembered how her twin had stood in the road staring at the same house on moving day. *Which one of them were you trying to warn me about, Linny? Richard or Kerry? Or both? I'm sorry I didn't understand. But I do now.*

There was no sign of Linny this morning though. *Still* no sign. Only Kerry in her dressing gown, running after Richard as he backed off the drive . . . and then the pair of them were lost to sight as Fern and Tina turned onto the main road.

'Trouble in paradise,' Fern muttered under her breath. It was something her dad used to say when he saw a couple arguing.

'What's that?' Tina was concentrating on the road. The traffic was surprisingly heavy for a weekday.

'Oh nothing,' said Fern, trying to ignore the shivery feeling in her spine. This morning was supposed to be about Linny. Not Richard. Not Kerry. And not Marte. But every time she caught sight of a red car in the passenger mirror, she found herself straining to try and make out the driver's face. What if it was him? What if Richard was following them?

Oh, Linny, I don't like this. I wish you were here. I wish . . . I wish you'd never gone. I'm coming to see you though, just like I promised Dad. Please, please be there . . .

The closer they got to the cemetery, the less likely it seemed. What would Linny be doing waiting by her own grave? But the thought of Linny *in* her grave was almost too much for Fern to cope with. The mere idea of it, coupled with nervous fantasies about Richard chasing them down in his car, made her feel positively queasy. And when they turned off onto the cemetery road and she caught sight of a red Audi a few cars back, she thought she might be sick there and then.

Shit. For a moment that was the only word Fern was capable of. Her brain seemed to be stuck in panicked swear-mode. 'Shit, shit, shit,' she gasped, almost choking on the acid taste in the back of her mouth.

'What?' asked Tina, stalling halfway across the road. 'What's happened? Is it your waters? Have they broken? Do I need to pull in somewhere?'

But the red Audi wasn't signalling. And although Fern could have sworn the driver was Richard – the same build and hair – he clearly wasn't following them after all, carrying straight on instead.

'No,' said Fern, as the car ground to a halt – and a blue van coming the other way also slowed to a horn-blaring halt. 'False alarm. Sorry.'

Tina was the one swearing now, as she battled with the ignition, but at last the engine kicked in again and they were off. Next stop, the cemetery.

Linny wasn't there. Fern knew it as soon as she got out of the car, leaning heavily against the door, trying to breathe away the fresh onslaught of nausea rising in her chest. She knew it as she limped across the gravel, every downward strike of her crutches a fresh cymbal crash against the peculiar stillness. She knew it when she reached the gates – *Abandon All Hope Ye Who Enter Here* – and stood looking out on the pockmarked greenness beyond. It was all wrong. Too neat and ordered. Too dull. What would Linny be doing in a place like this?

Tina shuffled along beside her, resorting to mouse-like steps in order to keep pace – to maintain a proper funereal rate of progress. She had the rose bush in one hand and a garden centre Bag for Life filled with tulip bulbs and a small gardening spade in the other. Now that they were here the thought of either one of them digging through the soil – digging over Linny's face like that – made Fern feel sicker than ever. But it was too late to change her mind. She'd promised her dad. Promised herself.

'We've been lucky with the weather, anyway,' said Tina, looking around appreciatively as if they were there for a picnic. 'The forecast seemed a bit iffy first thing this morning, but it's turned out nice.'

'Lucky' wasn't quite the word for how Fern was feeling. 'Scared' was a better one. 'Hollow'. 'Shaky'. 'Desolate'. All of them at once and then some, as if the world were spinning too fast, suddenly, the ground slipping away under her feet. She felt bitter and raw and aching and numb – a tangle of contradictory feelings swirling around alongside the bacon-flavoured bile rising in her throat.

265

'I'm going to be sick,' she blurted out, looking round in panic for a bin. That might have been one in the distance, but she'd never make it in time. *Oh crap.*

'Here,' said Tina, emptying her bag onto the path, sending tulip bulbs rolling off in all directions. 'Use this.' She held it open under Fern's chin, like a giant travel sickness bag, making soft encouraging noises as breakfast made its second appearance of the day. 'There. That's better.' And then she knotted the offending bag and placed it, warm and squelching, at her own feet, reaching into her capacious coat pockets for a clean tissue.

'I'm so sorry,' said Fern, wiping her lips. If only the ground would open up and swallow her, like it had swallowed everyone else round there.

Tina brushed away her apology with a deft flick of her wrist. 'What's a bit of vomit between friends, eh? You'll be covered in the stuff once the baby comes.' She gave a low chuckle as she scooped up the runaway bulbs, stuffing them into her pockets. '"Bag for Life" might be pushing it a bit now though. More like Bag for the Five Minutes It Takes to Reach the Nearest Bin, I think.' She picked up the offending carrier, holding it out by the scruff of its neck. 'Do you know where you're going from here? I'll come and meet you as soon as I've got rid of this.'

Fern knew where she was going. All these months later it was still burned into her brain. Seared into her memory. She could have walked there blindfolded, following the invisible spool of her grief, of her own unravelling.

'Linny,' she whispered, squinting into the winter sun as she lumbered towards the temporary headstone. Paul had asked her about choosing a proper one when the ground had settled, wanting to know if she'd had any further thoughts on the design or the inscription. He'd only asked the once though – Fern's near-hysterical reaction had seen to that.

'Linny,' she whispered again, just in case she was wrong. In case she *was* here after all, waiting for her. But the grave stood empty, like all the others. No tall blonde figures striding across the shorn grass to meet her.

It wasn't quite as awful as Fern feared, though, in the end. It was hard to imagine her sister there, at rest, sleeping away the whole of eternity, but the grave itself seemed peaceful enough. It was still bland and characterless – nothing like Linny – but yes, oddly peaceful, and a hundred times better than the hungry gape of earth she remembered from last time.

'I'm sorry I haven't been before,' said Fern, addressing the air rather than the ground. 'I . . . I couldn't bear to come. I felt sick at the very thought . . . I've just thrown up now,' she added, knowing that was the sort of detail Linny would enjoy. *Would* have enjoyed. 'In Paul's mum's Bag for Life.'

One word, she imagined her sister saying, tutting and shaking her head in mock judgement. *Tone-lowerer. And yes, before you ask, it does count. It's hyphenated.*

Fern could already feel the giggle rising up inside her, like her ill-fated bacon sandwich before it. 'It wasn't funny, really,' she began, replaying the full awfulness of it in glorious vomit-tastic technicolour. 'No, you're right,' she said. *Sick-sprayer. Puke-shamer. Barf-maiden.* 'It was the funniest thing I've done all week. Even funnier than chasing you under that lorry.' And now the giggle was spilling out of her, wild and unmanageable, and yet the harder Fern laughed the less she cared.

'Oh, the lorry! That was a classic. And with everyone watching too – all the new neighbours.' She wiped at her cheeks, eyes watering like crazy.

'Fern? Fern? Are you all right, love?' It was Tina. 'I couldn't tell if you were laughing or crying.'

Fern turned her tearstained face towards her mother-in-law and tried to force her mouth into proper word shapes. 'B-bit . . . both,' she stammered, which was the best she could manage. And then for some reason Tina started giggling too, the two of them stood there together, doubled-up and shaking, as if a cemetery full of bodies was the hilarious punchline to a joke they couldn't remember starting. And even though it was wrong on every single level – *not here, surely? Not now* – it still felt right somehow. It felt good.

'I'm glad we came,' Fern said afterwards, as she knelt by her sister's grave, patting the soil back into place around the rose's roots. She shifted her weight awkwardly from one knee to the other. It hadn't been too bad getting down, with help – her ankle seemed better again this morning – but she was starting to pay the price for it now. 'Thank you for bringing me,' she said. 'And for Linny's rose. I think she'd like that.' Yes, wherever her sister was now, she'd appreciate the splash of colour, even as she was laughing at Fern's elephantine clumsiness. At the lengthy manoeuvre it was going to take to get her back on her feet once she'd finished.

Still, doing the planting herself had been worth it. Fern let Tina take care of the watering though, happy to wait beside her sister, addressing her silent promises to the spider crawling up the wooden grave marker. *I'll get you a proper headstone as soon as I can. As soon as things go back to normal. And I won't stay away so long next time, I swear. I'll bring the baby, Linette. That's what we're going to call her. Paul doesn't actually know that yet, but what's not to like? A new little Linny. Not to replace you . . . I don't mean that. No one could ever replace you . . .* Only by then she was crying and Tina was fishing out a bulb-scented tissue and insisting on giving her space to talk to Linny on her own.

'I'll wait in the car for a bit,' Tina said. 'It's no problem. Just give me a ring when you're ready and I'll come and walk you back.'

Fern felt silly after she'd gone. Shy even, as if she didn't know what to say to her sister, now they were on their own. The spider had disappeared and Linny herself felt a million miles away again. Or maybe it was just that Fern had said everything she needed to say already. But she stood there dutifully for a while, relating her last couple of visits to the care home, passing on her father's message as instructed, although it pained her to do so: 'Tell Linnaea I'm thinking of her. Tell her I'll be there just as soon as I can . . . as soon as I get out of here.' And after that Fern limped along the graves to the nearest bench, to sit down for a minute, bathing her face in the feeble warmth of the sun. She wouldn't make Tina come all the way back down again, she decided. She'd be fine getting to the car park from here, once she'd had a rest.

She turned her head sharply at a sign of movement along the path. Was that Tina coming back to collect her already? No, whoever it was, they were taller and thinner than her mother-in-law, more man-shaped. It was definitely a man, she concluded, following his steady progress through the cemetery. Watching as he turned down onto Linny's row, clutching a bunch of flowers to his chest. Staring in slow disbelief as he came close enough to pick out his features, a sharp ribbon of ice shuddering down her spine.

Richard!

It *must* have been Richard's car she'd seen after all. He must have followed them all the way from Crenellation Lane, watching them turn off towards the cemetery and then looping back himself, further up the road. And now here he was, coming to finish what Kerry had started; to stop Fern poking round in his affairs for good. Perhaps he'd seen Tina off in the car park already and now he'd come to chase *her* down – a pregnant woman on crutches . . . It wouldn't be much of a chase though, would it?

Chapter 36

Fern stared around wildly, looking for someone – anyone – she could call for help. But there was no one there. And her phone? Where was her phone? She remembered slipping it back into her dressing-gown pocket after replying to Paul's text in the kitchen. And hanging her dressing gown over the back of a chair as she struggled into the change of clothes Tina had brought down for her. It was still there in her dressing gown, wasn't it? *No, no, no . . .*

'Stay there,' she shouted as Richard headed down the row towards her, her voice cracking in fear. 'I've already called the police,' Fern lied. 'They're on their way.' But either he hadn't heard, her strangled words carried away in the breeze, or he didn't care . . . or maybe he'd guessed that it was an empty threat. He carried on walking, wielding his bunch of flowers – blood-red roses – like a weapon.

The sick feeling was back with a vengeance as he drew near. Fern hauled herself up onto her feet, lunging for her crutches with shaking hands. A getaway was out of the question, but a sharp blow to her assailant's crotch might at least incapacitate him for a bit. She must have *over*-lunged though, losing her balance and toppling forwards with a fresh shriek of fear.

Strong arms caught her under the elbows, keeping her from

falling. *No*, she begged inwardly, *get off me! Let me go!* But the words caught in her throat. It was like Barry all over again, except Barry was just a plumber and Richard . . . Richard was a killer. A killer whose roses went tumbling to the floor as he helped Fern steady herself again. A killer who lowered her carefully back down onto the bench and handed her the crutches she'd been reaching for. Anyone would think he was just a concerned neighbour, not a murderer.

'Hey,' he said softly. 'Easy does it now. Are you all right?' He didn't *sound* much like a murderer either.

'Where's Tina?' said Fern, panic and adrenaline still coursing through her veins. 'Is she okay? My mother-in-law,' she added, realising that the two of them had never actually met.

Richard blinked. 'Tina?' he repeated. He looked more worried than wrathful. More confused than vengeful. Maybe he'd come to reason with Fern rather than kill her. Her shoulders sagged a little as she allowed herself to breathe again. Perhaps he just wanted to talk.

'The lady in the car, you mean?' said Richard. 'She looked like she was reading something – a notebook, maybe? – and I didn't like to disturb her. It's you I came to see. You and Linny.'

'*Linny?*' Fern was the one looking confused now.

'Your sister,' said Richard, as if there'd ever been any other Linny. He reached down and picked up the fallen roses.

Linny's favourite.

'But I thought . . .' *I thought you'd come to attack me.* 'I don't understand,' Fern murmured, staring at the single tear running down his cheek, and yet somehow she found she *did* understand after all. Richard hadn't come to silence her about his doomed relationship with Marte, had he? He'd come to lay flowers at his lover's grave. Impossible as it was, it was the only explanation that made any sense.

Richard.

Linny's lover was Richard.

271

'It was you,' she whispered. 'It was you all along.'

Richard nodded. 'She never told you, did she?' His face fell in disappointment.

'No,' said Fern. 'I knew she was seeing someone, but she wouldn't say who. Refused to say anything about you at all.' *Only that you were well off.*

If I'm not allowed to meet him, at least tell me something about him. Come on. One word.

Wealthy.

That's all she'd said. 'Wealthy' or 'loaded'. Wait, Fern remembered now.

He's. . . . he's Rich.

She almost set off laughing again at the utter stupidity of it all. At her *own* stupidity. *Oh, Linny. You told me his name and I wasn't even listening.* Except the laughter caught in her throat this time, stopping her breath, leaving her dizzy and faint. 'Sorry,' she stammered. 'It's a lot to take in. I thought . . .' But she didn't even know how to *start* explaining what she'd thought. Marte . . . the baby . . . Kerry . . . and Callie. The woman Callie had seen at the swanky bar – that must have been Linny all along. She should have felt it somehow, Fern thought. Known it. There was a time she knew everything about her sister. A time she'd have been hard put to say exactly where Linny ended and she began.

'It's taken me a bit of getting used to as well,' said Richard, sitting down beside her. 'Seeing you, I mean. What were the chances, eh? Of all the roads in all the towns . . . and we end up living across the street from each other.' He shook his head against the sheer vastness of the coincidence. 'Linny mentioned your dad's near Westerton, so it shouldn't have been *that* surprising maybe, but even so . . . I couldn't believe it when I saw you in the street last Thursday. I thought it was *her*. I mean, I knew she was gone but . . . I thought she'd come back for me. Crazy, I know.'

She did, thought Fern. She was right there, staring up your drive at you. It wasn't a warning after all, was it? It was a yearning.

Was that why Linny had stayed away ever since? Because it was too painful to see *him*?

'Yes,' she said, slowly, as yet another penny dropped. It was practically raining pennies. 'You called out her name, didn't you? *Linnaea.* I heard you . . . only, I thought it was my husband. I thought . . .' No, it was too hard to explain. Too much.

'I knew she had a sister,' Richard told her. 'But I didn't know you were twins. I didn't know there was an identical copy of her out there somewhere.'

'Not quite so identical anymore,' said Fern flippantly, meaning her enormous stomach and swollen limbs. Only sitting there, staring out over her sister's grave, it sounded like something else entirely. Something she couldn't bring herself to think about.

'What happened between you?' she asked instead, changing the subject. 'She took it hard when it ended, I know that much, but even then she refused to talk about it. About you.' All this time she'd thought it was *her* Linny was ashamed of, without understanding why. Too embarrassed by her own family to introduce them to the man she loved. But perhaps it was the other way round. 'Did she know you were married?'

'Not at first,' he said. 'Which was my fault entirely. I don't know what came over me that night. I mean, we were fine, Kerry and me. Things had been tricky for a while with the whole trying for a baby thing . . . we'd worked through that though. We'd decided to let nature take its course. If it happened, it happened, and if it didn't, we still had each other . . . But there I was at this networking do in the city – an utterly tedious affair. I wasn't even drinking because I'd driven to the Park & Ride, and then . . . and then Linny walked in. Just minding her own business, going through the motions like me, I expect, only . . . well, you know Linny. She could light up an entire room just by stepping into it.'

'Yes,' Fern agreed. 'She could. She did.'

'And before I knew what I was doing . . .' He shook his head. 'I should have been honest with her about Kerry from

273

the start. There shouldn't even have *been* a start. But there was something between us. Something neither one of us was strong enough to fight.'

Fern stole a sideways glance at the perfectly ordinary man who'd somehow stolen her sister's heart. Nose a little on the big side maybe. Chin a little loose as it headed down towards his neck. First grey streaks of hair already clinging to his temples. And married to boot. What had Linny seen in him that she couldn't?

'She tried to break it off with me a few times, but I always managed to talk her round. I told her I'd leave Kerry. Told her the marriage had been over for a while and it would be better for everyone in the long run. I promised we'd start over, properly this time. No secrets. No lies . . .'

No secrets. Did she think Fern would judge her? Was that it? *One word – home-wrecker. Yes, it's hyphenated.* Of course she wouldn't. Well, not for long anyway. She never could hold anything against her sister for long.

'But then Kerry told me she was pregnant,' said Richard.

What? Fern was thrown for a moment, until she realised Kerry must have lost her baby too. *An entire street of lost babies,* she thought, wrapping her arms around her stomach.

'And that changed everything,' Richard went on. 'Not for me, I'm ashamed to say, but for Linny. She ended it properly then, just like that. Cut me off dead. She said I had a family who needed me now and she wouldn't be the one to break it up. And that was it. She wouldn't see me. Wouldn't take my calls . . .'

'Were you there?' asked Fern. 'At the funeral? I remember thinking you might be – whoever you were – but . . .' *All those people who loved her. Who thought they had a claim to her.*

'No,' he said. 'I wasn't even in the country. I didn't know she'd . . .' He wiped his eyes on the cuff of his shirt. 'Not 'til later. Much later. I called her that day, you know, the day she . . .'

The day she died, thought Fern, finishing the sentence for him. *The day I died with her.* 'How did she seem?' she asked. 'What did she say?' *Tell me. Tell me everything.* But there was fear mixed in with her hunger for details. What if the answer was something she didn't want to hear? *She seemed down and distracted – not like her usual self at all. She said she'd had some kind of row with you the night before. Said she'd decided to cycle into work to try and clear her head . . .*

'She never answered,' said Richard. 'I rang her from the airport while Kerry was in the toilets, to tell her there *was* no baby anymore. That it never made it past a few weeks and I'd only stayed after that out of guilt and duty. I know it was shitty of me but if Linny *had* picked up, I'd have begged her to take me back. To try again. But she didn't and I didn't leave a message because I thought I saw Kerry coming and . . . and when she never rang me back, I knew it really *was* over.'

She was over, thought Fern, helplessly, wishing she could stop the new film playing in her head. The one where Linny heard his ringtone above the dull roar of the traffic and lost concentration. Lost control. A short jerk of her handlebars in the wrong direction as Iggy Pop's 'Fall in Love with Me' started up inside her arm pouch and then . . . and then . . .

'And Kerry,' said Fern, blinking away the final scene. 'Did she know about all of this?'

Richard shook his head. 'No. At least I didn't think so at the time.' He gave a deep sigh. 'There was a photo on my mobile . . . oh this must have been getting on for a year ago now, while Linny and I were still seeing each other. And the photo was right there on my screen when I went to make a call, and it shouldn't have been.' He touched his hand to his pocket as if he could feel the picture through the fabric of his trousers. 'I was terrified it was Kerry, that she'd been going through my phone and found it. That's all there *was* to find, as well. I never kept anything else. No texts. No call history. Nothing. Except for that one photo. A drunken selfie we'd taken in our hotel dressing gowns when we stole away for the weekend, that I hadn't got round to deleting yet. Because . . .

275

because . . . I don't know, because I was head over heels in love with your sister – totally besotted – and I couldn't bear to lose a single part of her.'

Besotted, thought Fern. Linny was the woman in the city he'd told Eddie about, wasn't she?

Richard shook his head. 'And perhaps on some level I *wanted* Kerry to find out. Wanted her to accuse me and get it all out in the open. Wanted her to leave me so I'd be free. But she never said a word and I thought I'd got away with it. Perhaps she was worried I'd leave *her* if she said anything . . . if she made me choose. Let's face it, she'd have been right, wouldn't she?'

No contest, thought Fern. *Poor old Kerry never stood a chance.*

Richard pressed his knuckles into his temples and sighed. 'And then a few weeks later she told me she was pregnant and that was that . . . I don't know now though. Maybe there never *was* a baby,' he said, slowly. 'Maybe she made the whole thing up to trap me. Or punish me. That's a terrible thing to say, isn't it? A terrible thing to think.' He gave a low, bitter laugh. 'But it worked, didn't it? I came back to her. We're still together. Just about, anyway . . . until yesterday, when she said that you'd been round wanting to talk to me. When she accused me of having an affair with *you*. Of picking up again where we'd left off . . . That's when I knew. I knew she *must* have seen that picture of Linny on my phone after all and committed it to memory . . .'

I doubt she could have forgotten it if she tried, thought Fern. The image must have seared itself into her brain.

'And then when *you* moved in across the street, she must have thought you were her: the woman in the photo.'

Fern nodded slowly. *Yes. I know exactly who you are* – that's what Kerry had said when they met in the street that day. *I didn't realise you were pregnant though. When's it due?* She must have been busy doing the maths. Trying to work out whose baby it was. And then she must have confided in April. It all made sense now. After Fern left the party, Kerry must have told her everything:

276

That's the bitch he was having an affair with. I recognised her from his phone. And now she's here, just across the street from me, rubbing my nose in it. Picking up where she left off . . . No wonder April's attitude towards her had changed.

'I guess that explains the hate campaign,' she said.

'What do you mean?'

'Someone posted hate mail through our door,' Fern explained. 'They vandalised the car and the garden and wrote a threatening message on the side of the house in red paint. I'm surprised you didn't see it.'

Richard frowned. 'Gosh, that's terrible. It doesn't sound like Kerry though. I don't know where she'd have got the red paint from either . . .'

'She was there again last night. We caught her watching the house,' said Fern.

'Shit, I'm so sorry. I should have told her the truth last week, when you first moved in. I should have guessed it was all going to come out anyway. Seeing you – seeing *Linny*, every time I catch a glimpse of you across the road – it's brought it all flooding back again. I keep worrying I'm going to say her name in my sleep. And then yesterday . . . I should have confessed when Kerry first confronted me but I panicked. I denied everything. I told her I'd never even met you until last week. Which was true, of course.' He sighed again. 'I guess that makes me a coward as well as a cheat.'

'I guess it does,' agreed Fern. *That poor woman,* she thought. *What must she have been going through these last few days?*

'But this morning . . . this morning I knew I had to come clean. I was going to tell her, I swear I was. I'd even called in sick to work. But I wanted to talk to you first. I wanted to know why you'd come to see me. I . . . I guess I thought you might have a message for me.'

'A message?'

'From Linny.' He laughed. 'Listen to me! Even after all this time, I still can't get her out of my head. It sounds crazy now I'm saying it out loud, but I thought she might have said something to you . . . Before she died, I mean. Something about how much she loved me. That's all I needed . . . one last thing to hold on to before I gave her up for good.'

Fern could see the desperation in his face. The longing.

'I know it's selfish,' he said, cradling his head in his hands, his fingers clawing at his hair. 'And Kerry deserves better. So much better. But Linny . . .'

'No,' said Fern. 'There never was any message, I'm afraid. I saw how much you meant to her though, if that helps. I saw how miserable she was when it was over.'

Richard let out a low sob.

'But you have to tell Kerry,' she insisted. 'No more putting it off. She deserves to know everything. *I* deserve for her to know everything too. Do you realise how scared we've been, thinking there was someone targeting the house? Wondering what they were going to do next?'

'I'm so sorry. It's all such a mess. I really *was* going to come clean this morning and hope against hope that Kerry would forgive me. But then I saw you heading out with your mother-in-law and I didn't even stop to think. I got in the car and followed you. I thought if I could *talk* to you, if I could hear Linny's voice through you, one last time, then . . .' He gave a long, shuddering sniff. 'And then when I realised where you were going, when I saw you turn off to the cemetery, I panicked. I wasn't sure I was ready to see her . . .' He nodded his head towards Linny's grave. 'To see her like this. I've thought about coming so many times but I've never . . .'

Fern reached for his hand and held it, tight. He didn't deserve her sympathy after the way he'd treated Kerry. But she understood *why* he'd done it. She understood his love for Linny, the way it eclipsed everything else. She understood his loss.

'I was exactly the same,' she said softly. 'But it's not as bad as I thought it would be. I think it did me good to come here and talk to her.'

278

'I brought her roses,' said Richard, staring at the bouquet in his lap. 'I had to drive all the way on into Lonford to find them – I was scared you might have gone by the time I got back – but they had to be red roses. They were her favourite.'

'Yes, they were,' agreed Fern.

They lapsed into silence. Fern was thinking about Linny, wondering what she'd say if she could see the two of them now – her sister and her lover holding hands on a bench surrounded by dead people.

'So what *did* you want to talk to me about yesterday?' asked Richard. 'I forgot to ask.'

Marte. Fern had forgotten too for a moment.

'I thought you might know something about Marte,' she said. 'Marte Hortlassen.' *I thought she was the one you were having an affair with. And then afterwards I thought you must have killed her. I thought that's why Kerry was trying to scare us out of our own house . . . to stop us poking into the past.*

'Who?' If the name meant anything to Richard, he wasn't letting on.

'A Norwegian lady who lived at our place years ago, back when it was shared accommodation,' said Fern. 'She was expecting her first child – I've discovered that much – and fell out with her grandparents over it. But no one seems to know what happened to her after that. She just disappeared off the face of the earth. And no one can tell me who the father was, either. Not Sean, that's all I know, although she let him think he was.'

'Eddie,' said Richard with surprising certainty. 'I bet you anything it was him. I dread to think how many little Edward Gumleys there might be running round out there.'

He pulled a face, looking more disapproving than he had any right to, and Fern let go of his hand.

'I don't even know him that well,' Richard went on, 'but we got hammered in the pub last Christmas after a "Crenellation Lane Social" April had organised – I mean *really* hammered – and it turned into a confessional of sorts. I blabbed that I was thinking of leaving Kerry for someone else and he told me I'd been a fool to marry in the first place. How he was free to sleep with anyone he fancied . . . and then reeled off a long list of all the women on the street, past and present, who'd succumbed to his charms at one time or another. I couldn't tell you many of them now. Couldn't have told you next morning, even – it was all a bit of a haze afterwards – but if it's a local Lothario you're after, then he's your man.'

Fern didn't have any trouble believing him. There was a reason April referred to Eddie as the Casanova of Crenellation Lane. But being a flirt, a womaniser, didn't make him a murderer, or did it? What if he'd taken exception to the idea of a baby tying him down? What if he held his carefree single life in the same regard as other men held their marriages? Or what if it was the opposite . . . what if it was the thought of Marte starting a new life with Sean that had tipped him over the edge? He'd certainly been rattled by the news that Marte was back . . . Fern thought about the charming killer in *Blood Lovers*, and the poor Norwegian girl he'd buried in the woods. What if it wasn't just fiction?

Chapter 37

It was Fern's turn to head back to the car now, leaving Richard to say his goodbyes in private. She was grateful for the slow limp back up the hill on her own. Glad of the space and quiet to collect her thoughts and untangle the knot of feelings jostling for space inside her head. Inside her heart. It wasn't *her* Linny had been ashamed of, then. And it wasn't *her* Kerry had taken such an instant dislike to. It wasn't even *her* April had turned against. Not really.

And then there was Richard. She ought to hate him, now that she knew who he was: the adulterous wedge who'd come between her and her sister, bringing secrets where there'd never been any before. And what if it really had been him distracting Linny that day? What if it was his selfish phone call that sent her careering into the wheel arch of that lorry? But of all the odd mixed-up feelings Fern felt towards the man, hatred wasn't one of them. Jealousy? Yes, childish as it was, at some level she envied him his bond with Linny, resenting her own exclusion from their introverted bubble of two. And pity. Endless pity. Pity for him. Pity for Kerry. Pity for herself.

At least Richard wasn't a killer though. At least she and Tina were still in one piece. And Paul. Paul was coming home again. As for Eddie . . . Fern shivered when she remembered how unguarded she'd been in his car that day, asking all those questions about Marte. But that was before she'd suspected Marte was dead. The most she'd suspected Eddie of back then was having a fling with April. And now Fern didn't know what to think. She wasn't sure she had the mental – or emotional – energy to think *anything* very useful. Her thoughts kept coming back to Linny and Richard.

She filled Tina in on the whole sorry story as they made their way home, after a brief diversion to find a toilet. Fern's bladder could be relied on to interrupt the most important of narratives.

'You poor love,' said her mother-in-law. 'As if you didn't have enough on your plate with this wretched Marte business. How are you feeling now?'

'Tired,' said Fern. 'Tired and sad.' It sounded pathetic even to her own ears but that was the truth of it. That's what the crazy cocktail of emotions had all boiled down to, somehow, in the retelling: a weary sadness. As if she was too exhausted to fight her grief anymore, or too exhausted to stoke it – maybe that's what she'd been doing all this time? Too tired for hatred or regrets. Peace was all Fern wanted now, which in a funny way was exactly what she'd found at her sister's grave. And that's what she held on to, all the way back home, pushing aside any thoughts of Marte, until they drew up outside the house and saw Sean there, waiting for them.

Fern could see the anger, spilling off him in waves, before she heard it. Before Tina had even opened the car door. And then when she *did* open the door and came round to help Fern, Tina got it with both barrels.

'Where do you get off questioning my mum like that?' he demanded, flecks of spit catching the sunlight as they flew. 'Hounding her, I should say. Poking round in my private affairs?' He must have been working at Yasmin's. Fern could see a loaded wheelbarrow the other side of her neighbour's gate.

Tina seemed unusually lost for words. 'No . . . that's not . . . I mean I didn't. I wasn't.'

'Sticking your fat nose in where it's not wanted. She told me all about it. Digging up the past. And *you*,' Sean said, jabbing his hand trowel dangerously close to Fern's stomach. 'You're just as bad. All your endless bloody questions.'

'We got talking, that's all,' said Tina, finally finding her voice, stepping between Fern and the trowel. 'I came round to see you, if you must know. To ask you about the lawn. But you weren't there and your mum was kind enough to invite me in.'

'Well . . . well, that still doesn't give you any right to be raking through my private life like that. Yes, I knew Marte, all right? Yes, she was having my baby – *my* baby – and she lost it. And yes, she ran off and left me broken-hearted. Is that what you want to hear? Happy now?'

'Not really, no,' said Tina. 'I don't appreciate being spoken to like that under *any* circumstances. And I *really* don't appreciate you threatening my daughter-in-law. You put that spade down, do you hear me?'

Wow. This was a whole new side to Tina. The woman was on fire.

'I . . . I wasn't threatening anyone,' said Sean, suddenly running out of steam. He looked down at the trowel in his hand as if he'd never seen it before, rubbing at a patch of paint on his finger. 'I only meant . . .'

'I don't care what you meant,' said Tina briskly. 'I'm telling you it's unacceptable. And you can forget about the work we agreed on. I'm perfectly capable of tidying up the garden myself as it turns out. Come on, Fern, let's go and sort out that rose bush, shall we?'

Fern could barely keep up, hobbling after her mother-in-law in awed admiration.

'What rose bush?' called Sean. 'What do you mean?' But Tina didn't even look back.

It was all an act though. She visibly deflated again the moment they got inside and shut the door, like a blown-up balloon released before the knot was tied.

'I'm sorry, that was stupid,' she said, sinking down onto a kitchen chair. 'He's never going to open up to us about Marte now, is he?'

'You were great out there,' Fern told her. 'I wish I had half your sass and fire.'

'Really?'

'Absolutely. And to be honest, he probably wasn't going to tell us anything anyway. That's if there's anything *to* tell. Maybe he's as clueless as the rest of us. Maybe Marte really did run off,' she said wearily, not believing it for one second. 'Maybe she didn't *want* anyone to find her.'

'But you *saw* her,' insisted Tina. 'With the baby she was carrying six years ago. The baby Sean thought was his . . .' She shook her head as if she was weary of it all too. 'And the writing on the lawn last night. That's got to mean something, surely?'

'I don't know,' said Fern. 'I just don't know anymore. Maybe when Paul comes back he can . . . You will tell him, won't you?' she begged. 'You'll tell him what you saw last night. That it's not all in my head?'

'Of course I will. He'll probably think we're *both* barmy, but yes, I'll tell him. We're a team, remember?' Tina forced a smile. 'Albeit a team missing the most vital element of any investigation.'

'What do you mean?'

'A working kettle,' said her mother-in-law. 'What else?'

Fern grinned, thinking it was a joke, but then wasn't so sure after all. Tina looked pretty serious, sitting there rubbing her temples.

'I can't think what I'd have done with the receipt if it's not in the box or my purse,' she said. 'And my brain's so caffeine-deprived I'm all out of ideas.' She pulled herself up suddenly, slapping the table with the flats of her fingers. 'Do you know what? Screw that weedy little salesman. I'm going straight to the manager this time, with some more of that sass and fire. *I really don't appreciate your attempts to deny me my consumer rights,* that's what I'm going to say. And if they still won't give me my money back, I'll damn well buy another one somewhere else. Needs must.' She paused for a moment. 'Will you be all right if I pop out again? I'm assuming you don't want to come with me . . . it's a fair trek from the car park.'

'I'll be fine,' said Fern. 'And you're right. We *do* need a kettle. I bet even Cagney and Lacey have the odd hot drink to see them through the day.'

Tina grinned. But then her expression darkened again. 'Promise me you won't go and see Eddie while I'm gone. Not on your own. I still can't believe he'd be capable of anything like that, but . . .' She left the rest of the sentence hanging there, unsaid.

'I promise,' Fern told her. 'I won't even *think* about Marte until you come back.'

But she was already thinking about Marte before the door had even closed behind her mother-in-law. The business with Sean had brought the whole tangled mystery right back to centre stage in Fern's head. Their previous questions had met with bland denial and evasion on his part, so why had Tina's conversation with his mother provoked such wild anger this time round? What had changed?

Fern stared out at the lawn, recalling the pale message picked out against the gloom the night before: *MY BABY MY BABY.* It should have been scary – it should have been downright terrifying – but of all the frightening things jostling for Fern's attention over the last few days, the ghostly message wasn't one of them. Maybe it was because Tina had seen it too this time. Maybe it was a twisted form of relief to think of ghosts out there in the real world instead of them being phantoms in her own head.

Fern still wished she could go back in time and do it all differently. Wished she'd turned around at the front doorstep the first time she'd seen the house. Or the second. But her feelings towards Marte had shifted subtly over the last day or so. It wasn't sympathy she felt exactly but . . . a sense of responsibility. As if their fates were inextricably linked somehow. As if Fern was the one Marte had been waiting for all this time. Fern and her baby.

The baby was kicking wildly now, kicking or punching, or elbowing . . . a hammer of angry little limbs pounding against her belly as if Linette was trying to get out.

'Shh,' she said. 'It's going to be all right. I promise.'

My baby. My baby.

Fern hobbled into the dining room and sat down at the freshly tuned piano. Maybe some music would calm her down. 'Shh,' she said again, opening up the Satie score to good old 'Gympnopédie, No. 1', settling into the first few bars in the hope that the baby would settle with them. But the notes in the melody were all wrong. The F sharps and the C sharps sounded more like naturals and the Es were practically E flats – a discordant clash against the clumsy, plodding chords of her left hand. The first time she put it down to error on her part, to tiredness and stupidity. But it was the same when she tried again. And again, the beautiful haunting tune turned harsh and ugly under her faltering fingers. And the baby – oh, the baby. What was it *doing* in there, pummelling her insides to a pulp? What was wrong with her?

'It's you, isn't it?' Fern said out loud, addressing the empty room. 'It's been you all along: The piano. The fridge. The kettle. Why are you doing this to us? To me? What is it you want?'

But there was no answer. Of course there wasn't. Why couldn't Marte come back and talk to her in person like she had on the day of the viewing? Why couldn't she tell them what she wanted – *revenge on my killer and a proper burial*, wasn't that what all ghosts wanted? – and then leave them in peace? Why did everything have to be so cryptic? An initialled heart on the mirror. A name on a window. A message scrawled across the lawn.

MY BABY

MY BABY

The words kept turning round in Fern's head. The same words Sean had used, like an unconscious echo: 'Yes, she was having my baby – *my* baby – and she lost it.' Maybe this wasn't the first time the message had appeared, and Tina had been onto something when she went to ask Sean if he'd seen it before. He must have been doing the garden here six years ago as well, she realised. *The one who did the lawn.* That's how Ant had described him at the antenatal meeting. But Fern was sure he'd only said 'lawn' singular, not plural. Maybe the upper lawn wasn't there back then, or maybe . . .

The thought made her gasp out loud. What if Ant didn't mean that Sean was the one who *mowed* the lawn at all? What if he remembered him as the one who *graffitied* over it? Fern had a sudden vision of a younger Sean taking his anger towards Marte out on the grass, staking his claim to her unborn child with a bottle of weedkiller. What if the words were *his*, from six years ago, not hers?

MY BABY

MY BABY

Fern and Tina had certainly seen the angry side of him today, and how quickly his mood could change. How he'd gone from threatening Fern with the trowel to looking down at it in surprise, as if he'd never seen it before, rubbing nervously at that patch of paint on his finger . . . a *red* patch of paint! Fern hadn't even thought of it at the time – hadn't stopped to put two and two together. But maybe the painted warning on the wall *hadn't* been from Kerry after all. Maybe it was Sean. STAY OUT. *Stay out of it. Stay out of my business. Stay out of my house.* Perhaps coming home to find Tina questioning his mum about Marte the day before had tipped him over the edge again. Just like it had six years ago, when he burned the message into the lawn . . . If Fern was right, that meant it wasn't a message from beyond the grave at all. It must have always been there: a slight colour variation caused by using the wrong seed to try and patch it up afterwards, which the evening dew and the outside light – and a bit of ghostly help from Marte – happened to pick up. Fern gathered her crutches and hobbled outside for a closer look.

The baby was going crazier than ever now as she stood on the patio, staring up at the lower lawn. 'Come on, that's enough now,' Fern pleaded. 'You're hurting Mummy.'

Was it her imagination or was there a lighter, tuftier line there in the grass, over towards the middle? Like the start of an M?

MY BABY.

The image of a baby swam behind Fern's eyes. A tiny red doll of a thing, wrapped in a matching red blanket, with a yellow name embroidered in the corner.

No! She forced the picture away again, refocusing her mind on the lawn. If she squinted hard enough, she could make out the start of a curve a little further along . . . the beginnings of a B, maybe? And yes, there was another one directly below it.

MY BABY.

The wild pummelling in her belly grew stronger than ever.

'What is it?' Fern whispered. 'What do you want with me?' She wasn't sure if it was the baby she was talking to anymore though, or Marte, as she stared at the lawn, searching for evidence of more letters. The faintest trace of lines further along *could* have been a Y once upon a time. Or maybe this latest theory was just that – a theory, her brain's way of trying to explain the unexplainable. Sean was the one to ask, but the mere thought of facing him again was enough to set Fern's heart racing. She could still hear the anger in his voice turning to desperation as he'd shouted after them: *What rose bush? What do you mean?* Could still see the fury contorting his features as he'd met them from the car, spade waving like a weapon: *She told me all about it. Digging up the past . . .*

What rose bush . . .

The rose bush! Of course!

It wasn't *Linny's* rose Sean was worried about, was it? It was the one at the top of the garden. The one he'd planted to remember his poor dead baby. Or to mark the spot . . .

What if *that's* why Sean was so desperate to hold on to the gardening contract from one owner to the next? Because he didn't want anyone else digging around in the flowerbeds? What if *he'd* killed Marte in a jealous rage and buried her in the garden as the quickest way of hiding the body?

If she'd stopped to think about it for half a second Fern probably wouldn't have headed up there on her own, scooping up Tina's new trowel, the one they'd taken to the cemetery, as she passed by the back door. If she'd thought about it at all, she'd have waited for Tina to come back, instead of hauling herself up the steps on her hands and knees, losing one of the crutches on the way up and letting it bounce its way back down without her. But Fern didn't think. *Couldn't* think of anything else – only of Marte waiting for her at the top of the garden in the shadow of the old folly. Marte and her baby cuddled one inside the other beneath the rose bush. Fern knew it, like she'd known about Richard and Linny, with a sudden, ferocious certainty that defied all logic. As if she'd always known it. As if the answer had been there in her brain all along, biding its time. Waiting for the final piece of the puzzle to click into place and spur her into action.

Chapter 38

Fern was a raw and muddied mess by the time she reached the top of the garden, her ankle throbbing with a new fierceness, and the knees of her maternity jeans already black and torn. But she scrambled on, belly dragging low over the unmown grass, the crenellated folly wall casting long, undulating shadows across the topmost bed. And there it was: the rose bush. Marte's rose bush.

Fern started digging, fuelled by a sudden rush of energy, but the densely packed soil was riven with wooded roots, her trowel striking uselessly around the rose's shank. She followed the bed along another foot and tried again, thrusting down amongst the smaller, weedier plants, biting her lip with determination. The going was easier now, the little spade striking through the earth again and again and again, each assault more frenzied than the last. She pawed at the ground with her left hand between strokes, scratching up the earth with her bare nails, sending mud and worms flying behind her, like a cartoon dog after its bone. Like a desperate woman after the bones of the desperate woman before her.

The blood in her ears was pounding so loudly that she couldn't make out the actual words when they came, not at first, just the hatred boiling underneath them. Just the roar of anger tearing up the steps to find her. *Sean.* And then he was right there behind her, hauling her backwards, her ankle twisting and tearing under her weight, her back a hot spasm of pain, fear rippling through her belly. And now he was spitting, flinging the words straight into her face, his mouth twisted out of shape as he shook them into her.

'Stop it. Get out. Leave her be, you interfering little bitch.'

Fern wheezed with the pain. A double pain – ankle and stomach vying for her terrified attention. 'Let go. You're hurting me.' *Now* she thought about Tina. Paul. Anyone. Why *hadn't* she waited, instead of dragging herself up here on some hare-brained rescue mission that was already six years too late? In plain view of any psychotic local gardeners. Sean must have been watching her from Yasmin's. Must have let himself in at the side gate she'd forgotten to lock. If there'd been *any* doubt in Fern's mind about the man – about what he'd done, what he'd been hiding all these years – it was long gone now.

'She's *mine*,' he spat. 'Her and the baby. *My* baby.'

'Yes,' said Fern. 'But what have you done with them? What did you do?'

'Mine,' repeated Sean, taking no notice. 'Not *his*.' His gaze flicked to the far side of the garden. To Eddie's. 'Why would she say that?' he snarled. 'Why would she lie?'

'Perhaps she was confused,' said Fern, changing tack. The last thing she wanted to do was antagonise him. 'Your brain does funny things when you're pregnant . . .' She closed her eyes as the pain in her stomach eased and the pain in her ankle took over. 'I think I might have got confused too. I just wanted to put in a new rose bush for my sister. Only this doesn't seem like the best spot after all.'

But Sean didn't show any signs of hearing, other than the tightening of his fingers on her arms. Fern swallowed hard, trying to fight back the fresh waves of panic.

'Please, let me go now. I think I need to see a doctor. I've done something to my leg. And the baby might be . . .'

'I'd have taken care of it. She knew that,' he said. 'Taken care of both of them. Her, me, Mum and the baby. Like a proper family. That's all I ever wanted. Why did she have to go and ruin everything?'

'My mother-in-law will be back any minute now,' Fern told him. 'She'll be looking for me.'

'You can't tell her,' Sean hissed, unpredictable anger giving way to unpredictable fear, the sudden shift no less terrifying and no less dangerous. 'No one can know. I didn't mean for her to get hurt. I barely touched her. It was the way she fell. The edge of the table . . . Everyone else was out and I didn't know what to do, and the trench . . . the trench was right there ready for the new plants. I'd spent all afternoon digging it.'

'Yes,' said Fern. 'An accident. Of course it was. I understand. I won't tell anyone, I swear.'

Sean's fingers shifted upwards over the tops of her shoulders.

'No one can know,' he said, his voice little more than a whisper now. 'Mum needs me. I'm all she's got.'

'I won't tell a soul,' Fern promised. 'But you have to let me go. You *have* to. Otherwise they'll come looking for me and *then* they'll know. Tina will be back any second now. And my husband,' she gasped, her eyes watering as his fingers stretched around her neck. She could smell the damp earth under his nails. 'I think I heard his car on the drive . . .' she lied, fighting for breath as fear turned to terror. 'Please,' she begged.

'No one can know,' Sean said again, his thumbs pressing deeper into the front of her neck while his fingers tightened round the back.

Pressing.

Tightening.

Squeezing.

Crushing.

The baby had fallen still. It was Fern kicking wildly now, limbs thrashing as she struggled to breathe, hands clawing uselessly

292

at Sean's. If she still had the spade she could have fought back, but the trowel lay useless in the hole behind her and he was so strong. Too strong.

Her lungs were burning all the way up her throat. All the way up to the backs of her eyes.

Please, she shouted in her head, screaming it over and over inside her flaming skull. *Please. Please. Please.*

Please let me go.

Please let it be over.

But maybe it already was. The agony of those first moments – seconds? minutes? – eased into meaninglessness. The fire was fading again already. Fading. And, for one tiny oxygen-starved moment, Fern felt glad, terror turning to euphoria. She was going to find Linny. They were going to be together again. But then she thought of Paul, of the baby, and knew she couldn't leave them. *Wouldn't* leave them. She summoned up what little strength she had left and kicked.

'Aggghhhrrr!' There was a wild animal howl of fury that matched the cry in Fern's head. But it wasn't hers. At least, she didn't think it was. Her throat was too raw – too burned – for any sound at all. But the noose of fingers around her neck had loosened somehow, cold air gasping back through the tight press of her windpipe.

'Take that!' Another feral cry, tearing through the confusion, and this time there was no mistaking where it had come from. Tina.

There was a terrible *thwack* that seemed to hang in the air, sending another spasm of pain up Fern's spine, circling round the tightness of her belly. Then something warm leaking down her legs, and a loud *whump* like a body hitting the ground. And then . . .

Nothing.

* * *

The light was dazzling. Too bright. Too bright.

There it was again. Shining in her other eye this time.

And then a voice, murmuring something soft and low. Telling her she was a good girl.

Good girl. Good girl.

Telling her it was going to be okay. Telling her—

The baby!

'My baby,' Fern said. Tried to say, her tongue knotting itself round the words and finding them gone.

Please. My baby.

And then the voice was talking to someone else, someone she couldn't see, her eyes still too dazzled from the brightness. She closed them again, or maybe they were already closed, sinking back into the soft black nothing she found waiting for her. And Linny was already there in the dark, just as Fern had known she would be, already reaching for her hand, mirrored fingers closing round hers.

'I still remembered how to play it,' Fern told her sister, as if they were halfway through a conversation, the words coming loose and easy now. '"Gympnopédie, No 1". But the notes were all wrong. *Your* part was all wrong. I tried, but I can't do it without you. *You're* the melody. You always were.'

'Yes,' said Linny, 'I know.' Fern felt her smiling through the darkness. Grinning. 'Because that's the easy part, you idiot! I only had one note to think of at once. But you? Entire chords stretching up and down the keyboard? It was you, Fern. It was always you. Always the depth. Always the strength.'

'But I don't know how to be strong,' said Fern. 'I don't think I can.'

'Yes, you do. You already are. Look at you. Look how far you've come already. Look how far you're going to go. You and Paul and the baby . . .'

'The baby's fine,' said the voice, but it wasn't Linny's voice. That wasn't Linny's hand squeezing hers anymore. Linny was gone. 'Heartbeat's a little high,' said the voice, 'but nothing to worry about. He or she's a proper little fighter, just like their mum. You're doing a great job there. Good girl, Fern. Stay with us now, that's it. Just 'til we get to the hospital.'

Linny? thought Fern, trying to call for her, eyes blinking back into brightness. Into daylight. But the strangled noise that came out sounded more like 'Tina'. Maybe it *was* Tina she was calling for.

'Tina?' said the voice. Kind brown eyes and a bearded face smiled down at her. 'The lady who was with you? She's fine, my darling, don't you worry. The police just needed to have a quick word with her and then she'll be following on to the hospital. And your husband. She said to tell you she'd spoken to him and he's on his way too. So nothing for you to worry about, okay? It's all going to be all right.'

And Sean? thought Fern. What had happened to Sean? But then her throat tightened all over again and she couldn't breathe. She could feel his hands back around her neck, squeezing. Crushing.

'You heard the cute ambulance guy,' said Linny from somewhere far away. 'You're a fighter, like your baby. Come on, where's that lust for life?'

Fern forced the breath back down into her lungs. In. Out. In. Out. Felt the grip on her throat loosening. She sang along to Iggy Pop inside her head, imagining the two of them crazy-dancing round their teenage bedroom, her and Linny, loose hair whipping against their faces as they flung themselves round like wild things.

Just like old times.

She imagined her and the baby dancing round the bedroom. Only she wasn't such a baby anymore. She was a proper toddler now. Blonde hair and blue eyes, and fearless, like her Aunty Linny. Like her mum. Fern imagined bouncing her up and down on the bed in time to Iggy Pop, drinking in her wild shrieks of laughter.

A love for life.

Chapter 39

She dreamed of cold hands unzipping her stomach. Reaching in to take her baby.

Please. My baby.

Dreamed of cold hands slicing it out of her while she slept.

And when she woke up the baby was gone.

Fern couldn't work out where she was at first. Everything looked fuzzy and strange when she opened her eyes. A white ceiling. A ring of blue curtain. And then a pale face looming out of the strangeness.

'Hello, sweetheart. How are you feeling?'

Fern felt like she'd been asleep for days. Maybe she had. 'Tina?' Her voice was cracked and dry, catching in the raw throb of her throat.

'Yes. It's me. I'm right here. No, no don't try and sit up. You need to take it easy. But it's okay. It's all okay. You're safe now.'

Fern almost believed her for a moment, and then she remembered. 'The baby!'

'Shh,' said Tina. 'The baby's doing fine. They're taking excellent care of her, I promise you. You've got yourself a beautiful little girl there. All her fingers and toes. Everything in full working order. Just arrived a bit early, that's all.' She smiled. 'Couldn't wait to meet us.'

Fern couldn't quite process what she was being told. They'd

obviously made it as far as the hospital, but she didn't remember anything after that. Nothing real, anyway, only dreams. How could she have given birth and not remember it? She felt along the low sag of her stomach, to double-check, and felt a dressing of some kind, a soreness. But no baby. 'And she's all right? Are you sure?'

'Of course she is. The doctors need to keep an extra eye on her while she gets her strength up. While you get *your* strength up. Don't worry, Paul's with her now and you'll be able to see her soon, I promise. Hima and I've been getting regular updates and she's doing really well.'

Hima? Who was Hima?

'Hima's the midwife who's been here keeping an eye on you after your C-section,' explained Tina, reading her mind. 'She's lovely. You'll like her.' She glanced over her shoulder as if Hima might have crept up on them unannounced. 'She just popped out a minute ago. I can go and find her though. Let her know you're awake.'

'What about Sean?' asked Fern. She didn't want to know, didn't want to remember, but without the full story she couldn't even begin to process a happy ending.

'He'll live,' said her mother-in-law, abruptly. 'Not sure he deserves to, quite frankly, after what he did – after what he tried to do – but yes, he'll live.'

'What happened?' Fern swallowed. Oh, but it hurt to swallow. And already he was right back in her head again, hissing his hatred into her face. Hands tightening round her neck. But she had to hear it. She had to.

Come on, you're stronger than this, she told herself firmly, pushing the feel of his fingers away again. Breathing in. Breathing out.

Tina hesitated. 'I'm not sure now's the best time to be . . .'

'Please. Just tell me.'

'All right then, if you're sure. But stop me anytime you want to, okay? If it gets too much.'

Fern nodded.

'Okay. So I was driving past the health centre when I remembered,' said Tina. 'Remembered where I'd left the blinking receipt, I mean. I don't know what made me think of it really . . .'

Even when it came to life and death drama, she still insisted on starting at the beginning, thought Fern incredulously. Still focusing on every little detail. But she kept her thoughts to herself, letting the story run its meandering course.

'And then it came to me all of a sudden. It was tucked under the tea bags for safe-keeping, wasn't it? Which *did* make sense when I thought about it . . . kind of, anyway, so I decided to turn round and come back for it . . . and bumped into Yasmin on the pavement, looking agitated. She wanted to know if I'd seen Sean anywhere, which I hadn't, not since our little confrontation outside the house. She *had* just seen him, before I got back, charging down from her top garden with a face like thunder. And when she stopped him to ask what the matter was, he . . . well, that's just it. He didn't stop. Barged right past her and out into the street.'

Tina paused for breath, leaning in to squeeze Fern's hand. 'Are you sure you want to hear this?'

Fern nodded a second time. 'Keep going.'

'All right. Well, *our* gate – your gate, I mean – was open, banging backwards and forwards in the wind, and I don't know . . . I just had this horrible hunch. And when we came round the corner into the back garden and saw him there . . . and saw you . . .' Tina shuddered at the recollection. 'I remember telling Yasmin to ring 999 and then I . . . I . . . I don't know, really. One minute I was down at the bottom of the steps, looking up . . . and the next thing I knew I was right there behind you. Behind him. And one of the crutches was there in my hand and *boom*. Down he went. Still breathing, but out cold, thank goodness. And then the police were there and the ambulance and . . .' She shook her head as if she couldn't quite believe it, even now, rubbing away a stray tear with her thumb. Then another. 'And they said I couldn't go with you because they needed to take a statement from me . . . and . . . and . . . you were so pale when they put you on the stretcher. Pale and lifeless. I thought I was too late.'

Fern looked at her mother-in-law, at the tears streaming openly down her face now. 'You saved my life,' she told her, part of her brain acknowledging the ridiculousness of the words even as she was saying them, as if they'd come straight out of a black-and-white war film or a disaster movie. 'You saved my life,' she said again, a sly giggle escaping out the corner of her mouth.

'Stop it. It wasn't funny,' said Tina. 'It *really* wasn't.' But Fern could see the corners of her mouth twitching through her tears, a matching giggle bubbling up under the surface. And then suddenly Tina was laughing out loud, even while she was crying. They both were, just like at Linny's grave. Like an overflow of emotion spilling out in every direction at once. It hurt to laugh – it hurt like crazy, but somehow Fern needed it. And maybe Tina did too.

'You saved my life.' Fern couldn't get over how funny it was. *My mother-in-law saved my life. In the garden. With a crutch.*

'I tell you what,' said Tina, reaching into her pockets for a tissue. 'We'll have to let Eddie know the truth.'

'About his baby?' Fern forced herself to keep a straight face, because that really *wasn't* funny. That was about as far from funny as it was possible to get.

'No,' said Tina. 'I mean, yes, of course, but that's a job for the police, I think. I meant about using crutches as murder weapons. He told us he didn't think it was sexy enough. I think he'll change his mind when he hears about me, don't you?' She winked.

No, no, no, thought Fern, with a fresh splutter and a sudden image of her mother-in-law's green lacy underwear. Tina was definitely Lacey now, no two ways about it. 'But you didn't actually kill him,' she pointed out. Which was a good thing, wasn't it? A good thing for Tina, anyway. 'So it's not technically a murder weapon.'

'Details, details,' said Tina, drying her eyes. 'Anyway, enough of this. I'll have Hima after me for over-exciting you if we're not careful. How about I go and find her, and then rustle up that husband of yours? He didn't want to leave your side for one moment, you know. But I told him the baby needed him too now. Your beautiful baby girl.'

My baby, thought Fern, hugging the words in tight, feeling a sharp tug of longing deep inside her. *My baby.*

She *was* a beautiful baby, she really was. *Linette.* And the first time Fern held her, she felt . . . there *were* no words for the feeling. Fern was struck dumb by the sheer weight of wonder and responsibility nestled there in her arms. The sheer weight of love. And she knew then, in that first brush of skin against skin, how little the rest of it mattered. Sean. Marte. Even Linny in a way. As long as she could keep this little bundle of arms and legs and snuffling lips safe, then nothing else could ever touch her. Could touch *them*. And the moment passed again, and the old thoughts came crowding back soon enough, with newer, equally frightening worries for companions, but there was a strength in that first primeval touch, in the silent vow she made to protect her daughter now and always. And somehow the strength stayed with her. Or maybe it had been there all along. *Always the depth. Always the strength.*

It helped that she and Paul were finally on the same side again, like a proper team. A family. They'd always been stronger together.

'I can't pretend to understand it all,' he'd admitted, squeezing her hand so tight that Fern feared for her fingers. 'And even now, with everything that's happened, I still can't quite believe she was there . . . Marte, I mean . . . right there in our house, watching us . . .' He shook the thought away with a shiver. 'Or maybe I just don't want to believe it . . . but I do believe you. I love you, Fern. I love you so much, and if you say she was leaving messages for us this whole time, then that's good enough for me.' He tightened his grasp even further as he hunted for the right words, as if he were trying to squeeze them

300

out of her knuckles. 'Oh, sweetheart, I'm sorry it took me so long. When I think what could have happened . . . what *did* happen. If it wasn't for Mum coming back when she did . . .' That's when the rest of the words abandoned him altogether; his grip on Fern's fingers finally easing as he dissolved into messy, un-Paul-like tears.

'Shh,' she said, pulling him into the soreness of her swollen chest and wrapping her arms around him. 'It's all over now. I'm still here, aren't I? And Linette. We're all still here, together. That's the important thing.' She meant it too. What difference did it make now who had or hadn't seen the steamed-up scrawlings on the glass? Fern knew she wasn't crazy – that was the main thing – and so did Tina. Paul didn't have to believe in ghostly Norwegian spirits or his own sister-in-law's visitations, just so long as he believed in her. Besides, maybe there *was* nothing more to believe in now, with no sightings of Linny on Crenellation Lane since moving day, and Marte finally gone.

It was strange, given everything that had happened, but the longer Fern stayed in hospital, watching Linette grow stronger with every passing day, every passing hour, the more she found herself thinking of Crenellation Lane as home. Paul seemed a whole lot less keen on the place since the police had excavated the back garden, taking away the bones of one unidentified female and her five-month foetus, but the horror had faded for Fern now. Now that Sean had confessed and Marte had been found, it was just a normal house again, she was sure of it. Just bricks and mortar, with an impressive, tiled hallway and a warm yellow light coming in through the upstairs windows. They were pretty much stuck with it now, anyway; bodies in the back garden weren't much of a selling feature.

Actually no, it wasn't just bricks and mortar – it was more than that. At least it had the potential to be so much more than that . . . Yasmin had visited twice already, bringing flowers and hand-knitted baby booties, as if she hadn't done enough already, putting Tina and Paul up while the police were going over the house and garden. Drugged up in a hospital bed wasn't *quite* how Fern had imagined meeting her next-door-neighbour, but she seemed like a well-meaning, no-nonsense kind of woman, with an endless supply of cheerful stories and advice. She could have been Tina's long-lost twin. No wonder they got on so well. And Eddie, he'd visited too, looking slightly unkempt and tired around the eyes, but putting on a cheerful face for the occasion, showering Fern and Linette with attention and flirting with all the midwives. He admitted that the last few days had taken their toll, making him rethink his priorities somewhat, but then he was back to grinning again, claiming it was invaluable research for his next book, and that he'd always known Sean was perfect villain material.

Richard had popped in briefly as well, to see how mother and baby were doing. To assure Fern that it was all out in the open now – Kerry knew the full story – and to apologise again for his part in his wife's less-than-friendly welcome campaign. It *was* her, he said – everything except for the painted message – but she'd been beside herself with guilt ever since she found out the truth. Fern still couldn't see it, the thing that had attracted her sister to him, but perhaps the man had hidden depths. Depths that belonged to Kerry now. And even though there was a tacit understanding between the pair of them that they wouldn't speak of Linny again, that officially Richard wouldn't even *think* of her anymore, Fern still found comfort in knowing how fiercely her sister had lived on in other hearts as well as her own.

Kerry came too, the day after her husband, which was the most surprising visit of all. She and April turned up together, laden with chocolates and magazines and awkward, stuttered apologies that Fern hardly knew what to do with. But she smiled and said she understood completely, that she hoped it wouldn't be too hard for Kerry, having her living across the road, and that maybe they could start again.

'Yes,' said Kerry. 'I'd like that. I think in a funny way it might be a good thing having you so close. It might help us face our problems head-on and see if there's anything in our marriage worth saving. Maybe if I'd done that in the first place – tackled Rich about the note someone put through our door, and the photograph I found on his phone, instead of hiding behind my fear – things would be different now. But the way he was looking at her in that photo . . . your twin . . . I couldn't remember the last time he'd looked at me like that. It sounds pathetic but I was too scared to make him choose, in case he chose her.'

You were right to be scared, thought Fern, feeling a fresh pang of guilt on her sister's behalf. *He told me as much, himself.* But maybe there *was* a way forward for Richard and Kerry now. Now that Linny was gone. Now that it was finally all out in the open.

'I'm so sorry,' Kerry said again. 'I don't know what came over me, terrorising a pregnant woman in her own home. The writing on the wall – that wasn't me, that must have been Sean – but everything else . . . Oh! I'm just so ashamed. Dumping dog poo on your doorstep, for crying out loud!' She shook her head, in disgust, or disbelief. 'If you *do* decide to press charges, I honestly wouldn't blame you. I swear, though, I've never done anything like this before and I'd never have hurt you. I was horrified when I heard what Sean put you through. I wish I'd put dog poo on *his* doorstep instead,' she added with a nervous laugh. But then her face fell again. 'I just couldn't bear the thought of losing Rich when things were finally getting better between us . . .' She stared at the floor, red-cheeked with embarrassment, and it was all Fern could do not to crawl out of bed and hug her. What a mess.

'Oh,' said April, looking equally shame-faced. 'We brought you something else as well. I bumped into your husband yesterday morning and he mentioned getting an electrician in to check out the wiring . . . something to do with an exploding kettle?' She dug into the jute bag by her feet and pulled out a replacement Rapid Boil 750. 'So we got you a new one, ready for when you come home.'

Not *go* home, Fern noticed. But *come* home. As if she belonged on the street with everyone else now.

'And so I can pop round for a cuppa after work,' said April. 'See how you're settling back in.'

'Thank you,' said Fern, finding she'd already forgiven the nurse for her cold behaviour. 'That's really thoughtful of you.'

'Yes,' piped up Tina, who'd been sitting there quietly the whole time, reading an article about baby massage in one of the magazines they'd brought. 'It's one of life's essentials, isn't it? A kettle.' And, to give Tina her credit, she did actually wait until they'd gone, until they were halfway through the door anyway, before pointing out that she and Paul had stopped off to buy a new one that morning. 'Still,' she said, beaming. 'You can never have too many kettles, can you?'

With every visit, Fern felt the pull of Crenellation Lane a little more. Against the odds, given everything that had happened, but there it was: the urge to be home with her new baby; to get started on that new life she and Paul had talked about; to transform the house back into a proper family home. A happy place. *Their* happy place. With every visit she imagined that new life more clearly.

Even her dad made it to the hospital to meet his new granddaughter, although Paul was under the strictest of instructions from Anne and the other care home staff that the visit was a short one. It almost broke Fern's heart, seeing him wheeled into the ward like an invalid, like an old, old man, but he was surprisingly lucid, given his unfamiliar surroundings.

'She looks just like you and your sister at that age,' he said, his voice choked with emotion as he reached forwards in his wheelchair to stroke Linette's soft down. 'My little blonde angels. I still remember the day you were born . . .'

And there it was, the same old speech as always. But it resonated with Fern in a way it never had before, watching the two of them together. 'I was too scared to even touch you,' he murmured, his

304

face cracking into a proper grin as baby fingers tightened round his. He wasn't scared today.

'Oh yes,' he told Linette. 'The spitting image of your mum, you are. And your aunty, of course, only she's not with us anymore, I'm afraid . . .' He broke off, turning briefly towards the door as if Linny might be about to walk in and surprise them all. 'But we mustn't be sad about that now, must we? Not on such a happy occasion. I don't always remember everything these days, I'm afraid, sweetheart – bit of a silly old grandad like that – but I won't forget this. I won't forget meeting my beautiful granddaughter.' He paused a second time, as if he were physically committing the scene to memory. Trying to make it stick. 'But if I do forget, you and Mummy will just have to come and remind me again.'

'You won't be able to keep us away,' Fern promised.

She sent a silent smile of thanks to Paul and Tina, over his shoulder, basking in the pleasure of having all her family, old and new, together in the one room. Almost all, anyway.

As for Linny, she was the last visitor of all, waiting until Fern was asleep that final night on the ward, creeping into her dreams with uncharacteristic quietness. No blaring music. No raucous laughter. One minute it was just Fern and the baby, and the next minute there she was, staring down into the cot, whispering advice to her new niece:

Never let anyone tell you you're not good enough.

Never give up on your dreams.

Never do tequila slammers on an empty stomach.

Never eat garlic bread on a date.

And never let your mum do karaoke in public. She's terrible, she really is.

She blew a kiss to the baby and another back towards the bed. 'Catch you later, Sister Midnight.' And then Linny turned on her heel, her ridiculous red platform heel, and headed for the door, slipping out into the brightness of the corridor beyond.

Epilogue

Fern stood on the tufted grass of another cemetery, watching the coffin disappear down into the rain-clagged ground. One coffin, two bodies. It's what she would have wanted – Marte's grandparents were in full agreement on that. A proper English burial beside her own mother, all three generations reunited at last.

They pressed their hands into Fern's after the ceremony, thanking her over and over again for everything she'd done, but couldn't be persuaded to come back to the Queen's Head with everyone else. They had a long journey ahead of them, and the sooner they got going the better. Perhaps the proximity to Crenellation Lane was too much for them. The road where it had all happened, where Marte had lived and died. And of course, Crenellation Lane had been her killer's home too, until he found new lodgings at Her Majesty's pleasure, awaiting trial for manslaughter and attempted murder. The Hoskins' house was up for sale now – Sean's mum had gone into residential care – and indeed an offer had been accepted just a few days before. Fern and Paul wouldn't be the newest arrivals on the street for much longer.

'All right?' said Kerry, gently jigging Linette up and down. 'Are you ready to go?'

Fern glanced over at Paul, still cradling the baby sling against his chest, despite having relinquished the baby within minutes of their arrival. He was deep in conversation with Richard and Eddie a few graves along.

'*I'm* ready,' she laughed. 'Not so sure about our husbands though. Maybe if we start walking, they'll get the hint. Are you all right with Linette or do you want me to take her back now?'

'More than all right, aren't we sweetheart?' said Kerry, cooing into the baby's blonde wisps of hair. 'You stay and have a cuddle with your aunty Kerry. Let your mummy hobble up in peace.'

Tina and Yasmin were halfway back to the car park already, and April was meeting them at the pub once her shift had finished. It wasn't a proper wake – of all the people there, Eddie was the only one who'd really known Marte, given that Nicky and Ant hadn't been able to make it. But everyone agreed they needed to mark the occasion in some way, as a sign of respect. To mark the laying of old ghosts to rest, quite literally as far as Fern was concerned. Not that there'd been any trouble on that score since her return home, thankfully. The dreams, the messages, the crazy electrics and general sense of unease were long gone now. The house was just a house. Even the piano stayed in tune these days. Ever since the day they found Sofia. That's all Marte had ever wanted – Fern was convinced of it – justice for her daughter. *My baby. My baby.*

'I bet you wish you'd brought your crutches now,' said Kerry, as they set off towards the car park at a slow limp.

'A bit,' Fern admitted. 'But I'll be fine. April said it's healing nicely.'

'That's good,' said Kerry. 'Oh, and speaking of good news – or not, as the case may be – I hear your mother-in-law's found a buyer for her house?'

'Yes, that's right. Cash buyers, no chain. Couldn't be more perfect, really. She could be in in a few months.'

Kerry frowned. 'She's not worried about taking on the Hoskins' place after everything that happened then?'

307

'Tina?' said Fern. 'No, she's made of tougher stuff than that. It's only a house, at the end of the day.'

'And you're not worried about having her on the same street? I'm not sure I could cope with living that close to *my* mother-in-law. She'll be round all the time, you know.'

'Yes,' said Fern. 'She will. I never thought I'd say it, but it's been kind of nice having her here. And we'd have struggled without her these last few weeks, what with a new baby *and* a busted ankle. It'll be nice for Linette too. Paul's the one who took a bit of convincing, but the thought of free babysitting on tap won him round in the end!'

'And here's the man himself,' said Kerry, as Paul came speed-walking up to join them. 'I suppose you've come for your lovely baby,' she told him.

'No, that's fine,' said Paul. 'Don't wake her now if she's asleep.' He turned towards Fern. 'I just wanted to check you were okay. That pregnant lady back there – the blonde in the Fair Isle jumper – she's the spitting image of you and your sister, don't you think? I honestly thought it *was* Linny for a moment.'

'Really?' Fern slipped her hand into his. 'I can't say I noticed.'

Acknowledgements

It's hard to believe that *The Woman Before*, which started life as a germ of an idea in the aftermath of moving house, is now a full-blown novel out there in the real world. But it wouldn't have got that far without the help of some important people. Big thanks to my fabulous writing friend and beta reader Lizzie Strong, whose cheery emails and encouragement helped get me from the first chapters of what was then called *Crenellation Lane* to this finished book. And thank you to all the wonderful Write Magic writers who kept me company on Zoom sprints during the editing process, bringing a real sense of fun, community and motivational accountability to what would otherwise have been a very solitary experience.

Huge thanks, of course, to my awesome editor, Rebecca Jamieson, for taking Fern, Tina and Linny under her expert wing, and to all the amazing HQ Team. I'm so pleased my book has found its home with you.

As this is probably the closest I'll ever come to an Oscar acceptance speech, I'd also like to thank my mum for all her support over the years, and my dad for his (and for introducing me to *The Writers and Artist's Yearbook* at an impressionable age!). Thank you to all my family and friends for your ongoing interest and encouragement and for your kind promises to read *The Woman Before* when it's out . . . and thank you to you, lovely reader, for having done just that!

An enormous thank you, finally, to the main characters in *my* story, Dafydd, Lucy and Daniel. Thank you for everything you do, from reading drafts and offering well-timed pep talks, to being there and being you. None of this would mean anything without you.

Dear Reader,

We hope you enjoyed reading this book. If you did, we'd be so appreciative if you left a review. It really helps us and the author to bring more books like this to you.

Here at HQ Digital we are dedicated to publishing fiction that will keep you turning the pages into the early hours. Don't want to miss a thing? To find out more about our books, promotions, discover exclusive content and enter competitions you can keep in touch in the following ways:

JOIN OUR COMMUNITY:

Sign up to our new email newsletter: http://smarturl.it/SignUpHQ

Read our new blog www.hqstories.co.uk

🐦 https://twitter.com/HQStories

📘 www.facebook.com/HQStories

BUDDING WRITER?

We're also looking for authors to join the HQ Digital family! Find out more here:

https://www.hqstories.co.uk/want-to-write-for-us/

Thanks for reading, from the HQ Digital team

If you enjoyed *The Woman Before*, then why not try another gripping thriller from HQ Digital?

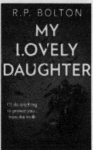